# Clouds Over Okotoks

## by H. Lee Disher

**DORRANCE**
PUBLISHING CO
EST. 1920
PITTSBURGH, PENNSYLVANIA 15238

Dorrance Publishing Co
585 Alpha Drive
Pittsburgh, PA 15238
Visit our website at *www.dorrancebookstore.com*

ISBN: 978-1-4809-3014-8
eISBN: 978-1-4809-2992-0

*Dedicated to my two maiden aunts:*
**Aunt June Morrison,**
*whose passions included fine arts, ballet, and anthropology,*

*and **Aunt Helen Disher,***
*who had a sly sense of humour and always loved a good story.*

# Preface

I love this country. Canada has been my home for over sixty years, the bulk of them spent in the province of Ontario. I feel I have travelled quite a bit in this land of my birth, but I doubt I've even seen one-tenth of it. No matter where you are in this country, the landscape, the geography moves you, seeps into your soul. I want to celebrate that. This novel is a salute to the province of Alberta. It is primarily a work of fiction, but there are some details and accounts which are factual. Excepting "Dewdney Common," actual street names mentioned in the town of Okotoks have been used. I have attempted to use totally fictional character names for the citizens of that town who appear in this book. If, by chance, there is any resident there whose name is the same as one of the characters in this novel, it is not you I am talking about. Okotoks is a wonderful town still, I believe, considered to be one of the ten best places to live in Canada. Its annual rodeo usually takes place at a local hockey arena not at the Agricultural Fair Ground.

The description of the Canadian Football League match between the Calgary Stampeders and the Saskatchewan Roughriders (June 1999) is based on the sports report of that event in *The Calgary Herald*, as are the results for the professional competitors at the Calgary Stampede (July 1999), excepting the insertion of a fictional competitor, Randall LeCroix. The same is true for the chuck-wagon races of that year in July, except that Troy Dorchester drove a wagon for The Hamptons in that event rather than for the fictional Tranogco corporation. I thank those grain growers with whom I conversed at the Agriculture buildings during a visit to the Stampede in 2003 who informed me about growing barley, oats, and canola and such and put me onto the wonderful website of the provincial government's Department of Agriculture, "Ropin' the Web." Pops Davis' Christmas tree farm is a fiction. Southern Alberta is not conducive to raising such trees *en masse*. Surprise of all surprises perhaps, in a provincial election in May 2015, Rachel Notley and the NDP party won with a majority government ranking.

Historical data on Okotoks was gleaned from a visit to the town museum and from the town's own website. Historical references to rodeo in North America come from sources listed in the Acknowledgements. Biographical data on Catherine deHueck Doherty is based on prefacing remarks to her own works and on the website dedicated to her. I trust I have been faithful in recounting such facts in my own words without plagiarizing the efforts and work of others.

H. Lee Disher

# Acknowledgments

A number of sources were read and consulted in the preparation of this book. They include:

Eamer, Claire and Jones, Thirza. *The Canadian Rodeo Book*, (Western Producer Prairie Books, Saskatoon: 1982).

Fredericksson, Kristine. *American Rodeo*, (Texas A&M University Press, College Station, TX: 1985).

Scanlan, Lawrence. *Wild about Horses*, (Harper Collins, New York, NY: 1998). *[He also makes note of the bizarre ritual of the Sredni Stog peoples of ancient Ukraine that I also came across in* The Scientific American *(December 1991 edition).]*

Tinkelman, Murray. *Rodeo, The Great American Sport (a photo essay)*, (Quill, New York, NY: 1982).

Doherty, Catherine de Hueck. *Poustinia*, (Madonna House Publications, Combermere, ON: 1993).

Doherty, Catherine de Hueck. *Sobornost*, (Madonna House Publications, Combermere, ON: 1992).

Doherty, Catherine de Hueck. *Strannik*, (Madonna House Publications, Combermere, ON: 1991),

Doherty, Catherine de Hueck. *Molchanie*, (Madonna House Publications, Combermere, ON: 2001).

Doherty, Catherine de Hueck. *Uródivoi*, (Madonna House Publications, Combermere, ON: 2001)

Quotations from *The Philokalia*, (Deb Platt, translator, 1999) appear with permission. Source of origin http.//www.digiserve.com/mystic/Christian/Philokalia/humble.html. *[The exception is the quote at the end of chapter 6 which I made up].*

Besides the versions of retelling used in this novel, there are other variations on the legend of Napi and Big Rock and on the *pysanka* tradition of Russia and the Ukraine. I adapted my Napi legend from the one included in the town's website www.okotoks.ca. I first learned of the *pysanka* tradition while studying Russian language during my undergraduate years in the late 1960s. I share the legend as I remember it.

I wish to sincerely thank several people who kindly read through manuscripts and revisions and offered suggestions, corrections, and wise counsel during the gestation period of this novel, which stretches over several years. They are Alyssa Nichols; Grace Bradish; Paul and Julie Ciufo; Arthur Lake; Bonnie Staib, archivist of Madonna House, Combermere, ON; Kathy Coutts, historical assistant, Okotoks Historical Museum and Archives; and my wife, Diamond Fotiadis. It's been quite a journey. Finally, thanks to the editing team, staff, and Tina King, my Project Coordinator at Dorrance Publishing for enabling this novel to be published.

# Chapter 1:
# Field Trip

Two seconds to midnight. If the whole span of cosmological time for the existence of our universe were compressed into a daily clock, that minuscule segment would represent the length of humankind's appearance on planet earth to date. That is as awesome as it is humbling.

It was also the beginning of the fascination for the grade nines from Dewdney Junior High in Okotoks, Alberta, who were on a two-day class excursion and field trip that would take them to the Royal Tyrell Museum in Drumheller and then onto Dinosaur Provincial Park some 130 kilometers further south the following day. Dr. Arthur Newbury had been selected from the museum staff of paleontologists to be the tour guide for that class. When he met and boarded their bus at Airdrie, where he resided, that intriguing piece of information was his opening salvo as he sought to captivate keen young minds on the verge of visiting his vocational world. It was a short speech, a teaser intended to awaken curiosities, and, as far as he could tell, it worked. He ended by offering a balsa-wood model dinosaur kit to the first student who could spell "paleontology" correctly. Alex Davis leapt at the chance and failed just as quickly as he began: "p-a-i-l...." Before Tyler Stedman, "Lumpy" Jenkins, or other somewhat brighter students in the class could offer their attempts, Raja Punkara had answered correctly with precise enunciation.

Dr. Newbury settled down into a empty seat in the middle of the bus as the class, their parental escorts and their teacher, Ms. Carol Morton, settled into window-gazing, animated conversations, some road songs, and the usual bus-ride routines while the commonplace yellow and black carrier beetled them along through the last stretches of hills and fields towards their destination. The Insect Express was how Tyler imagined it, trying to convert the temporal magnitude of the cosmos into spatial terms.

A few kilometers outside Drumheller, a whole bus-load of "Ahs!" and "Whoas!" and "Oh, my Gods!' emerged from dropped jaws. The landscape altered dramatically. Great craters plunged beneath the surface. Grassy areas disappeared as stone, rock and sand replaced them. Trees were spindly or just AWOL from the Creator. If it hadn't been for the town of Drumheller itself in the middle of this wasteland, one might have thought one was in another part of the cosmos, some place like the planet Toth in the *Star Wars* movie series. The bus descended into "Craterville," wiggled its way through town past an oversized purple raptor with a slide inside that designated the local tourist information bureau, around a corner, slightly uphill, and then off into the Royal Tyrell Museum parking lot.

Surrounded by Badland terrain, the museum looks like a biological research laboratory in the middle of some desert. It harbours vital knowledge on which the grade nine class of Dewdney Junior High knew they were going to be tested. It delights in unveiling its marvelous treasures to all who visit.

The class immersed itself in prehistory, spellbound at every turn as each exhibit area and its attendant interpretation discharged its wondrous powers. Students who had never visited before were utterly astonished. Those who had, like Tyler and Alex, were nonetheless entranced on this return visit. Fossil displays and hands-on exhibits of geological and biological phenomenon served up as appetizers beyond the foyer stimulated their intellectual taste buds. The soup and salad room that followed introduced them to the various subdivisions of paleontological research, gave them a view of staff at work in the on-site laboratory, and grabbed their cerebral glands with plaster-cast replicas of prehistoric plants, insects, fish, reptiles, and amphibians and a full-scale skeleton of the dinosaur that started it all: an Albertosaurus, a carnivore unique to that part of the world, like the one discovered accidentally by Joseph Burr Tyrell while heading up a map-making and geological expedition in 1886. After that came the entrées showcasing the evolving process of three major geological eras, Paleozoic, Mesozoic, and Cenozoic, and their various subdivisions: Cambrian through Devonian to Permian; Triassic, Jurassic, and Cretaceous; the Tertiary (from Paleocene to Pliocene); and Quaternary (Pleistocene and Holocene).

Five hundred and forty-four million years of creation in evolution that followed four thousand million years of Pre-Cambrian time were represented. Each one of them was a smorgasbord of revelations, mystifying adaptations and residual unanswered questions. The loudest of sporadic exclamations among Ms. Morton's protegés erupted in the Jurassic area.

"Hey, guys! Look at that Stegosaurus!"

"Wow! Were Brontosauruses really that big?"

"Holy liftin' Pterodactyls!"

"Tyler! Tyler! Here, over here! Here he is! Tyrannosaurus Rex, the uncontested king of the oldest jungle." Alex Davis could scarcely stop his eyes from widening nor stem the flow of adrenalin straining his excitement. He was fourteen going on seven again. Alex always acted somewhat younger than his years. He was having the same reaction now he had had when he and his cousin had visited the Royal Tyrell twice before.

"All right, Alex, I'll be over in a sec. Don't wet your pants!" ("Oops!" Tyler murmured within himself. "I hope the others don't take me seriously about that. I promised Alex I wouldn't cause him any more embarrassment about his little problem.")

Tyler made his way over to the Tyrannosaurus exhibit, making an earnest effort to share his cousin's momentary euphoria.

"What kept you?" Alex asked. "Look at this sucker! He gets bigger every time I see him."

"That sounds like you," Tyler began responding, "the bigger, the nastier, the more fascinated you become. Tyrannosaurus Rex must have been terrifying in his day, but he really was kind of awkward and operated mostly by surprise attack. I'm holding out for more the Eohippus display. They were the only prehistoric creatures other than Mastodons and Sabre-toothed tigers that most closely resembled species still in existence today. They were smart. They were swift and sure-footed. They could out manoeuvre His Tyranno Clumsiness any day of the week. Starvation killed them off. Predators never got the best of them."

"Yeah, yeah. I know. I know. And they looked like miniature horses, just like those little ponies that prance around on Sable Island off the coast of Nova Scotia out in the middle of bloody nowhere. You and your horses. I don't get it. They smell awful when they're wet, and the turds they drop are disgusting."

"I hope you never get stuck behind an elephant, Mr. I-have-a-passion-only-for-big-creatures. Just the thought of being crapped on by your beloved Tyrannosaurus Rex drums up a nightmare or two I'd prefer not to have."

"Okay, okay. To each his own, I guess."

The museum tour was complete by noon. Lunch followed. Then Dr. Newbury presented a film and an illustrated lecture in the auditorium.

By 2:30 P.M. the class was checking into a local hotel for their overnight stay, changing into swim trunks for an afternoon pool and water-slide break. In the evening, their bus would take them just outside of Drumheller for a Rosebud Little Theatre performance of "Arsenic and Old Lace" and then back in time to bed down before the second leg of their journey.

After swimming, Tyler and Alex scrambled to get changed for dinner so they could get seats in the restaurant beside Stephanie Wells and Enid Evans. Well, Alex was eager.

"Golly, Tyler, did you see those two at the pool this afternoon? Haven't you noticed how nicely they are starting to sprout!"

"Shh! Maybe I have, Alex, but I'm not about to take any pages straight out of *How to Grow into a Sexist Pig*. Jeepers, one way or another you seem determined to wind up with a soggy crotch today. That's not going to score you any points with anybody."

"Okay, okay, just hurry and get in line. Perhaps I'll just wait until your little sister fills out!"

"Now, you're cruisin' for a black eye. Good God, man, she's your cousin too, like I am."

"Damn, I keep forgettin' that."

"Well, it will be better when you keep remembering."

"I'm sure it will. I suppose I'm just jealous because I don't have anyone else to protect. My mother's learned how to fend for herself exceptionally well, and my father's a lost cause."

"Oh, I don't know. If it hadn't been for Uncle Louie, I probably would never have developed a liking for horses."

"Yeah, right. But you like riding them. He just likes bettin' them. 'A bottle and a racingform, son, that's all the support a man really needs.' Some motto. Someday I'll have the guts to ask him where a son's supposed to find a father for support when the first one he has dies young and the replacement doesn't give a shit."

"Come on, cuz, let's go eat and leave off rubbing any more sore spots."

"Enid Evans can rub my sore spot any time she likes."

"Come on. Get your brains back north of your neck line. You'll be flunking puberty worse than you manage English grammar."

"I don't know about that. At least I know I'm in puberty. Where are you?"

"I'm right here, heading on to dinner with my horny-toad cousin, waiting to have a decent meal, then out for a taste of live amateur theatre and feeling like I'd rather not be the one to offer you lessons in manners and self-control."

"Hey, it's okay. Maybe you're where a son of a useless step-father goes when he needs support."

"Or maybe you'll realize that Ola is doing a pretty good job of being father as well as mother. And Pops. You get to live with Pops too."

Both boys stopped, exchanged a revelatory glance, noticed small puddles of tears almost leak out, then joined the file of classmates into the restaurant. They were too late to get a seat at Stephanie and Enid's table. They wound up sitting with "Lumpy" Jenkins and plain and frumpy Martha Yellan who was fully into puberty with a face full of pimples and blackheads. They managed making it through dinner anyway without staring, without snickering, without incivility. Small talk and school talk filled the void and silences between bites and gulps. Ms. Morton blew a middle C on her pitch pipe precisely on the hour of 7:00 P.M. indicating it was time to finish up, wash up, and be on the bus at 7:20 for the ride to the theatre.

The stage performance was comical enough, if somewhat dated. Alex liked crazy Uncle Teddy. The ride back to the hotel was uneventful. Most of the students were already bushed and nodding off. There was a short-lived moment of excitement when the driver cut one corner too close. The back wheels hit gravel and began to skid and swerve. A mix of hysteria marked by screams and exhilaration marked by laughter rippled through the seats. Within ten minutes everyone had settled down again. By the time they reached the hotel it was already past "lights out" so students made their separate ways to their shared rooms to bed down for the night.

Tyler and Alex had a third-floor room with two double beds. They changed into their night-wear, brushed their teeth, and slid in under their separate covers. Tyler turned to face his cousin.

"Pretty fine day, wasn't it? Lots of mental stimulation, some exercise, some fun, fairly decent food."

"Yeah, but the best part was seeing Stephanie and Enid in their bathing suits."

"Let it go will you? If you don't stop thinking about them, you will have an accident in your sleep-wear. You're only fourteen. Don't you think sex can wait a few years, like when it might mean something, when you might have some idea of what you're actually doing? Just go to sleep, okay? See you in the morning."

They exchanged "Good nights" and were sleeping deeply within minutes. In the morning, it was Tyler who woke up with a couple of soggy spots in his crotch. He hoped that didn't mean he was being more immature about puberty than Alex was. He hoped his mother wouldn't notice anything dried and caked on when she put his bed-pants in the laundry on the weekend. He rose, shook Alex awake, showered, and waited till his cousin was ready to head down for breakfast.

The day two excursion to Dinosaur Provincial Park included a couple of morning stops en route. There was a one-hour visit to an abandoned coal mine and about a fifteen minute break when the bus pulled over at a scenic lookout. Cameras flashed. Mouths gaped. Exclamations burst forth again. They were staring from the edge of a precipice across a narrow crater in the middle of which were some of the tallest, weirdest rock formations in Badland territory. Pillars of piled stone of varying heights, mixed hues and textures balanced precariously before them. Ages of glacial activity and water and wind erosion had left them standing there, bulbous and top-heavy like the spindly legs and feet of some upside-down ossified giants. The phallic symbolism wasn't missed by a bus-load of thirteen- and fourteen-year olds. Remarkably, nobody ventured to name that out loud. *"These geological marvels, unique to Western North America, are known as hoodoos,"* began the sign affixed to the railings of the outlook. *Aperitifs* in stone.

The school bus rambled along back gravel roads and through a few tiny hamlets until a turn sign for Dinosaur Park appeared just past Patricia. "Hey Lumpy!," someone shouted out, "Isn't this where your old lady's from? Patricia?"

"No, you moron. She's from Picture Butte. It's three times the size of this place."

"Right. And she is a beaut! Mind if I come over and take her picture some time?"

"Mind if I stuff a knuckle sandwich right down your throat?"

A high E-flat squealed out from Ms. Morton's pitch pipe—her code for "Knock it off!."

Not many kilometers later her grade nine homeroom class was descending desolate canyon spaces similar to those around Drumheller but far less civilized. It was difficult to believe one was in the same province. Nothing they had read about or studied in class quite prepared them for the actual experience. They knew about big skies, huge suns, limitless horizons, but where were the crops? Where were the railroad lines? The grain elevators? The trees?

H. Lee Disher

The rolling hills? The fields and meadows? Dirt and dust, stone and rock, pebbles, canyons, calcified mud slides, fissures, scrub-brush, sparse tufts of grasses, and the meandering Red Deer River and its tributary creeks—that was it for miles and miles and miles, about twenty-six square miles worth. *"Welcome to Dinosaur Provincial Park—A World Heritage Site."*

There was time before lunch for the class to be subdivided into two groups. Group A was given a tour of the on-site staff research centre and a lecture on fossil-hunting and collecting. Group B was led on a couple of "discovery" walks on trails just outside the research centre. Then they switched.

After lunch at the park snack bar, the class assembled with park staff to receive equipment and instructions for the afternoon dig. They were on fake parchment paper in Bedrock script:

1. Always carry your hand pick with the head down.
2. Always wear goggles when hacking away at rocks.
3. Don't swing hand picks within three feet of another student
4. Chip stone away slowly, carefully; brushing loose gravel and dust gently away
5. Make sure you have solid footing; no reckless climbing.
6. Bring samples in a collector bag to resource tent for labeling and identification.
7. Walk, don't run.
8. Keep your hat on at all times. Apply sunscreen liberally.
9. Stay within the confines of the area assigned to you.
10. Work side by side in pairs.

Tyler wondered if Moses got similar instructions before he received the Ten Commandments. He wondered if he would have to keep Alex focused, not wandering off to see if Stephanie and Enid needed any help, creating opportunity to sneak a peek or two down their tank tops. He wondered why he was momentarily imagining that possibility too.

Heading off to the dig site on the park buses was very much like riding across a sci-fi movie stage set. Hills, swales, mounds, buttes, and mesas of mud and sand over 75 million years old spread themselves over hundreds of acres of earth. Vegetation was so sparse it could hardly provide sufficient food for animals let alone shelter. (There are sections of parkland by the river bed that are more lush and provide a habitat to numbers of deer, foxes, and such and a number of bird species). The fluctuating sculpting of this tract of land began

13,000 years ago as Ice Age glaciers made their retreat. It continues through the lifelong meanderings of the Red Deer River and its creeks and tributaries, aided and abetted by other forms of prairie water run-off. The solid blocks of stone, rock, and earth that protrude, intrude, merge, or divulge themselves throughout the park are the result of sand and mud deposits left by rivers 75 million years ago. They look like old ogres caught in the midst of a strip-tease performance, or, in Alex's mind, like "snake-o-sauruses" shedding skin. Ages ago, a palm springs paradise. For centuries since, a scene from the middle of nowhere. An incredibly rich depository of compacted and compressed prehistory.

The section for geological and paleontological exploration assigned to Alex and Tyler was a three-foot square at the base of a seven-foot outcropping. Already on the face of the small cliff they could detect the striations of several centuries of geological activity and the exposed markings of wind and rain erosion of recent years. The bottom layers where they were supposed to be working were comprised of alternating bands of caked mud, sandstone, and limestone with a wider segment of harder, granite-like rock near the base. Yellow-brown, gray; yellow-brown, gray; yellow-brown, gray; yellow-brown, gray and clots of taupe mixed with speckled pink. The mud and sandstone came away easily. The limestone required a little more effort. The ironstone could barely be dented by a hand-pick and needed sharper, heavier treatment from hammer and chisels. One worked around it, not through it. The two boys picked away with some degree of interest for about half an hour, dislodging a few pieces of flint, a couple of arrowhead imprints, and some ossified fragments from a bison's shin bone. These were only mildly exciting since almost every other student in the class uncovered similar treasures. These were predictable remnants of the Neolithic Age when early ancestors of the Peigan, Sarcee, and Blackfoot tribes roamed the area in search of meat and water.

Alex stopped to swipe some sweat from his forehead and, gazing upwards, saw something crawling that caught his attention. It was about five inches long, with an amber-brown segmented body, six legs (or were there eight?), head, antennae, and, yes, a curled tail. "Scorpion!" He began to shimmy up the slope swinging his hand pick at the scavenging creature that was now moving more quickly to evade its attacker.

"Alex, get down," Tyler uttered in a loud whisper. "Leave the poor thing alone. It's not bothering us. No climbing! Remember? You'll get us in trouble. Ms. Morton will yank us off the project and send us back to the resource station to help with cataloguing."

"Oh, let her blow a couple of F-flats on her blasted pitch-pipe. I can catch this

H. Lee Disher

little sucker and give him a good whack. There's no rule says we can't take dead insects out of the park. Just think, I can put it in Martha Yellan's desk someday."

There was no stopping him. Alex scrambled toward the top, flailing his hand-pick at the scorpion and just missing. Cascades of loose gravel slid down the slope from the soles of his feet. His hand pick chipped away bits of sandstone and softer shales. A few small chinks tumbled down in front of Tyler with a couple of them glancing off his left shoulder. "Hey, watch it Flintstone. Wait till I move aside if you're going to start quarrying like a wild man."

Tyler moved. Alex continued his pursuit. Near the top, the scorpion was running out of  room. More solid rock made its footing more slippery. It slowed and rested. *Whack. Chink. Whack. Chink.* On the third whack, Alex crushed the helpless critter. At the same time, a large chuck of rock broke away, bounced down the cliff-face, and struck Tyler square on the right knee. Ms. Morton, two parent supervisors, and a cluster of gawking classmates rallied around the spot where the scream was heard.

Mr. Evans, one of the supervising parents, rode with Tyler and Alex as one of the park attendants named Wayne drove them to the nearest hospital in Brooks. Tyler winced a few times with the pain and shot reproving glances at his cousin. Most of the time was spent in suspended silence. A couple of times Alex whispered back, "I'm sorry, man. I'm sorry." Tyler shook his head in disbelief. His knee continued to swell. "Alex, shut the hell up!"

The emergency department in Brooks was backed up some. The best that one of the nurses could do while they were waiting was to slice Tyler's pant leg open above the knee to relieve exterior pressure. The knee was swollen, yellowed, and impossible to walk on. Mr. Evans helped Tyler make a couple of trips to the bathroom while they were waiting. Triage meant that a sous-chef with a sliced finger, a young mother with a baby who seemed to have stopped breathing, an old man with severe stomach cramps, and a fifty-something woman who had broken out in hives received attention first. The nursing station had already had the foresight to call in the x-ray technician. The doctor-on-call made a cursory examination of Tyler's knee, ordered the x-ray and an ice pack and sent him back out until the film was developed. During that wait Alex reached into one of his pockets and held out a clenched hand in Tyler's direction.

"What have you got there?"

"I wasn't sure I wanted to show you. I wish that chunk of rock had missed you, I really do. As a geological exploration it wasn't a lost cause. Look, behind that piece that fell off was this sliver of ironstone that lay on the ground next to the dead scorpion. Look! It contains a perfectly preserved ammonite!"

"Whoopy ding, Alex. I suppose you showed it to Ms. Morton?"

"Nah. There wasn't time. And she was hardly in the mood. Maybe someday. Maybe I'll just hang on to this as a souvenir of our friendship."

"Friendship? I feel like you've stung our friendship with that scorpion's tail. Lucky for you, we're relatives. I don't get to choose you, so I'm stuck with you."

The whole emergency treatment process took a good three to four hours. The net result was a hairline fracture of the patella, a large contusion, and significant swelling. The doctor secured Tyler's knee with a tight Tensor bandage and suggested a consultation with his own physician back home as soon as possible in case an actual cast would be needed. Mr. Evans handed over the twenty-five dollar fee to cover the cost of crutches. Off they went to the parking lot where the park attendant had returned with his van. An earlier cell phone call from Mr. Evans had suggested an estimated pick-up time. They were only twenty minutes later than the estimate.

"The school bus will be leaving the park in another fifteen minutes," the park attendant informed them. "I'm headed to Calgary for the weekend anyway, so we've arranged to meet the bus at the Trading Post on the highway in Strathmore."

"Thanks," said Mr. Evans. Alex clambered into the rear seat of the van. Mr. Evans helped Tyler settle into the middle seat where he could stretch his whole right leg out sideways. "Are you comfortable, Tyler? ...Good. Okay, Wayne, I'm going to hop in the front and we're off."

"We won't get a seat across from Enid and Stephanie when we meet that bus," Alex commented, taking a stab at conversation as the van turned onto the Trans-Canada Highway just outside of Brooks.

Tyler glared wide-eyed at his cousin. "Don't talk to me, Doofus!" and then whispered, "And keep your naughty, hormonal fantasies to yourself."

Alex had "Oops!" written all over his face. Up front, Mr. Evans, Enid's father, smiled and chuckled inwardly. He was a teenager himself once, not that long ago really. Well, actually, it had been over twenty years.

By mentioning the girls, Alex had drawn Tyler's attention back to the previous night. The bed pants with the crusty crotch—would his mother notice? Probably not. The bandaged knee would arrest a good deal of her attention and become a focus for the worries and anxieties she continually maintained over her son—the ones to which she gave expression and the ones she struggled to keep to herself, and that mix of both by which she signaled her disapproval of his recreational passion. Tyler himself worried how

H. Lee Disher

the fractured knee was going to affect his coming summer holiday plans. How much horseback riding and preparation for novice rodeo would he not be able to enjoy? Would it heal before he went off at the end of August to a dude ranch in Montana? As for the bed pants, he could wash them out in the sink when he got home and let them dry overnight before putting them in the laundry.

These were the thoughts that continued to preoccupy Tyler's mind during the bus ride home after they made the transfer at Strathmore. All around him his classmates shared and compared their discoveries, remembered funny incidents that had occurred and struck up several rousing choruses of "One Hundred Bottles of Beer on the Wall," "Four Strong Winds," "I Just Wanna Fly" (by Sugar Ray), and assorted other recent hits and bus-riding songs. Time and kilometers flew. Prairie passed into the outskirts of Calgary which moved on towards foothill country. By 7 P.M. they had arrived back in Okotoks. Clouds of just about every shade of grey came to camp out over Southwestern Alberta; sodden, heavy-laden clouds that chilled the air and unfastened their burden of rain the next day, drenching the ground like gods vomiting after an all-night orgy.

# Chapter 2:
# 35 Dewdney Common

It was Friday night and most students were met by family members gathered in the junior high school parking lot. Alex's mother was still working that day, busying herself about her beloved cash crops. Wallis Wilton, her neighbour was there to pick Alex up and take him out to the homestead. He was a smart-looking man with well-weathered facial features, strong shoulders and forearms, and large, red-palmed hands. His face was gentle with a cleft chin, chapped thin lips, a long, medium-sized nose that looked just right, and slightly squinting, deep-set, pensive blue eyes. Close-cropped brown hair stuck out beneath his Allis-Chalmers cap, which topped off his farmer's garb: unzipped denim jacket, green-and-blue checked shirt, overalls, and brown leather cowboy boots.

He missed Alex getting off the bus for his attention was caught up in the slim, eye-fetching appearance of Ms. Morton standing off to one side of the bus door conversing with a couple of parents. Her straight, black hair was nicely cut angling downward from front to back in graduated flips. Her face was pleasant, if somewhat angular and accentuated by two large dark eyes. She sported a navy blue felt cap, a light black suede jacket over a white turtleneck and black nylon slacks and gray suede walking shoes. *There's a word for a woman who looks like that,* Wallis thought to himself. *Demure. Yes, that's it. Demure.* He hadn't really looked much at women for the past two years. Ms. Morton just stood out that day, perhaps because she didn't much resemble Amy. Amy was taller, more buxom, a brunette with lots of bravado. Two years ago she succumbed to the ravages of a rare form of liver cancer at the young age of thirty-eight.

Alex came up to him overflowing with talk. "Hi, Mr. Wilton. Guess my mom did have to work today, eh? She wasn't sure when I left. We had a good trip till I dropped a chunk of rock on Tyler's knee. Banged him up pretty sore. But he's going to be all right. The doctor in Brooks said so. But he's gotta see his own doctor here soon in case he wants more x-rays or to put a cast on. Wait till you see what I found out there. I'll show you in the truck on the way home."

While he stepped up into the passenger seat of the pick-up, Wallis opened the driver's door to get in, caught Ms. Morton's eye, and just politely put his left hand to the tip of his cap. When he got in and started the engine, Alex had noticed where Wallis's attention had been drawn. "That's Ms. Morton, our teacher. Not bad looking for an older babe, eh?"

"I don't think she'd appreciate you calling her a babe, Alex. I don't think that's what I'd call her. I figure she's just a very pleasant-looking young woman. Demure, to be more precise. Yessir, we can do that with this fascinating English language of ours—fish around for a word that means almost exactly what we want to say. I suppose that's already part of your education, but you may not value that very much right now."

"It is, and I guess I don't really. But Ms. Morton does. She just loves the English language."

As Wilton and Alex drove away, Ms. Morton was heading over to the Stedman family to have a little conference about Tyler. As soon as the crutches had touched the parking lot, Myra Stedman's hands had sprung up to her cheeks catching her mouth in mid-gasp. Then, her right hand flung itself down to grip her husband's left hand as if she was clinging to the guardrail on a roller coaster. Jules Stedman was fighting to maintain a composure of patience and serenity while, at the same time, Rebecca, their nine-year-old daughter, was exhibiting edgy excitement and shouting: "Look, Tyler's got crutches and a big bandage on his knee. Cool!"

Ms. Morton had watched Tyler swing over to his family, overhearing Alex shouting from across the parking lot: "It's all my fault, Aunt Myra, Uncle Jules. Tyler will explain it. I have to get going along with Mr. Wilton. My mom will have chores waiting for me to do." Now she was making her way over to exercise her damage-control skills. She had some years of practice helping nervous and over-protective parents like Myra Stedman settle into calmer states.

After offering her own sincerely apologetic preliminary remarks, Carol Morton reached into her purse to pass on a brief report from the attending physician which she had advised Mr. Evans to procure. That, and Tyler's own optimism, sufficed to spread the oil on troubled Stedman waters this time round, enough to reassure Jules and to enable Myra to put on a pleasant face, to mask her reservations. Ms. Morton exchanged sincere parting words with Tyler's parents and went off into the school. The Stedman family proceeded with their drive home, Tyler promising Rebecca that he would take off his bandage when they got there so she could have a look at his bruised and swollen knee.

The Stedmans had moved to Okotoks from their apartment in Calgary thirteen years ago, just after Tyler had turned one. They bought a split-level, three-bedroom house on the crest of the small escarpment at 35 Dewdney Common. They came during the second wave of growth spurts that converted a once drowsy, stable, but dwindling small town of boiler plants, lumber mills, and oil-related industries into the second fastest growth dot on the provincial map. The commuter era had begun in 1976 when the town's population doubled almost overnight, returning it to the size it held in its days of earlier glory in 1906 when the railroad made it a shipping terminal for lumber and agricultural products. Dewdney Common was part of a newer subdivision with similarly named streets. Sometime during the 1880s, Dewdney was the second name of the village that began as Sheep Creek out of humbler origins as a trading post in 1874. A federal government treaty of 1877 encouraged settlement in an area that was "home" to nomadic Blackfoot tribes. In 1897, six years after rail service replaced the stagecoach run on the Macleod Trail, the railway opted for the present name: Okotoks. (It rhymes with "folks," not with "fox.", though in the early days it did and many oldtimers still say it that way.) A number of the streets in the original town below the escarpment are named for members of the primary founding family, the Linehams. It was John Lineham whose sawmill operation and generous benefaction provided much of the impetus that converted a laid-back railway town into that turn-of-the-century metropolis. By 1904, Okotoks had reached official town status.

Surrounded by foothills, with Rocky Mountain views just a forty-five-minute drive west, the town nestles in a wide, flat-bottomed-bowl-shaped valley where Sheep Creek has grown to river width. The present name reflects the predilection in many Canadian communities to honour our nation's aboriginal ancestry. Plains tribes were not given to river travel, so good river-crossing points became significant. Not far west of the present town, a huge rock measuring 41' x 18' x 9' sits in the middle of a hay field. The rock itself could be anywhere from 50 million to 150 million years old but was left where it now sits by erratic glacial activity only 10,000 to 18,000 years ago. There are numbers of other rocks similar to it plunked down sporadically in isolated places in Western Alberta. It happens to sit near a low-water place in the Sheep River, and the Blackfoot word for "big rock" is Okatoks. As well as being an important geographic point of reference, the great stone weighing some 16,500 tonnes has native legend and spiritual significance attached to it. It does not figure in the official town crest, an almost cartoonish rendition of the crest on the Alberta provincial flag embraced by the motto: "Prudence, Progress, Industry."

Being employed in middle management in one of the Calgary-based oil companies in the late 1980s, Jules Stedman typified the kind of new resident that had been migrating from the big city for a decade or more: embodied icons of the town motto. The Stedman home was more than modest but not out of keeping with the homes of other neighborhood families whose earnings in Calgary stretched a lot further 34 kilometers south. Their home was on the curve of a crescent-shaped street and from the wide bay window in the living-room one could look across sports fields behind the Community Centre and the playground area that spread out from the rear doors of Dewdney Junior High. The living-room was twenty-four feet long and turned into a dining area at the back of the house that formed the base of an L-shape. Beside the dining area, there was a very decent kitchen with stainless steel appliances (including a gas stove, dishwasher, two-door upright refrigerator with a cold water and ice-maker dispenser in one door), marble countertops, and lots of cupboards finished in light teak. Beside the front door framed by two wooden pillars opening onto a small cement portico, and beyond the northwestern section of the split-level, was a sloped concrete driveway that led down about an eight-foot decline to a two-car garage. The Stedmans had an automatic garage-door opener and the driveway was heated underneath so that snowfall in winter melted into a drain. In 1995, Jules had the concrete replaced with interlocking brick. Stairs off of the front hall led upwards to the bedroom area and downwards to the family room. Tyler's bedroom and Rebecca's were at the front, separated by a washroom and a linen closet. Tyler occupied the bedroom at the end of the hall. The master bedroom took up the entire back side and included an en-suite bathroom and walk-in his and hers closets. There was a patio door that led onto a small balcony overhanging their backyard. From that balcony and through the master bedroom windows the Stedmans had an impressive view of the town below: the central shopping district, a corner of Riverside Park, and a fair piece of the Sheep River and one of the bridges under which it flowed slicing the town in two. From the kitchen windows, one could only glimpse the tops of roofs and trees, the tower in the middle of the restored railway station that now served as a cultural centre and tourist information bureau, and a few steeples. Downstairs, off the front hall, one came to a landing area that had storage closets, a laundry room, and a half-bath on the right. Jules's den on the left was large enough for a pull-out sofa and could be used as a spare bedroom. A second set of steps led down to the family room which almost covered the entire lower level area. A square of space to the left of the bottom of the staircase comprised the furnace room. In the family room, there was a gas fireplace in one corner with an arrangement of seating around it, a ping-pong table and games area for the kids, and a corner bar.

Patio doors led off the back of the room giving access to the terraced backyard area where Jules and Myra had spent some quality time creating rock gardens and several perennial and annual flower beds. Unlike some of their neighbours, they did not have a swimming pool. A raised gazebo in the northeast corner of the backyard looked through an opening in the trees of the escarpment offering views of the town similar to the perspective from the master bedroom. There was a flagstone patio area just outside the lower sliding doors on which, in summer, a gas barbecue and grill not only sat but received a rather regular workout. There was a back door at one end of the kitchen that opened onto a small porch that held up one end of an outdoor clothesline. Steps from the porch brought one down onto a grassy, sloped area that eventually merged with the yard below via a set of stone steps flanked by two cascading rock gardens.

Since moving in 1986, Myra had put 35 Dewdney Common through a few rearrangements of furniture and decor. The contemporary art deco look of their Calgary apartment—black and white and chrome and glass—virtually disappeared upon moving in. All that remained were three black and chrome kitchen stools that became bar stools and a lampstand of curved chrome that featured three separate globular lamps on seven-foot arching tubes attached to a round base. These items found a home in the family room. The first phase was a Colonial and Western look that seemed after three years to clash with the both the split-level style and the spirit of industry and oil that was driving the new West in Alberta. So the first attempt at contemporary brought the Laura Ashley look to the Stedman dwelling with softer, pastel carpeting, replacing basic brown with calf-skin throws and printed-fabric furnishings, patterned wallpapers, and a new rustic pine dinette set. By 1997, Myra was tired of all that. After months of itching and pondering, the most recent make-over removed all wallpapers in favour of latex paint in cranberry, slate grey, and teal shades and ripped out all the broadloom except for the family room carpeting and replaced it with hardwood flooring. Ceramic tiling covered the hallway, kitchen, and bathroom floors. Colour coordinated rugs were purchased for the bedrooms. A large Persian rug graced the living-room floor and a small, matching one lay beneath the dining-room table, chairs and buffet with hutch that were now made of cherry wood. A hot-tub was purchased for the outdoor patio. The Stedmans were economically blessed and socially progressive, comfortable without becoming ostentatious or boastful, just like many other residents of the town they had adopted as home.

Okotoks was a picturesque place, an energetic place, a safe place to raise a family. People left doors unlocked and walked the streets at night without fear. Neighborhood Watch happened unofficially, instinctually without any need for programming or training. The Wojniewskis on the east side of the Stedmans watched obsessively.

"Come on in the house, Tyler. Don't linger on the porch." Myra Stedman's light command betrayed all her attendant undercurrents of anxiety. She knew it was probably already too late.

She had caught the flip of a lace living-room curtain next door rolling back into place. She had already begun to imagine the birth of gossip. Magda, abrupt and disdainful, remarking to Yannis, "So the Stedman boy comes back from trip on crutches. Dat school never has enough adult supervisors for dose outings."

Yannis, equally terse but faintly smiling, "Ya. Ya. But look on de bright side. Dere vill be no kids playing ball hockey on the street for a vhile, tramping all over our front yard and garden patch vhen deir ball goes astray. Unt less noise!"

"Ya. But I bet dere vill be a few indentations in the lawn from crutch tips getting in and out of dat van."

Myra consoled herself with the realization that her insecurities were far more valid than such selfish, petty concerns.

Tyler swung himself through the front door as his father held it open. Rebecca and Jules Stedman trailed in after him. When their jackets were dutifully hung up, Jules took Tyler's overnight bags to his son's bedroom and returned to join his family around the kitchen table while Tyler recounted his version of the school trip story. He talked about changes made to the Tyrell Museum since the last time the family had visited there. He mimicked Alex's excitement over dinosaurs in an amusing but favorable manner. He described the trail leading out to the dig site on the second day and the unfortunate event that brought about his cracked kneecap. The not-always-patient endurance of the trip to the hospital, the boredom of the waiting room and his understanding of what the doctor told him closed off his part of the conversation which his mother had interrupted with inquisitorial questions in several instances.

Rebecca drifted in and out between fascination and disinterest, pausing to make gurgling sounds in her chocolate milk which got her glares from her mother resembling shots fired from an alien's ray-gun. Jules Stedman listened with his characteristic patient, relaxed intensity, the picture of a man who had once been a boy, the picture of a father who could image the steadfast love of God as if it caused him no effort to do so. In fact, he worked hard at presenting such an image almost constantly because it was so diametrically opposite to the portrait painted for him by his own father during his childhood and adolescence. He had developed as great a measure of success in such interior, personal work as he had in his actual daily work as Vice-President of Marketing and Sales at the Calgary office of Trans-National Oil and Gas Company Limited (Tranogco).

"Well," Myra injected after letting out one more exasperated sigh, "I'm going to have to track down Dr. Krupka and get Tyler in to see him some time on Monday." Her upset-apple-cart face was conspicuous.

"Sounds like a plan." Jules spoke up while rising from the table. "Let me know when you're done with the phone. I've got some calls to make to Singapore." His leaving was Rebecca's cue to ask Tyler to take her to his room to show her his bruises and his little collection of Badlands souvenirs. Everyone moved away to enjoy some relief from the tension and irritation that comes out of situations you wish could be otherwise and mishaps one can't reverse or fix automatically. Bear up. Find patience. Move on. Unless you're like Myra Stedman.

Washing up before bed that night, Tyler removed his bed pants, soaked the crotch, and hand scrubbed it with soap and then rinsed. He struggled to put them back on over his still somewhat sore and swollen right knee as the damp patch stuck to his bandage. He grabbed up his crutches and swung himself back to his room where he eased himself into bed confident the evidence of his other accident would be dried into obscurity by morning.

Saturdays at the Stedman house frequently followed a similar pattern. Myra got up with Rebecca and took her to figure-skating lessons at the arena or soccer practices depending on the season. Jules installed himself in his home office to catch up on paperwork for his employer. Tyler slept in and did some household chores or homework after waking. Myra Stedman looked after lunch the way she managed most of the meals she prepared—with microwave-able foods or oven-ready entrées or occasional pots of canned soup. Afternoons were spent either with the children out playing, or family shopping expeditions, or collective yard work. But Saturday suppers were always Jules Stedman's responsibility. He worked from scratch, used fresh produce and other ingredients, and introduced his family to a variety of international and vegetarian delights. Tyler and Rebecca regarded Saturday suppers with eager anticipation. Myra harbored a reserved, dubious enthusiasm. Featured on the menu the day after Tyler's return would be meatless chimichangas, five-bean salad, and tropical fruit enchiladas for dessert. (Myra had already registered her request for no jalapeños.) Saturday evenings were spent watching TV or going to a movie together; watching the hockey or football game of the week; or viewing games live at the Saddledome or McMahon Stadium. Tranogco executives enjoyed a four-pack of complementary season's tickets for the Flames and the Stampeders. Sometimes these games were played in the afternoon. Six days of the week, from Monday through Saturday in fact, the Stedmans pretty much mirrored the dormitory-town living patterns of most of the other citizens of Okotoks. That's how that Saturday passed, ending with the family glued to the tube in the family room watching the Flames lose a Stanley Cup playoff match.

Some Sunday mornings, the Stedman family also appeared conformist by attending worship at St. Paul's United Church. Yet Sunday was by and large an atypical day measured against the routines of their neighbours. Sunday was a day they spent ten miles southeast of Okotoks on the old Davis homestead, an acreage of farmland reduced in size from its former grandeur. Grandpa Davis was now housed in the two-bedroom cottage that used to be the hired hand's residence. Tyler and Rebecca's Aunt Ola lived in the larger house managing what was left of the family cash-crop farm, and assisting "Pops" with a few horses,a sizeable vegetable garden, a couple of acres of woodlot, and his Christmas tree operation. She did all of this with no help from Uncle Louie who had "flown the coop" or been "given the boot" eight years ago, depending on whose version of the story one was party to. At the moment, Sunday was still a good night's sleep away.

Which was what eluded Tyler. His bruised and slightly-fractured knee throbbed even when he elevated his right leg with an extra pillow. He couldn't get comfortable in bed. So he got up made the effort to stagger to the washroom to fetch a couple of ibuprofen tablets from the medicine cabinet, which was his pharmacist mother's recommended medication. He made his way back to bed and was just beginning to feel some pain relief when he turned his face towards the digital clock radio on his bedside table. It was 11:58 P.M., two minutes to midnight. That set his mind churning in several re-runs of the previous two-day foray into paleontology, a bit of amateur theatre, the antics of his cousin and other classmates, the unfortunate accident during the dig, the onset of adolescent sexual awareness, and coming home to his mother's apprehensions about his cherished dream. It might have been around 2:30 A.M. before he finally nodded off.

# Chapter 3:
# Grandpa's Acreage

Sunday thus came soon enough, a bright, balmy, cloudless late spring day. Once out of town, the sun shone larger and more brilliant. Ponds appeared like rippled fun-house mirrors. The tributary creek of the Sheep River that kept them company looked like a garter snake slithering low-down in the fields, keeping pace with their van. The foothills were a parade of every shade of green imaginable: hunter green, sea green, lime green, olive, clover, prairie-grass green, Granny Smith apple green, moss green, English ivy green, char-treuse, fern, willow, emerald, Kelly green, water-cress, bottle green, deep green. Perhaps the only shade missing was that aged, tawny green look of weathered copper roofing so prevalent in Scandinavian cities. Sprouts of oats, alfalfa, rapeseed, and hay aligned the fields like battalions of saluting soldiers on parade. Corn stalks were already higher than a cowboy boot in some places. Where fences didn't separate the fields, stands of poplars used as wind-breaks did, or small sections of mixed coniferous and deciduous woodlot. Per-haps Tyler noticed the countryside more than usual this day because the song playing on the car radio was by a group named Green Day called "Good Rid-dance (Time of Your Life)." It was that kind of day, a-whole-day-at-the-farm Sunday for the Stedman family, a day to put all worries, troubles, fears, and other stressors into some cold storage vault or morgue drawer labelled "good riddance" at least for the time being.

The family van turned right off of Highway 7 onto an extension of 434 Ave. S. That was a new designation for 911 emergency purposes. Formerly it was known as Macmillan Line, named after one of two original homesteaders in the area. It was one of two spur trails that once divided below Calgary and passed around Okotoks rejoining the Macleod Trail East of the town. Many locals still called it Macmillan Line, including "Pops" Davis, whose family had lived on it as long as he could remember.

When they arrived on the farmstead, the laneways were still drying out from yesterday's rain. They drove in through a couple of puddles until they stopped beside Pops' cottage. Ola was off at St. Bartholomew's Orthodox Church in South Calgary. She would not get home until after one P.M. Pops had just finished up the lighter barn chores that he could still handle before they arrived. Freshly barn-scented boots and coveralls "perfumed" the mud-room through which the town-dwelling Stedmans passed to greet him. He was there in the middle of the one large room that occupied half of the cottage and comprised kitchen, dining area, and sitting room. He remained seated in the Saratoga rocking-chair by the wood stove wearing a pale blue T-shirt, jeans and white sport socks, bald as a cue ball with a rim of monk-like white hair joining his ears around the back of his head. A wide grin almost connected his ears at the front writing joy all over his partially-wrinkled face like a telegram typed in Bodoni bold. Rebecca got to Grandpa first with kisses and a hand out ready to receive a few happy-to-see-you-again Milk-Duds which she would soon share with Tyler, who came up next to exchange hearty pats on the back. He could drop the crutches to do that.

"My, my, my, young man," Pops remarked, "I heard you met up with a little accident, or did the accident meet up with you? Sure hope it's not too serious."

"At the moment it's tolerable sore, Pops, just a lot of swelling and some nasty big bruises."

Jules came up and hugged Pops hello. Myra made her way to receive and return kisses of affection. "Hi, Dad. You're looking well. Still sticking to your salt-free diet?"

"Yep. Don't have much choice really, what with you checking up on me frequently and Ola tracking my calorie intake and cholesterol levels more closely than a hawk spying on gophers in a hay field. Doc Herbison was pleased when he looked me over three weeks ago."

"Doctor Herbison is ten years older than you are and starting to go blind as well as dotey," Myra interjected. "He should have become fully instead of semi-retired seven years ago when he started downsizing his practice."

"He'll be happy to hear you're still worrying about us both. By the way, I'd appreciate it if you'd not try to patronize me by using old-fangled words like 'dotey.' Now, how would you kids like a few games of Parcheesi before lunch. Alex is tied up this morning helping Mr. Wilton clean up his henhouse. Damn weasel got in and went on a real rampage. Ola's left a big pot of rabbit stew simmering on the stove, a dozen home-made rolls on the warming shelf ..."

"Rabbit st ....!!" Myra began to protest.

".. and there's a couple of cheese and cucumber sandwiches in the refrigerator for your mother."

To which Myra reacted with a mild "hrmmph!" of exasperation and then headed off to the spare bedroom through the door to the right of the wood stove where there was likely laundry that needed ironing and folding.

She and Ola had reached some agreements. There were still some things Myra could do for her father and some of the clothing detail was one of those things. Myra used ironing as a form of soul massage. It helped put the lid on the simmering pot of her own uncertain self-esteem which had developed increased uneasiness since Ola's entry into the family circle. How could she avoid being compared to a woman who was the consummate home-maker and also worked for a living and ran a business no less? It was Myra who did most of the comparing more than anyone else. Where was the place for the dutiful daughter once the very competent daughter-in-law had appeared on the scene and was living on site?

Ola was more than willing to let Myra do whatever she wanted to do, whatever helped sustain the father-daughter connection. That too roused slight irritation in Myra, that she didn't have to fight or argue about such things. Ironing was one reassuring exercise. Every smoothed wrinkle, every nicely-pressed crease was like smooth, glutinous gravy in that stew pot that kept the bits of jealousy and hunks of envy and chunks of inadequacy-feelings in check, subdued beneath the reassurance that blood is thicker than vodka. But the floating seeds, the floating seeds remained disturbing—seeds of self-loathing and seeds of contempt for a sister-in-law locked into a role of usurpation. Such seeds, Myra knew, must never, never be permitted to sprout. Press and fold. Suppress and hold.

"Parcheesi would be fun, Grandpa," Tyler remarked while Rebecca was already busy laying out the board on the kitchen table, "but I'd really love to go out to the barn and see how the foal is doing, and Striker."

Striker was a chestnut stallion that Grandpa had given Tyler several Christmases ago (the same year he footed the bill for Rebecca's figure-skating lessons: skates, outfits, the works.) Something just as special had come with that gift—a genetic transfer in the bloodstream of Davis males of a love for horses. Louis, Myra's brother, had indeed grown more fond of betting them than of riding them which was the primary source of his current disgrace and unofficial divorce from family affairs. He was unsuccessful in transferring his passion to his adopted son, Alex, who as a toddler just screamed and wailed whenever Louis set him on a horse. In recent years, well after Louie's departure, Alex developed a middling affection for things equestrian. When Louis picked up two-year-old Tyler one day during a family visit and did the same, his adorable nephew yelled, "'ets' go. Giddy-yup! Me love horsey." He did, and he loved riding. Tyler was a natural. His interest and his fever soared not towards thoroughbred racing, nor to show-jumping, nor to such a British import as steeple-chase, nor polo (for which there was a playing field on the outskirts of Okotoks), but to all things cowboy and rodeo. It was no transient fantasy. As he grew older he had been practicing, literally learning the ropes, and the saddles, bridles and bits, the commands, the techniques, the responsibilities, the joys, and the upsets that turned such dreams into realities. This fall he would be entered in his first junior competition in his own town. The junior and high school circuits were just his stepping-stone to the novice ranks and—when he was eligible and proved good enough—the pros. Louie's encouragement and support had evaporated in 1991, but Pops still carried the vibrant chromosomes of horse sense and he was as readily present and available for boosts of stimulation as fresh milk in a refrigerator.

"Why, of course!" Pops replied, "How silly of me to invite a young boy who's just got out to the country again to stay indoors, especially when he's got horses on his mind."

"I don't mind playing a couple of games, Grandpa. It's only ten o'clock. Plenty of time before lunch to get out to the barn as well."

"Deal. Jules. What colour would you like? Seems Rebecca has already fixed on red for herself."

Grandpa won the first game and engineered the second so that Rebecca would triumph. Tyler didn't mind. His concentration focused just as much out the dining-room window toward the horse barn as it did on the game at hand. That barn, an equipment shed, a small granary for storing hay, and a derelict privy were the only out-buildings left on Grandpa Davis' portion of the farm. After Louie's departure, Pops had severed a couple of sections and sold them

H. Lee Disher

to Wallis Wilton. He put the proceeds into an educational fund for Tyler and Rebecca. The management of the bulk of the 2,300 -acre farm had been progressively handed over to Ola: eighteen hundred acres devoted to cash crops in three separate parcels. Three hundred acres were woodlot within which Pops developed his one-hundred-acre Christmas tree farm. By 1998, Pops only held title to about fifty acres of which one was set aside for his homestead, out-buildings, lawns and a sizable vegetable garden. The rest was taken up by forty-nine acres of rolling pasture and grazing land for the horses. Ola's home, lawns gardens, the implement sheds and grain storage facilities occupied about forty acres. The remainder of the land was bush and stream and access lanes. Tyler's gaze couldn't take it all in at once, the bulk of his outdoor attention was filled with images of Striker, the foal, and their stable-mates. Unquestionably as the dice rolled and the little plastic pieces made their way around the board from one station of safety to the central home base, his mind was precisely divided: half here, half there.

There was where all four of them went after the second round of Parcheesi. Spare boots kept just for walking around a farm were worn. Good thing, since while the lawns, lanes, and pastures had pretty much dried up after recent downpour, the barn yard itself was still quite mucky.

There were still five horses on the farm: Striker, a healthy, handsome chestnut quarterhorse with a pair of white fetlocks on his forelegs; the new foal now nine-months old; Belva, the foal's mother, a piebald Narragansett filly; Charro, a blonde Appaloosa mare with an off-white mane and tail, sturdy haunches and firm, lean withers; and Tacitus, an old Percheron work-horse that had kept Pops company for years pulling a small hay-wagon, dragging out logs from the woodlot and cart loads of firewood, inspecting fences and ploughing up a small patch of ground for growing a few vegetables. It was a bit of old-fashioned hobby-farming for two.

"I named him Tacitus as soon as I acquired him," Pops recalled. "I just figured the two of us would wrack up a bit of history together. When I left school after grade eleven, I had developed a liking for Latin somehow. Tacitus was my favorite author, teaching me the value of keeping our past in perspective, even if it's only one's own perspective. I found a copy of his works in the original, with an English translation included, in a used book store in Lethbridge. Some days I just poke around in it for fun. *'Nullam ob eximiam artum; sed quod par negotiis neque supra erat.' ('He had talents equal to business and aspired no higher.')* That was written about some patrician who befriended senators and never made waves, like this ever-obliging animal here."

Tacitus gave them a nod and a flutter as they passed by his stall. Charro neighed from across the way. In the stall next to Tacitus, the foal was standing nestled up to Belva. Striker was not the foal's father. Belva had been bred by Koan, a black Galieno stallion owned by Wilton next door. The foal was already showing signs of strong, well-formed legs, high haunches, a durable back, and a noggin bedecked by a silky mane and bearing the appearance of a feisty, spirited steed.

"I've been thinking about naming him," said Tyler. "It's been a toss-up between Julius and Luigi, a way of sort of honouring either my father or my free-range uncle. But now I'm leaning towards Ironstone, something black like the rock that just cracked my knee-cap."

"Ironstone sounds like an excellent name!" replied Pops.

"But what a curious and unhappy reminder," Jules interjected.

"I know," Tyler continued. "But he looks like the kind of horse who has mind of his own and who would throw something at you in a minute if you weren't paying attention."

"I reckon you're getting' the hang of discernin' horses," Pops commented.

"I had a good teacher," Tyler added appreciatively.

"Yeah, the same guy who knows his way around a Parcheesi board," Rebecca piped in.

Pops winked a brief thank you as they moved on to Striker's stall. The stallion whinnied hello and pawed the floor with his right foreleg as soon as Tyler came into view. Tyler lifted a handful of hay which was readily received, and then reached into his jacket pocket to produce three cubes of sugar hastily scoffed from Grandpa's kitchen on the way out the door. The sugar disappeared in an instant with a gratifying smack of horse lips and a couple of joyful snorts.

"I know, Pops," Tyler said avertingly. "It's not a good thing to hand over sugar to a horse. I just couldn't reach the apples on the way out. They weren't on the table today. Do you think we could saddle him up after lunch and I could have a little ride?"

"But Tyler, your leg!" Rebecca worried out loud.

"I'll just need a little help getting on and off Striker. I'll be fine riding him."

Pops and Jules pondered Tyler's assertion as brother hushed younger sister into promising not to say a word about the possible jaunt to their uneasy mother, the dream-blocker.

"Okay, but it will cost you," Rebecca answered agreeably.

"What's the penalty this time?" Tyler asked.

H. Lee Disher

"Three games of Candyland and one of those sea mollusk fossils you brought back from the Badlands."

"You got it, sis," Tyler replied. Within him, a sigh went off, the kind of sigh that settled into satisfaction, that had it found its way to words would have uttered: "Oh, the things we do for love and for a little self-preservation. Small but worthy sacrifices nonetheless."

A clanging triangle sound, another family-ritual-when-needed, told the barn party it was lunch time. Myra hadn't forgotten all her country traditions after marrying out of them and moving into town. Jules was urban-born and raised but relished every opportunity to experience rural spaces and patterns and customs Myra and the Davises had introduced into his life. Especially he valued the peace of mind that came to him whenever he got out to the farm, out of his hamster-cage existence even for a few hours, even though he always brought some of his cage surroundings with him since corporate vice-presidents these days were expected to work long and tirelessly in service of keeping a company's edge over the competition. Rodent proclivities.

The barn-visiting quartet kicked off their boots in the mud-room and filed in to their places at the kitchen table.

"You'll have to serve up this stew, Pops," said Myra. "I can scarcely stand to look at it let alone smell it." She turned to the refrigerator to collect her sandwiches.

"Tyler's going to name the new colt Ironstone," chimed Rebecca.

"Ironstone? How come?" Myra asked.

"It's a black rock like that chunk that Alex loosened that came crashing down on my knee," answered Tyler.

"How appropriate," Myra remarked, "a horse whose name will be as a warning to you, an omen, perhaps, prompting you to consider a more civilized recreational pursuit."

"Mom," Tyler went on, "you let Rebecca risk figure-skating."

Jules and Pops began keeping mental score.

"Yes, there's always risk she will seriously injure herself; but she's well coached and supervised. She isn't allowed to try a higher risk move until those training her believe she's ready. But you can't anticipate what a wild horse is going to do. Rebecca's in a sport that's about grace and finesse which would be true for you if you'd develop an interest in show jumping and dressage as I once did, but you've got your heart and head set on rodeo. And it isn't only fear of you're getting injured that causes me concern. Forgive me for worrying, if you must, but I'm a mother. It's my job."

"And we all love you because you do it so well," Tyler replied. "I'm not being facetious about that, Mom. I mean it honestly and sincerely. Because I know you worry, I try to exercise good sense as well as horse sense. And I've been trained and coached by Pops and one of my high school gym teachers. And at dude ranch again this summer I'll get more guidance and safety tips from guys who know rodeo as well as you know pharmaceuticals."

"What's that about your mother and the farm?" inquired Pops.

"Not the farm, Dad," Myra replied. "Pharmaceuticals—drugs that I deal with weekly working half-time at the pharmacy. Which reminds me, here are your noontime pills."

"Could I have a little more stew, Grandpa?" Rebecca asked.

"Why sure, sweetheart, just let me swallow these little nuisances first."

There was not unanimity regarding the main course, but all five of them enjoyed the fresh apple pie that furnished dessert. The last forkfuls were just being consumed with the last sips of tea or milk when Ola's car was heard driving up her lane and screeching to a stop.

# Chapter 4:
# Aunt Ola's Farm

"Stupid chickens! Go back home where you belong!" was what she shouted as she got out of her car closing the driver's-side door. "Shoo!"

What Tyler and Rebecca heard through grandpa's open kitchen window was "Stoopit Shickenz! Go bagome ver you belonk!." Thirteen years in Canada had not totally eradicated Aunt Ola's Ukrainian accent. It resurfaced on those rare occasions when she became over-excited. The adults had developed their own means of not noticing it so well that Tyler and Rebecca almost choked stifling their titters.

Uncle Louie, their mother's brother, had been Ola's "rescuer" from the disaster of Chernobyl. From the get-go, his motives were less than noble. With Myra gone off and married to Jules, and with increasingly less help from his father, managing the farm had become increasingly difficult. It needed a woman's presence and domestic skills and other arts to make it run more smoothly. His gambling and drinking habits were well known throughout the area, which made him ineligible as a mate in the eyes of just about every available single woman for four or five hundred miles around. The Chernobyl disaster in the Ukraine afforded Louie a golden goose opportunity. A couple of long-shots that paid off handsomely had served to finance two of his own trips to the ravaged foreign region and covered the costs of bringing Ola over on a two-month respite visit. He behaved himself well enough to present a charming, welcoming, charitable character, which in the better part of himself he actually was. Correspondence was kept up over the next several months. Another visit for Ola was arranged and she began to fall in love, more with the land and the landscape and the comparably more favourable prosperity of this other country in many ways resembling her own. Louie was more of an infatuation, a romance which to a nineteen-turning-twenty-year-old Ukrainian girl without much experience in such matters was an unavoidable enticement-in-waiting. When Louie began talking seriously about love, about living together permanently if she was willing to emigrate and become married, Ola's resistance lasted about as long as it takes the sand in the top of an egg-timer to filter down into the bottom half. Well, maybe two or three more flips thereof.

But, there was a secret truth that needed unveiling. Ola had been married to a young, nuclear plant worker in 1984. A year and two months before the 1986 explosion, they had had a child, a son named Alexandr. Ola's husband, Uri Oosterov, was one of the first ones to die from radiation poisoning. As a personnel officer, he had been doing some negotiating with a few workers in a lunch room not far from the main reactor when the meltdown occurred. One of the first to be hospitalized, he lasted only a week and a half. Louie would have to accept Ola as a widow and a young mother with a toddler and bring both of them to Canada. Louie was unperturbed, even delighted by this unforeseen wrinkle. After the requisite negotiations with the Department of Immigration and $10,000 later, Ola became a landed immigrant in Canada destined for citizenship within eight-months of becoming married for the second time in her life to a young, affable Alberta horse-farmer and grain-grower named Louis Davis of RR 4, Okotoks. Her son, Alexandr, was approved for immigration too on condition that the same Mr. Davis legally adopt him. Agreed, but it would be easier just to call the boy Alex.

That was the fall of 1987. Pops, Myra, and Jules had hopes that it would help Louie settle down and cause his conversion to responsible living. Even people not prone to betting would have known the odds were very high against that. Within two years Louie already had one foot and a couple of suitcases out the door and a mistress in Calgary, a young woman from Nova Scotia who had come West seeking improved employment and life opportunities. Too bad for her too.

Ola might have been good for Louie, if he had stuck around, allowed her to form him into that better self she believed was there, and let her steadfast, austere yet sincere Eastern spirituality afford him a least a fraction of moral and common sense. He ran off before she had much chance for that. What did prove true was that Ola was good for the farm. Romantically naive perhaps, but she was in most other ways very bright. Her domestic skills were impeccable, tireless, and replete with old-country values of frugality, recycling, handcrafted artistry, and diligence. Her aptitude with figures, bookkeeping, and farm management were high calibre. Her strength and work ethic found outlets beyond the house in her own agricultural endeavours. Realizing Louie's uselessness and Pops' limitations, she was the one who encouraged the decision to downsize the horse breeding operation to a mere hobby, retain a manageable eighteen-hundred-acre cash crop in parcels, and allow Pops pretty much free reign over the woodlot parcel plus Christmas trees, and his own garden.

Ola grew up on a farm outside Chernivtsi, a small town in the shadow of the Carpathian Mountains. She met Uri at business school in L'viv. He was studying accounting. They were young but mature adolescents. Love and marriage and moving to Chernobyl, where Uri found employment, happened in rapid succession. Ola found secretarial work for an agricultural collective. At the time of the disaster she was off at a training seminar in Odessa . She remained there until it was safe to return to her newer home. A wealthy neighbour had offered to buy up her parents' small estate, orchards included. They accepted and had followed Ola and Uri to Chernobyl, hoping to enjoy early retirement. Within six months they grew listless, recognizing that letting the orchards go had broken their spirits and no alternate pursuits enticed them. The disaster resolved their irresolution when fallout spread into their neighbourhood, their drinking water, and seriously infected their lungs. They were moved to a state-care institution in 1987 and died within months of each other in 1991. They were still in their early fifties. Ola went back for an annual visit after her emigration year and attended their funerals four years after their dreams and lives had already crumbled.

Rural Okotoks was her opportunity to re-live her family's farming passion. It brought hope and smiles back to her parents in their dwindling last years when she told them about it, and brought them, illegally, some samples of sour cherry jelly she had made from the fruit of a pair of spindly Morello trees she had bullied into surviving on a sandy slope that trundled out of a wood-lot to the edge of one of her Alberta fields. There was something Chekhovian about Ola.

"I'll look after them, Mom. They got out of Wilton's outdoor pen. What a mess that weasel made of the coop! Ten dead, two missing, five injured, and blood and feathers and broken eggs everywhere!"

All this spilled out of Alex who came racing up from his mother's right as he saw her driving in headed towards the loose birds. As he rounded them up, picking up a couple of strays and starting to head the escapees back next door, Pops and the Stedman family were making their way over from Ola's left to greet her.

"Tyler! Rebecca! Uncle Jules and Aunt Myra, Hi! I'm just about done helping Mr. Wilton. I'll be over in about fifteen minutes," Alex shouted as he kept about his business.

"Wilton would do better with sheep! They're even more stupid but easier to manage than chickens," Ola continued muttering to herself louder than she thought.

"Oh, I don't know about that," Pops interjected as he drew near. "Sheep cost more to look after. Speaking of sheep, how was the flock at St. Bartholomew's today?"

"Don't tease me so, Pops, you know I take my faith seriously. We're a small, but committed congregation of 80 or 90 dedicated souls. We do what we need to do to stay strong."

"Yep, I reckon so. And I reckon the tithe they get from you does a lot more than keep fresh gilt on all those golden onions serving as dome and spire tops."

"Pops, that's all the fun you're going to have with me today over my religion. Be careful when you speak about fresh gilt, there's another way to spell that you know." Ola flashed a wink at her father-in-law then turned to the others. "Myra, Jules, so good to see you. Rebecca, you look as perky and clever as ever. Tyler, still strong, handsome and yet so sad to see you temporarily crippled. I was sorry to hear of your misfortune."

"But it is temporary, Aunt Ola. It doesn't come close to the sorrow you've had to bear."

"Thank you for your sincerity and kind sympathy, young man. Other teenagers could take a lesson or two from you, which is why I'm so happy you are Alex's cousin. I'm afraid he's got more of his stepfather's saucy and wild spirit in him than my simplicity and stability are able to counteract—either by genetics or by exemplary behaviour. I pray that you may have influence with him as you seem to have over horses."

"A horse is a more conquerable challenge, but thanks for your vote of confidence, Aunt Ola. He and I aren't exactly on speaking terms right now. If you have prayers that speed up healing cracked knee-caps as well as relationships, I'd appreciate some of those."

"There are prayers for every situation and occasion, Tyler, but we can never rush God's answers nor seek to predetermine their outcome. Well, I'd like to go into my house and change. Would you all like to come in for a visit. I can put on some more tea if you haven't had too much with lunch. Myra, Rebecca, perhaps you'd like to see the quilt I'm just finishing up."

"We'd be delighted," Myra replied. "Jules, however, has brought along some work he has to get done by Monday, so he's going to hibernate awhile in Pops' den. Tyler thinks he'd like to help Pops in the horse-barn and he has promised to be very careful. Alex will likely want to join them when he's finished helping Mr. Wilton."

"Me too!" cried Rebecca.

"Maybe later, dear. You also like visiting Aunt Ola and learning stitches from her. I also know she has great recipe for fudge she'd be happy to teach you."

"Fudge. Did you say fudge?"

"Yes, she did," Aunt Ola replied, "and she'd better hope I've got all the ingredients on hand. Come on in."

The members of the small clan went their separate ways: Jules back to Pop's domain, Pops and Tyler off to the barn, the women into Ola's house. They went, six differing body-spirits, to their separate endeavours: a pile of work, a bundle of risk, an immersion in domesticity. Alex returned from rendering assistance to Mr. Wilton in time to notice one older bent form, and one pair of jeaned legs swinging on crutches disappearing around the corner of the granary. He rushed in that same direction

"Tyler! Pops! Wait up! You're not going to the horse barn without me!" The slower-moving pair stopped in their tracks until he caught up. Tyler heaved a sigh and decided to tolerate his cousin's presence. Together they walked steadily to where the horses were stabled. Pops went into the stall where the tack was stored and pulled down a bridle and bit and a saddle.

"What! You're going to go for a ride, Tyler? Not without company! I'll get my saddle down and take Charro. She can't keep up with Striker, but she can keep you both within sight." Alex was never one to want to miss out on any bit of excitement or adventure if it was anywhere close to him, even in spite of his aversion towards smelly horses.

"Shh! Keep your voice down. It might just carry all the way to Ola's house and I don't want Mom and her to hear. They think I'm just here to help Pops with some chores and a couple of scrub downs," Tyler admonished his cousin, whose eagerness was indeed harder to tame than the vigor of any horse.

"Which means we also have to sneak out the front door of the barn and make fast behind the hedgerow so that they don't see us. Pops can take Tacitus out for a walkabout giving us a bit of cover."

"You young bucks! Always scheming," Pops remarked. "Come on, Alex, if Tyler's going to get mounted we'll have to help saddle up Striker and hoist your cousin aboard."

The pre-ride preparations ended, Pops led Tacitus out to the front dooryard as Tyler and Alex snuck by on the west side at a slow trot, almost out of view of Ola's living-room windows, an unnecessary precaution as it turned out, for at that moment Ola, Myra, and Rebecca were in the kitchen collecting fudge-making ingredients. Jules however watched the ruse in progress from Pops' den, flashed a smirk that didn't quite mask his own resident anxiety, and returned to the stack of financial reports that didn't jive, scratching his brain for a way to reconcile the figures that were beginning to give him incipient vertigo.

"I'm a little low on corn oil, but we can substitute liquid honey," Ola offered up while Myra helped Rebecca begin to blend milk, melted butter, brown sugar, eggs, vanilla, and caramel chips. "I never worry about the pinch of salt. It's always suggested, but I've never known it to make any difference whatsoever. And, of course, chopped nuts are optional. Let's make some with and some without. The art is in the stirring and patient watching. The science is having an accurate candy thermometer."

Slowly, steadily Rebecca moved the wooden spoon through the melting mass in the stainless steel saucepan on the medium-high burner, her other hand holding fast to the handle to prevent slippage.

"I hope Tyler's careful out there in that barn. Horse behavior is sometimes unpredictable, especially a mare's protective comportment when there's a new foal around."

"I share your anxiety, Myra," Ola commented. "It has to be a mother's, how do you say, idiosyncrasy? I'm amazed it was Tyler who came back wounded from the field trip. I would not have been surprised had something happen to Alex. I'll never get used to it, but I'm getting better at expecting it. I have to say, however, that I've had some rather bizarre showings in my dreams lately."

"Another showing! Oh please, share it, share it," Rebecca shrieked from over by the stove.

"When you've finished stirring and the fudge is poured out and cooling. I promise."

"Ola, I have to say I find your showings weird, beyond my realm of spiritual experience. Sometimes they augment my anxiety. Often they're so cryptic I listen to them the way I might read a science fiction novel. And I have to confess that I encourage Rebecca to treat them so, even though they indeed fascinate her."

"They are part of my faith, Myra. I could teach you the practices of *poustinia* and *sobornost* if you like. Or perhaps you'd like to borrow a copy of *The Philokalia*."

"I'll continue to pass for now. I have a hard enough time keeping up with any regular rhythm of personal devotion in my own life as it is."

"No pressure. To each one's own. But beware of spiritual starvation. St. Diadochos of Photiki said:

> *Everything longs for what is akin to itself: the soul, since it is bodiless, desires heavenly goods, while the body, being dust, seeks earthly nourishment. [The Philokalia, Vol. 1, p. 259]*

Now, Rebecca, let's put this thermometer in the pot and see how our candy is doing."

A more rapid pace was being set on the foothills of the back west acres and onto the trails of the woodlot. Tyler was hugging and flowing with Striker as symmetrically as a streetcar keeps balanced between rails beneath and an electric feeder-wire above. Alex was not far behind astride Charro. In the woods the pace slackened till they were trotting within two metres of each other.

"So far, so good, Tyler. But you know Striker's going to take off when we turn for home and gets a whiff of hay up his nostrils waiting for him back at the barn."

"That's what a good bridle and bit is for, Alex, and a hefty squeeze of the thighs. You have to stay in control. Love the beast, but never loosen the reins beyond measure."

"Who are you quotin' now? Some old American cowboy?"

"Grandpa."

As they neared the opposite end of the woods, a coyote unnoticed by the riders was detected by Striker who decided without the incentive of hay to break into a full gallop. Charro followed suit but not at a speed Alex couldn't handle. Tyler yanked back on the reins, began yelling "Whoa fella! Don't get so excited boy! Whoa down! Whoa down!" He pressed Striker's flanks with his thighs as hard as he could, but his muscles had already weakened some as a result of his cracked knee. Striker was beginning to respond but had gone several metres off-track. The shortened route back to the barn was now heading straight for a clustered rock-pile in mid-field. The horse needed no encouragement to gain speed again making ready for the anticipated jump. Up reared the forelegs with the hind legs soaring and tucking swiftly and neatly behind. The rocks were successfully cleared, but the landing was hard enough to begin to jostle Tyler sideways, just enough of a slide to topple him to the ground, where he hit, praise the Lord, on his left side and then rolled forward a couple of rolls. Striker continued riderless to the barn as Alex pulled up on Charro and dismounted to check on his fallen cousin.

"Damn! Rocks again! You and rocks just aren't getting' along these days. Are you okay?"

"Basically, Alex, yes. Sore now on my left side. I'm sure I'll have some bruises to show for this. Better just go to the barn and fetch my crutches. I'll have to hobble in from here."

"You got it, Hopalong. I'll be back before you can say Butch Cassidy and Sundance."

Alex didn't even have to go all the way in. Pops and Tacitus met him at the corral gate, already carrying Tyler's crutches.

"When Striker flew in alone, I guessed there'd been a tumble. Is Tyler all right?"

"He figures he'll be bruised on the other side of his body now too, Pops, but other than that I reckon he's okay. Want to help with the rescue? I'll put Charro back in his stall for now."

"Sure. That's the easy part. Explaining it to his mom and yours is going to be an Inquisition I'd rather not have to face. The only amusement will be watching them go through it good cop-bad cop style. Ola will probably make me polish silver and brassware for a month as penance."

Picture another twinning of youth and age disappearing down a slope on a mission of mercy. A faithful Percheron plods behind them straddled by a set of crutches. The dumped rider, now sitting up, breaks into mirthful laughter at their approach, the laughter of disbelief. If he could kick himself for his uncharacteristic stupidity, he would, but both his lower limbs are too sore or out of joint for such an exercise in self-castigation. The mental messaging circulating through his brain has the pattern of: "Well, if I'm determined to do rodeo, I'll have to get used to being spilled. Of course, it would help if I wasn't already cracked up while I was in training." He accepted the assistance of his rescuers uncontested.

Picture a trio, an elder book-ended by teen prodigies ambling back up the hill on six legs and a pair of crutches like a spider turned contortionist. The faithful Percheron plods behind without a care in the world, just a steady heartbeat for the humans who love him, with whom he shares a history.

"A pair of foxes were frolicking out in the woodlot darting through and around the trees. Here and there they were leaping, falling upon one another and rolling around together like Jack and Jill in the old nursery rhyme. They are actually chasing a pair of squirrels who elude them time after time escaping up one tree trunk after another, flying from branch to branch overhead. They are free spirits at play under a watchful eye. But a cloud appears in the sky like a patch now covering that eye. While it can no longer see, one squirrel runs over a fox-trap and is caught by the hind-leg. The snap of the trap sends the other animals scurrying. The foxes disperse, the other squirrel squeals running frantically in circles, feeling helpless to rescue his friend. An old shepherd dog appears, the colour and shape of wisdom. He approaches the trapped squirrel and has enough jaw power to grab hold of the upper clamp and lift it enough to release the captive. The dog licks the squirrel's wounds, and soon it is able to limp away with its friend squeaking gratitude and *"Adieu"* and *"Gloria, gloria, gloria, Deo!"*

"You call that a religious showing? I call that a fable, Ola." Myra presented her case with a cultivated pragmatism.

"Oh, but quite often animals are featured in the spiritual exercises and visions of the Desert Fathers. St. Olaf of Odessa had a multitude of such experiences which have been retrieved in his collected works. They are often allegories, as I believe this showing of mine to be.

"Oh, oh!" was Rebecca's comment as she turned her gaze from the quilt and conversation in the living-room out the window where she noticed Pops and Alex helping her brother wiggle toward the house next door and old Tacitus trailing behind. "Something's happened to Tyler again. Maybe your showing showed up in real life pretty quick this time, Aunt Ola."

All three rose quickly and left the house like the father in *The Night Before Christmas* who sprang from his bed "to see what was the matter." Jules, still puzzling over paper in Pops' den, was distracted by a rush of commotion and clatter and a cacophony of questions and truncated conversations making their way collectively through the mud-room to Pops' kitchen table.

"He what? I don't believe this!"

"What did you hurt this time, Tyler?"

"Easy, ladies, easy. One a time. Let's head in single file and try to settle down."

"Sometimes I wish I couldn't predict such things. I'll go get some ice for our wounded squirrel". As she headed to the freezer compartment of the refrigerator, Ola muttered within herself, "I really hope this isn't a foreshadowing of other wounds to come." But who was she to mistrust the powers of *poustinia*.

*Poustinia* is the Russian word for desert. It has a long-standing association with a form of Eastern spirituality based on solitude, fasting and prayer. The Eastern Orthodox fathers whose writings have been collected in the *Philokalia* are one source of meditative literature and theological thought used in Ola's version of such a devotional practice alongside the Christian Scriptures. It was a form of spirituality virtually unknown in the West until Catherine de Hueck Doherty helped popularize it amongst Canadian lay Catholics during the 1960s. Catherine and her first husband, Boris de Hueck, emigrated to England as refugees from the Russian Revolution and shortly thereafter arrived in Canada in 1921. A son, George, was born to them. Boris' health failed. Catherine's experience of poverty seeking to support her son and ailing spouse not only wore her out, it wore out her marriage. It was annulled. An agent discovered Catherine's excellent speaking skills and sent her out on a relatively lucrative lecture circuit. Spiritually, Catherine grew more and more ill at ease feeling distance from her calling to follow a Christ who was a friend of the poor. She gave her life to God's service in October 1930 making her own vow of poverty. She and George slummed it in Toronto during the early Depression years. She gathered younger men and women around her who founded a co-operative, mendicant venture based in Friendship House and adhering to the spirituality of St. Francis of Assisi. Scandal and rumour shut their fledgling operation down. Catherine moved on to an invitation to set up a Friendship House in Harlem in 1938 and found herself connected to early stages of the Civil Rights Movement in America. Rejection and persecution tracked her wherever she went lecturing, or on fund-raising jaunts. But it was internal staff turmoil that brought down her American Friendship House project. She returned to Canada in 1947 with her second husband Eddie Doherty whom she had married in 1943. They settled in Combermere, Ontario, where she hoped to retire and recover from the traumatic years of setback and disillusionment.

Soon, however, she was serving as a nurse and community worker in and around that area of the Ottawa Valley. Along with Eddie she developed a newspaper, *Restoration*, and set up a training centre for Catholic lay workers. A host of encouragements came Catherine's way from bishops, papal secretaries, and many who came to Catherine and Eddie's training events. In April 1954, they established Madonna House, a site for community living based on poverty, obedience, and chastity. Catherine began to fashion a wedding of her old country Eastern spirituality with her new world monastic-style Catholicism. Madonna House sprang up in other centres in Africa, the Americas, the West Indies, Asia, Europe, and Russia. Catherine's vision inspired them all, a vision of spiritual devotion, farming, household living, fine art, drama, theology, philosophy, science, and bare-bones economic existence. The concept of *poustinia*, of hermitage and desert spirituality provided the framework. The rule of love provided the guiding principle. The gospel was being translated into simplified, relational, supportive living in an increasingly technological, depersonalizing world. Over against revered and inculcated individualism, Catherine offered *sobornost*: a search for unity with the Holy Trinity in mind, heart and soul. Catherine de Hueck Doherty died in December 1985, a full four months before the disaster of Chernobyl and a good full year before Ola Oosterov sought refuge in Canada as the bride-to-be of Louie Davis.

That there was an active, vital Ukrainian Orthodox congregation on the southern edge of Calgary within a half-hour's drive of rural Okotoks helped make her new situation all the more attractive and bearable. It was there at St. Bartholomew's that she met with some lay people in the congregation who had experienced retreat time at Madonna House in Combermere. They introduced her to Catherine Doherty's work and witness. Ola herself attended retreats at Combermere and at a Madonna House in the Okanagan Valley in British Columbia. Her faith had a focus to which she could easily adhere. In the back corner of the field by her spindly cherry trees, Ola had her own private one-room cottage constructed for her own self-imposed times of solitude, a place she willingly and lovingly shared with others who wished to avail themselves of it similarly. One might suspect that she didn't quite fully embrace the concept of poverty since she still held title to a large parcel of land that returned relatively handsome profits. Yet Ola and Alex, and Pops for that matter, led pretty much a no-frills existence. Ola's generosity to her church and throughout the surrounding valley and to local Okotoks community service groups had become legendary. Her cash crop business was one of the very few that was still run as a labour-intensive rather than technologically-efficient operation. She hired dozens of manual workers. Ten percent of the profits of each year's harvests was handed over to some reputable religious organization working in developing countries. In recent years Ola had favoured the Canadian Food Grains Bank. "Little, be always little, poor, childlike." That was part of Catherine Doherty's Little Mandate. Ola took it straight to her heart.

• • •

Stature-wise, Ola was a tailor-made follower of *poustinia*. Five feet four inches tall at most, somewhat stocky but not stout, just strong and solid. She had fine angular Slavic features, fine blonde hair, a pale complexion, her eyes and lips somewhat withdrawn like her character in general—until you sought her opinions. Those she served up straight and uncompromising yet fair as far as they accorded with her perception of gospel principles. She would have done Louie a lot of good. Perhaps he did know that and it terrified him, so he fled. Tyler loved Aunt Ola as a kind of second mother. He trusted her judgment. He marvelled at her showings. He welcomed her concern evident in her simple preparation of an ice pack for his new-grown bruises. He experienced and appreciated her love that was wider than an Alberta sky, which is only about ten kilometres narrower than a Montana sky. And he was looking forward to seeing plenty of both of those vistas of heaven as the school year ended and summer holidays approached. By then the crutches would be tucked into a cupboard with the hope that they would become interesting artifacts in their own right some distant historical day. He had no intention of needing them ever again. He prayed to God for a full and speedy recovery, for the wisdom and strength he would need to turn his love of horses into a passion and finesse for rodeo, for the wit and heart to continue to be blessing to his friends and family—a support, a trusted crutch for others; a young man of faith in his own right. That would have been a safe bet for Uncle Louie to make.

As Tyler seemed soothed and comforted, Myra's anxiety escalated. She resolved to ground him for two weeks and seriously entertained the prospect of cancelling his Montana vacation. All this she kept to herself making pretense of being at ease. The momentary panic and concern that afflicted the whole family settled into a hearty and simple roast beef dinner, prepared with Ola's gospel touch, graced by Pops' opening words of thanks and capped off by savory cherry cobbler and ice cream. While Myra, Ola, and Jules tidied up the dinner dishes, Pops and the grandchildren engaged in a few more spirited rounds of Parcheesi. Then, farewells were exchanged as the Stedman family boarded their mini-van, backed out of the lane and turned down the road for home in town. One critical incident aside, the Stedmans scarcely realized how idyllic such a Sunday experience was compared to the hullabaloo, turmoil, disjunction and disassociation more common among perhaps 90 percent of other Canadian families on that or any other "typical" day, for some of whom even going to church left no evident imprint or was an ordeal of its own.

# Chapter 5:
# Class Act

Sunday subsided into sleep. Monday morning meandered in. Families in Okotoks mustered for another weekly venture into the mundane—work or learn, eat, drink, sleep, shop, cook, clean, launder, set out the trash and the blue box, share surface conversations, listen to the radio, watch TV, dream if you're fortunate, consider plans for the summer. Jules left for Calgary at 7:30 A.M. Myra dropped Rebecca off at Thompson Public School at 8:10. Alex waved from the front lawn of Dewdney Junior High as they turned the corner leading to the public school. Tyler stayed with his mother in the car; he had an appointment to keep. Loudspeakers carried the sound of simulated, clanging bells. Alex and Rebecca filed into their separate classrooms in their different schools to join their own circle of classmates. Except for a handful of recently-arrived Muslim students from Iraq, there was a wide measure of homogeneity in dress and deportment among the student body at both schools. Students of Anglo-Saxon, East European, East Indian, and Asian heritage all wore Tommy Hilfiger, Guess, or Gap clothing, Nike, Adidas, and Air Jordan running shoes. Reeboks were only worn by adults.

Dr. Krupka was waiting for Myra and Tyler in his office at the district health centre. After a physical inspection of the damaged area and close scrutiny of the X-rays, Dr. Krupka confirmed that there was only a hairline fracture of Tyler's left knee-cap. The bruises and swelling however seemed to have been aggravated and more recent contusions on Tyler's right leg invited inquiry. Tyler was not long confessing the risks he took riding the day before and the resultant accident.

"You're a very fortunate young man," Dr. Krupka observed. "You've probably added at least a week to your recovery period. Keep the tensor bandage on tight until the end of June. You might be able to ditch the crutches a bit earlier than that. Stay on the ground and get appointments at the McDaniels Clinic for physio-therapy starting in July."

Myra breathed a sigh of relief and then stared at Tyler as if to burn Dr. Krupka's words into his skull. Tyler returned his "What, Mom?" glance as they were leaving the doctor's office and she lowered her hammer, "Staying on the ground will be easy because you are grounded for the next two weeks! Don't argue."

Myra dropped a sullen and silent Tyler off at school by 9:30 and then proceeded downtown for coffee with some of her co-workers before starting her ten-to-four shift as an assistant pharmacist at Kingman's Drug Store on Elizabeth Street in the centre of town.

Rebecca's day in grade six would be filled by morning journals, exercises in long division, the parts of a flower, chapters fourteen and fifteen of *Black Beauty* for Reading Response, forty minutes of soccer, and a session on the establishment of Edmonton as part of a compulsory history of Alberta course. Recess and lunch break fell in place at their usual times. All her exercises and experiences in learning were engineered by the affable and competent Mrs. Barnaby.

Tyler's grade nine class was given time to prepare for Tuesday's end-of-session test on *Who Has Seen the Wind?*; some exercises in multiplying complex fractions; and music "hour" with Mr. Dillenberger, who was also Stephanie Wells' uncle. That filled in the morning. The afternoon was pretty much given over to graduation planning. In art period, each student made a large black silhouette of his or her own profile on black construction paper. These would be posted around the walls of the gymnatorium during the ceremonies. Physical education period was given over to modern dance, which meant learning some of the latest hip-hop moves. Enid Evans and, somewhat surprisingly, Kevin Noseworthy were the instructors *de jour*. The school-day closed with speeches from the nominees for Valedictorian and the secret ballot election. Alex had been nominated out of popularity, not for his scholarship. He came in third. Stephanie Wells was both bright and popular. She wound up runner-up to Raja Punkara, a conscientious scholar, help-you-on-a-moment's-notice

H. Lee Disher

kind of friend, and star volleyball player. She was second-generation Canadian after her grandparents emigrated to Alberta from Bengal province in India at the end of World War II. It's probable the prevailing currents of political correctness tipped the balance in her favour in a close-of-the-century grade-nine classroom in Canada. No one mentioned that as they shared celebration cake and ice cream provided by the indomitable Ms. Morton.

Carol Morton had graduated with her Bachelor of Education degree with top honours in 1983 at age twenty-three. For her Bachelor of Arts degree she had majored in English and History. She was now thirty-nine and would not see forty until March 2000. She discovered a knack for teaching Junior High School pupils. Their enthusiasm, their burgeoning independence, their hormonal moods were conducive to her own high-energy approach to life, her restless mind and her controlled temperament that seemed to know when to be firm and unrelenting, when to ease up, when laugh out loud, and when to admonish in love. She rehearsed in her head the boundaries between closeness and detachment with all her students and found she had treated other people around her all her life the same way. All of her suitors so far had given up on forging any real connection with her, though one patient and slightly resilient soul had dated and befriended her for seven years. Vulnerability frightened her. Intelligence, politeness, occasional wit, and coolness became her allies in self-protection and exercising control. She was something like a female panther. Her students respected her, received her as an adult friend and mentor who learned along with them, welcomed her as "one of the gang" during in-class parties, class trips with sleep-overs and games of Marco Polo in the pool. She made time for them for extra help before or after classes or during lunch break because she wanted each student to "get it," whatever the troublesome subject was. She was the den mother who sat up with you at night in the hotel if you needed to talk. She told your parents straight: what you did well, where you needed brushing up, and *that* included life and social skills as well as academic aptitude. She knew that ice cream and cake was a good way to wind up a valedictorian election.

After the bell rang at the end of that school day, Tyler and Alex stayed for a soccer practice. Alex was a keen goal tender. Tyler, mostly because of his height and size, played defence—not particularly well, but good enough, and intimidating just by looks to many opposing players. If only they knew how few violent, rough-housing genes Tyler harbored within his psyche, they might have kept the ball on his side of the field more often. For the rest of this season, however, Tyler wouldn't have any effect on any opponent. Injury and crutches had sidelined him. Just before heading out to practice that day, Enid Evans hinted to Tyler that Stephanie Wells wouldn't mind if he got up the nerve to ask her to the Graduation Dance.

"I'll think about it, Enid," he replied.

"Well, don't think too long, or you might miss your chance."

"And who's taking you, Enid?" Alex jumped in having overheard with excited interest.

"Oh, I don't know. Perhaps some wild, red-headed guy who plays goal on the soccer team, if he's interested."

"Interested! I'm exspastic! Consider it a date!"

"Okay, Alex," Enid said, unable to restrain a smirk, "but I think you meant to say 'ecstatic'."

"Right. Ex-tak-tik."

Enid smiled and skipped away, still chuckling.

"Whoa, Tyler—Grad Dance: me and Enid, you and Stephanie, if you just get up the nerve to ask her. Is there a God or what?"

"Check with your mother, she's more familiar with the Almighty than I am. Anyhow, as I said, I'll think about it. Come on, you've got a practice to attend to."

Ola was busy that afternoon interviewing new applicants for field labour. Wallis Wilton offered to go to town to bring Alex home from school. She thought she detected something eager in his eye about the prospect, something she hadn't noticed in a couple of years. Perhaps another "showing" would unveil more for her. She watched Wilton get into his pick-up and drive off wearing, was it? Yes, it was a pair of shined shoes!

Wilton arrived at Dewdney Junior High School after most of the students had gone home for the day. He went to the office area to report his presence and his objective and found a sign taped to the doors: "Meeting in progress. Please go to Staff Room (Room 102) to check in." He kept walking down the corridor to his left, reading numbers on room doors, turned to his right at the end of the hall and approached Room 102 where the door was slightly ajar. He heard the sounds of a meeting just about breaking up. Staff were discussing one last concern about the graduation ceremonies. It seemed there was going to be a shortage of chaperones for the dance.

"Well, let's sleep on that overnight," said Mr. Purnell, the principal. "That's about all the time we allotted for today's meeting. Motion to adjourn?" Moved, seconded, and carried. The staff began to file out separately. Mr. Purnell noticed Wilton standing by the door.

"Can we help you?"

"Oh, I'm Wallis Wilton. I'm Alex Davis' neighbour. His mother is busy today and she sent me in to pick him up and drive him home. I'm just letting you know why I'm here."

"Thank you, Mr. Wilton. You'll find Alex out back on the playing fields. Soccer practice should be over in about ten minutes."

Mr. Purnell excused himself as he passed by on his way to leave some papers in the office and then head out to his own car in the parking lot. One staff member was left in the room tidying up the coffee mugs and straightening the furniture.

Wilton spoke up. "Excuse me, aren't you Ms. Morton. We met the other day when the field trip buses came back from the Badlands. Wallis Wilton, Alex Davis' neighbour."

"I don't recall actually meeting, Mr. Wilton. I do remember you being there to pick Alex up, and...yes, you tipped you cap towards me as you got into your truck I believe."

"I suppose I did, Ms. Morton. I always try to be polite, especially when I see someone so striking as yourself. I hope you don't think me forward, ma'am, but I figure you dress yourself as smart as you must actually be from what Alex tells me about your teaching abilities. It's a habit of mine to complement people on things I appreciate about them, even perfect strangers."

"It's not such a bad habit, Mr. Wilton, though I suppose some might consider it forwardness."

"Well, thank you, ma'am. If you can stand another piece of forwardness, I'd like to say that I caught the tail end of the conversation at your meeting. If you're short chaperones for that Graduation Dance, I'd be happy to volunteer. My Friday night calendar isn't very full after I've got my chores all done for the day."

"That's very kind of you to offer, Mr. Wilton. I'll let Mr. Purnell know in the morning. If we need you, his secretary will call you. Perhaps I'll see you there then?"

"I'd welcome that opportunity, Ms. Morton. Wallis—my first name's Wallis."

"Carol."

"Good to actually meet you, Carol. That sounds like the end of practice whistle. I have to go round Alex up."

"What an appropriate metaphor, Wallis. There are times I wish I knew better how to harness some of Alex' willful wildness. If he actually applied himself more, he might not only appreciate me as a teacher, he might be surprised at his own ability to learn."

"I think I know what you mean, Ms. Morton, uh, Carol. Hope I see you again soon."

Good-byes were exchanged. Heartbeats flared up a few notches. Interests were twigged. An original errand took precedence for Wilton. Ms. Morton sat down in the staff room to give tomorrow's test on W. O. Mitchell one last going-over. She caught herself gazing out the window, short-circuiting a passing day-dream in mid-course. She had seen these winds before and had avoided being swept too far. A gaping cloud seemed to smile at her. A pick-up truck left the curb in front of the school headed for RR 4 Okotoks. Two male occupants were being variously transported. Personal chinooks happen.

H. Lee Disher

# Chapter 6:
# Shopping Spree

Thursday that week was an early dismissal day, a good time to go shopping for semi-formal wear. The small ripples of excitement generated by graduations in Okotoks were swallowed up in larger waves engulfing the whole province. Calgary was awash with Stampede preparations as usual for that time of year. Lesser tides had been generated by the local Canadian Football League opening game. It was a West Division battle featuring the once-mighty Saskatchewan Roughriders going head-to-head with the Calgary Stampeders, winners of the coveted Grey Cup championship in 1998 and looking for a repeat in the coming season. Jules Stedman had tickets for six in the Tranogco box seats for that night.

Anyone who has ever raised adolescents knows that getting young teen boys to go shopping for a new suit is like trying to have sex on an elephant. (Actually, a bartender in Las Vegas had just concocted his version of a new drink by that name that year. Sex-on-an-Elephant: one part rum, one part Grand Marnier, a splash of grenadine, and a spoonful of chocolate syrup. Sounds impossible. Tastes wonderful. But it has to be quick, so it's a shooter. The more conventional Sex-on-an-Elephant is a mix of Amarula and pear liqueur). Hot tickets for a season-opening football game were more than sufficient incentive enticing Tyler and Alex into an afternoon trip to the mall even if the shopping excursion would be drawn out and close to tedious. Having Myra and Ola along on the same outing made a more improbable chemistry. The parking lot at Southgate Mall was crammed almost full when they arrived. Jules dropped everyone off at the west entrance doors and said he had to head over to the office for several hours' of catch-up work. (Yeah, right! The truth was he had a few documents to file and could spend the rest of the afternoon watching baseball and golf on television in the executive lounge and enjoy a relaxation break in the hot tub. It was a workable, plausible way of managing his aversion to shopping with others. It wasn't about trusting their judgments when it came to making decisions. It was about the process they used on the way there.) Myra wasn't fooled, but she accepted it as a compromise. Better that than winding up accused of torturing him, (one of the darts he had tossed her way during a few of their infrequent marital spats). Jules agreed to return for them at 5:30 P.M. at the same doors. That would ensure getting to McMahon Stadium sufficiently ahead of game time to secure a parking spot within easy walking distance of the entrances even during rush-hour traffic. That was the plan. His plan—reasonable, logical, fair. "All agreed," was his assumption—his flawed assumption.

Myra checked the mall directory board to get their bearings. If they headed left and kept going clockwise they could check out three stores on the same path and then double back to one more in the centre aisle section. She had a plan too, you know. Ola was still fascinated by the fact that so many people could show up in one place to shop at once without having to stand in line for hours. And the choices, the multitude of choices! Even after over ten years in Canada, she couldn't quite get over the comparisons to life back in the Ukraine. Not that she wanted to return. She had read enough, wrestled enough , and wrung her brain nauseous searching for a way to redress global political and economic disparities. She wound up settling for a response from her faith, from the writings of St. Paul, Philippians 4:11-13:

> *Not that I complain of want; for I have learned, in whatever state I am to be content. I know how to be abased, and I know how to abound; in any and all circumstances I have learned the secret of facing plenty and hunger, abundance and want. I can do all things through Christ who strengthens me.*

Tyler and Alex were doing their best to follow along without feeling being dragged along. In fact, they were warming up to some state of excitement at the prospect of their first full suit, maybe even a tuxedo! Jackets and dress slacks were for boys, weren't they? Suits—suits were for young men. And ... no more clip-on ties!

Rebecca, on the other hand, thought malls were some of the most wonderful places on earth next to Disneyland. Things to do, things to see, people walking around like crowds at a fair, splashes of colour, barrages of sound, food to eat, drinks to drink, movie theatres, and other entertainments along the way. People were generally happier at Disneyland and in higher spirits. You might still overhear some arguments, the screams of some whining child, the complaint of customers about the pricing. At a shopping mall such occurrences were more frequent, more real because it was mostly only real people working and visiting there. Characters only showed up at Christmas and Easter and sometimes around Hallowe'en. No matter, malls were busy, alive, and loaded with fascination. Rebecca knew if she endured, went along, she too would be rewarded—a chocolate chip yoghurt cone, and maybe, a new outfit for her too. She kept her eyes peeled noticing items she might like for her birthday, or Christmas, or for school, or for taking to friends' parties, or to buy for the members of her family about whom she truly cared. She kept her ears alert trying to take in all the sounds she caught. She felt the frenzy of those were frazzled, the niggling frugality of those who came in search of bargains, the joy of those who found just what they were looking for, the disappointment and frustration of those who didn't, the energy of those who were in a hurry, and the sloth of those who weren't, who were maybe only there to people-watch and gawk and saunter and stay cool in an air-conditioned asylum for the economically insane. On occasion, she had the good fortune to see a shoplifter being nabbed. If she grew up to become nothing more than a professional shopper, Rebecca would have considered herself fulfilled. Shopping malls were as cathedrals to her, each step taken on terrazzo flooring was like a genuflection on hallowed ground.

In addition to its regular features, the mall this day was plastered with Calgary Stampeder sweaters and paraphernalia rooting the team on from every store window and at every fountain. Not to be outdone, the promoters of the annual Stampede had made sure their flyers, posters, displays and other enticements were liberally brandished throughout the facility. For over a century now, the first two weeks in July had brought a singular kind of fever to Calgary and area and the world-renowned Stampede revitalized everything Western and cowboy and pioneer-like as recurrently as black flies infesting Northern Ontario in June.

Myra and Ola, however, were especially agenda-driven that day. Their sons were graduating junior high. Their sons needed suits. Their sons deserved to learn the sound techniques of clothes-shopping these two women had developed over the years. First, both of them agreed, check out all the available offerings where you are. If nothing grabs you, move on to another mall, a different store. Second, keep track of what you tried on where and what you liked the most. If you think you've found what you want, never buy it right there and then. Take it off. Leave. Think about it. Come back. Try it on again. If it works for you, buy it, cash or charge. Myra parted company with Ola at this point. If the outfit truly screamed "It's you! It's really you!," then you could break the rule and purchase it on the spot not allowing someone else to snatch it away from you. Ola had experienced losses by wavering. She shrugged it off with an, "Oh well, perhaps it wasn't meant to be ." Myra and Ola also parted company on best value, best quality, best price. Ola was willing to pay more for something well-made that would last a while—even with growing children to outfit. Myra would use charge cards. Ola wouldn't have one. She had, in recent years, began to use a bank card which to her was the equivalent of always paying cash. She had also learned about lines of credit and how to attribute many purchases even for household or personal use as business expenses. She wouldn't, however, pay more than anything was worth in her opinion of fair market value. Myra was more of a sucker for things claiming to be "on sale."

Myra's route took them first to Le Chateau, then to Bootlegger, on to The Gap and then back to Jack Fraser's. There were a couple of more exclusive men's wear shops at Southgate Mall, but Myra and Ola both agreed there was no need to shell out extra dollars there on suits for growing adolescents. They could well put the extra money that would cost into new dress shoes and decent neckties.

Nothing Tyler tried on at Le Chateau seemed to suit or fit his more solid frame. Alex put on an off-white dress suit that only needed the cuffs let down on the sleeves. The pants came unhemmed. He thought he looked "boss." Myra and Tyler admired it on him. Ola looked it over and said, "We'll see." Bootlegger had mock tuxedos with possibilities for both young men. The Gap had very little in the dress suit line. Most of their formal wear still looked casual. There was a light gray suit that fit Alex rather well. Ola felt it was splendid. Myra reminded her that gray was a colour more suited to older men. It rather clashed with Alex' red hair. Jack Fraser's barely had anything in Alex' size, but there was a double-breasted black suit that seemed almost tailor-made for Tyler. He looked, what would Wilton say was the right word? "Debonnaire," yes, that would be it, debonnaire!

Time out for thinking things over meant heading to the food court. Rebecca got her yoghurt cone. Tyler and Alex settled for Banana Ramble and Peach Passion from Orange Julius. Myra got a cinnamon coffee and Ola a cup of chai (not quite like in the old country) from Timothy's. The conversation began with Rebecca asking about when they were going to take in the Stampede this year, and would her friend, Charlene-Berenson-next-door, be able to come with them, and would she be able to get some real cowboy autographs herself this year as Tyler always did. Myra and Ola took turns trying to settle those questions down relatively quickly for now. The more pressing considerations to be made were about the suits they had come to select in the first place. Alex was still stuck on the off-white outfit in Le Chateau. Myra agreed. It looked good and the price was great. Ola paused before offering her opinion. Her eyes declared she was about to put her foot down.

"It looks good. But it's not made well. He'll bust out of the stitches before the dance is over. And, Alex, think about it, you in something white around food and punch!"

The gray suit was also out, so that left the mock tuxedo at Bootlegger. It would cost more, last longer, and actually give Alex a little more class, even if he considered it to be a little less cool. A slightly different tux looked good on Tyler too, but the double-breasted ensemble at Jack Fraser's was destined to win the day. It wasn't a label popular among teens. That didn't matter much to Tyler.

In the course of all this decision-making, Stephanie and Enid and their moms showed up at the next table. Exclamatory greetings were shared. The mutual purpose of the outing was confirmed among them.

"So," Alex asked, "has my date figured out what she's wearing to the prom?"

"If you really want to see," Enid replied, "meet us at Mariposa in twenty minutes."

One group went off in one direction. The other group headed in another. Suit stops and purchases were made separately at Jack Fraser's and then at Bootlegger. Alex was actually eager to keep his on so he could show Enid how he would look. Ola suggested, rather decided, it would be better to keep the tuxedo as unwrinkled as possible until graduation day. Tyler, Myra, and Rebecca smirked slightly and giggled inside themselves. Once again the wild young red-haired stallion had to be reined in. It was a good move. The next move was down the corridor, round the corner to the Mariposa outlet.

The store was busy with numbers of mothers and daughters searching for the same magic, a means of turning a teenage girl into a princess or a diva for a day. Some moms and daughters would settle for taffeta or chiffon and lace and frills and puffed sleeves in other stores. Here most of the dresses were silk or satin—sleek, sometimes too suggestive for fourteen- and fifteen-year-olds. Some moms succumbed. Others refused. As the Stedman and Davis party made their way towards the back of the store, Enid Evans emerged from the dressing rooms. She was stunning in a high-neck, shoulderless, low-cut back, black, shimmering evening gown not quite ankle length, with a slit running only above the knee on the left leg. Alex' eyes bulged like protruding golf balls, his heart accelerated, and it took a monumental effort to keep his hormones in harness. Then, Stephanie came out and stood beside Enid, complementing and slightly overshadowing her friend. She was wearing a similar-styled form-fitting dress: deep mauve, leg slit on the right calf, half-open back, squared-off neckline just below her collarbones and spaghetti straps that didn't cover her bra straps at the moment. New lingerie was the next item on order. She was gorgeous in her simplicity and stature. Alex gave Tyler an elbow below the diaphragm and found his cousin virtually frozen solid. Tyler was transfixed. The boys' faces and stares registered all the attention and admiration the girls craved. The mothers and Rebecca were all mesmerized by the moment.

"Lovely, absolutely lovely," Myra spoke, breaking the spell. "Frances (Mrs. Evans), Doris (Mrs. Wells), you look utterly astounded and delighted, and you should be."

"Thank you, Myra," Mrs. Evans responded, "indeed we are. And this must be Mrs. Davis, Alex's mom. Enid's told me many interesting things about your son, and they aren't all bad."

"I'm relieved to hear it, Mrs. Evans. Ola is my name. Alex seems quite taken with Enid. It's good to see young people choosing sensible, enjoyable friends."

What they didn't all see while this conversation ensued was Tyler venturing to make his way toward Stephanie.

"If it's okay to use an older-fashioned word, Stephanie, I'd have to say you look just fabulous in that dress."

"Thank you Tyler, I know your compliments are always sincere."

"If ... uh ... if ... no one else has asked you to be their date for the grad dance, I'd be honoured if you'd consider being mine."

"Tyler, to be honest, I haven't dreamed it any other way. I've just been hoping you'd ask. I'm honoured to accept."

"Well, aren't we being formal. I guess this dating thing can be somewhat awkward. I mean us to just go to the dance as friends and have a good time. You don't have to stick with me all night."

"Okay, Tyler, let's just leave it at that and see how the night works out."

"Good. Well looks like we've got to be headin' out. My dad's picking us up at 5:30, and we're already eight minutes late. Bye."

"Bye, Tyler. See you in school."

The Stedman and Davis party made their way out of the store towards the mall exit. Before they had cleared the entry-way to *Mariposa*, they heard a couple of rather loud shrieks of joy back in the dressing-room area. Turning back they saw Enid all buoyant and congratulatory, almost jumping up and down with her arms on Stephanie's shoulders saying "Yes, yes, oh my God, oh my God, I'm so happy for you, Steph!"

Alex knew exactly what that was all about. He slapped Tyler square on the back and shouted, "Way to go, man, I wasn't sure you had it in you!"

"Had what?" Myra asked.

"As Pops would say it, Aunt Myra…gumption!"

"I see," Myra said, not sure whether she did or not. Ola saw. She knew she would soon see more beyond the suits and the satin and the celebrations, and it might not all be pretty. These were passing thoughts that only occupied her mind until they reached the west door entrances where Jules would be waiting somewhat impatiently to take them off to the big game. Ola had no clue about Canadian football. Football in the Ukraine and in Europe is what North Americans call soccer. Hockey she could grasp. Hockey was something from the old country she understood, even though they played it rougher in North America. If they had had a women's team in Chernobyl when she was growing up, she would have tried to be on it. She would have been a swift, feisty, sneaky little player like Valery Kharlimov or, who was that little guy that used to play for the Flames? Oh yes, Fleury, Theoren Fleury. Myra put up with football and hockey the way she suffered through occasional hemorrhoids by sitting still and quietly enduring them. It was still a family outing and where family went, she went.

It was actually closer to 5:45 when they got to the pick-up point. They had made a quick stop at The Gap store for a top Rebecca had fallen suddenly in love with. Jules was sitting on the steam generated by his own internal com-bustion engine whenever lateness messed up his master planning. He had learned not to make any kind of deal about it, almost realizing that shopping is not an exact science nor a precise art when it comes to timing. You have to allow leeway and expect it to take longer than you expect. He had driven around the circumference of the mall just to settle down his upset and frustra-tion. When he met them, he was gracious, glad to see them and genuine in sharing their sense of accomplishment in finding appropriate suits. Myra had also learned to help simmer down her husband's steam offering an apology for being late, which she didn't truly believe was necessary except as an interpersonal coolant. She rather enjoyed watching Jules' ears lose their redness, his face relax, and his breathing pattern return to regular. Ola enjoyed watching her sister- and brother-in-law fence without "losing it" in front of the children. She never fully got onto the Western obsession with clocks and time. Life took whatever time it took, didn't it? There wasn't much time to argue or admonish one another even had they wanted to.

Rebecca was not long in the van before she began plying her father with questions about the Stampede, when they might be going, and such...all the way from the mall to McMahon Stadium. The others found Jules' attempts at sincere but evasive responses somewhat amusing. There were still spots left in the stadium parking area overflow section. It would be a slightly longer walk to the entry gates than Jules had anticipated. The shoppers were still in good shape following their afternoon junket at Southgate mall. It was Jules who had let his muscles relax too much, having over-stayed his hot-tub session. They made their way into the stadium and to the glassed-in box seats about thirty feet above centre field tucked under the press box above them and overhanging the fifteen rows of gold section mid-field seating.

It was an intense atmosphere before the opening whistle. The Roughriders had a number of returning veteran players and could be expected to launch a threat to West Division supremacy. The Stampeders for the 1999 season were riddled with question marks. Last year's main stars had moved on. Quarterback Jeff Garcia had landed a job with the San Francisco 49ers in the National Football League in the United States. Star running-back David Sapunjis had retired and all-star defensive back Allen Childress had also gone south to play in the NFL. Dave Dickenson was being given the nod as starting quarterback for this year. He had not had a lot of experience in his back-up role in 1998. Newcomer Kelvin Anderson at running back and wide receiver Allen Pitts were carrying a huge load of fan and media expectations on their shoulders. If the "Stamps" were going to repeat their winning ways of the previous year, such hopes were saddled on these two workhorses as the go-to guys in order to accomplish such a feat. The other aces-in-the-hole resided in the continuance of a competent, winning coaching staff still headed by Wally Buono and assistants like George Cortez and Bob Vespaziani.

Over 31,800 fans jammed McMahon stadium. Near the end of the pre-game festivities, Stampeder veteran Rocco Romano rode around the field on the "touchdown" horse (the Stampeder mascot) carrying the Grey Cup on his shoulders. The Grey Cup victory banner for 1998 was hoisted into place above the press box. The home team fans were revving in high gear.

It didn't begin well. After the opening kickoff by Saskatchewan, Dickenson was sacked on the Stampeders' first play of the game. He got sacked four more times during the first half and seven times in all during the game as well as taking numerous hard hits from the Saskatchewan defence. Calgary's weak offensive line appeared leaky. Guard Jay McNeil left the game early on with a knee injury. On the second play of the game, Dickenson was forced out of the pocket and managed a nine-yard run. The rest of the opening quarter and first part of the second quarter continued in shaky fashion for both teams. The Roughrider placekicker managed a field goal putting three points on the scoreboard for the visiting team. The Stampeders managed to grind out a rushing touchdown for Kelvin Anderson following a short punt by Roughrider kicker Cory Stevens.

Late in the second half, Dickenson's arm became something like a magic wand. He found a way of connecting with his favorite receiving targets, Vince Danielsen and Allen Pitts. A sixty-seven yard drive was capped off by a perfect seventeen-yard pass to Pitts in the end-zone. The local crowd came alive again with their guys now ahead 14-3. Mark McLaughlin had made sure of getting the one-point converts after both Calgary touchdowns. However, before the half was over, Saskatchewan quarterback Reggie Slack engineered a series of nine rushing and passing plays finishing with a short lob pass to wide receiver Fred Bailey in the Calgary end-zone. Though Saskatchewn missed the convert, a more subdued home crowd watched the players leave the field at half-time aware that their team was only leading by four points.

During half-time Jules went for a beer, Alex and Tyler went to the men's room. Then they found Jules, visited an adjacent concession and helped him bring back hot-dogs and Pepsi for everyone. Myra, Ola, and Rebecca also took a ladies' room break and bought Rebecca a bag of popcorn from one of the other vendors beneath the stands. Before they returned to their box-seats, Ola passed a booth featuring fresh-made giant pretzels and decided to indulge herself, at which point Myra said to herself, "What the hell, I'm going to get myself a large chocolate bar." While some high school marching band was strutting their stuff out on the field and hitting the odd flat note, the Stedman and Davis group snacked and told Jules about the boys' suits. Alex made a dash for three orders of French fries with ketchup they could share among themselves. Some of the ketchup got slopped onto Alex's jeans and the toe-end of one of his running-shoes.

The third quarter had some more spark to it. Right around the half-way point, Dickensen completed a pass-and-run play to Danielsen that resulted in a touchdown. In quick response, Saskatchewan marched down the field after McLaughlin's kickoff and soon threatened to score. Then, a controversial play held the fans in momentary suspense. Eric Guilford, a Saskatchewan receiver, caught a pass at the goal-line, but then appeared to drop it. The loose ball was pounced on by Calgary's middle linebacker, Willie Hampton. Whistles blew and the referees and other officials consulted. Then, the head referee stood in a gap separating the two teams and announced the combined ruling. Guilford's catch was considered caught and the ball ruled dead before he dropped it. The Roughriders retained possession of the football and on the next play, quarter-back Reggie Slack dove in over the goal-line behind the lead blocking of his centre. To drive their hopes forward, Saskatchewan made a convert, leaving them trailing again by four points. Well into the fourth quarter, Saskatchewan kicker Cory Stevens sent a long punt into the opponents' end-zone that Calgary conceded for a single point. This heightened the tension in the stands, everyone knowing that Saskatchewan was just a field-goal away from being able to tie the game. However, in the final five minutes, Dickenson managed to direct another sixty-three yard march that wound up with Kelvin Anderson punching his way over the goal line for a second time. McLaughlin's convert that followed was good. Calgary was now well ahead leading 28-18.

All opportunity for Saskatchewan evaporated, and that's how the game ended. The Stampeders were now four wins and zero losses in a home opener after winning a Grey Cup championship. Nevertheless, question marks about the ability of the Stamps to repeat as champs had surfaced during the game. All those sacks, the loss of McNeil, a suspect offensive line, a blocked punt by Saskatchewan's Steve Anderson, and forty-seven missed tackles by Calgary trying to bring down Saskatchewan's Eric Guilford as he was returning Stampeder punts. Obviously for Calgary, there were evident weaknesses leaving lot of work to be done and plays to polish.

The Stedman and Davis contingent would head home relieved but weary. It could be a tough season for football in the West. Saskatchewan didn't look all that shabby and might be the dark horse team in the league. The British Columbia Lions were firing on all cylinders right out of the pre-season and the initial starting gate. The perennial provincial rivals, the Edmonton Eskimos, could be counted on to contend against the Stampeders for top-dog honours. That was a provincialism Ola understood. She had been raised in it fiercely half-way across the globe. She kept receiving reports from relatives, making her own observations as the Ukraine again became a nation in her own right following the breakup of the Soviet Union. It had been a long time coming. There was a very long road ahead.

The road from Calgary back to Okotoks is only twenty-five kilometers once you hit the outskirts of the city. It was a little heavier traffic-wise that night as other mildly-impressed football fans rambled home. The ambivalent spirits in the Stedman van were ironed and steamed by a spray of clichés and consolations: "The Stamps came up with enough gusto to win." "They've still got a good chance to return to defend the Cup!" "Hockey season is just around the corner and the Flames might be a contender this year too." "The Stampede is coming soon." "Those suits look just great!" "Yes, they do." "Thanks, Mom." "Yeah, thanks Mom."

Before long, the turn-off from the Macleod Trail (Highway 2) to Highway 2A leading to Northridge Drive and the Sheep River Bridge appeared. Within five minutes the lights of Okotoks twinkled "Welcome home!" An upstairs curtain that flipped aside and back briefly from the house to the right as the Stedman van parked in the driveway at 35 Dewdney Common did not escape Myra's eye making her sense of "welcome back" somewhat spoiled. Another imagined conversation crossed her mind, one that wasn't far from the truth.

"It vould be nice if they could just get out of dat van qvietly unt slip into der house vithout makink zo much noise! Vy do dey vaste zo much money going to a football game you can see on de TV at home? Look at all doze parcels of new clothes doze kitts vill hartly ever vear! Vaste, vaste, vaste, all dese Nort Americans do is zo much vaste!"

"Ya, Magda, I know," Yannis mumbled as he yawned into his pillow. "Now get back from zat vindow unt crawl back into zis bett, Mrs. Wojniewski. Your poor husbant is gettink colt vile you are vasting all ze heat we yust hatt a few minutes ago."

A short stretch of travel awaited Ola and Alex. Shortly after their arrival home, he was in bed sound asleep. Ola sat in the kitchen with a cup of lemon tea pondering various meditations: memories of the old country, her parents, Uri and other victims of radiation poisoning; musings on political freedom and the lack thereof; and premonitions about teens entering into opposite-sex relationships, two of whom she knew rather well. She wondered and worried not so much about whether the relationships would last, but whether the adolescents themselves would. There was an acid reflux reaction in her stomach she found distressing. She pursued it with prayer. What came to her were the words of St. Theodorus the Ascetic:

*Restlessness requires patience. Something out of sorts is a sign of spiritual displacement. Give it time to settle, become sorted, find its place in God's grand scheme. Then wait for wisdom. Trust in the Lord at all times*

"We'll see," Ola murmured to herself.

"I'm sure you will," a voice seemed to utter back.

Low-hanging stratus clouds spread their restlessness over Okotoks.

# Chapter 7:
# Graduation or Commencement?

June was whirl of a month. Waiting for it to reach its final days felt very abbreviated. Crops in Ola's fields were well sprouted and surging with biochemical reactions headed toward fruition. Wilton shipped three hundred aging layers to Kemper's Processing in High River. They would wind up inside chicken wieners. He bought four hundred new chicks. He met his milk quota for the month. He bought himself a new suit. The horses in Pops' barn relished running around the paddocks. Tacitus helped till the vegetable patch. Seeds were sown. Louie phoned out of nowhere wanting to check the date of the big day. Suit cuffs and pants were hemmed. Pharmacy customers began to stock up summer and vacation supplies. Tranogco completed a friendly takeover of Gastech, a smaller oil-refining operation. Jules was instrumental. He also spent a week in Dallas enlisting three new American customers. He was in line for another promotion. Rebecca was joyfully into playing weekend soccer and skipping rope with her playmates after school. Requisite exams were taken; final marks tabulated and report cards issued. Student record forms were filled in.

Graduation Day arrived like a train two days' ahead of schedule, though it wasn't. Florists and hairdressers all over town were absorbed in frenzy. The limousine service had all its vehicles booked solid. Restaurants that took reservations had turned down a few hundred last-minute callers. Engravers put the finishing touches on plaques and trophies. Decorated gymnatoriums were getting the final inspection by custodial staff. Chairs set out by student recruits were set more evenly in line. Sound systems were checked. Diplomas and awards were wrapped and set out on the distribution tables. Places for presenters and dignitaries were assigned. Cosmetics were being liberally applied to young women, making them appear three or four years older. Young men were showering with smelly soap, applying after-shave they didn't need yet and trying to rub in the right amount of gel to make their hair behave as they imagined it should. Wallis Wilton asked Alex about hair gel, figuring he might give it a try. He struggled with the royal blue tie suggested by the salesperson who sold him his new navy suit. "Regis has set the trend, you know, of wearing solid complementary colors." Carol Morton thought about wearing her black, backless evening gown with a white lace shawl but opted for something more germane—a two-piece light linen maroon suit over a deep teal blouse, maroon high heels and a three-tone handbag, the third tone being tan. She chose a fine gold chain to set it off. Tyler and Alex had already had their preview of what Enid and Stephanie might look like. The final version with hair-style and make-up and accessories added bowled them both over even more. The girls were equally impressed with their dates *de jour*. Indeed, as Wilton did say, they looked "debonnaire" despite any sense of temporary discomfort they may have felt in such not-so-usual attire.

The whole graduating class was an outstanding ensemble of young adult-looking teens who seemed to have matured rapidly in the space of a few hours. The girls who opted for frills and flounces were as comparably beautiful as the ones who chose slim and sleek apparel. Raja Punkara wore a splendid sari with a left-leg side split as a concession to American fashion. Kevin Noseworthy, who refused to wear a suit and tie, didn't look out of place in his Garth Brooks' look: black slacks, black cowboy shirt and silver lariat string-tie. The hat, of course, came off during the singing of "O, Canada." He had to keep it on his lap or chair during the ceremonies.

One by one they filed across the stage receiving their diplomas and audience applause and pausing for obligatory photo shoots. Special awards were almost predictable: Raja received most of the academic prizes, except for the French and history awards which went to Martha Yeallan. Athletic honours were bestowed on Enid Evans and Kevin Noseworthy. Smiles and snuffles of amusement passed through the assembly as the award for Home and Family Studies went to Larry "Lumpy" Jenkins, and the prize in Industrial Arts and

Technology was given to Stephanie Wells. The surprise of the evening was reserved for the Staff Award, a hundred dollar prize and a keeper medallion plus one's name inscribed forever on the school plaque kept in the front lobby display case. The award was given to the student who, in the opinion of the entire staff, represented all-round excellence in academic accomplishment and athletic achievement, school spirit, social skills, and general deportment. For the year 1999, the winner was Tyler Stedman! Myra at last had tears she could not contain. Jules' eyes watered too. Rebecca whistled and whooped out loud. Ola felt familial pride. Alex led the class in cheering. Tyler shook some at first, blushed and then gathered himself in grateful and gracious acceptance. He still had a slight limp and, at the moment, a glottal lump. Uncle Louie winked from his seat at the back of the hall, gave Alex a thumbs-up, sent an envelope up with a student usher to Ola, waved good-bye and made his exit. Myra, Jules and Ola had acknowledged his presence stiffly earlier on. During the ceremonies Pops never turned his head back once. He did drop it during the diploma presentations as he sniffled into his handkerchief then made a swift recovery.

Raja made a marvellous valedictory address, expressing thanks not only to the teaching staff who had guided them this far and to classmates with whom the journey had been shared but also to parents and other influential friends who had contributed to their years of growing up, learning and developing self-awareness and character. She offered insightful and wise-beyond-her-years counsel to her classmates about keeping as many options open from here on in as they could. The future for her generation was offering no guarantees, no promises for job security, various options for valid relational supports, and a world still waiting for lasting peace, viable justice and freedom from poverty and oppression.

"Some writers have dubbed us 'Generation Next.' It feels more like 'Generation We-Don't-Know-What's-Coming-Next!' Study and train broadly. Cultivate caring for others and people skills. Stay versatile and as optimistic as possible. If you have a God, walk with that God. If you don't have one, you might consider looking for one. You'll probably need it. Farewell, Dewdney Junior High. You've been good to us. We won't forget you. We'll be back to visit perhaps. But there are other doors we must pass through now. The future is pulling them open. Here we go, ready or not. But for now, at least, we feel ready for the next few steps."

Principal Purnell closed with congratulatory remarks. The words of the school song appeared on an overhead screen for audience participation while the junior string orchestra squealed out the tune. The ceremonies were adjourned for refreshments in the lobby while the gym was converted into a dance hall—chairs away, punch tables up, disc jockey into position. *"One, two, three o'clock, four o'clock rock.* Testing. Testing." Mr. Dillenberger had engaged the services of a local young college couple, Ben and Breanne, who had started up their own DJ business. St. Paul's United Church had previously employed them for several youth dances. Young teens loved them. Ben and Breanne seemed to know just what songs were popular and danceable and how to help young teens have a great time. Part way through the evening they would delight the crowd with their own lip-sync parody of Brittany Spears and Justin Timberlake which they liked to call "Not-Quite-in-Sync". It was bound to be a grad dance to remember.

Myra and Jules embraced Tyler with congratulatory hugs after cake and ice cream and left for home with Rebecca in tow. Ola stretched out her arms on Alex's shoulders and just nodded her affirmation and quiet pride. Then she pulled an envelope out of her purse and said, "This is from your step-father. He didn't stay long. It's a card that says "Well done!" with fifty dollars inside. I'll take it home. You can bank it Monday. Enjoy the dance. Mr. Wilton will bring you home." Alex managed to plant a quick kiss on her before she left. "Why is Wilton bothering to drive all the way back into town to take me home?" he wondered to himself. By then the first song from the DJs was already playing.

There was the usual wait-and-see, let's-just-enjoy-the-music initial period during which maybe only two or three couples danced. To be accurate, it was one couple, two pairs of girls and one group of six girls and one guy acting goofy. No date, but he knew how to try to attract attention. After about half an hour, more young people and Mr. and Mrs. Dillenberger ventured into the dancing area. Alex and Enid, Tyler and Stephanie joined in. Standing by the refreshment table, keeping watch were Ms. Morton and her escort, a man unfamiliar to all except a few. Alex and Tyler made their way to the punch bowl after a few dances.

"Well, hi, Mr. Wilton, surprised to see you here."

"I'm somewhat surprised myself, Alex," Wallis Wilton responded, "but I'm thinking about running for School Board Trustee in the fall, so I figured some exposure to public education wouldn't hurt."

"Neither would exposure to certain public educators either, eh?" Alex teased back jostling Wilton in the ribs.

"Come on, Alex," Tyler commanded. "Don't let him kid you, Mr. Wilton, he's as nervous as you are and happy as I am to see you here."

"I suspect you're right, Tyler," Wilton replied tipping an imaginary cap.

H. Lee Disher

Ms. Morton couldn't help overhearing with undisguised admiration and a delight she tried to keep secret.

The free punch was consumed within the first hour. Pop and chips sold frequently from the canteen. During one memorable foray, Martha Yellan and "Lumpy" Jenkins cleared the dance floor with an inspired display of hip-hop attended by gales of laughter and raucous applause, shouts and whistles. Wallis Wilton took a couple of chances to take Carol Morton around the dance floor. They looked just fine despite a few traces of awkwardness. Some of that was attributable to the fact that they held hands and didn't dance apart as they circulated even during fast songs. They talked whether they were dancing or not, speaking about present joys and tribulations of teaching or farming, about their discontent with the present provincial government and their dis-ease with the rise of the Reform Party in Alberta. They shared little of the past other than "currently still single, my choice I suppose" and "currently widowed, not my choice" "Sorry, to hear that." "I'm getting over it. Life goes on and it's better if you go on with it."

The time came for Enid and Stephanie when a bathroom break seemed in order. "Oh, my God, Steph, I swear, during that last slow dance I think Alex was getting a hard-on!"

"You think?" questioned a voice emerging from one of the stalls. "Enid, if his fingers were all on your back what else could it have been?"

"I wasn't inviting you into this conversation, Debbie."

"It's a public washroom, sweetie. Don't say anything here you don't want heard in public."

Tina Lewis and Rachel Kendrick gathered around Debbie Berenson egging her on. "So, tell us, Evans, what was it like? A stubby bottle top? Or a decent zucchini?"

"None of your business, Gutter trash!"

"Just curious, puke breath! By the way, tell your chummy there if she'd like the skivvy on her date I do happen to live next door and I have caught a shot or two of him in his boxers."

"Frankly, Debbie," Stephanie spoke up, "I'm not that interested in gossip like that."

"Gossip, schmossip, sister, our Mr. Congeniality Tyler is turning into quite the hunk in more ways than one and if you're not interested others certainly are, including me. Why, I could steal him from right under your nose anytime I want."

"Maybe so, Debbie," Enid cut back in, "but that's assuming that Tyler would even consider being attracted by the likes of you. All the doors the future seems to be pulling open for you are heading straight into Slut Street."

The disputation might have turned to hair-pulling and punches had Ms. Morton not entered the washroom at that moment and, seeing a cluster of girls registering some degree of agitation, asked, "Anything wrong, here?"

Dumb stares and silence met her there.

"Good. Then I suppose you're all on your way back to enjoying the dance, right?" the teacher continued.

"Come on, Enid, that's your favorite 'N Sync song the D.J.s just started playing. Aren't they the pair who do that Brittany and Justin take-off?"

One pair left the bathroom. Another trio wasn't far behind.

During the same break, Tyler and Alex took the opportunity to step out-side for fresh air.

"Whew, it was getting warm in there, wasn't it"

"You bet, cousin," Alex replied. "My armpits were starting to sweat. They don't even do that during a heated soccer match."

"Puberty happens."

"I know, I know. During that last slow dance with Enid, I was getting a stiffy! In fact, I think I had an accident."

"Chernobyl was an accident, Alex. What you had was a minor mishap."

"Chernobyl was a disaster, cuz. But let's just let the past be the past, okay. I'm here in Canada now. I'm safe. It's the country I've known best and have grown up in. I just wish I wasn't growing up in it so fast some times."

"Maybe some of that happens because you're rushing things along your-self. If you want to slow it down, don't dance so close just yet. Enid likely won't like you any less. In fact, she might appreciate a little more space and respect, and some relief from not being put in situations of worry, uncertainty, and even embarrassment."

"How do you know? How do you know she won't think I'm a cold fish? A guy who's timid and unsure when she's looking for someone who knows what's what?"

"I don't know, Alex. Maybe that stuff happens later. I'm willing to play it safer for now—safer for everyone involved. Now, if you're cooled off, why don't we visit the john on our way back in so you can 'freshen up' as grown women like to say."

"Why, Tyler, you big tease," Alex shot back with a feigned Alabama accent. "What would I evah do without you? To the john it is, and then, back to the action! With all due discretion, my friend, with all due discretion. God, I'm starting to use words the way Wilton uses them!"

When all had returned to the dance floor, the party proceeded mirthfully. The Brittany-Justin parody was hilarious. The rest of the music was conducive

H. Lee Disher

to joy, celebration, and the gestation of budding relationships. Tyler and Stephanie, Alex and Enid exchanged sincere "Thanks, I had a wonderful time" remarks and managed a couple tentative pecks to the cheek. It was the same when Wallis Wilton left Carol Morton at the door of her condominium, except that he asked if he might see her again some time. She agreed and hoped it would be soon. He was already figuring that out as he drove home in his pickup. Summer was already smelling sweeter than the scent of the first fresh cuts of hay that drifted in his open windows.

# Chapter 8:
# Physio and Free Time

Summer holidays for Tyler started with a weekend with Pops and Ola and Alex, about whom Tyler had some feeling of restored relationship. He was on the edge of offering his cousin forgiveness. Riding was forbidden, but caring for the horses—brushing and grooming them, bathing them, feeding them, cleaning their stalls, taking them for strolls, letting them run loose in the paddocks—sufficed. It can't be genetic but there is something very instinctual happening when a human being and horses truly connect. There's a rush in the blood, a sensation surrounding the spine, an almost-electrified cerebral hum and an empathic vibration deep in the gut experienced by both animal and individual. Tyler was supersaturated. The human-equine harmony was his ontology of being, his heaven on earth. Pops Davis had seen it surge through his own offspring and land squarely upon his grandson. That gave Pops no small gratification. Ola noticed it too and stored it in her soul's files for future reference. Alex was happy just to see Tyler happy and to have his undivided company for the bulk of the weekend.

Beyond time in the horse barn they worked and played together: cutting lawns, beating rugs, weeding Pops' garden, washing and drying dishes, helping with haying time, cleaning out the "Bunkie" for Ola's hired workers, giving

Wilton a hand with his chickens, playing catch with a baseball, tossing a Frisbee, engaging Pops in Parcheesi, and challenging one another in Nintendo games. Everything furthered the restoration of their friendship. Alex anticipated coming days together at Tyler's house in town as opportunities to advance a couple of other relationships the two of them had begun to cultivate. Wispy cirrus clouds overhead echoed such hopes.

On the Saturday evening they were surprised to see Mr. Wilton dressed up and heading into town. "What do you think that's about, Tyler?"

"I don't really know, Alex, maybe a friend of his died and he's going to pay his respects."

"I think he's more likely on his way to a Social Studies lesson," Ola suggested, having caught the drift of their curiosity.

"Oohh!" chimed two young voices in unison. Tyler thought he had a speck of understanding. Alex didn't really have a clue. He was just pretty sure that Social Studies classes didn't happen on Saturday nights.

Pops stared at Ola across the table to see if she was registering any signs of disappointment that the eligible gentleman next door was exploring more distant pastures. There was no facial hint, but wasn't that an ever so slight tremor in her hand as she sipped her tea? Pops knew about humans and horses and their various cravings for wild oats. He knew it in his veins.

Alex wouldn't come to Okotoks until the national holiday on Thursday. Family fun and feasting and fireworks were in the offing. Most of Monday Tyler would spend at the McDaniels Clinic. There was an initial consultation with a resident physician, another set of x-rays to be taken, an assessment made and a regimen recommended. The intake period took an hour and a half. Then Tyler was introduced to Brad, his personal therapist, who would get him started on the program that very day.

Lying prostrate on a padded table, Brad had Tyler bend his left leg upwards and sideways to see how much flexibility was present. When he reached about a 80-degree angle pain in his patella began to smart. Brad nudged Tyler's lower limb towards 90 degrees and got a loud "Ouch!" in response.

"Sorry, Tyler. You've already come a good way down the road to recovery. What we're going to aim for is 150 degrees of bend or better, just like here on your right side. Look over in that wall mirror and see. Now flip over on your back while I fasten a couple of one-kilo ankle weights and get you to try some simple front leg lifts."

There were another series of exercises to perform while standing and walking up and down a ramp. The best part was the last fifteen minutes spent receiving soothing electro-therapy above, below, and through the injured knee area.

"You did just fine, Tyler. Make an appointment with the receptionist for Wednesday and Friday, and the same three days next week. If you have access to a hot tub, you can spend ten minutes in one twice a day. Don't be impatient, you'll be in therapy at least another four weeks. It isn't just flexibility you need to regain, it's also about the ability to withstand impact."

"But, I can keep my reservation for dude ranch in August, can't I?"

"Yes, especially if you stick with this program."

"Brad, I may just be one the best program-stickers you've ever counselled."

"Motivation is always the next best thing to miracles, Tyler. See you on Wednesday."

As he made his way to reception to book his next appointments Tyler was thinking miracles were more within Aunt Ola's realm of experience. Myra was in the reception area waiting for him. "I've got the momentum of my own motives that should be sufficient inspiration for me for now," Tyler continued musing, "but it may not be sufficient to overcome my mother's apprehensions."

Add in Rebecca's soccer games and practices, household chores to look after while Mom and Dad were at work, cutting the Berensons lawn while they were away camping (making Rebecca's life more boring since that meant her best friend, Charlene, was away too), hanging out with classmates (Stephanie and Enid included) at Riverside Park, knocking back sodas and cherry cokes at Fleer's Restaurant, watching rodeo videos and tearing into some novels by Louis L'Amour, *The Virginian*, and A. B. Guthrie Jr.'s *The Big Sky*, and Tyler Stedman's first weeks of summer holiday were shaping into a sporadic but steady circadian rhythm. The only irregularity in the routine was the welcome interruption of two days at the Calgary Stampede.

# Chapter 9:
## Stampede Expedition

For almost ninety years the annual Stampede has been transforming the city of Calgary and a good part of the province of Alberta into something between a week-long to ten-day combination of Hallowe'en and a circus. People who have never ridden a horse, never even visited a farm and who rarely, if ever, use words like "How-dee!" and "Yee-haw!" in ordinary conversation take to the streets and public transit systems dressed in cowboy and cowgirl gear, get giddy and foolish and go watch other people and animals perform. They become part of gathered throngs that include a large contingent of tourists (often easy to spot because they aren't wearing Western attire) and a raft of real farming and horse-riding and cow-savvy folk who bring their lifestyle, their ethos into a world-class arena in a truly celebratory manner. What began as Guy Weadick's dream of a first-class rodeo show on Canadian soil in 1912 has evolved into a Fest of the West. The rodeo ring is a grandstand-style performance venue that winds up each night after the chuck-wagon races with a full-scale song-and-dance entertainment production accompanied by fireworks and pyrotechnics. Agricultural barns—where farmers and ranchers can put their animals on display; compete for best-of-breed prizes; and share the stories of grain-growing or milk, beef, or egg production, where a few can actually talk turkey—have been surrounded by midway rides and carnival games of chance, souvenir and clothing booths, fast-food vendors, and special exhibits like the Canadian Country Music Hall of Fame and an authentic heritage cabin. In recent years a variety of Stampede-week lotteries and an on-site casino have dispersed their seductions across the fair. The Stampede Showband has been strutting their marching musicianship around the grounds since 1971. Stampede Showriders perform precision horseback riding to music. Often on the opening weekend the Royal Mounted Canadian Police sends its Musical Ride team to the Stampede. The Round-Up Centre has become an indoor mercantile mecca. Smelly soaps, massage chairs, vegetable-chopping gizmos, leather goods, the latest in handy-dandy cleaning fluids, hot tubs, and such seek to suck the dollars out of your wallet or add charges to your credit card. The Corral Centre has become an arena for corporate-sponsored special shows like piggy races or dogs doing tricks. The Pengrowth Saddledome, added to the grounds when Calgary was awarded a National Hockey League franchise, is the main venue for marching band and indoor motocross competitions, heavy and light horse performance events, show-dog trials and team cattle-penning contests. Representatives of five regional native communities— Stoney, Blood, Peigan, Siksika and Blackfoot—set up an Indian Village just east of the south gate. It's a circle of teepees that native families actually live in for the duration of the fair and that are open for public inspection on a rotational basis during certain hours. Native dances are performed frequently in an open-sided pavilion. Corporate sponsors bring in other performances by X-treme bike-riding daredevils, skate-boarding wizards, high-diving teams, or musical groups that belt out country and western tunes at Nashville North or rock away the evening on an outdoor stage near the Round-Up Centre. A lot of this comes free with the price of admission.

The Calgary Stampede has become an Ed Sullivan-style "really big shew!" It spills over into rotating free breakfasts and entertainments at local malls and surrounding communities each day of its duration. In the mornings, in a small plaza in the city centre there's a daily Stampede warm –up promotional show. Pancakes and bacon are served up free from the back of the chuck-wagons that will be racing later that evening. Some local people treat the Stampede like a week-long Italian wedding and wouldn't miss it for dying. A pocket of locals treat it like a plague and categorically avoid it. After you have attended for several years a lot of the excitement and glitz wears thin. You go to see what's new, or simply out of a sort of patronizing sense of obligation. You pick and choose the times to drop in, the performances and events you select to catch. If you're an adolescent member of a gang of other adolescents, you pick a day and attend *en masse*. Wednesday, July 14, 1999 was an excellent day for that, thirty dollars let you ride all the rides on the midway all day as often as you wished. Jules and Mrs. Punkara (Raja's mother) dropped off two van-loads of raging hormones at the city centre on their way to work. They would come back at midnight for passenger pick-up for the trip back home.

Nothing much happened on the Stampede grounds until after 10:00 A.M. or even 11:00. But the gang knew about chuck-wagon breakfasts and the preliminary entertainments downtown at Rope Square that were currently being sponsored by the Fluor corporation. And, in fact, Raja and Enid were part of a modern dance troupe that was included in that morning's performances. Why not go early, chow down and cheer your friends on. Surprise swept over the youthful onlookers from Okotoks when Lumpy Jenkins also appeared among the dancers. He had looked pretty smooth on prom night, but nobody knew he had moves in him like they witnessed that morning. Now he had no secrets withheld about what he did in some of his spare time. When the dance troupe finished, there was a howling pocket of raucous whistles and catcalls from a certain small section of spectators that day.

At 10:30 A.M., the little group of recent graduates from Dewdney Junior High boarded the rapid transit coaches for the two short stops south to Stampede Park. If you had to pick them out of a vast mass of cowboy hats, blue jeans, scarves, checkered or patterned shirts, boots and shiny silver buckles that day, you only had to focus on the group collected around the young woman with a big pink feather protruding from her hatband. Martha Yellan wasn't always the coolest dresser, but she always managed to get noticed.

After disembarking, filing through the entrance gates with pre-paid admissions purchased at Kingman's Drug Store, and making a natural necessity pit stop, the whole gang proceeded to line up at a midway ticket booth more than willing to part with thirty precious saved-up or parentally-donated dollars. Enid scanned the daily events calendar in the Stampede program brochure and started plotting out a group itinerary for the day. They would stick together enjoying and screaming their way through midway rides until lunch time. Splintering would happen in the afternoon. About half of them would snap up rush seats for the afternoon rodeo and work in a visit to the Indian Village. Two young bucks in their group were keen to take in the extreme motocross competition at the Saddledome, generally tool around on the midway and go "chick" hunting. Stephanie (who seriously disliked rodeo), and Raja and Kevin Noseworthy planned to tour the agricultural barns, take in whatever dog-and-pony show was happening at the Corral and shop. Kevin was actually just interested in Raja. A rendezvous point in front of the heritage cabin was set up for 4:30 P.M. So it was that, after lunch, the smaller groups dispersed but not before Alex accidentally squirted ketchup on Lumpy's left pant-leg. Kevin gave Lumpy's right leg a matching squirt and said, "There you go, Lump. When they dry they'll look like a set of mini-chaps!" Lumpy wore his condiments proudly. Later that afternoon, his deftly launched elbow would drive a double-scoop ice-cream cone accidentally on purpose up Alex' nose. Enid would manage to drop crushed ice down Stephanie's back and receive a face and blouse-front full of return-the-favour cream soda. Good thing Enid brought along a spare blouse in her back-pack. Several sets of fingers would get sticky and gooey tearing apart three strawberry-syrup-and-whipped-cream-covered elephant ears. Alex re-christened them "buffalo butts."

"Ooooo yuuck!" Martha gagged.

Even from high up in the bleachers, Tyler was a keen observer of the afternoon rodeo events. It was part-way through the second set of go-rounds with competitors seeking to accumulate one of the top twelve total scores. He noticed ropers and steer-wrestlers who broke the barrier, who made a toss or a move too late or too soon. He held himself mildly amused by the opening cow-milking contests and chuckled as loud as anybody at the "little tykes" sheep riders. He was awed by the agility and abilities of the demonstration trick riders. He cheered on the women barrel racers with enthusiasm and winced in exact anticipation of an unsuccessful bull rider's forced dismount. He focused discerning attention on the saddle-bronc and bareback riders and felt every body-wrenching jolt of those who stayed aloft for the requisite eight seconds. He knew some of the novices from their days on the high-school circuit: Scott Turner, Josh Burrell, Kyle Gunnarson, and Shane Butterworth (there was always another Butterworth competitor coming along). Some of the pros he knew by reputation: Denny and Rod Hay, Chad Klein, and Jason Delguerico. His personal idol was Randall LeCroix. These were among the best of the best on the North American rodeo circuit, having passed the rigors of just qualifying to compete in the world's richest ten-day showdown. Here they were in the midst of their second go-round trying to place in the top six, if they hadn't already done so in the first go-round. They needed to stay aloft and they needed a good score. Only 50 percent of that was up to them. The other 50 depended on the horse they drew for a mount.

Among novices in saddle bronc, Shane Butterworth was bucked off. He would still make it to the semi-finals having placed second in the first go-round. Another young Albertan, who rode fourth that afternoon, fell from the saddle before the eight-second buzzer. Josh Burrell had a wicked ride on a sorrel mare named Helen's Fury. The stands erupted in loud cheering as he hung on through numerous severe twists and high-hoofed leaps. Anticipation of a great score held the watchers breathless.

"Don't get your hopes up," Tyler commented to Enid and Alex who flanked him.

The announcement came soon enough. "Josh Burrell...has been disqualified." Tyler had seen what so many had missed. Just around 7.6 second mark Josh's free hand had slipped down to grab the saddle-horn for a milo-moment. Kyle Gunnarson had an admirable second ride, but his points total left him in seventh place, one spot shy of the semis. Scott Turner wound up in second place scoring 66. Brad Phillips, an up-and-coming young star from British Columbia, took first place honours with a 69-point ride on a wild, black stallion named Russian Roulette.

"Even my mom would have bet on a horse like that," Alex remarked.

"I doubt that Aunt Ola would bet on anything, cuz, but your renegade step-father would have," Tyler returned.

"Right," Alex muttered back, "but let's just leave him out of it for now, okay?"

Three of the afternoon's competitors in novice bareback bronc also suffered buck-offs. Of the three left scoring, one of them rode a not-so spirited steed to a score of 49. The higher scores of 68 and 73 were awarded to the second- and first-place contestants who would place fifth and sixth in the cumulative standings at the end of the day and be in a position to advance to the finals.

There are no novice calf-roping contests at the Stampede.

When the pros went to work in saddle-bronc, Canadians fared well. Dan Black from Maple Creek, Saskatchewan, with his flashy, bright red chaps and scarf to match came out ahead of the pack scoring 77.5 after a torturous bout aboard Blitzen, a randy, piebald paint horse provided by Kesler Rodeo Company. Right behind him were three Albertans: J. R. Reding out of Beiseker scoring 77; Guy Shapka from Alix snagging a 76.5; and Shawn Henry from Wainwright who tied another Saskatchewan contender with a 74.5. One other rider marked out not having his spurs above his mount's shoulder when he emerged from the chute. Two others were bucked off, including Denny Hay, who would still make it to the Sunday finals on his aggregate score.

The bareback bronc competition was even tougher. Nine out of ten riders stayed on and scored. Bobby Doyle of Oregon was ripped out the back door hitting the turf heavily re-injuring a previously broken left radius. Dazed and sore, he pushed himself up on his good arm, got to his feet and left the field wincing and favoring his left arm amid the applause of an appreciative crowd while the announcer hollered, "Now that's real gutsy try in a cowboy, ladies and gentlemen. Keep clapping 'cause that's all the reward he's gonna get today. And don't worry, as soon as he's able, Bobby boy will be right back at it."

The other nine scores ran as low as 77. Coming out on top was Larry Sandvick of Kaycee, Wyoming. Red-shirted, silver-studded black chaps flaring in the afternoon sunlight, he survived a frantic, gut-wrenching ride atop Ice Maker to net the top score: 86. Right behind him, scoring 84.5 was a local favorite, Jason Delguerico from Strathmore, Alberta; and then, Tyler's idol, Randall Lecroix from St. Albert scored 82.5 with an equally exceptional ride on a mahogany bay Canadian called Lights Out. Tyler found it hard to choose between the two who both exhibited superb spurring and incredible control as their mounts flung them sideways, straight back and then forwards again in turgid jerks and jolts. It was like watching two men holding onto hurricanes. Tyler got his group to give Randall a standing ovation. A Texan, Chris Harris, placed fourth, followed by another American, Mark Garnett from Colorado. Right behind them was Cam Morris from Patricia, Alberta.

"Patricia! Isn't that where someone thought Lumpy's mom was from?" Enid recalled.

"Yes, but they were wrong," Alex remembered. "Patricia was that two-street hamlet we skirted around on the way to Dinosaur Park. The whole village must be this guy's relatives."

When Larry Sandvick toured the ring as the afternoon winner, the small gang from Okotoks cheered as wildly as did the rest of the crowd.

Tyler watched and commented on the calf-roping competitions with intensified interest. He felt the disappointment of five riders who misfired and recorded no time and the heartbreak of one contestant who almost made it until his cinch knot slipped and the calf stood up and skipped free. Three of the four who succeeded that afternoon had impressive times. Tim Williamson of Madden, Alberta clocked in at 9.9 seconds. Blair Stroh from Elkwater came second logging 11.5. Stan Smith out of Texas tied off in 14.3 Kurt Goulding from Duncan, Oklahoma took a longer time roping his prey and setting it down. 21 seconds was a distant fourth-place finish. But it was always better to complete the task than to fail. Cumulative points mattered. Tyler was still envious, his best time yet was 34 seconds.

"God Almighty, Tyler," Stephanie exclaimed when she met up with his group at the Heritage cabin "I can't understand why you're aiming to put yourself through all that risk and punishment. And besides the cruelty those horses and bulls and calves receive is abominable!"

"Well, Steph, I can't imagine anything more exhilarating."

"But I don't get it. You're such a gentle soul. Why not take up show-jumping? That would make sense to me."

"You sound like my mother. She's probably even more anxious about my dream sport. But, hey, everyone has his or her wild side. Rodeo is where I plan to exercise mine."

"Hey!" Enid yelled, "When you two stop rehearsing your future marital spats, you can catch up with the rest of us by these food booths over here. We're hungry. We're skipping the visit to the Indian village."

Tyler and Stephanie were not long rejoining the rest of the group gathered half-way down the midway where there was a little green space and a couple of commandeered picnic tables near the pioneer heritage cabin. Some chowed down on beef or back bacon on a bun. Some had burgers. Two had large corn dogs. Everyone had fries and a cola. Martha Yellan alone socked back two large pieces of vegetarian pizza. All through supper stories were swapped: about the afternoon rodeo, about how the sheep were even smellier than the pigs and how fabulous the circus dogs were at the Corral. The two stray guys gave rave reviews on the extreme motocross competitions, a somewhat graphic report on the "babe" watch and passed around a photo of the two of them pretty near crapping in their drawers as they were flung high up and around in the "two-person bungee whirly-gig kind of contraption" they couldn't remember the actual name of.

"Forty-five bucks a person a pop, but, man, what a pop!" one acclaimed.

"Best forty-five bucks I've spent in a long time!" added the other.

Alex wondered what it might be like to have forty-five spare bucks to blow at any one time. Ola was not stingy with his allowance or his occasional wages, but she had taught him thrift and the virtues of sensible spending, one of the rare ways in which Alex did manage to evidence sensibility. The fact that the evening rock concerts were free with the price of admission suited him just fine.

There was still time after supper for more screeching on midway amusements. Off they went as a group from one swirling, twisting, racing conglomeration of metal and flashing lights to another. Kevin Noseworthy lost his supper when he emerged from the Gravitron and stood the rest of the rides out as the gang continued to take several more spins of varying degrees. At

7:00 P.M., a half-hour downpour sent all of them into the cattle-barn enclosure for cover.

"Oh God! I don't know if I could ever get used to this!" commented Lumpy while screwing up his nose.

"In my parents' home country," remarked Raja, "cows are sacred."

"Does that mean that Alex just stepped in holy shit?" asked Kevin making great guffaws.

"Oooo! Yuck!" cried Martha, as if on cue.

Alex started chasing Kevin down an aisle intent on "adding some dung decoration your nice new jeans, Noseworthy".

Enid snickered.

"What?" Stephanie inquired.

"Oh, it just struck me that, to Alex's mom, almost everything is sacred."

"'Tis," Tyler agreed as he noticed the rain clearing.

Then Tyler put fingers to lips and let out a shrill whistle summoning Alex and Kevin back to the fold. The small flock from Okotoks made their way to the stage area sponsored by one of those major soft-drink manufacturing companies to get themselves situated for the evening concert by Nickleback. Tyler would have preferred going to hear Paul Brandt at Nashville North but that was an age-of-majority venue where beer and alcohol were served. No matter. Just lingering outside the canvas door flaps would have still been within earshot. Still, group consensus rules at times and along with his recently-graduated friends he would put in an hour and a half of suffering the slings and arrows and outrageous volumes of a band that wasn't among his favorites. He and Stephanie and Kevin Noseworthy and Raja decided to stand just back from the edge of the mosh pit area that soon engulfed Alex and Enid, Lumpy, Martha, and the two "babe-seekers." The recently-dampened ground was predetermined to become a muck pit fifteen minutes into the performance. Diehard Nickleback fans were not disappointed. Crashing drums and cymbals, jacked up amplifiers emitting squealing, visceral guitar chords and arpeggios and thrumming bass notes, raspy voices belting out repetitive, suggestive lyrics about getting high, falling in and out of love, being drunk, getting laid, or driving your teachers and parents insane fed them what they came for. Bodies in the pit pushed, clashed, slipped, bumped, sprawled, and fell into one another, with some getting ceremonially hoisted and tossed about. At one point, Alex emerged topless above the crowd with mud-markings up and down his chest and back and arms like war-paint. During the following song, he was up again being passed one way while his trousers got flung in the opposite direction.

"Nice boxers, eh!" shouted Lumpy.

"Whoo-hoo!" went Enid. "We want to see what's in them!"

Alex clutched his underwear tightly to his waist at that point as he descended ungraciously toward the ground and then fought and crawled his way in search of retrieving his pants. Which he did. Eventually. After someone or two someones shoved a couple handfuls of muck down his butt. He made his way back to Enid and suggested they might take a breather. Agreeably she came along as he led her back to where Tyler and company were standing.

"Too much!" he exclaimed.

"You mean 'What a rush!' rather than 'That's enough of that!' don't you cousin?" Tyler remarked. "But I have to say I've now seen you getting carried away both figuratively and literally, and that's as much 'too much' for me as the concert itself."

Just then a huge "Wooo-hooo!" went up from the audience.

"Oh my God!" Stephanie yelled out, "I don't believe it! Look it! Martha's thrown her bra up on the stage, and the bass guitar player has stuck it on his head!"

"You Canadian youths, you are just so uncivilized!" shouted Raja making mock ethnic parental tones as she fell into fits of laughter with the company of friends around her.

When the concert ended, Martha and Enid and the two "babe-seeking" guys went backstage to get autographs from the band while the rest of the gang headed out to snap up some more elephant ears before the booths shut down for the night. They all met up again near the main gate by the Round-Up Centre, and left the park together to meet Jules and Mrs. Punkara waiting for them in a designated pick-up area near the corner of 11th Avenue S.E. and Macleod Trail South. One wound up but weary bunch was ready to head home.

Three quarters of Okotoks would already be asleep when they arrived. Six of them would have to be awakened before disembarking from the vans that carried them. Alex would spend the night at Tyler's house. Jules tossed his nephew's muddied clothes straight into the laundry basket and packed him off to bed naked, with an old sweatshirt tied around his mid-section, and his bare butt reflecting glints of light from the low-wattage ceiling lights in halls and stairwells.

"Someone may have to save that butt someday," Jules thought to himself. "I hope it won't have to be me, and I'd bet Pops Davis's farm it'll never be Louie."

Tyler flashed his father a good-night smile as he crawled into bed next to an already dozing cousin. A knowing smile it was, the kind that signals "Yep, I'm thinkin' what you're thinkin'."

Not long after sunrise on Stampede closing Sunday, calf-ropers, barrel racers, and steer wrestlers who have made it to the top ten showdown event are exercising their own mounts for the day, taking a few practice runs, then cooling their horses down and giving them a good grooming. Those who have warmed up at home load up their trailers and head to the park. Those who are already on site stable their horses in the barns behind the grandstand and head out for a hearty breakfast.

One hundred and fifty miles northeast of Calgary on a prime acreage of ranchland thirty miles south of Hanna, Alberta, the twenty-five select bucking horses and fifteen of the fiercest bulls that are prepared to appear at the Stampede showdown that afternoon enjoy about an hour or so of lazy morning grazing, a good half-hour four-mile sprint on a grass track and a fresh morning feeding. The bulls are allowed a sustained pen run. After eating they are given a thorough medical inspection and then taken to a customized stationary chute for final grooming. A rubber squeezing apparatus coordinated with the animals' breathing patterns holds them still while the barbers and groomers go to work. The state-of-the-art mechanism then flips each animal sideways so that the farriers can "do their nails." Well-coiffed, hooves trimmed, the other stars of the show are loaded and transported to Stampede Park looking their best, coats shimmering, feeling frisky. These are not glamorous horses with large noses, faces that could break a camera, and heavy-set legs, but if you expect them to buck well, they need to feel super. Bulls are bulls: brutish, bulky, ugly as gigantic toads. Try to make them pretty and you wind up making them more than pretty mean. The meticulous handlers ensure that their charges arrive at maximum readiness: horses hot to twist and trot, bulls pumped and set to snort and sworl.

The Stedman family left the church service at St. Paul's United, Okotoks, in casual summer Western dress. They too were Stampede ready. They would meet up with Pops, Alex, and Wallis Wilton (who would drive his neighbours to town that day) for barbecue chicken- or beef-on-a-bun near the Canadian Country Music Hall of Fame around noon. Wilton made a stop in Okotoks along the way to pick up Carol. Ola also planned to join them all meeting them at grandstand gate B at 1:00 P.M. She had a luncheon meeting at St. Bartholomew's after worship to share in planning for booths of Ukrainian foods, clothing, and artisanship at an upcoming multicultural festival in Calgary in late August. Eagerness, anticipation, and excitement registered on all their faces with trace-lines of apprehension evident in the women's looks, excepting Rebecca. Rodeo is wild. Rodeo is intense. Rodeo makes pain public.

Jules and the female contingent all had A section seating in the stadium. Alex and especially Tyler were all agog at the prospect of having access to pen-side views made possible through Pops' and Wilton's local cowboy connections. *"Dear Diary,"* Tyler began journaling in his mind, *"Today is bound to be a thrill-of-a-lifetime day. I get ring-side seating, access to autographs, up-close-and-personal cheer-leading opportunities, and who knows, perhaps chances to kick boots, shake hands or rub shoulders with local and North American rodeo heroes. Bring it on!"*

Soon enough, there they were, four lucky *hombres* witnessing pacing, deep-breathing, anxiety-reducing rider exercises, the steeling of eyes, the tightening of muscles, the steadying of nerves. The immersion in intensity in the pen and chute area is such that one imbibes it. Nostrils swell with the stench of rawhide, leather, horse hair, sweat, dung, hay, hemp, animal and human steam.

Sunday is super payday. Six events. Winner take all in each for a cheque of $50,000 and championship trophy and bragging rights. The seven top aggre-gate winners of the previous nine days of competitions (six in bull-riding) put their skills to the test along with the reigning Professional Bull Riding World Champion, the current World and Canadian Champions in all other events, and the Calgary spring indoor Royal Rodeo winners in each event. The first goal is to place in the top four out of ten with quickest time or best score. Then it's a give-it-your-best-shot sudden death contest for all the marbles. There's no richer rodeo pot to play for on the planet during the regular season.

The announcer welcomed the afternoon audience, thanked the warm-up Stampede band, introduced officials, judges, key Stampede organizers, clowns and two of the day's competitors, withstood a mother-in-law joke from one of the clowns and then barked, "Let's Rodeo!"

Calf roping topped the afternoon bill. Tyler paid special attention to toss-ing techniques, dismount moves, tying speeds and cinching manoevures. Two Americans and two Canadians placed in the top four. During the second runs Fred Whitfield of Hockley, Texas and Marty Becker of Manyberries, Alberta were too hasty trying for the quick snag out of the chute. They both roped out. It was Cliff Williamson, moving more slowly, more methodically who snagged top-dogging honours. He rode a horse named Crown that he had borrowed from a previous winner, Greg Cassidy. His time was impressive at 8.6 seconds. The crowd cheered wildly for the odds-on local favorite. After nineteen years on the circuit, Cliff soaked up all that well-deserved praise and celebrated a Stampede win that felt like a crown on a season that had made him Canadian rodeo's first million-dollar winner.

The competition shifted closer to Tyler's side of the stands for bareback bronc riding. Two out of eight riders were bucked off in the preliminaries. Aggregate scores placed only one Canadian in the final four. All riders survived both final trials. Scott Lund from Bozeman, Montana wound up fourth with scores of 80 and 81.5. Third place fell to Eric Swenson out of Bonham, Texas after rides scoring 84 and 82.5. Davey Shields Jr., the lone Canadian from Hanna, Alberta had a great first ride scoring 86.5 and a lesser result of 82 after his second mount. It was Chris Harris of Arlington, Texas who proved indomitable that day outscoring his opponents with a fantastic first ride atop Blue Ridge scoring 88 points, one shy of J. C. Trujillo's 1990 record of 89. His second foray scored 84.5 making him a clear overall winner.

Barrel racing laurels fell on Rachael Myllymaki from Arlee, Montana, who rode her horse Scott around the loop twice with identical times of 17.53 seconds, just enough to edge out two others hot on her tail: Kristin Weaver from Temecula, California whose times of 17.53 and 17.59 left her .06 seconds shy of first place; and Jody Hollingworth from Valleyview, Alberta who also came close with rides of 17.67 and 17.77 for a combined time of 35.44.

The steer wrestling prize and trophy was swooped up, or rather slammed down by Mickey Gee of Wichita Falls, Texas edging out gritty competition from Todd Boggust from Payton, Saskatchewan, and Jeff Solomon of Havre, Montana. Gee's times were 4.6 and 4.7 for a net total of 9.3 seconds. Boggust made him nervous with a remarkable first throw-down of 3.8. His second tackle took 5.5 seconds leaving him net 9.4. Solomon's total was 9.7 seconds adding a 4.7 to a 5.0.

Was a Canadian comeback possible? Something like watching old 5934, a steam engine on the Canadian Pacific Railway dubbed "Dominion," gliding past the grain elevators in Carstairs with coal and freight cars in tow seemed to be building momentum in the stadium that afternoon. Two events left. Only one Canadian winner during the first four.

The saddle bronc competition was next. Randall Lecroix did not make it to the final four but Tyler made a point of getting Wilton to introduce him to an also-ran hero. Randall was appreciative of a younger admirer's encouragements and consolations.

"Why don't you come up to St. Albert some day and take part in my training camp. Here's my card."

Tyler's jaw just about dropped into his boots. "You serious? You mean it? Th...tha...that would be utterly fantastic!"

H. Lee Disher

"Yep, son, I mean it. Word gets around, you know. I've heard about your enthusiasm and it's been my pleasure to meet you too."

Speechless, thrilled, ecstatic, Tyler returned to his fence-rail lookout to watch the tide shift. The final four couldn't have been more thrilling. It featured all the earmarks of a classic showdown. The brothers Denny and Rod Hay were poised for a duel with Dan Mortensen from Manhattan, Montana and Billy Etbauer out of Edmond, Oklahoma. The first elimination round ended tightly. Rod scored 84.5. Billy was awarded an 84. Denny pulled off an 83. Dan scored 82. It was anybody's trophy up for the taking. Etbauer put the pressure on with a second outing that scored 86. Denny drew Airwolf as his mount, a horse that Rod had ridden the previous year in 1998. Disappointment spilled from his heart throughout the whole stadium when he was bucked off. Mortensen fared better the second time out scoring 84. Rod Hay sat down behind the chute on Zorro Bandit, a horse that had been assigned to brother Denny once before. The chute opened. The ride was hair raising. The eight-second buzzer buzzed. The crowd held their breath. The judges submitted their score. The announcer made it public. "It's an 86 folks! Just enough to make Rod Hay this year's Stampede saddle bronc champion by a .5 differential. Yahoo! Alberta's back. Canada's still in the hunt."

The America-takes-on-Western-Canada showdown was settled that day in no-bones-about-it fashion, or rather no-bones-left-undisturbed manner, when Jason McDonald from Spear, New Mexico emerged the winner in bull-riding. The final four event was anti-climactic. Two of the four riders were bucked off. Mark Freeman was the only rider other than McDonald to survive and make it to the winner-take-all round. McDonald, the only contender wearing a protective helmet and face-mask, had made it by virtue of being awarded a re-ride after his first mount threw him. He stayed on and scored 82. Freeman netted a 77. In the last round the bulls won first bucking both of them off. Up and on it one more time, Freeman got bucked off, but McDonald hung on scored another 82 and emerged the champion. Having ridden four bulls in order to gain the victory, a reporter asked McDonald how his groin muscles felt. "If they were any better," he replied, pun in mind, "I couldn't stand myself."

Americans won four-out-of-six in 1999. Later that day, winners continued celebrating. Non-winners this time round packed up their gear, their mounts and headed down the road for the next stop on the circuit or back home for a little rest-up and mending time.

The Stedman-Davis group with special guests Wilton and Morton found their way to the top-of-the-stadium Clubhouse Dining Lounge where they had reservations for a mammoth smorgasbord starring Alberta prime rib of beef roast and B.C. salmon, western ranchers' chicken and pork, and all the vegetables, salads, and other fixings one might imagine and drool over plus a great selection of desserts. Grand appetite-pleasers done up in grand style made their own grandstand performance. Good thing Ola was present to put restraints on Alex's eyes that grew far too grand for his gut.

Affable conversations over dinner were followed by grounds-strolling time: time for the men to inspect some agricultural exhibits; time for Rebecca, Alex, and Tyler to take in a few more midway rides; time for Ola and Myra to take Carol to visit the Country Music Hall of Fame. Such fill-in time becomes requisite before returning to the grandstand for the evening chuck-wagon races and the current extravaganza version of a song-and-dance show plus pyrotechnics. The final Sunday features the top four out of thirty-six chuck-wagon racing teams who have compiled the lowest aggregate times over the previous nine days of racing in a final showdown for $50,000, the ATCO Gas Championship Chuck-wagon trophy and bragging rights. In the business field, ATCO is one of Tranogco's biggest competitors.

Guy Weadick introduced chuck-wagon races into the Stampede in 1923. When the world was getting increasingly engrossed in fascination with the automobile, this throwback to a previous era, reminiscent of chariot races in the Roman Empire, was added to the Stampede entertainment platter like cheesecake on a dessert tray. It caught on. Nostalgia seldom fails. Transplanted into an arena setting was that wild, frantic, "yee-haw we're headin' to town" insanity invented by cowboys of the Old West too long out on the range, sleeping under the stars, filling their bellies on grog served out the back of a covered wagon and gathering around fires for stories, songs, and playful banter, and deciding that instead of plodding along into town when opportunity knocked they would race their wagons instead. Last one to arrive bought the first round of drinks. Just imagine: dust flying, fry-pans clanging, foodstuffs, and even stoves springing loose and free, teams of horses heaving, panting and charging, reins flapping, whips whipping, shouting, hollering, whooping riders, and, sometimes, canvas tearing, wheels falling off, wagons tipping, horses stumbling, cowboys toppling, bones breaking, bodies being crushed, injury, crippling, and occasionally death. What a way to go! Or not. That's the part that disgusted Myra.

Well into the 1940s, chuck-wagon races were occasionally held in the open in downtown Okotoks. A couple of trees in front of the railway station anchored a perfect figure-eight loop which is needed at the start of such a race.

If a race happened to be on or in progress when a train stopped by, the engineer would let passengers disembark to spectate before moving on.

Within the confines of an enclosed track, not all the risks are minimalized. The first Stampede chuck races featured heavy draught horses making slower times, suffering broken limbs, shattered hips or serious, fatal injuries at times. Wheels still came off, wagons tipped over, teams and wagons collided causing havoc and sporadic disaster. Crowds ate it up nonetheless, recognizing prowess and precision, saluting victors, yet also prone to that rather indefensible perfidious bloodlust that also infused the throngs of the ancient Roman Coliseum with temporary sadism.

Tyler was eleven years old before he could nerve himself to watch chuck-wagon races. He had seen *Ben Hur*. Nightmare visitations of abused and tortured horses precluded his ability to venture anywhere near the Stampede racetrack at night. When it became clearer that safety measures had been enacted: drivers switching their wagon teams to thoroughbreds instead of draught horses, replacing metal camp stoves with a rubber drum, altering the sharp angles on the barrels in the opening figure-eight, rules preventing switching lanes after the final turn, then Tyler risked viewing the spectacle. That, and the fact that , when he turned eleven in 1996, Tranogco had finally been successful at the spring auction where corporations and other consortiums bid for the right to sponsor a wagon. That meant that corporate executives like Jules and other company employees could enjoy ground level viewing sections at each night's races. Corporate sponsorship was introduced in 1979 to level the playing field so that cowboys didn't have to solicit their own supports or underwrite all their own costs of feed, horse-breeding, travel, wagon ownership and maintenance. Since then, corporate logos and nomenclatures adorn competing chuck-wagon canvasses. Chuck-wagon drivers and outriders are grateful for both sponsorships and safety measures. Their primary concern is not only to cross the finish line first, but to cross it penalty free. A panel of judges scrutinizes every race looking for infractions of any thirty-five or more rules. Some of the penalties are definitive (e.g., five seconds for each barrel knocked over), others are discretionary (e.g., offering assistance to an outrider horse).

The Half Mile of Hell track was lengthened to 5/8 mile in 1974. The basic race requirements have remained the same since the beginning. A wagon is pulled by a four-horse team and accompanied by a driver and four outriders. The whole team must complete a figure-eight turn before taking to the 5/8 mile circuit. At the starting line, the lead outrider or barrel peg man steadies his own horse and the two lead horses on the wagon team. A second outrider behind the wagon must lift the "stove" barrel into the back of the wagon. Outriders three and four hold tent poles with a taut piece of canvas stretched between them. These poles must also be shoved into the wagon before they mount up to follow in the wagon's tracks. Outriders' horses have no stirrups hanging off the saddles and the riders wear running-shoes, not boots for faster traction. All this action happens very quickly at the sound of a klaxon that initiates each race. The first ten seconds or less as the team negotiates that figure-eight often prove the most crucial. Getting onto the track first is a huge advantage. Penalties can be incurred for tipped barrels, false starts, outriders missing their mounts, poles and stoves off the ground ahead of time, poles left dragging, drivers assisting outriders, blocking another team's lane or any other form of interference, outriders crossing the finish line ahead of the wagon or lagging too far behind, and even wearing mismatched colours. Timing is everything. Intensity infuses spectacle.

1999 had been good year for the Tranogco team headed by driver Troy Dorchester who was 1998's rookie driver of the year and a third-generation chuck-wagon captain in his family out of Westerose. They had placed in the top five four times during the heats in the winner-takes-all round. In the final four they faced tough competition from teams sponsored by Fountain Tire, Copen-hagen Inc., and Serval Integrated Energy Services. Drivers for those teams respectively were Jim Nevada of Airdrie, Buddy Bensmiller of Dewberry, and Kelly Sutherland of Grande Prairie who appeared to be on a roll again and headed to being crowned king of the chucks.

The Stedman-Davis group and friends found their way into the Tranogco cheering section for the final night's showdown. Black and gold flags and pompoms waved ecstactically displaying the company colours, gung-ho to cheer Troy on. The voice of Joe Carlson announced the line-up for the evening's racing card as he had been doing for almost forty years. The teams appeared in the arena and headed for their starting places. The klaxon klaxxed. The Copenhagen team faltered, tipping over a barrel. Troy had the Tranogco wagon tight behind Sutherland who was leading the pack. On the back stretch, Sutherland opened up an almost three wagon lead. On the final turn, Fountain Tire began to lose ground. Tranogco and Copenhagen charged towards the finish seeking to catch Serval Integrated. Sutherland was uncatchable. "Ladies and gentlemen, the winner of the fifty thousand dollar showdown and the ATCO Gas Trophy, for the sixth time in his career and third year in a row is Kelly Sutherland and the Serval Integrated Energy Services team! In second place, Troy Dorchester and the team from Tranogco, followed by Buddy Bensmiller and the team from Copenhagen, Inc., in spite of an added five seconds for tipping over that barrel at the start. In fourth place, also making a valiant effort, Jim Nevada and the team of Fountain Tire. Hats off to Kelly Sutherland, King of the Chucks once again."

And that was that. The Stedman-Davis contingent made their way into stadium seats to enjoy the Grandstand Show, marvelled at impressive fireworks, filed out of Stampede Park until sometime next year in early July, located their respective vehicles and made their various ways home partially satisfied, partially dejected, feeling like family just as racing chuck-wagons has a history of being a family enterprise and passion. Myra had kept her eyes closed during most of it, but she wouldn't have missed a family outing. Principles trump personal antipathies.

# Chapter 10:
## Reciprocity and Receptivity

When the Stampede was over, the Stedman family spent one laid-back lazy week at a rented cabin on Lake Kananaskis. Rebecca didn't mind as the Berensons were also staying at a lodge in the same vicinity. Tyler settled into more reading, rodeo videos and daily exercises designed to strengthen his recovering leg.

After that, Tyler was due to spend the rest of July at Pops' place. He and Alex spent several hours each day helping weed the garden and harvest what was ripe and ready. Four or five other hours were spent helping Ola and her hired workers with the second-cut of hay harvest. Ola drove the tractor hauling the wagon following the worker who dragged the baler around gathering up the mounds of hay that had been swathed the previous day or two. One worker stood on the wagon stacking the tied bales hoisted towards him by Tyler and Alex and another worker who followed along on the ground. It was dusty, heavy work, not manageable by anyone with allergies. For these labours Ola paid her teen helpers five dollars an hour. Eighty to a hundred dollars a week came in handy later in the summer going to movies, buying ice cream and sodas, choosing new clothes and running-shoes, and helping to foot the bill for their week at the Lazy J Dude Ranch in Montana in August.

What Tyler relished the most was morning and evening hours spent in the horse barn. All Pops had to do pretty much was point. "There's the feed. Tacitus gets a double share. This here is a special growth supplement and bone-builder, add a quarter of a litre to Striker's water every second day. Ironstone gets that special feed for foals. Move Belva and him across the way. It's time they had their stall cleaned. Do the same with Charro after that. Striker and Tacitus can wait for clean digs until tomorrow. Grab a few bales of fresh hay from the loft to spread around." Tyler moved from one chore to the next with a lilt in his body, a smile on his face, a whistle on his lips and the diligence of an army recruit obeying a benign sergeant-major. Five horses neighed, whinnied, snorted their appreciation, and enjoyed every occasional lump-of-sugar treat their temporary caregiver offered them. When morning barn chores were over, each horse was led lovingly out to the paddock, where water and feed troughs were checked again and replenished as needed. All that before 7:30 A.M. left Tyler with an ample appetite for breakfast.

The evening duty roster meant bringing the horses back into the barn. Two of them got a complete brushing down one night. The other three were groomed the next. If a chilly night was expected, body blankets were attached. Hooves were inspected and anti-cracking gel applied to splits and dried-out areas. Manes and tails were checked for tangles, burrs and other attaching seeds. Snags were straightened, snarls were removed and "cling-ons" discarded. All of this activity served to help strengthen Tyler's knee during its recovery period. He only wore a tensor bandage now whenever it developed aching from being over-strained. He knew that the second week of his stay at Pops' place was the fourth week since his physio-therapy had started. That was the week Brad had said, he could ride horses again with minimal risk. He stared his favorite stallion in the eyes before leaving the barn each night. "Next week, Striker, you and me and those foothills trails. It's a date." A vertical nodding of the head, a pawing on the floor of the stall and a friendly anticipatory snuffle characterized a spirited creature's response. Synergy.

Alex continued spending morning and evening hours helping Wilton with his chickens. Egg collecting, feeding, roost-cleaning was always best done in the cooler times of day. The smell during hotter hours was truly nauseous. The weasel, by the way, had been trapped, skinned, tanned and tacked up on the backside of one of the coops. Wilton's idea of poetic justice. It was wonderful having Tyler almost fully healthy again. They could play more active games in their free time. One-on-one soccer was popular, as was tossing a football, and occasional wrestling for fun. Despite Ola's ambiguous feelings, there was also target practice.

Alex was so impressed by the weasel hide, Wilton had asked Ola's permission to present his young farmhand with a used shot-gun of his own. It had to be re-registered in her name or Pops' name with Alex listed as an occasional user and learner by special permit. It was the one facet of farming Ola would have preferred to do without, but critter-control was a necessity if you wanted to keep your domestic animals safe and your crops protected. Traps and shot-guns were preferred to poisons. Ola used all free-release traps. She had only shot one coyote in all her years in Canada so far. It was rabid and headed for the horse barn. There wasn't time to fetch Pops.

A hundred meters back of the horse barn, down in a small valley was a training corral, which when not in use served as a great place to set cans and other objects on fence posts and take aim at knocking them off with dummy shot. Dummy shot came with a plastic casing filled with baking soda. It cracked on impact and exploded into dust. On Tuesday of Tyler's first week on the farm, he and Alex had finished their farm labors early in the afternoon. Alex suggested this would be a terrific opportunity to head down to the corral with his fire-arm and a pack or two of dummy shot. Tyler said he'd be happy to watch.

"Watch!" Alex exclaimed, "What fun is that? I'll show you how to load the gun, hold it snug, aim and fire."

"Well...I don't know."

"Don't worry. You can't hurt anything, even if you miss."

Alex shouted that out as he went to the house for gun and ammunition and came back running, racing Tyler to the corral. When they arrived Alex got busy setting up targets: an empty bean can, an empty oil can, an empty tomato juice can, an old Coke bottle, an empty plastic ketchup bottle, a mud-died rubber duck he used to use in the bath-tub, and a Barbie doll that Rebecca had forgotten she even had at Pops' house. Alex stepped back to the opposite side of the corral, loaded the gun, and fired off several shots that knocked down two cans, one bottle, and the rubber duck. He put the gun down, hurried over and reset the targets. Then he helped Tyler load the gun, lifted it till it was nestled into Tyler's right shoulder, showed his cousin how to take a sighting and how to aim a little above the target to allow for a slight drop after firing. Tyler's first two shots went zinging wide of the mark over and between fence rails. The third shot dinged the post beneath the Barbie doll. The fourth shot whizzed into Wilton's adjacent field and smacked into the side of a grazing cow. It said *moo* in a way that sounded like "Ouch! Hey watch it, buster!" as it turned a bovine stare in Tyler's direction.

"Oh my God! Sorry," Tyler said apologetically fluttering inside as he imagined "What if the shot had been real?"

Alex was flopping into the fence and slapping Tyler on the back in hysterics. He couldn't decide what was funniest: Tyler hitting the cow in the first place, or the cow's virtually human reaction, or Tyler's muttered appeal for pardon. This was an historical incident in their friendship he would joyfully remember and readily retell repeatedly whenever an opportunity presented itself. Tyler wasn't long in sharing in the hilarity of the moment and laughed at himself as much as Alex did in every subsequent recounting though Tyler never touched a gun again.

But he did pick up a lariat. The corral posts became targets of a different sort for him. Pops had showed him how to tie the rope and how to throw the basic overhand and side-arm tosses. Wilton took time to teach him four other manoevures and made a wooden calf using an old saw-horse for the body. Tyler first practiced for many spare hours from a standing still position. He was working out the basic principles so that when he was riding, he could throw the lasso one-handed with rote-memory precision, the held end wrapped snugly around a saddle-horn. Those were some of the rides he and Striker enjoyed that last week of July, circling around the corral, closing in on the wooden calf, letting the lariat fly—round the neck, under the forelegs, the back legs, and around all four legs. Wilton had elevated the calf on a central metal pole, leaving just enough room for the rope to slide beneath the wooden limbs. Visions of rodeo stardom were running their own circles through Tyler's consciousness.

•  •  •

Ola continued having visions. On the Friday of Tyler's first week visiting, she left prepared casseroles and salads in the refrigerator for supper that day and lunch the next, complete with heating and serving instructions. She had stopped working at 4:00 P.M. and begun her own twenty-four hour fast and spiritual retreat at her cabin in the outback. That was as close as she could come to keeping an original Sabbath.

The cabin was 30' x 40' of one-room simplicity. A fireplace set against the north wall had a stock of wood laid by in case of cool weather. A match-holder hung on a hook set in the mortar to the left of the grate opening. A black mesh metal fire-screen and a wrought-iron poker were the only accessories. An ice-box

H. Lee Disher

in which to keep water and juices sat on the floor beneath the west window. To the left of it were a wooden trash bin and an apple crate that served as a recycle box. Two willow-cane chairs and a similar settee with plain blue cushions were placed in the middle of the room around a braided rag rug. One small square table could be moved next to wherever one was sitting. A Bible and a hurricane oil lamp were set upon it. To the right of the fireplace was a small divided orange crate on which there was a knotted prayer rope and a simple wooden cross. On the shelf of the crate were four volumes of *The Philokalia* and some of the writings of Catherine DeHueck Doherty. In the bottom portion of the crate were a supply of lamp oil and several kinds of unscented candles and candle-holders. Up against the east wall was a three-quarter bed with white sheets and pillow cases, a green woolen blanket, and a quilt Ola had made in the Bethlehem Star pattern. To the left of the head of the bed a small clothes rack was attached to the wall. At the foot of the bed was a vinyl-padded *prie-dieu* Pops had made from old barn board. It was his gift to her for her first Christmas in Canada. To the left of the door as one entered from the south side was a small oak washstand with a ceramic jug and basin, towel and face-cloth hanging on the towel bar, and a cake of scented oatmeal soap. The drawer in the wash-stand held a supply of Kleenex, Q-tips, aspirins, and Band-aids. A five-gallon galvanized-steel water container sat next to it on a small stool. Wooden shutters on the two small windows on the east and west sides were shut or opened to admit or block light. Toilet facilities were in an outhouse twenty meters to the right of the cabin at the end of a stone path. A closet to the right of the entry door held two spare roll-away beds and bedding when the cabin was used by visiting retreatants. There was also a cot available for anyone who brought along a sleeping-bag. When she first set up the cabin, Ola had hung several Orthodox icons on the walls. She found them too distracting during her first spiritual seclusions and removed them to her bedroom in her own house. When she made the cabin available to other pilgrims in 1990, she realized only a few of them had any Eastern Orthodox affiliation. The only adornment which hung on the otherwise barren west wall to the right of the window was a wall-hanging woven by a woman named Sylvia from Chalk River, Ontario. She sent it to Ola after her visit to the cabin in 1992 as an expression of her appreciation for the insights and fulfillment she experienced there. It was part macramé, part tapestry featuring a clockwise circle of symbols — a torch, a full moon, and a larger sun at nine o'clock all in browns and red tones. It represented the path to spiritual knowledge outlined by St. Hesychios the Priest in "On Watchfulness and Holiness":

*While we are being strengthened in Christ Jesus and beginning to move forward in steadfast watchfulness. He at first appears in our intellect like a torch which, carried in the hand of the intellect, guides us along the tracks of the mind; then He appears like a full moon, circling the heart's firmament; then He appears to us like the sun, radiating justice, clearly revealing Himself in the full light of spiritual vision.*

—*Philokalia (Vol. 1, text 166, page 191)*

Ola entered the cabin, opened a small canvas shoulder bag, and hung a night-dress and a housecoat on the clothes pegs next to the bed. She crossed the room to the ice-box and took out a container of bottled water, opened it, took a swallow and moved to sit down in one of the willow-bough chairs. She straightened her back, closed her eyes, set her feet square on the floor about thirty centimeters apart, laid her arms on her knees palms up and began to breathe deeply, slowly blocking out all distracting sounds or absorbing them into her consciousness so everything was part of the wholeness of the moment. As she paid attention to her breathing she concentrated on erasing any racing and random thoughts and worries that were on her mind at the time, opening her intellect to God's Spirit, preparing her heart to be receptive, inviting God's presence with her in this time and space apart. She felt and heard her heartbeat slowing. She imagined cluttered thoughts flying out the windows experiencing a holy emptiness of consciousness. It took a good fifteen minutes to reach that state of readiness. She was in no rush. She began an unvoiced prayer: "Come, Holy God, into this present moment. Let Your Spirit awaken within me as it visits my soul. Make me receptive to Your grace, attentive to Your voice, open to Your wisdom. Speak if You desire, or just attend me and fill me with Your warmth and love. Remind me that I am Yours and that You are mine. Steady me to stay here in Your company for this Sabbath day. In the silences, hold me in the palm of Your hand. In the conversations, let me be an ardent and patient listener. In the visions, let me behold Your power and Your glory. Let Jesus be my torch, my moon, my sun. I pray in his holy name. Amen."

She stayed put in that stillness, in that sense of reassurance and holy belonging for a good two hours, moving only occasionally to sip more water. Water that became for her as the living water Jesus promised from the well of God that springs up to eternal life and never runs dry. Water that merged into spiritual experience. Birthing water. Birthing Spirit — enhancing life, affirming connection, informing faith.

She repeated this process at 9:00 P.M. that night and at 6:00 A.M. and noon the next day. In between she proceeded with self-designed meditations on Psalms 84, 111, and 128 and a selection of readings from Volume Two of *The Philokalia*: "On Self-Emptiness," "On Being Humble," "On Readiness," and "On Attaining True Wisdom". During the course of this retreat she had two clear messages from God and three visions. The first of the messages was an emphatic underlining of Psalm 128:6 : *"May you see your child's children."* It seemed early on in the game to be realizing Alex would someday marry and start a family of his own. Ola would have preferred something about a less worrisome and less rambunctious adolescence for her son. The second of the messages was a personal commendation to stay her course: live simply, hold fast to faith, love generously and treat your workers justly. There was one other blessed coincidence when after completing her 6:00 A.M. devotional she picked Volume 1 of *The Philokalia* and opened it to Text 196 [page 197]:

> *... the sun rising over the earth creates the daylight; and the venerable and holy name of the Lord Jesus, shining continually in the mind, gives birth to countless intellections radiant as the sun.*

Ola's first vision was of a factory converted into a cathedral. Steel girders in the ceiling were replaced by ornate wooden struts and cross-beams. Frosted and checkered glass panes became stained-glass windows set in Roman arches. Workers on the assembly line became worshippers seated in pews and rising to sing songs of praise, kneeling to pray. The boss' office became a chancel complete with altar, a business suit gave way to alb and chasuble and stole. The work orders posted on the wall became Scriptures read from a lectern; shift supervisors turned into lay readers. The mechanical room on one side of the factory and the restrooms on the opposite side became transepts presided over by statues of Mary and Joseph furnished with banks of votive candles for personal supplicatory devotions. The upper level cafeteria became a choir loft with workers on break and cooking and serving staff chanting canticles. They were chanting verses six and seven of Psalm 84 which must have been the inspiration behind the vision:

> *As they go through the valley of Baca they make it a place of springs...They go from strength to strength, the God of gods will be seen in Zion.*

In Ola's vision, they were chanting in Ukrainian. "Baca. Baca. The Valley of Baca. What does that word mean?" she asked herself. She went to her Bible and checked the footnotes beneath that psalm. "*Baca*: tears, sorrow, desolation. Baca," Ola repeated to herself, "Baca, desolation. Baca sung in Ukrainian. Like *fabrika*, our word for factory. *Baca. Fabrika*, Desolation turned to a place of springs. A factory becomes a cathedral.

"Oh!" she almost cried out loud, "Chernobyl! Chernobyl will recover strength! God's power of restoration will be seen there! Someday. Someday. O Most High and Holy One, I praise You, I glorify You that such a day may come. May You continue to be present and honored in the midst of Your people there."

Her second vision was more easily deciphered. Birds were threading kernels of some kind and stringing them around young conifers. The branches were almost overloaded. Rabbits rejoiced in circle dances around the bases of the trees. Stars popped in the heavens like fireworks. Parcel after parcel from beneath the trees grew legs or wings and paraded outwards in all directions dispersing themselves throughout the earth. They seemed to be carried on the wind that brought the birds in as it drew them out. Images of fecundity and fruitfulness, rejoicing and celebration. What else could these mean but that she could look forward to a bountiful year of grain crops overseen and assisted by the blessing of God's *ruach*—God's Spirit, God's breath, God's wind.

Her third vision was enigmatic, bizarre, and seemed unfinished, partial. There was something like a crater with its sides carved into amphitheatre seating, a sunken coliseum of stone and clay. Pastel speckled dots lined what might have been the grandstand area. Faces in a crowd? Some kind of athletic event seemed to be in progress. Something with horses. It wasn't polo.

Maybe she had just had too much Stampede on the brain in recent weeks. The scene was surreal: history and fantasy fused with reality. It was more like a circus act. A gaunt rider on a horse came into the centre of the ring. The horse was grotesque. It was pale and transparent as if made of glass or plastic so that Ola could see its every muscle as it moved, its blood vessels, its vital organs, and some exposed nerves. He was being pursued by an indistinct young rider on a gray steed that had eight legs. It moved very fast, virtually flew across the ground. Behind the younger rider came a female rider on a white-hot horse blazing like natural phosphorous exposed to air. Neither the horse nor the rider were consumed or harmed by the flames. The scene took on a racing format as riders and charges moved in circles around the arena and began dodging one another so that soon it became confusing. You couldn't tell who was chasing or leading whom. But the gaps between them all began to shrink somewhat. Where was God? Ola scanned the whole crater from top to bottom and side to side. A divine figure like a golden angel seemed to appear in a kind of windowed box in the centre of the seating area, stepping up towards the public address system to offer on-site commentary, or perhaps just to make an announcement. The vision faded into obscurity and took up residence in some back corner of Ola's mind. She had had strange presentations before. Not all of them had come from God she discovered. The Devil can invade solitary spaces too. Her discipline was to store such images away for a time. If they didn't recur, either they weren't important or they were demonic distractions unworthy of further attention. This vision had happened on Saturday afternoon, hardly the time for a bad dream or a nightmare but possibly a time for nonsense.

When her Sabbath was ended, Ola offered a prayer of thanks, packed her night-wear in her shoulder bag, made notes about replenishing water supplies and toilet paper in the outhouse and took a woodland trail back to her house. A simple supper of cheese and crackers and a few grapes would suffice for her and maybe a dish of ice cream. There was a slightly uncharacteristic buoyancy in her step thinking of Chernobyl reborn, the prospect of an abundant harvest and the reassurances she had received from the Almighty.

•　　•　　•

Saturday was the day the tensor bandage came off, the day to begin to refurbish left leg muscles without assistance, the first day Tyler was free to risk riding again. He itched to saddle up Striker right after morning barn chores and breakfast, but there were still four hours of farm work to put in and corn in the garden was ripe for picking. Pops could still manage to boil up hot dogs and corn on the cob during Ola's absence.

As Tyler handed Striker a handful of hay after cleaning his stall, he stroked the horse's mane and gently chided: "Now don't you make any other plans for this afternoon, fella, 'cause you and I have a date that's been long overdue. And don't even think about getting too frisky! We're just going to take it easy since I can't afford to fall off when you decide to go jumping rock piles."

A whinny, a snort, and a toss of the head in reply. A reassuring pat, a wink before turning to leave and the whistled opening notes of "I'm an Old Cow Hand from the Rio Grande" came from Tyler. Something slow, something soothing, something he had heard years ago from Pops' collection of country music, something to prime the pump of a requisite patience. The afternoon would come soon enough.

After picking the corn, Tyler made up a bag lunch to take over to the bunkie, a small four-bedroom cottage where the hired hands stayed from mid-May through to harvest time. Saturday was tidy-up time and often Ola took Alex or Tyler along to help her. This day, she had assigned full cleaning duties to Tyler. It was usually a four-hour job, so arriving a little after 10:00 A.M. Tyler reckoned he'd be finished by 2:00 in the afternoon.

Kitchen first. The workers were responsible for cleaning up their own dirty dishes and had left their breakfast plates, pans and cutlery air-drying in the plastic rack to the left of the sink. But there were counter-tops, shelves, appliances, and a table and chairs that needed dusting, a floor to be mopped, a refrigerator to be cleaned and sanitized inside and an oven needing attention. That's where Tyler started, by placing newspapers beneath an open oven door, taking out the racks and spraying the interior of the oven with Easy-Off. While the cleansing foam took effect, he proceeded with the dusting. He returned to the oven to wipe it out with a damp cloth rinsed and wrung out in a pail of water. When the oven was clean, he turned his attention to the refrigerator. Then he mopped the floor. The kitchen sparkled when he was done and he broke into a smile that would have made Ola wink.

After kitchen patrol, Tyler diverted his elbow grease and sanitizing prowess to the bathroom. Then, having wiped away the sweat that had formed on his forehead and chest cavity, he sat down and ate his lunch. "I hope Ola doesn't let Mom know I'm good at this, even though I do find it rather satisfying."

It was nearing one o'clock when he began to tackle cleaning the bedrooms being careful to put the workers' personal things back where they were after he had dusted, scrubbed and vacuumed. Some clothes and bed linens obviously needed laundering but that too was the workers' own responsibility not his. In two bedrooms in particular, aerosol spraying helped mitigate bad odours. In the third bedroom, there were some magazines left lying open on the dresser and on the bedspread. Not *Rod and Gun*, *Playboy*, *Popular Mechanics* or *Penthouse* that he had noticed before in grown men's domains; no, these were magazines lying open at pictures of naked men and young boys in individual poses or in pairs or groups doing rude things. Tyler knew homosexuality existed but this was as close as he had come to confronting it. Fright was what he felt more than disgust. He translated his fear into completing his cleaning with haste, all the while assuaging himself with the reassuring thought that at least that worker hadn't snuck in while he was vacuuming, had a shower, and appeared before him dripping wet and flinging a towel open and asking, "So, do you like, eh?"

At 2:00 P.M. he fairly flew out of the workers' cottage and burst into Pops' kitchen out of breath to gulp down a glass of ice water and head out to the tack room. Pops was already there to meet him with his saddle all soaped and shined, bridle and bit looped over the horn, stirrups attached and spurs in hand ready to clip on to the heels of Tyler's boots.

"Help me saddle up Belva and I'll ride with you, Sport."

"At your service, Pops. That will be just great. Do you think Wilton would mind if we rode along the ridge back of his place?"

"Nope. I figured that's where you might like to go so you could have a safe run with some speed in it, so I already checked."

"Golly Grandpa, you're almost as psychic as Aunt Ola!"

"Naw. I just never forgot what it was to be a boy with a hankering after horses."

"Are you sure you'll be all right on Belva? Why not Charro?"

"Ironstone will be all right without his mother for a while. It's time she got a little more exercise to take off some her maternity fat. Charro thinks she's Striker's running mate, thinks she can match him stride for stride. Belva has more horse sense than that. She won't egg him on and he won't want her to get too far out of sight."

It took only minutes for the two riders to saddle up. It took only a few more minutes to amble out of the barn, round the paddock and hit the trail leading to the foothills at an even, easy trot.

Grasshoppers leapt, crickets chirped, mice scampered unseen in the fallow field around them. Milkweeds nodded, buttercups bowed in the breeze, Queen Anne's lace sashayed to and fro, an occasional daisy shimmied. Thistles and burdock minded their own business as the grasses glistened golden and green. Wales had settled momentarily in southern Alberta as Tyler called to mind Dylan Thomas' "Fern Hill". It was poplar boughs instead of apple under which Tyler was "young and easy." The houses had a similar lilt. He was "famous among the barns." Time let him play "and be golden in the mercy of his means." To their right they heard a whirr of tractors hauling squeaky wagons through the grain fields, the sound of workers singing, joking and whistling. Further to their left, Wilton's hay field lay buzzed, scattered with stray remnants of a second cut. The next visible fields over bore ripened barley and oats well on their way. From further down the road the scent of fresh-spread pig manure stung their nostrils momentarily.

"Whew!" Pops exclaimed, "that's some powerful lung disinfectant!"

"Only thirty points shy of lethal!" Tyler shouted back. He chuckled to himself imagining that if Alex were here he would have said, "Don't put any of that on your fork, Dork!"

The borderline toxic scent diminished as they made their way into the woodlot starting their gradual, curved ascent into the foothills. Freshness filled the shade. Sunlight leaked through leafy crevices. Several low-hanging boughs needing trimming were noted and pushed back by hand during the ride. A harmony of humankind and horses glided along like a hum sustained. An older Butch Cassidy and a younger Sundance Kid doing no evil, up to nothing but good.

After the edge of the woods, there is a brief rise to climb and then, the hilltop and a path undulating over two hills leftwards till you reach a flattened ridge. On a carefree, unhampered outing like this where time is not an issue, on a blue-sky day of such extensive clarity, you do not keep moving when you first reach that hilltop. You pause, breathe deep, take a 360-degree scan of the horizon, allow the vista to infiltrate your being. More than the usual limit of 33.5 kilometers of straight-ahead vision applies. You've reached the Western borderline of the Prairies. East is very much down east and for flat out mile after scarcely interrupted mile there's a continuum of fields and streams. West is on the rise, knoll after knoll, waves of grass surging green upon green up to the distant forest's edge as conifers creep and cluster as if they are climbing stairs or playing leap frog until they run out of room, run out of soil, thin into rock and pay homage to their overlords. On a day like this day, you can see them looming farthest West the lords, the dukes and duchesses, the robust princes and princesses among peaks on the earth — the Rockies. Here beyond Okotoks they play backstop to Lake Kananaskis. Their summits will preside in silence over a not-so eventful Summit of G-8 nations in July 2002 and sit in state eons after. They are majestic. They are purple-robed or blue-skinned or twenty-five shades of grey. Rugged, rutted, precarious, daunting and often dusted with snow like whipped-cream on a sundae. You have to stop to pay your respects on a day like this day. You have to hum "This Land is Your Land" in your heart. You have to say "awe." And if you're even one nanogram of a believer, you have to acknowledge your Almighty with thanks. On a day like this day, you have to pause to imagine Tyler and Pops astride Striker and Belva stock still on that hilltop at that moment of first reaching it, wordless and wor-shipful, held and beholden, a fusion of atoms and chromosomes and soul, a sheerness of belonging in some overarching schema. Blessed assurance.

After that reverent pause, they ride on two hills to their left to the top of the ridge behind Wilton's acres. Time to let the reins out, to let fly, to release oneself into another form of spiritual and natural merger. Tyler bent over Striker at a gallop like the scene on Keats' Grecian urn. Beauty is truth, truth, beauty. You know. You just know. Just ask Pops for a witness. Not a single misstep. Not a jot of imbalance. Not a whiff of discomposure. Throughout the whole looping circuit of racing forth, making graceful turns and sprinting back several times in succession there is a smooth and fluid symmetry and synthesis. Such a beauty can compel you to tears. Pops has a damp hanky. Tyler savors an inner glow. Satisfaction sustains them all the way back home, through a simple, succulent supper of hot dogs and corn on the cob; through several laidback games of Parcheesi with Alex, some spirited conversation and a telecast of a Blue Jays baseball game; through a peaceful night's sleep. For Tyler it lasted through the rest of his stay with Pops and Aunt Ola while enjoying similar rides every day except Wednesday when it rained.

The more exceptional day, however, turned out to be the following Saturday, the last day of Tyler's stay. In fact, up until late afternoon, it was a relatively similar day to all the rest. Barn chores, garden work, spare time and play time with Alex, time for riding horses and for horsing around, and only a little time spent around Ola's barns and fields—which left time later that afternoon for Tyler to offer to help Alex with Wilton's chickens.

Tyler took a few pecks to the back of his wrists from hens unfamiliar with his presence among them as one who gathers eggs. One hen even made an advance on him with a flurry of squawking and shed feathers, so he quickly backed off and let a giggling Alex look after that one. Mr. Wilton excused himself part way through wondering if the boys wouldn't mind finishing up. He had to get ready for an appointment he said. Tyler and Alex didn't mind. They had a little play fight stuffing straw down each other's shirts and managed to break a couple of eggs in the process. Without rags or paper towels handy, they just wiped the sticky yolk and albumen on their jeans. They emerged from the coop to take the eggs to Wilton's shed behind his kitchen and noticed a car pulled up in the laneway they weren't used to seeing around Wilton's place, a car they were sure they had seen elsewhere before but couldn't just place at the moment.

"Here's all your eggs, Mr. Wilton," Alex yelled from the shed through the open kitchen door as he and Tyler placed them on the shelves set aside for that purpose.

"That's fine, boys. Thanks for your help," answered Wilton coming towards them through the kitchen, smelling of musk after-shave and dressed in handsome navy slacks, white shirt and tie, blue blazer, and black Oxfords.

"Whoa, Mr. Wilton, look at you!" Alex remarked, wide-eyed. "You got a heavy date tonight or something?"

"As a matter of fact, Alex, Tyler, I do." And, turning towards an unseen guest seated at his kitchen table, he said, "I'm ready if you're ready."

"Oh, I'm ready," she replied, "I was ready when I arrived here."

"Then, off we go," Wilton responded, "dinner at Sergio's and then, what's the name of that play at the little theatre?"

"Wingfield Follies. It's a one-man show by an actor from Ontario about a city man who takes up farming. You'll love it!"

And with that the two of them passed by Alex and Tyler whose mouths fell and hit the floor.

"Ms. Morton?" they shouted in stereo.

"Hello, Alex. Hello, Tyler. Enjoying your summer?"

They were too stunned to answer soon enough. Ms. Morton and Wilton keep moving, got into her car and drove off smirking all the way out of the lane. Alex and Tyler dashed over to Ola's kitchen. The more impetuous young man couldn't contain himself.

"Mom, Pops, did you know Mr. Wilton has a girlfriend? Do you know it's my teacher, Ms. Morton?"

"Yes," Ola replied. "She's been out here several times. They met at your graduation, remember, when they both acted as chaperones for the dance."

"Maybe that's when they met, Mom. But Wilton started taking a shine to her the day he picked me up from our field trip to the Badlands. 'Demure' he called her. Too shy to admit he found her 'attractive' as well. Good thing he hasn't had to deal with her in a classroom. We've got our own different adjectives for that," Alex ran on.

"Well," Tyler interjected, "if that doesn't shut down all the elevators in Vulcan!"

"Huh?" queried Alex.

"Oh, just another expression I picked up from Pops."

"Yep," said Pops agreeing, "I reckon that pretty much sums it up."

Ola smiled, shaking her head somewhat mystified as she sat down with them all to supper. Alex remained stupefied in surprise as assorted dinner chatter continued. Out in the barn, Belva cast a sideways glance at Striker over in his stall, the kind of look that says: "You just keep your distance, fella."

# Chapter 11:
# Where the Girls Are

Riverside Park is a popular gathering place in Okotoks, particularly in summer. Parents, mostly moms, with toddlers and infants congregate around the wading pool. Older children, some accompanied by parents or guardians or baby-sitters enjoy the roped-off portion of the Sheep River set aside for swimming. A bit further downstream old-timers, night-shift workers and young men with a day-off or who are currently unemployed may be found fishing. Couples, singles, joggers make their way around the pathways and garden walks around the park's perimeter. Some stop at benches or under trees to read, have lunch or a snack. A playground area filled with swings, slides, monkey bars, teeter-totters and a couple of sand-boxes attracts a number of children. Morning, noon and evening (when there are no soccer games) Rebecca Stedman and Charlene Berenson and their friends cluster there and play with seemingly endless energy, chatter, laughter and occasional arguments over whose turn is next. Weekdays there are supervised programs led by young adults hired by the town for the summer months. The northeast corner, away from the playground is where the young adolescents hang out. Tyler, Lumpy Jenkins, Kevin Noseworthy, Raja Punkara, Stephanie Wells, Enid Evans, and (when her parents permit and can't contain her any longer with piano lessons or household chores or good books she should appreciate) Martha Yellan gather whenever they can. Someone usually has a Frisbee or a football to toss around; some bring baseballs and gloves and play catch. Others from their graduating class also show up now and then. The conversation and activity may take a different twist however. Those who can't stand one or more of the "intruders" find some excuse to leave and go elsewhere. Or after a while the interlopers are not so politely told to "buzz off!" Alex, whenever he is visiting Tyler, is always welcome. Comic relief always enhances company. Conversation is sporadic. Sometimes it involves the whole gang. More often it is one small group here, another small group there, a pair of people talking in another separate space. No one is ever too far out of ear-shot of what's being said and some persons flit from one conversation to another. Group activity can occasionally burst out into a game of dodge ball or frozen tag. The topics of the day range from what was on TV last night, to new clothes recently purchased or being noticed at the mall, to what happened at the last sleep-over or backyard camp-out, to the odd memories of life in grade nine at Dewdney Junior High, to what is worrisome or exciting about high school in the fall, to what anyone did on his or her holidays with their parents, to how about we all go to such and such a movie this weekend or let's grab a video and meet at so-and-so's house to watch it. They talk about who can stick it out through " *I Know What You Did Last Summer*" without getting freaked; or who can watch *Silence of the Lambs* without once closing their eyes or feeling on the edge of being sick. They talk about rock and pop and alternative music: who's in, who's out, who's cool, who's wicked, who's a bust, and who is way too twisted.

That's the surface conversation. The sub-text, the whispered private interchange, is about mating and dating, and adolescent hormone control (or not); about fears and already-experienced pleasures and mishaps and imagined fantasies; about zit remedies, cosmetics, and underarm deodorants and bad-breath control; about smoking and drinking (Dare we? Dare we not?); about where to get the best burger, best ice-cream, and best cheesecake in town. Such is the stuff that comprises teen summers. It's about where the girls are or where the boys are as the case may be. No question however about favourite French fries and cherry Cokes—that would be at Fleer's, the restaurant where this same gang tends to congregate shortly after the street lights come on. It's where belonging is expressed in teasing one another—Raja about her brains, Lumpy about his weight, Martha about her affection for things French, Kevin for his dream of becoming a movie star, Stephanie for her "have-to-be-cool" clothes, Enid for her forgetfulness, Tyler for his decency, and Alex for just about anything. Lumpy's sister, Monica, works as a part-time waitress. She is quite well-developed at age nineteen. Once, on his way back from the men's room, Kevin slipped Monica a toonie if she would make a point of bending low in front of Alex as she served up his fries. She even undid an extra button to make a more ample display of her cleavage as she leaned into ask her favorite Ukrainian customer if he'd like more gravy.

Alex gulped and began spluttering, "H-holy sh...Sh, Shaint, ah I mean, Saint Bart's."

"What's that?" inquired John.

"St. Bartholomew's, my mom's Orthodox church in Calgary. I said I'd go with her this Sunday m-m-morning. S-so I can't come to the junior high play-ground and join you guys for slo-pitch then."

"Okay," Lumpy replied, "but I'm pretty sure my sister's coming to play catcher for all sides."

"Martha!" Raja chimed in somewhat uncharacteristically, "maybe you could make a video for Alex to watch later in the day. Mostly home plate action, if you get my drift, and...if Enid doesn't really mind."

"That would be a hooter or two," Enid shot back. "Whoops, I mean a hoot. Wouldn't it, Alex."

"Too much!" Alex replied. "That's *too* spelled t-o-o, not t-w-o, you minks!" His face turned redder than his hair.

This gang pretty much has reserved booths and they know every song on the jukebox that you can punch in on the fifties replica consoles on the wall beside each booth. They know when a new song has been added and what former song it replaced. They know how to say to Alex: "If you play 'Back Street's Back' one more time, your cherry Coke is going straight down your pants!"

He did once. Lumpy doused him. The waitress brought a rag and her own cascade of laughter as she said she couldn't have thought of anything more ap-propriate herself. She returned with a replacement cherry Coke for Alex and when he went to pay, she said, "Not a chance! This one's on the house. I wouldn't risk giving you anything more to change." Wild snickers consumed two booths full of teens for more than a few minutes.

"Alex," commented Tyler as he turned to face his cousin, "this one's a def-inite entry in my journal tonight."

"Tyler, you keep a journal?" Stephanie inquired.

"Well, I just started it a few months ago."

"I bet it makes pretty interesting reading."

"I don't know about that, Stephanie. But if you'd like to swap your diary with me for a day or two, I might let you have a peek."

"Hmmm. I think not."

"Right. That's why diaries and journals are usually stamped 'Personal.' On the not-so-secretive ground, Alex is in town till Sunday. Would you and Enid like to take in a movie with us tomorrow night?"

A brief exchange of passing glances preceded her response, "We'd be delighted, kind Sir Stedman. Our choice?"

"Your choice, fair ladies, *enchantés somme nous*."

"Oh, *oui, oui*, Stephanie!" exclaimed Enid. "Aren't our suitors getting *très charmants*?"

"Please," Alex cried out, "don't say anything like 'wee-wee' when I still got cherry Coke soaking in my pants."

"On that soggy note, I suggest we adjourn," interjected Raja.

Which they did, giggling and chortling all the way out the door. All the way to their various homes. All the way into their recollective dreams *de jour*.

The next day was preparation day for movie night. Myra was somewhat surprised to find her nephew, Alex, and her own son hovering around the toiletries section of Kingman's Drug Store. She excused herself from behind the pharmacy for a few moments.

"May I help you?" she asked smilingly as she approached them.

"Uh, we were wondering if the store brand hair gel is any good," Tyler answered.

"Well, I imagine it's as good as any of the name brands. But right now, you two are standing in front of the colognes and aftershaves. A little early yet to be worrying about razors, isn't it?"

Alex began to stutter a response when Myra caught on. "Aah! Might there be plans for a night out with some young ladies in the works?"

Half-embarrassed flushes began appearing on their faces.

"I suggest Stetson for you my dashing young nephew—bright with a bit of its own bravado and brashness, but not overpowering. As for you my son, something a bit more subtle like this light musk down here—earthy, leathery like the smell of a fine saddle."

"Thanks, Mom," Tyler muttered appreciatively as the two young bucks headed for the front cashier grabbing up a bottle of store brand gel on the way down the aisle.

"I hope it doesn't work too well...yet," Myra sighed to herself, remembering how the scent of Stetson was among the lures that drew her to Jules in their courting days.

Helping her mother clean up the dinner dishes that evening, Rebecca wondered momentarily what had gotten into her brother and her cousin. She had never known them to spend so much time showering and grooming at that time of day. Catching her daughter's look of consternation, Myra whispered aloud, "Date."

"Oohhh!" Rebecca replied, her face awash with comprehension, "This will make for creative gossip with Charlene over the phone tonight."

Myra held back from asking what "creative" meant, hoping the chit-chat would be confined to imagined kisses (sloppy or otherwise) and perhaps a dreaded hickey or two. Note to self: set aside time for "birds and bees" consultation with Rebecca this summer, sooner than expected.

The cineplex at the Southgate mall had six separate small auditoriums with screens and digital surround-sound. Categorized ratings narrowed the choices for Tyler, Alex, Enid, and Stephanie. They'd have to wait for *American Pie* to come out on video and hope to catch it that way with or without parents at hand. They themselves weren't yet as far along the post-puberty road of adolescence as the teens in that film were. *Bowfinger* was un-intriguing to them, whereas *The Blair Witch Project* was but, unfortunately (and rightly so), labelled Restricted. They had heard great things about *The Sixth Sense*, but both that evening's viewings were already sold out. Tonight it was either *Wild, Wild West* or *Big Daddy*, another in a series of inane celluloid vehicles featuring Adam Sandler.

Stephanie had already seen *Wild, Wild West* and said it had kind of sucked, which pretty much decided the matter. Tyler wasn't much of an Adam Sandler fan. Alex was in stitches for most of the film. It was just as much fun watching him react as it was paying attention to what was on screen. At one point a spray of Coke flew out of Alex' mouth, spotting his own jeans and Tyler's and Enid's. Good thing there wasn't anyone sitting in front of them. Not nearly as severe a splatter as the Coke-at-Fleer's-Restaurant incident. Just holding Stephanie's hands, Enid's hands, and having feminine heads fall snugly on their shoulders was a quite acceptable comfort level for both boys. By the end of the film, the arm-around move was not met with any rejection. Just that once, when she broke into a laugh, Enid's head came up and crashed into Alex's chin, causing him to bite his tongue—cause for another moment of enhanced amusement and the non-protested acceptance of a make-up peck on the lips. Uninhibited cuddling during the cab ride home felt okay. The "Thanks and good night!" kisses at the doorsteps were affirming and encouraging without a sense of over-stepping any limits.

"And, by the way, next Friday night I'm having a backyard birthday bash," Stephanie was eager to inform them. "We'd love it if you'd both be able to come."

"We wouldn't miss it!" came a stereo echo.

"Not if you cut our legs off at the knee!" Alex burst out.

"Seems to me, you just about did that to your cousin," Enid shot back at him teasingly.

"All is forgiven," replied Tyler, "that's like ancient history."

"It was! It was ancient history we were exploring at the time," Alex continued.

"How insightful, my dear Watson," Tyler jibed. "Come on, cuz, home to Dreamsville, and thanks to you fine young ladies, we will certainly have pleasurable ones."

"Why Tyler, darling, you're evah so persistently a gentleman," said Stephanie in a put-on voice of a Southern belle but with complete sincerity. "Good night."

"Good night," again came in tandem as one last kiss was bestowed on young female cheeks by two tender and smitten suitors.

"Psst!" Alex asked Tyler as they made their way along the three blocks to Dewdney Common, "is 'persistently' a good thing?"

"As long as it's connected to good and decent behavior, yes."

"You mean like when a person acts kindly, politely, respectfully, and considerately most if not all the time and not rudely, crudely, roughly, or snobby or nervy or pesty or conceited-like?"

"I think you've got it."

"Yeah, I get the idea, but it sounds like awful hard work."

"Not so bad. Think of it like taming wild horses."

Alex considered it an idea amenable to pondering, which deepened his appreciation of his mother's sustained processes of meditation on Christian Orthodox thought.

Alex was still jubilant as they approached Tyler's place. "I'm in love, Tyler, I'm in love!" he shouted springing down the sidewalk. At the edge of a flower bed, he flipped into a few cartwheels then landed him on the Wojniewski's lawn.

From a hastily raised upper bedroom window, an older woman's voice cried out, "Gett off zat grass, dju stupit Djukrainski!"

Alex and Tyler hastened into the Stedman house. The glow of a couple of scented candles illumined an upper window frame in the Berenson house. Inside that room Rebecca and Charlene were enjoying a sleepover. They too had witnessed the late-night arrival of the two young bucks. An imagined mock conversation occurred.

Rebecca as Stephanie: "O Tyler, Tyler, you give me goosebumps. My breasts feel leaky!" [fits of giggling].

Charlene as Enid: "O Alex, sweet Alex, you make me feel all sweaty and tingly inside." [uproarious laughter].

A thump on their bedroom wall was followed by a parental admonition: "Okay, girls, have your fun, but keep it down a little, okay?"

Getting ready for bed, across from the upstairs bathroom, Tyler waited for his turn to brush his teeth. He was glad Rebecca, whose bedroom was adjacent to the bathroom, wasn't home that night. She wouldn't hear the "tcht, tcht, tcht" sound of her cousin masturbating. Tyler hoped his mother and father were still downstairs out of earshot. "Is he thinking of Enid? Or Lumpy's sister?" Tyler wondered to himself. Before he had finished formulating the questions, the answer came to him: "Both!"

He awoke the next morning feeling his own embarrassment. In the midst of some subconscious state of sleep, he had had his own wet dream again. He hoped it had nothing to do with what a wilder part of his adolescent being might wish to give Stephanie for her birthday.

As it was, the following Friday came soon enough, and when Sunday should show up, Tyler would be off with packed bags, unflagging zeal and a tag-along cousin for a week at a Montana dude ranch. Alex bought a new Blink 182 CD as a gift for the birthday girl. Tyler, after several days of self-debate, risked purchasing a silver-plated friendship bracelet engraved with "Your lassoed friend, Tyler." Stephanie received it with two sincere kisses and some tears.

It was a bash with splash and teenage panache. Alex found it far easier to hold his hormones in check as the evening wore on and cooled even more when the girls wore coverings over their swim-wear. Kevin, observing Raja, also fought to rein in spontaneous blood rushes or jumped into the deeper water to hide some of the evidence. Lumpy also developed occasional flourishes that brought teasing remarks from his male buddies about having a second reason for conferring such a nickname upon him. Boys will be boys until later adolescence or young adulthood truly turns them into men. Well...most of them, for the most part.

The girls were noted to be neither totally unobservant, nor flushed at times with their own sporadic discomfiture. Barbecue food and soda pop, including the newest arrivals of Pepsi Blue and Vanilla Coke were a hit. Stephanie's cousin, Paula, from Red Deer, balancing the male-female ratio, took a shine to Lumpy. They danced into the darkness of night to a host of "Big Shiny Tunes," other alternative music selections, some 80s classics and a few country selections. It was a slower Rolling Stones ballad that almost halted Stephanie and Tyler in their tracks and drew them together as if glue was forming between them. It was a song Jules had shared with Tyler from his own vinyl collection and transferred it onto cassette tape. It was a song that seemed doubly fitting for a budding rodeo star and his girlfriend who had just consumed birthday cake. It came from an album named *Sticky Fingers* and its title was "Wild Horses." The refrain insisted that such horses would be powerless to separate connected lovers. "... *Couldn't drag me away,*" it repeated. For the time being, it suddenly became "their song."

Out on the Davis' ranch that night, Ola had a recurrence of her circus-like vision: a fiery female rider, a young Vikingesque cowboy on an eight-legged gray mount, and that bizarre see-through steed with some kind of wraith on its back. No one in the stands was shouting "Olé!" No fluke. This movie-like image deserved spiritual attention. "God," she prayed, "I await Your revelation."

The clouds over the moon that night made it look like it was moaning. The revelers in town didn't notice it. Burgers, cola, chips, cake, tunes, joshing like ping-pong, the hormonal tango put stars in their eyes and air under their feet. "*Happy BIRTH-day, Stephanie We-ells!*" Tomorrow will bring whatever.

# Chapter 12:
# Dude, Where's My Horse?

Whatever else it meant for the rest of the citizens of Okotoks, the Sunday following that particular tomorrow was breakaway day for Tyler and Alex. They were headed for a week's worth of dude ranch experience in Montana. Jules and Myra had booked coincident vacation time. Rebecca and her friend Charlene would join along for the week. After dropping the boys off, the rest of the travellers planned to enjoy a leisurely circle route up through the Great Divide to Glacier National Park stopping at Kalispell and Flathead Lake, then crossing the Montana-British Columbia border up through to Cranbrook and some time in the Okanagan Valley, before veering east again through Roger's Pass to Lake Louise, Banff Springs and eventually back home. A week of hiking, fishing, swimming, touring, relaxing, relishing the mountains and the valleys unique to that corner of the world; a wondrously diverse vista ranging from plains and foothills to forests and ice fields through semi-desert and back, all of it royally interrupted by the Rockies, indeed, by purple mountain majesty. Aunt Ola would do the fetch-and-return run collecting the boys at the end of their stay.

The state of Montana shares more similarities with Alberta than the other provinces of Canada. The two of them make excellent geographical siblings.

Alberta is the fourth largest province in her nation. Montana is the fourth largest state in America. Both share a similar range of topography from plains through foothills to mountain regions. Both have a designated section of "badlands". A long history of South-to-North-and-back cattle drives charted their paths of interconnection. Turn either one of them sideways and flip them over and their borderlines almost match. The differential being that Montana is about six-tenths the size of Alberta. The population of the province is about three times that of the state. Both of their western borders resemble half a spine. Indeed, native peoples have named the Great Divide "the backbone of the world". The Forty-Ninth Parallel separating the one from the other is, for all intents and purposes, almost an imaginary line. Through its entire breadth of almost four hundred miles, there are not that many official border crossings. The main one is found by following Highway 15 for seventy-five kilometers south of Lethbridge. There are a few others in the mountains in the Glacier National Park area, but only one main one where Coutts, Canada meets Sweetgrass, U.S.A. High chainlink fencing topped by barbed wire running east and west of that point is much more a simple indicator than any kind of deterrent. Illegal crossings have far more to do with seeking refuge than with smuggling. Police on both sides of that border have far greater concerns to which to attend, concerns and crimes that vastly outnumber and outweigh border offences. And since crossing that border at any unofficial point simply gets you from one large uninhabited area to another, there's not much point in making the venture in the first place. "And miles to go before you sleep, steal some sheep or earn your keep" is scarcely enticing even to a veteran law-breaker.

Eighty percent of Alberta's people are urban dwellers. Great Falls, Montana, the densest population centre in the state, is mainly a large town. More than ninety percent of Montanans are country people. Montanans speak English a little slower with a bit of drawl and a slight twang compared to plainer, quicker Albertan speech. One could compare them as On-the-Fly Country versus Big Sky Country. Cowboy culture finds a niche in both. That suits Tyler Stedman just fine.

Heading south through High River, the Stedmans stopped at Fort Macleod for early lunch. Time was taken to tour the replica museum of an 1874 Northwest Mounted Police outpost and for a side trip to the more infamous locale of buffalo massacres by native peoples known as Head-Smashed-In-Buffalo-Jump. Legend has it one unfortunate brave wandered underneath that cliff at the most inauspicious moment. Broken skull, broke-down life. Buffaloed beyond a doubt. "A bison-cranial extravaganza!" Alex remarked. Unison groan response.

High, hot prairie sun accentuated a draggy afternoon drive over to Lethbridge, south to the border and on into the Safflower State twisting off westward towards Great Falls for snack time. Then they travelled further south to Canyon Creek, a ten-minute drive northwest of Helena in Jefferson County. Good thing Myra had the presence of mind to pack a large cooler full of bottled tap water. A couple of pit-stops and a few breaks for photo opportunities did little to deter them from arriving at their destination a little past their 6 P.M. check in time.

"Yahoo!" came the synchronized duet from the back seat as they passed under the overhead log sign reading "Lazy J Cattle and Guest Ranch." Nestled in foothill grassland abutting the edge of mountains, this little haven for cowboy wanna-bes exceeded the claims of its brochures. The laneway in took them past two corrals full of horses and ponies, a field full of big horn cattle, a pond cluttered with ducks and geese, an outdoor swimming pool and basketball court, a roping and riding arena, two sets of stables and a large cow barn, three granaries, a hay mow, a smoke house and a two-story outhouse. A grove of aspens led up to the main lodge surrounded by eight to ten separate cabins. All of it cut from local fir and Jack pine and covered in red cedar shingles. Behind the main lodge, waiting to be discovered were horseshoe pits, an archery range, a rifle range, a separate barn full of tack and riding gear, and the entrances to several walking and riding trails. It was too much to take in all at once, even for the widest of eyes; but a whole week in laid-back Montana in such a setting would be more than sufficient time to imprint a young man's memory banks for life.

There was time for Tyler and Alex to register, find their cabin, store their luggage, bid the other Stedmans and Charlene farewell, and make it to their designated dining-room table for Sunday evening chuck. Those other pilgrims from Okotoks made their way back to Helena to dine and bed down for the night before moving on into glacier territory the next day.

"Welcome, bucks and does and buckaroos, to your great Western getaway week at the Lazy J! My name's Jacob Kershaw. This is my wife, Sally; our son, Deke; and our daughter, Allison. We'll be your hosts and servants this week along with the rest of our staff and promise to do all we can to make your stay enjoyable and rewarding. If ya want to work and keep busy, you can do as much of that as you like. If ya'd rather sit back and just mope around, that's okay too. Some things are on a schedule. Most things can happen when you're ready for them to happen. Mind you, comin' in on the end of meal times might get you into cooler and less appetizin' food. But in case you miss a meal altogether, we've got our fast order kitchen winder open every day from 7 A.M. to midnight.

"Now by lookin' around I reckon you've already noticed that we only accommodate a maximum of thirty people at a time. By mid-week, you'll already be gettin' to recognize and know each other pretty well. This week we've got eight couples, two families of four, four college lads from Wisconsin, and our two youngest residents who will just be startin' senior high school in September just rolled in from outside Calgary in Canada. Two of our couples and one of our families also come from Canada, the provinces of British Columbia and Manitoba respectively. Four couples and our other family are from right here in Montana and our other couple flew in all the way from Delaware. For now, let me invite you to introduce yourselves to the other folks at your own table which means there'll be five groups of six people chattin'.'"

Tyler and Alex were seated with the Gresham family from Billings, Montana which is clear across the other side of the state. Bill and Ellen Gresham were high school physical education teachers. Their daughter, Kaitlyn, eighteen years old, six-foot-one, blonde, blue-eyed, and slim, was a freshman on a volleyball scholarship at UNLV. ( "University of Nevada at Las Vegas," she translated for them.) Their son, Keeshawn, an adopted Black child, was fifteen years old, stood five-foot-nine-inches in his lanky but muscular frame and was a sophomore at Lewis and Clark Collegiate Institute in Billings. Obviously, they were here for an active vacation. "Lazy" wasn't often in the Gresham family lexicon. Tyler had similar intentions. Alex was simply allergic to words like "slow," "settled," "idle," or "sluggish."

A clatter of cowbells interrupted the conversations. "Sorry to break you up, folks; but I just wanted to let you know supper is about to be served. Tonight's menu features Black Angus steak, baked potatoes with sour cream if you wish, carrot and wax bean medley, house salad with ranch dressing (what else?) and sourdough cake for dessert—vanilla or chocolate. Enjoy!"
It was as delectable as the continuing conversation was amicable.

After dinner Tyler and Alex undertook a further lay-of-the-land investigation as feasible as darkness would allow. Beyond the dining-room in the main lodge was a check-in desk and lounge area, a side-room extension beyond the desk area featuring a large-screen TV room and a hot-tub corner. There was no bar on the premises but adults-of-age were permitted to bring their own poison. On the upper level of the lodge was a divided loft area with two double-bed suites with a shared washroom, and one *en suite* chamber to the left; a library and reading lounge and pool table on the right. The Kershaws had booked the college men into the rooms in the main lodge and a newlywed couple into the *en suite*. The two guest families had the larger outdoor cabins. Seven other cabins were occupied by the other seven couples, which left the tenth and smallest cabin for Tyler and Alex. It was furnished with two pine wagon-wheel beds, a pair of dressers, a shared closet, a writing desk and chair, a pair of easy chairs, and a separate washroom with sink, toilet, and stand-up shower. Just fine.

"What else could we need?" Tyler mused out loud. "No, Alex, don't even think of answering that. Breathe deep and let this fresh, clean mountain air sweep the sewage from your brain." Tyler passed that message to his cousin through sheer facial expression and a few selective non-verbal cues.

"Hmmm," Alex replied releasing a chest-full of temporarily-trapped mountain atmosphere. "You're onto something there, Cuz."

"Come on, let's fill our lungs some more as we stroll the grounds a bit. Then, let's see if we can have a turn at the pool table."

"Lead me on, bro, I'm headin' ."

"Right, Alex, just don't get talking like that around Keeshawn until we get to know him better, okay."

 "Okay, dude, you da boss!"

"ALEX!"

"All right, all right, I got ya."

The environment was comparable to Pops' and Ola's place. The scents of horse and cow manure were muffled by pine and fir and cedar and hay. A gurgling sensation came from mountain stream waters. The mustiness of damp road dust and gravel mingled with strong smell of sage, and something uncharacteristic to which Tyler couldn't put a name. The cattle now in their barns shuffled hooves, mooed, swished as they brushed sides one with another and murmured as in the Christmas carol—*"The cattle were lowing...."* Geese on the pond still honked intermittently. Ducks quacked, splashed, fluttered. Most of them waddled up onto the bank to snuggle down for the night. The sounds of the horses and ponies in the stables were muted. Soft, slow munchings; floor scuffles, subdued whinnies, the quiescent susurations of sensate beasts circling and gently lowering themselves as they settled down to sleep. "Noble, graceful, particular," Tyler noted to himself, "even in the process of readying themselves for bed; the yin-yang combination of pattern and unpredictability." At random, the cackle of crickets, the croaking of frogs, the occasional whoosh of bats' wings or maybe an owl's could be heard. The sound of their own boots stepping about was the largest disturber of the peace. The ranch complex was surrounded by the silhouettes of shrubs and trees, hewn timber and split-rail fencing that seemed like sensual shadows serene and non-threatening, playing hide-and-seek with minimal, but sufficient outdoor lighting. Night games, nocturnal rituals were in effect—*le déroulage du jour*, as the French say so symphonically.

Their stroll tacked onto a rather lengthy travel day had its own distinctly soporific effect. Alex and Tyler stared yawning at the lodge and meandered instead back to their cabin. The pool match could wait. 10:15 P.M. felt just as late as midnight. Sleep sounded swell for now. Within fifteen minutes, both of them were sunk in their bunks resembling those submersible pumps cast as plastic divers in bathysphere outfits that some people place in their aquariums.

•    •    •

The shrill clanging of the outdoor triangle announcing chow time at 7:30 A.M. didn't disturb Alex and Tyler. They were already up, washed, dressed and in the lobby waiting for breakfast by then. Most all of the guests in fact were up, except for a couple of residents in the main lodge. Several loud groans emerged from the college guys' bedrooms and one rather startled exclamation of "What the fuck was that?" Keeshawn and Kaitlyn, seated on a couch across from Alex and Tyler, glanced over at the two boys from Alberta. Four pairs of somewhat widened eyes met as the four of them expressed suppressed laughter.

The guests filtered into the dining hall sitting in the previous evening's arrangements. Three slightly tousled college lads drifted in about a half hour later along with their fourth mate who was bright-eyed and prepped for the day. Breakfast consisted of orange or grapefruit juice, stacks of buckwheat flap-jacks with maple syrup and butter or blueberry topping, hearty farm sausages, milk, coffee or tea. A sidebar of dry cereals, toast and fixings was available for those who preferred something lighter.

As the breakfast hour wound down, Jacob Kershaw appeared asking for a moment's attention. Tyler had noticed a new guest seated at table with the Adamson family from Manitoba and Paul and Laura Foster, the newlywed couple from British Columbia. Jacob Kershaw proceeded to introduce the newcomer to everybody.

"Folks, it is indeed a pleasure and an honor to introduce to you our special instructor-in-residence this week—Mr. "Buck" Youngman from Dalton City, Oklahoma. In the 1990s, Buck was three-times national calf-roping champion, once an overall grand champion, and five times placed in the top ten in saddle bronc and bareback riding. This man knows about horses, about managing them, training them, working with them and riding them. We're thrilled that he was able to find time to be with us this week and about a dozen and a half of you are going to gain a lot from his wisdom and experience. The other dozen will be headin' out tomorrow on a four-day cattle drive. But let's all of us do our darndest to make Buck feel especially welcome among us right now."

Eruptions of applause broke out in the dining hall alongside three or four "Yahoos!"

Buck Youngman rose from his seat, waved his fine brown Stetson and said briefly that he was excited to be there and was very much looking forward to the week ahead. He was a tall, thin but solid man, six feet three inches in height with long arms and legs, weighing no more than 190 pounds. He had sandy, brown hair with bushy eyebrows to match, narrow but kindly green eyes, a straight non-distinctive nose, wide mouth and square chin. Pretty much your picture postcard image of a rodeo star in his categories. Bulk and brawn were prevalent among steer-wrestlers and bull-riders. At thirty-six, Buck had retired from almost twenty years on the amateur and professional rodeo circuit. There comes a time when one more bruise, one more dislocated finger or broken bone is too much to take. His competing days had reached a point of completion. He still went down the road from rodeo to rodeo, but as a trainer or a cheerleader, and once in a while, a judge. Increasingly, he was spending more and more time as an instructor now that American college programs were growing in popularity; and summer camp opportunities abounded. He had come to the Lazy J as a favor to Jake Kershaw whom he had met on the Upper Mid-west circuit in the days when Jake worked as a rodeo clown. At several events, Jake had partnered with Buck as the heeler in team roping contests.

The Upper Mid-West circuit was also where Jake had met his wife, Sally, in her days as state champion barrel-racer. She knew her way around horses too. The idea of owning and operating a riding and cattle ranch was a dream they shared in common. It probably had as much to do with their courtship and eventual marriage as any other factor, physical, mental, emotional or spiritual. Now they were living their dream and loving every blessed minute of it, and quietly and quickly cursing and disposing of every not-so-blessed aggravating or frustrating minute. Late deliveries or short orders of supplies, last-minute guest cancellations, horses gone lame or stillborn calves, broken fences or water-mains, occasional arguments with banks over lines-of-credit or loan-payment extensions were minor inconveniences easily traded off against being around horses and cattle every day, bonding a family together around a business that they shared as a passion and living in a setting they seemed destined to inhabit. The human-animal-environmental daily interchange of atoms felt utterly agreeable for the most part. It was as if, yes...as if God had a hand in it.

At 9:00 A.M. the morning seminars began. The Adamson and Gresham families, the Ozmay couple from Delaware, the Irwins of Montana, and the newly-wed Fosters gathered on benches inside the cattle ring as Deke and Sally Kershaw shared a history of cattle-driving, handed out and went over copies of the route they would be following, demonstrated how to pack a trail kit and had their charges practice pitching and striking tents. Deke gave a small lecture on poisonous plants, snakes and other critters to watch out for, answered questions and concerns and negotiated what grub would be supplied.

In the practice corral, Buck Youngman and Jake Kershaw talked about the skills and secrets of calf-roping. Four college lads from Wisconsin, the other couple from B.C. named Meloche, the rest of the Montana contingent of couples named Bennett, Hirtzel, and Rollings, which sounded like the name of a law firm when gathered together like that, and Alex and Tyler all listened with fixed attention. Several metal and steel calf dummies were scattered around the corral. But first, some lessons and hints about tying a lasso were given. Buck then demonstrated several varieties of throw noting that an immobile calf was so much easier to snag than a moving one. The group divided up in practice pairs and it was soon obvious, as it was in Alex and Tyler's case, who was more suited to being the header and the heeler in team roping pursuits. Alex almost always had to throw his second rope before he got a snag. The college guys got into roping each other instead of the calf dummies which made for a few moments of hilarity as one gangly body after another was yanked down playfully into the dirt.

After a refreshment break, this class moved to the adjacent corral where each student had a couple of chances from a standing position at roping a live calf released into the arena while the others watched and cheered from the fence rails. Buck's tips on flipping the calf, cinching the three legs and tying off were well received, if not so immediately well-executed. Mrs. Rollings was the best and fastest of the women, faster than some of the male participants. Three of the four college lads had good speed and decent accuracy, after all, they were in a rodeo athletic program. There was no question however, that Tyler exhibited the most consistency and promise. Buck and Jake were equally well impressed by Tyler's skill and accuracy even if his speed-time left room for improvement. This, however, was only ground school. The real test-and-assessment criteria would show up in flight, on horseback.

That would wait for tomorrow because, after lunch, all the guests had free time till three P.M. At that hour, the schedule called for trail-riding. Everyone gathered at the stables to begin to befriend the horse that would be his or her mount for the week. Tack was provided for those who didn't bring their own. Assistance in saddling up was given to those who needed it

The Kershaw riding stable was populated by about forty healthy steeds: four Appaloosas, twelve Western Saddlebreds, fourteen Standardbreds, two Westphalians, four Palomino ponies, and four smaller horses with a Latin look. The latter was a breed unfamiliar to Tyler as well as other guests, a breed averaging only fourteen hands high that could pass for ponies. One of the Appaloosas belonged to Sally Kershaw. Allison's name was written all over one of the Westphalians. Deke and Jacob favoured two of the Standardbreds, but could ride almost any breed. Buck Youngman had brought along Venus, his own regal cremello Andalusian mare, whom he did treat as a goddess. While the others were preparing their assigned mounts, Jake and Deke brought out those four smaller horses and presented them, one each, to Tyler and Alex and to Gino Palabria, the shortest of the four lads from Wisconsin. Jake himself would ride the fourth one.

"Hey! What is this?" Gino asked as if in protest. "You want me to ride a pony?"

"These aren't no ponies," answered Allison Kershaw. "Ever heard of a Paso Fino? Part Spanish Barb, part Andalusian, part Spanish Jennet (a breed no longer in existence). They've been bred in Latin America since the time of the Conquistadors. History suggests Columbus brought them to Santo Domingo on his second voyage. Other voyageurs brought more so that, by breeding, these wonderful *caballos* spread through South and Central America, up through Mexico and across the border into the Southern United States. They've got footwork that's utterly amazing and a ride that's a smooth as gliding on glass."

"Whoa! I mean, wow!" Gino exclaimed, "like they say in bad movies, 'Dude, where's my horse?'"

The whole party began their ride together out the back of the barnyard through a deciduous woodlot into foothill trails until they reached a plateau 800' above sea level where the path divided westwards towards forests and mountains and eastwards towards sloping hills and plains. Sally and Allison had taken the lead with Jake and Deke bringing up the rear. The whole company paused on that plateau for one of those silent, rapturous moments when the panorama that defines places like Montana arrests your breath, catches your heart up short and massages your soul. Ego disintegrates. Time is suspended. Mind becomes as sponge in an ocean. Sounds are slight and aspirate—a hawk's wings flapping, a sniffing of horse's nostrils, a couple of throats gulping, the flickering of eyelids, a hushed creak of shoulder blades when heads turn, a few soft squeaks of denim on leather. Words, if any, are monosyllabic—"Oo!," "Man!," "Fffff!," "Ah!." The one diaphon that may escape is "Holy!" Big Sky Country was posing in all its captivating enormity. Tyler thought of similar vistas outside Okotoks. "Close in places, but nothing quite like this," he mused. "Maybe, in a couple of spots, some leaners. But this! This is a ringer!."

Jacob Kershaw had an intuitive sense about when folks had had enough scenic lookout time. "Well now, friends, this is where some of us part company. Deke and Sally and the cattle-drive group will continue on up the mountain trail getting used to staying slow in the saddle. Allison and Buck and I are taking our little rodeo academy back down towards those plains where we can get up some speed for a spell. We'll all meet back at the ranch around five. Supper is at six."

So, the cattle-drive party ambled on. Their trail would prove to be a wide, round circuit. Group two headed for the plains on a route over which they would later double back.

Tyler could tell there was something special about a Paso Fino. He didn't know whether Alex or Gino noticed. The footfalls, though always in the same sequence, were so steady in cadence he hardly shifted at all in the saddle. As they picked up pace on their downhill trails toward the plains they covered the ground with ease and began to outpace the other riders. Movement in the saddle remained minimal. When they reached the plain, Jake turned to the three of them and asked, "Well, boys, how do you like your ride so far?"

"Amazing!," "Incredible!," "Awesome!," came a rapid succession of responses.

"It's just like you said," Tyler admitted, "so smooth!"

"Wait till you experience high gear," Jake interjected. "In fact, these horses trot and pace so different from others their steps have names unique to their breed. That slow canter at the start, that's the classic *fino*. Gather some steam as we just did, and that's the *paso corto*. In a moment, when I give the signal for all of us to ride full out, you'll be whisked along on the *paso largo*. Enjoy!"

"Okay, group, pair off in your header/heeler teams and get ready to go for a good gallop. We got all kinds of room here, so spread out and don't bother about bucking against one another. There's another red flag fixed to an old telephone pole about two thousand yards straight ahead like this one hanging over me here. We'll make three or four runs there and back at my signal and on the count of three."

All the riders paired off with Jake riding alongside Buck. When Jake counted to three and dropped his right arm, they took off.

Exhilarating would certainly describe the experience for most of the pack. But for The Three Musketeers on Paso Finos a word like that barely scratches the surface. Flying at *paso largo* was not simply running with the wind, it was more like you were the wind, like vehicle and driver zooming through a sports-car test-drive in the desert. All is motion. Motion is all. *"Anda!"* Alex was as wide-eyed and brimful of delight as Tyler had ever seen him.

"Ecstasy, Alex. Sheer ecstasy," was Tyler's comment at the end of the first run. "That would be the right word for it, as Wilton would say."

"Oh yeah, you got that right, pardner, 'ex-taks-sty.'"

It was a rich start to a week full of treasure. It kept the two of them pumped up and talking well past supper, past lights out, past midnight until they both simply passed out.

• • •

The next morning, the cattle-drive party was to be up, dressed, breakfasted by 6 A.M. and out to the cattle barns with back-packs and tents in tow ready to hit the trail. No clanging triangle was sounded, but the Foster's alarm clock going off across the hall at 5:00 A.M., the shower running, the pair of padded footsteps down to the dining hall, the thunk of two back-packs dropping on the lobby floor was sufficient disturbance to arouse reactions in the collegians' quarters, nicknamed "the dorm" for the week. Three muffled grunts, two sustained groans, and a garbled verbal outburst that de-scrambled comes out "Jesus! That's ungodly!" emerged among the sounds of bedclothes being tossed into twisted knots and swirls.

For this day and the following three days, the rodeo academy had the run of the ranch. This day's seminars continued training in calf-roping, individual and team. Morning practice on roping dummies had each pair take turns at being header and heeler, and exercises in a variety of throws. No standing tosses at running calves however. This day, they rode. Yesterday's mounts from their trail ride were their chargers of the day. Jake and Buck acted as timers, judges and chute openers in a replicated regulation roping corral. The three women riders when not teamed as heelers to their husbands' headers, had their time in the ring as barrel racers. Teresa Rollings was still the best roper, but she took third place in the racing just seconds behind Betty Bennett and Gizelle Hirtzel. As for the male ropers, Buck's advice to Tyler, Alex and Gino working from Paso Finos was that, being closer to the ground for starters, shoulder-height or side-arm throws were more suitable than overhead tosses. He was right. Alex found that out after several missed attempts. Again, he proved better as a heeler than as a header in tandem competitions. Rodeo, at best, might someday be an occasional hobby indulgence for him, but never a serious sport. He was here to support Tyler and to have all the fun a dude ranch week afforded. No shortage there.

Wednesday turned out to be a rain day, a morning downpour dowsing the ground and muddying the rutted lanes and pock-marked corrals. Never unprepared, Buck conducted indoor seminars in the recreation lounge with commentary and class discussions of classic rodeo performers on video on the big-screen TV. It was as thrilling and fascinating as it was insightful to see and evaluate Bob Crosby's first all-round national championship at the Pendleton Round-up in Madison Square Garden in 1929; footage from the cowboys' strike at the 1936 nationals at the Boston Garden (October 30 to November 6); Charles "Sharkey" Irwin's winning saddle-bronc ride on Magruder at the Ski-Hi Stampede in Buena Vista, Colorado in 1927; Todd Whatley's first RCA all-round championship performance at La Fiesta de los Vaqueros in Tucson in 1947; Dean Oliver's prize-winning display of calf-roping in Reno in 1960; cousins Les and Reg Camarillo's win at the team-roping event in the 1974 national finals; Bruce Ford's consecutive wins in bareback bronc riding in 1982 and 1983 (the year he was the first rider to crack the $100,000 in winnings mark on the circuit). There was some footage of Canadian champion riders Kenny McLean and Mel Hyland. Other Canadian notables like Dale Trotter, Lorne Walls and Bob Duce were not part of this demonstration package. For fun and interest's sake, there was footage of some steer-wrestling and bull-riding including the amazing rides of "Freckles" Brown in 1962 that gained him the national title even though in October of that year he suffered a debilitating broken-neck injury from a buck-off. Five years later, at age forty-six, Freckles was still at it some fifteen years past normal retirement age scooping up accolades from an amazed crowd who watched him outlast the notorious bull Tornado at the 1967 National Finals. The clip ended with Freckles' documented reply to an interviewer who wondered about fears of injury and dying: "It never crosses my mind that I might get hurt; I don't even think about that. I think it's part of this mental process. You'd defeat yourself if you even thought about that."

Sometimes Buck asked the viewers to pay attention to the rider's or roper's techniques. "Check out the arm work." "Notice the spurring." "Observe the exceptional balance." "See how timing is everything in roping." At other times

H. Lee Disher

he asked them to watch the events through the eyes of the judges which meant paying attention to the animal's performance as well as the human competitors. Tyler was totally transfixed.

There was some debate over the afternoon options. A: Continue with the video series and listen to a lecture about rodeo sports injury and recovery, or B: go outdoors and practice roping anyway. Two of the women and two of the men opted for A on a self-instructed basis. The others, soon to become the dirty dozen, chose roping in the rain. After all, weather happens, even in outdoor sports competitions like rodeo. Times are almost always longer, but the games go on unless it's too slippery which increases the likelihood of injury to the horses and calves as well as to the riders. The morning rain had let up enough and soaked in enough that the practice corral was muddy but not slick. What a hoot! Chad Corriveau, one of the Wisconsin U. trainees put it into a poem he shared at the dinner hour.

> All of our skills were tested and tried
> in a half afternoon of ride out and slide.
> Kick up your spurs and swallow your pride,
> while your shirt and your pants drip with mud down inside,
> while your boots cake in slime as you're losing your stride,
> while the animals squirm or your tosses go wide.
> It's still rodeo, cowboy, and you won't be denied
> your catch, or your chance, or your piece of raw hide.
> Ride on! Yeah, ride on! Yahoo! Danger defied
> is the name of our game. Let our guts be our guide.
> In the risks we all share. In this sport, we're allied.

Thursday's activities hitched those risks up a few notches as the seminars shifted from calf-roping to saddle bronc riding. For the male participants, that was. Allison Kershaw spent time with Mss. Bennett, Hirtzel, and Rollings on honing their barrel racing skills. Buck and Jake used video sequences again as part of their instruction. Then, their class went out to a second horse barn at one end of which was a mechanical bronc surrounded by a small sea of crash mats. It was a reasonable facsimile of the real thing except for the softer landing area. Each man's partner acted as a kind of rodeo clown releasing the rein-strap under the horse's belly, disengaging a rider's hand hung-up in the reins after being bucked off, or helping a bucked rider break free from an imagined wild stomping horse. The mechanical bronc was programmable so that trap situations could be simulated as well as faults such as blowing a stirrup. Each participant was put through several wild and bumpy rides. Gino almost lost his breakfast. Alex had to be rescued from a hand-trap twice. Kurt Rollings got a bruised ankle from a mechanical hoof. Most of the critique from Buck was about flawed spurring sequences or flailing free arms. But he always noted the most admirable techniques and skills first.

The afternoon session of working with live bucking horses caused a few jitters lasting well through the lunch hour. Health and safety regulations however made it mandatory for every rider to ride with a crash helmet and a front and rear air-bag apparatus dropped over his shoulders and affixed to the saddle in such a way as to provide automatic release and inflation upon ejection. Legs were still at some risk, but most riders knew how to land on their feet and roll. Four professional clowns were imported for the afternoon session. All those precautions being in place, the buckaroos-in-training had a virtually accident-and-injury free "bums-on" workshop excepting a few bruises and one twisted ankle.

"Where does one go to get used to being thrown onto solid ground without protection?" Mr. Hirtzel asked.

"The amateur rodeo circuit," replied Buck

"Or the University of Wisconsin practice corral," Gino piped in, feigning a limp and a very sore back.

Friday was a marvelous day of trials and friendly "in-house " competition as each rider urged the other one on. It was a showcase day for Tyler Stedman, not yet sixteen years old, who was able to hold his own against older competitors finishing third in calf-roping and fifth in saddle bronc. Alex did not finish last in either category taking twelfth in roping and fourteenth in bronc. As a team, the two of them placed fourth in the team roping challenge. What observers, judges and other participants noted was that Tyler had "try" as big as Texas. If there were a prize for that, he'd have won first overall hands down. There were some belt buckle and bandana prizes handed out after dinner which was a classic Western-style steak cook-out on the patio. The college guys were lamenting just before dinner that the cattle-driving group would be missing out. At 6 P.M. that whole happy tribe rode in grinning and hungry like a posse returning with a captured outlaw. It was a glorious reunion and a great, great barbecue.

The cattle drive group had their series of awards as well: best-packed backpack, fastest striker of tents, most agile and accurate brander, best endurance rider, and round-up king and queen of the range—a prize awarded to the newlywed Fosters of Chilliwack, British Columbia. Tyler and Alex enjoyed re-connecting with Keeshawn and the rest of the Gresham family.

"I can tell you this fo' sure," Keeshawn remarked, "steak bar'b'cue beats the daylights out of wieners and beans around a campfire."

Alex and Tyler nodded agreement, then stared and smirked deeply one to another knowing intuitively each of them was wondering if Keeshawn had seen the movie *Blazing Saddles.*

There was a bonfire further out in the yard that night. The whole company sat around singing Western songs, sharing stories and legends of the Old West and tales of the Oregon Trail and of the early days of rodeo. A surfeit of serendipity as satisfying as hickory-smoked sausage and a fine European cheese enfolded them all.

The party broke up around 11:30 P.M. Tyler and Alex weren't tired so they walked out to the cow barns. That's when they heard the screaming.

"Get off me, you Italian pervert!!"

Tyler and Alex burst through one of the barn doors to see Gino astride Allison at the far end. As they ran closer they saw that Gino had ripped up her blouse, pulled down her bra and was in the middle of molesting and fondling her.

"Leave her alone, preppy boy!" Tyler shouted as he raced at Gino.

"Get lost, punks! This is a-none o'you business."

"Yeah. Well, we're making it our business."

Tyler reached out and grabbed Gino. With a strong burst of adrenalin he was able to haul the college student to his feet and land a solid punch in the left shoulder. Gino swung beneath Tyler's arm and caught Tyler a stiff blow in the midriff. Tyler doubled over and stepped back, releasing his grip on Gino. They began to circle one another. Tyler caught sight of his sneaky cousin and made a lunge for Gino. Gino took a heavy shove to his chest, reeled back and felt his lower calves come up against the bent torso of Alex, who had positioned himself on all fours behind the American hot-shot. As Gino fell to the ground he struck the back of his head on one or two of the metal poles in the grille-work at the front of a cattle stall. While he lay there dazed, Tyler grabbed up some lariat rope and cinched the fallen student's right arm to the gate.

All this gave Allison time to collect herself and semi-cover herself.

"Wow! Thank you, boys," she exclaimed. "I may just have to figure out some appropriate way to reward my high school heroes."

"Don't worry about that, Allison," Tyler replied. "We're just glad we were able to get here in time to rescue you. So...what about him?"

"My father will take care of him. I expect he and his buddies will be given the big spurred boot back to Green Bay first thing in the morning. That's after I call the cops in now and charge him with attempted rape, seeing as I also happen to have a keen pair of witnesses."

"Ah, come on, cut me some slack, hunh?" Gino pleaded from his tethered position. "I was just hoping to have a little fun. You did agree to walk with me away from the bonfire, Allison. I could even say you led me on."

"Forget it, you horny dipstick. Your word against mine. In fact, I believe one of the local deputies is a cousin of mine. And the evidence clearly shows I wasn't agreeable." At this she flashed open her torn blouse and then turned to head back to the main ranch. "Tyler, would you and Alex mind staying here while I make that phone call?"

"Not a bit."

The police arrived within half an hour, made their investigation, questioned the perpetrator, the victim, and the two witnesses. They charged Gino with attempted rape and took him off for a night in jail.

Tyler and Alex tried to settle into their beds in their cabin around 2:00 A.M. having been well thanked and complemented by Allison and her parents. Deke had given them two big thumbs up. The rush from spontaneous heroism left them still excited, but that wasn't all that had aroused Alex. "Holy, Tyler, I know we were like saviours and all, but did you see her tits! They were gorgeous!"

"And you are running again in overdrive, my horn-toad cousin, which doesn't make you much different than that scum-bag, Gino. Go stick your wiener in cold water and try to go to sleep."

A trundle of feet, a twist of a bathroom tap, a splash of water, more feet trundling, a flapping of blankets as Alex dropped onto his mattress with a dull thud. "Spoil sport," he muttered.

"So I am," Tyler thought to himself, "even though he is right about those tits."

•   •   •

Just after the crack of dawn on Saturday, the police brought Gino back to the ranch to be sent packing back to Wisconsin with his room-mates. His trial date would come up in November. He would be fined heavily and given the boot from college.

Saturday morning otherwise was free time to lounge around the ranch, assist with barn chores or to enjoy a brief, private trail ride. The afternoon and evening offered a stimulating day out for everyone at the Jefferson County

Rodeo near Helena. Four mini-vans full of vacationing buckaroos added their number to crowds of locals who were there to cheer on their personal favorites or native sons and daughters. Buck Youngman and Venus were guest celebrities who served as marshalls for the opening figure-eight parade of participants and clowns assisted by the marching tones of Helena District 7 High School band who worked the chords of "Big Rock Candy Mountain," "Don't Fence Me In," and "Home on the Range" into their repertoire. Then, as the announcer finished his opening patter and shouted "Let's Rodeo!," the coterie of visitors from Lazy J Ranch whooped and hollered and oohed and ahhed and cried "Ouch! That's gotta hurt!" with the rest of the assembly, from junior goat-tying and pony-busting competitions through amateur level saddle bronc, calf-roping and barrel racing in the afternoon to bareback bronc, steer wrestling and bull-riding in the evening. The winning times were not world-class. The techniques often left lots of room for improvement. But the enthusiasm and determination of the competitors, the shared disappointments when a rider was bucked off or a calf got loose, and the inspired display of some professional potential in-the-making more than offset the obvious limitations of an amateur county event. The excitement was augmented for Tyler and Alex as Buck and Jake arranged for them to have ring-side views right from the chute area, circulating among the day's competitors who embodied that strange mix of rough-and-tumble character laced here and there with decency and goodwill. It was a more than ample atmosphere in which Tyler found his own personal inducement to be in that number someday soon deepened and doubly underscored. Saturday night's dreams in one bed in the smallest bungalow at the Lazy J were magnificent and huge.

Sunday morning that same teenage sleeper from Okotoks, Alberta woke up just as affable and considerate and humble as was his usual public persona, nothing phoney about any of it. He and his more excitable cousin spent the morning helping Deke with chores around the stables, giving special attention and thanks to Chaparròn and Seda Lisa, the marvellous Paso Finos who had served as their mounts for the week. At 11:00 A.M. they returned to their quarters to pack up and then head towards the lounge and dining area to make the rounds of saying farewell and thanks to the other guests with whom they had shared one of the most memorable vacations ever. After lunch, Ola came down the lane of the Lazy J to gather her two passengers for their ride back home. Grace, smiles, and duty attended her.

During the nine-and-a-half hour journey home, the radio, for the most part, remained off. Alex provided an almost non-stop monologue as an entire cavalcade of stories issued in a week's worth of succession from his memory banks into verbalization with occasional help, correction or brief corroboration from Tyler. Descriptions of the ranch, their cabin, the menu, the backgrounds and appearance of the other guests, the stardom that attended Buck Youngman and Venus passed over into adventures in trail-riding, barn cleaning and horse-tending; onto successes and failures in roping and the unbelievable smoothness of riding a Paso Fino; to tales from historical footages of great rodeo performances and slip-sloshing roping in the rain; to riding a mechanical buck till you almost puked and Mr. Rollings' bruised and swollen ankle; through the drama, challenge, and success of his eminent cousin on ranch rodeo day; through Texas barbecues and bonfires and a re-telling, complete with American Black accent and jargon, of Keeshawn's hilarious story of how on the second day of the cattle drive just after the rains, Kaitlyn's horse got away on her a bit and dumped her smack into a mud puddle the size of an American football field end-zone, through his own not-so-private-wish-I-was-ten-years-older crush on Allison Kershaw (without saying anything about the attempted rape) and all the smells, sights, sounds, hard knocks and marvels of an amateur county rodeo "live and unplugged."

"Oh, Mom, it wasn't as high calibre as our own Stampede, but we got to watch it from so close up at ground level that even I could hear rodeo percolating in Tyler's bloodstream. Look, I still got some make-up from one of the clowns on my jacket!"

"Yes, I see," Ola acknowledged, "and if I'm not mistaken, you might still have a bit of horse dung stuck in the grooves on the sole of one of your shoes."

Her composure broke several times as she shared in the delight of her young passengers' joyous experience. It was like bathing in a solidarity in blessedness. Yet something sat sour in a small corner of her mind like a little acrid bit of indigestion attached to a small section of stomach lining, something she couldn't name or envision with even a drop of clarity. By the time they arrived home, it had disappeared. So had the clouds in the sky.

# Chapter 13:
# Home and High School

Routines resume in Alberta before the end of August. School starts up again during the last week. Family life reacquaints itself with parents working during the day or one of them keeping abreast of household chores and management, with children and teens being back in school, with older youth heading off to college or university, with shunting back and forth to extra-curricular activities and car-pooling, with calendars full of meetings and appointments and activities at the recreation centre and churches and charitable organizations and mens' and women's and couples' and singles' clubs, with people coming and going and eating and bedding down and rising at different hours. Quality time with family or between spouses and partners becomes a rare commodity reduced to minutes or a couple of hours on most weekdays. In Okotoks, such a whirlpool engulfs just about the entire population, except for older, retired immigrant couples like the Wojniewskis who observe such frenetic commotion with critical commentary and personal dooryard vigilance, easing the exuded tension only when their own children and grandchildren from the big city (Calgary or Red Deer) drop around for a visit. Myra Stedman knows there is no fairy-godmother-like power could possibly make such neighbours friendlier or compassionate, so one just does one's best to ignore them and not take their crabbiness or critique too seriously. Jules Stedman never does. Long weekend getaways to a lodge on Lake Kananaskis around Canada Day and late August are wondrous relief and welcome respite from such localized minor frustrations and other bothersome worries. Even those few days out of the usual hustle and bustle of late summer and autumn have a value akin to rare, protected orchids.

The rented cabin is a rather standard double A-frame design with one "A" fitted sideways into the other. A central stairway leads to upper level bedroom lofts, four in all. The interior is covered in soft, knotty pine planks and adorned with pioneer memorabilia: a scythe, an ox-yoke, a butter churn, a cross-cut saw, a harness and halter rigging for a cutter sled, a washboard and so on. A replica wooden-stove that works on propane anchors the kitchen area. The refrigerator looks like an old ice-box from the outside. An old electric two-sided flipping-door toaster is still used for toasting bread or bagels. Modernity mimics nostalgia. Jules does chop and stack wood for use in the fireplace. The cabin often takes him back appreciatively to his province's historic roots in lumbering and railways and agriculture. For the rest of the family, the cabin is a break-away place in which the reminders of by-gone days are either quaint or "cool" or one-more-damn-thing-that-has-to-be-dusted, sometimes with difficulty.

Jules is the only one who will spend time staring at the photos of old Okotoks he brings along with him—one depicting the main drag with a stagecoach stop by the Macmillan Hotel when the town was stilled called Dewdney and one circa 1909 showing the train station, three hotels, two livery stables, spires of four out of five churches, the outer edges of two grist mills and a sawmill, the Union Bank, and a cement plant in the background. In front of the train station the town band is welcoming a pair of arriving newlyweds. "The Eldorado of South Alberta" reads the caption. A third photo from the late 1930s shows chuck-wagon races around a tree-line figure-eight in front of the first brick train station built by the CPR in 1929 when the previous one burned in 1928. Jules the import, the one who grew up around Vegreville further north, is the one who can get caught up in reminiscence and legacy and telescopic time. He will often leaf through his coffee table copy of Okotoks' local history fascinated or amused or at times aggrieved by its progression of stories.

Aboriginal peoples of Blackfoot descent who named the site Okatok (to them meaning "the rock") invested their geographical reference point with myth making it holy ground. Gifts were left at the base of the rock in honor of the spirit Napi. Because of some disagreement over a coat, Okatok once chased Napi across the prairies. Napi thought buffalo, antelope or deer might defend him, but the rock just crushed them. Exhausted and fearing for his life, Napi called upon a bird to slay his pursuer. In some versions, the rescuer was a bat. With one hard downward flap of wings, Okatok was split in two. Okatok died and came to rest in the field near the Sheep River just west of the town that will adopt his name. Changing the "a" to an "o" was just some English translator's idea of intoning a Blackfoot dialect.

Exploration by white people led to trading posts and cattle drives on a north-south axis. A treaty in 1877 creating a settlement and private property rights at Sheep River Crossing sent Stoney, Sarcee and Peigan nomads into serious culture shock. By 1880 land in the area was leasing for one dollar an acre. Two original homesteads on the north and south side of the Sheep River, one belonging to Kenny Cameron and the other to John Macmillan, forced a split in the Macleod trail leading from Fort Macleod and the American states up to Calgary. By the 1890s settlement of the area was well on its way. A trading-post soon became a town.

Jules managed a slight chuckle each time he reviewed certain stories such as the ones about shoppers chewing on sow belly in the General Store. Large chunks of salt pork were stacked like cord wood on the floor. One might chaw one's way through one or two hundred feet of sow belly and never bite into anything like ham or shoulder meat. Or stories about "beef ring" Fridays. Without refrigeration local farmers formed their own kind of co-operative. Everyone in the ring brought one animal to the central abattoir for slaughter on Friday. When the butchering was done, each one received certain cuts of meat on a rotational basis as had been previously agreed. The boiler plant bathing story brought out a larger laugh. With steam boilers and plenty of water handy, local businessmen had a special bathtub installed on site for their weekly immersion at a few cents per dip. The practice halted abruptly right after the local coroner used the tub to thaw the frozen corpse of Tucker Peach in order to proceed with an autopsy. Later historic confusion transposed the setting of the story to the brickyards out at Sandstone, four miles west.

Lower on the guffaw scale was the epithet generated after 1913 when, with the discovery of oil in the Turner Valley, Okotoks became the heart of the oilfields. Gas carried on a west wind trapped between the river and the north escarpment sent some locals promoting their community as "a yard wide, a mile long and a smell all its own." One other story that never ceased to amuse Jules was one former resident's recollection of a tale his father shared about a carpenter who had fallen from a roof. Helpers rushed to surround him and one of them offered the fallen man a swig of whiskey. "No thanks," said the carpenter, "I can't go to heaven drunk."

Jules was well-versed in the legacy of Okotoks' leading town founder and benefactor, John Lineham. Lineham Lumber Mill, begun in 1891, whirred and throbbed at the heart of the local economy for twenty-five years. Mostly it spewed out railway ties for the construction of the CPR railway. John Lineham was a generous town philanthropist donating land for St. James Roman Catholic Church, for St. Paul's United Church, for Sheep River Park. He promoted lots of downtown tree-planting and served a term as mayor. The Lineham Lumber Mill barn still stands on Riverside Drive having served as a dairy producing award-winning butter from the 1920s to the 1940s, a teen centre, a restaurant in the 1970s and '80s and '90s. Now it was currently a pub on the upper level over top of a law office. John Lineham's family names are memorialized on several city streets—Elizabeth, Elma, and Lineham in addition to Martin Street. Several great-nieces and great-nephews still reside in town along with other descendants of John's brother, Will. Doreen Wells, Stephanie's mother, is one of them.

The early 1900s was the only other time until the recent decades when Okotoks was booming and bustling. For most of her history, she was a much drowsier, casual community like the rural regions still surrounding her. In those opening-of-the-twentieth-century years, there were exciting and busy days but not the hectic and frenzied days at the end of that century. Nowadays it seemed as if the residents of the town whether local workers or commuters were all caught up in a chasing game like Big Rock hunting down Napi. Jules would be prepared to trade some of now for some of then. How strange it was that his few, infrequent tastes of then were gained by escaping now and hunkering down in a rented cabin at Lake Kananaskis. Myra, Tyler and Rebecca mostly rolled with now. They just kept flowing variably as the currents of the Sheep River cut through the centre of their town. Seldom did they pause at Big Rock to offer the gift of their thanksgiving and respect.

Out on the farms of Pops and Ola and Wallis Wilton in those rural regions, life routines keep their usual seasonal and month-to-month cycles. You have to appreciate the land and live with it 24/7. You suffer from a perpetual co-dependency to the weather. The only change that comes at the end of this summer is that Alex has to be up and ready earlier to ride on a different school bus, the one that takes him to Foothills Composite and weekday reunions with his cousin, Tyler, and a gang of graduates from Dewdney Junior High—Enid Evans being one in whom Alex continues to take special interest.

A school with two stories and three wings, with separate male and female gymnasiums, a large auditorium with an orchestra pit, with chemistry and biology labs and computer science rooms, with more than two sets of washrooms, with classrooms offering an array of subjects not studied before: Design and Technology, German and Spanish, Business Law, Accounting, Dance and Drama, International Studies, Sociology, Psychology, Anthropology, and (in later grades) Calculus—such a school seemed for recent junior high graduates like landing in a foreign country. Sure, they had visited last spring and selected one or two electives they would take during their first year in addition to compulsory subjects, but now they were stepping onto new ground for three or four more years of educational adventure, struggle, challenge and, hopefully, accomplishment. At least a dozen of those new entrants came as a cluster, a foray of friends, keen, enthused and a bit overwhelmed.

The mystique only lasted about a month. Then the taunts and sarcasms from grades eleven and twelve didn't bite much. Then it felt as if they had been here for a longer while. Then it felt like school always felt, just a bit broader, but just as rigorous, intense, raucous, joyous, ho-hum, boring, lame, "Get out!," exciting, enticing, provocative as each day, each subject, each different teacher or support-staff member or fellow student helped it to feel. The head custodian was everybody's friend. The Resource Centre director (a.k.a. Librarian) wanted to be your buddy whether you wanted her to or not. The Guidance Department was a place you wanted to visit infrequently unless a course change seemed appropriate. The Main Office was a source of late slips and excuse slips and public address announcements and personal pages and crass, dumb or cutesy student radio broadcasts and the daily trumpeting of the National Anthem. And the vice-principal was The Henchman of Hell.

Extra-curricular sports, clubs and special interest groups were plenteous and various and served to define some of the high school sub-cultures: artsies, jocks, nerds, socialites and joiner/political nymphos. Loners and revolutionaries made themselves relatively easy to spot. Alex opted onto the football and soccer teams. Tyler would have too had not a brand new offering been added to the options that year. The University of Calgary was sponsoring high-school rodeo clinics during the fall, winter and spring at a ranch between Okotoks and High River. Interested students from any high school in the region were invited to participate. A parental car pool formed ferrying Tyler and a grade eleven student at Foothills Comp to and fro. Sometimes it involved a van coming out of Calgary carrying some city participants. When it was his turn to drive, Jules Stedman re-arranged his work hours to accommodate his son's burning interest. Pops agreed that Striker could be quartered at the training stables for Tyler's use. After school on Wednesdays and every Saturday morning, Tyler got to indulge his number one passion and to grow in skill and competence. He was not long surpassing some of his companions in the sport. Coaches noted that he was a natural with a lasso on horseback, at tying a calf and in the saddle on a bronc-machine. His balance and riding technique required some fine-tuning. Thank God for crash mats—he had a few more things to learn about falling. That mental discipline that Freckles Brown had adopted would still take some work. The recent memory of his knee injury made it hard for Tyler to keep worry about being hurt at bay. A couple of trial competitions at the upcoming High River Fair would be his first genuine opportunity to exercise his talents and to exorcise his fears before an audience of people other than coaches, peers, friends and family. Stephanie served notice that she would boycott the event. Myra Stedman retained her fears unexorcised. Thank God for "nerve" pills.

# Chapter 14:
# Ribbons all Around

T he Okotoks Fair pre-dated the turn of the twentieth century. It sprang out
of the pioneering spirit and agrarian economy of the Canadian West, a
spirit not quite as wild as the American West. In 1900, the Okotoks Fair featured 600 horses competing in show and dressage events, pulling contests and
round-the-loop races. A Victorian English flavour was evident in the cricket
and polo matches and rudimentary football (soccer in North America). Children engaged in sack races, pum-pum pullaway, and several versions of tag.
They played baseball with an untrimmed stick of firewood for a bat and a ball
made of tightly wound stocking yarn. There were makeshift barns for livestock
displays and tents featuring grain and produce, home baking and craft competitions. Prize-winning oats from the region won highest honours at the Paris
Exposition in 1902. Little "Big Rock" enjoyed a few moments of grander
global attention.

During the 1940s, rodeo competitions became the replacement events for
what some might consider more civilized horsing sports. But by then there
had been chuck-wagon races for over a decade right in the middle of town earlier in the year. Cowpokes displaced jumpers and jockeys and sulky drivers.
Competitive displays of stock, produce and home-craft continued. Children

became featured in talent shows, roping and goat-wrestling contests and 4-H projects. Sometime over the next couple of decades, the fair proceedings evaporated and Okotoks settled for hosting a significant stop on the professional rodeo circuit on Labour Day weekend.

In the 1960s, an enterprising business association in High River took a plunge into hosting the Okotoks fair somewhere near the nexus where summer folds into autumn. The Agricultural Society property on the edge of town got a facelift and an expansion and saw the construction of new pavilions, paved parking space, and a refurbished grandstand. The promoters brought in a midway with various spinning rides and hawkers enticing fair-goers to waste a lot of money trying to win a Kewpie doll or a big, fluffy teddy bear. There were also carneys in a sideshow: Bearded Lady, Alligator Boy, Human Pin Cushion. By the 1970s, they added a major Saturday night hoe-down, barn dance or concert featuring some travelling country music star or band willing to put the Okotoks fair on their itinerary.

It's a reasonably-sized show. Standing barns are crammed full of livestock. Stables house rodeo stock: bucking horses, riding horses, steers, calves, bulls and goats. Wood and brick pavilions become lined with displays of hand-crafts, baking, photography, produce and grain. Decorations and banners adorn downtown stores and businesses. Church groups and charitable organizations set up food tents and concession booths. Some parents and some of their grown children spend a good chunk of the weekend working one day in a church-support capacity and another day slinging food and drink for the charity with whom they volunteer. Travelling food vendors roll in as competition offering hot dogs, pogos, burgers, fries, Greek souvlaki, ice cream, candy apples, and candy floss. Permits are not given to outside sellers of beef- or bacon-on-a-bun, or sausage, or barbecued ribs, or steak. Local clubs and groups who buy from local producers have a lock on those items. One area pig farmer makes a tidy profit on deep-fried strips of pork rind sold as sow bellies while his wife offers up homemade fried donuts. In 1992, one venturesome area resident tried marketing chocolate-flavored wrinkled pancakes as cow pies. It was a one-year gig that flopped, even though for an extra seventy-five cents you could cover them with whipped cream or strawberry topping. A subsequent 1994 revival featuring chocolate-dipped cored apples as horse balls was a more dismal failure. Some folks....

By mid-September 1999, Tyler Stedman was fifteen going on twenty in terms of personal maturity and rodeo athleticism. He was as ready as he was going to be for the spotlight of an invitational junior rodeo corral for a couple

H. Lee Disher

of days. He had even cajoled Alex into joining him in the team-roping competition mostly for the fun of it. Cousin Alex would never had considered it if it was for experience's sake or a learning opportunity or a skills test. As for putting up twenty-five dollars per event to enter the calf-roping and saddle-bronc riding events, Tyler was on his own. He felt both eagerness and confidence circulating in his blood. Jules felt earnest supportiveness with a subdued parental pride. Rebecca was inflated by enthusiasm. Myra, in dissent, refused to attend. Ola was cautionary, outwardly encouraging yet inwardly struggling to sustain an equilibrium of hopefulness and prayerfulness. For all the chickens in Georgia, Wilton wouldn't have missed watching Tyler compete. And Pops was afloat on the same hay-wagon. Stephanie Wells made sure she was away in Manitoba visiting her cousins. She loved Tyler but still couldn't stomach rodeo; in fact, she had also begun to develop a self-conscious eating disorder.

Wilton, by the way, would come away from the 1999 Okotoks Fair with Best-in-Show ribbons for a pair of pullets and a Rhode Island red rooster as well as second prize ribbons for his Black Angus cows. Rebecca would win honorable mention for a couple of crocheted doilies she had fashioned under Ola's supervision. And Ola, well, who was going to beat out Ola Davis in the cherry pie, bumbleberry jam, hand-fashioned rag rug categories that she had been winning already for four years straight? She also took home first prize cash and honours for her upside-down peach crumble cake in the Open Dessert department. The greatest surprise was Alex receiving third prize in a youth essay contest for his 2,500-word account of seven heavenly days at the Lazy J, which he had titled "Hey Dude, Take Me to My Horse." In bold letters as their final remark, the adjudicators had agreed to write: "There's always something very positive to be said for exuberance!"

At the corral and grandstand, Friday night from 7:00 to 8:30 P.M. was set aside for the twelve junior competitors registered in calf-roping. A tight schedule that meant each of them had a maximum of one minute. A downed calf that stood up again or a breaking the barrier fault virtually meant pushing closer to the one-minute envelope. Focusing on getting it right was what absorbed Tyler this evening. Having Striker as his steady, reliable mount promoted the effort. In this amateur competition, ropers would be scored on their best two out of three attempts. You hoped you didn't add pressure by using up all your time on your first outing.

In the first round, Tyler drew the eighth go. Out of the first seven riders, four of them failed, three of them being in fact unsuccessful in completing their calf-tying, one missed his throw. The most successful competitor in that group had his calf roped and tied in 40 seconds flat. Very impressive.

"And now, roper number 92, a young fifteen-year-old contestant from right here in Okotoks ... TY-LER STED-MAN!" cried the announcer. A mighty whooping cheer rose up from the partisans in the crowd.

Tyler steadied himself in the chute. "Okay, Striker, let's do it!"

A 170-pound black calf came scampering out of the neighbouring pen. Five seconds later (the delay in professional rodeo is longer), Tyler's chute wire dropped automatically and Striker took off in hot pursuit. Tyler leaned to his right on a 65° angle swinging his lead lariat. As they drew within ten feet of the runaway calf, Tyler launched a magnificent side-arm toss that caught the calf's neck square on. Striker pulled up smartly. The rope tightened. Tyler slid down to the ground, flew to the toppled calf and set to rapid, rote-memory work tying off two front legs and one hind leg together then rose quickly to his feet with elevated arms signaling "Done!" The crowd roared with applause and waited intently for the announcement of the judges.

"Forty-two and a half seconds. No faults!"

General uproar. Tyler's face beamed. He couldn't quite pick out his family in their row, but he knew they were all smiles, that Rebecca had both tears and jiggles going, and that Ola probably fought back a tear or two as well. Pops' face was busy moistening his handkerchief. He heard some whoops that sounded like his father's. Where his mother was, he hadn't a clue.

One of the remaining four riders came in at forty-one seconds and another at forty-three which left Tyler in third place after round one. The pack had started to separate. It was going to be a four-dog fight.

During the second round, the order changed, Tyler wound up going eleventh. The other three leaders would all ride out before he had his turn. The young cowboy who clocked in at forty-three seconds bettered himself at forty-one for a net eighty-four. The rider who had clocked forty-one managed a forty-two and a half. Pretty consistent and a total of 83.5 The first-round leader got into trouble missing with his first toss, having to wield his second lasso in order to snag the calf. Lost time increased his score to forty-eight. Added to his previous forty, that dropped him to third place at eighty-eight seconds. Tyler set his concentration. When the chute wire dropped, Striker was the one who flew this time catching up to the cavorting calf within twenty seconds. Tyler had it roped, thrown and tied off in a blur. The crowd erupted in a surge of joy. They knew before the judges made the announcement, "Thirty-eight seconds, clean!"

"That's right, folks," the announcer shouted, "give it up for your newest homegrown hero, Tyler Stedman, leading the way at eighty point five!"

In rodeo there's seldom anything such as a sure thing. Three seconds wasn't a huge cushion. Besides, this event was slated as best two out of three, so victor's laurels were still up for grabs.

In that third round, the original leader redeemed himself tying off in thirty-nine seconds for a best net of seventy-nine seconds. Mr. Consistency pulled off a forty for a best net 81. The third competitor who had shown steady improvement breezed out of the gate, caught his quarry and roped off in an amazing thirty-five seconds moving him to first overall with a total best time of 76. Anything better than his previous thirty-eight would give Tyler the crown. A repeat would place him into a tie-breaker. Anything else would still leave him in second place by half a second. Victory was not to be. Riding out third this time, Tyler was as engaged as ever. Just as his calf was released, some yokel in the crowd bellowed "Yee-haw" into a plastic imitation megaphone that came out with a horse's whinnying ring to it. Uncharacteristically, Striker bolted breaking the barrier. Their time was a blistering thirty-six seconds, but with the obligatory ten-second penalty tacked on it meant forty-six was the best total Tyler could accumulate that evening. He knew the barrier-breaking was a fluke. The judges did not award him a re-ride. They must not have heard the horn in the stands. He knew he and Striker were a winning team. The crowd realized it too and embraced a selfless, talented young man with loud ovations when he received his second-place medal and shouts of "You go, boy, 'cause you've got what it takes."

That Friday in September 1999 had an extra-special festive feel in Okotoks, Alberta by day's end, a super-special jubilant feel at 35 Dewdney Common. Myra, however, remained uncertain, uneasy and unconvinced. Nonetheless, Tyler Stedman had his first rodeo prize, $125 to add to his bank account and a major exclamation mark across one of the passions of his heart.

Further accentuation was forthcoming.

Saturday afternoon at the corral began with the team roping event. Ten teams, two hours, two pieces of scoring—combined times plus individual judging of headers and heelers. It was as wild as it was intense as it was at times almost hilarious. It was a good thing that for Alex there was a sense of fun in it. At times, it seemed as if some sneaky yahoo had greased the calves' legs with Vaseline or mayonnaise or something the way the ropes sometimes seemed to slip and slide on and off and out of place. During the second round, one poor header got himself pinned under a calf and wound up bound to a hind leg by an over-enthusiastic heeler. With Tyler on Striker taking the lead and Alex on Belva bringing up the rear the pair of them didn't disappoint the crowd with a respectable sixth place finish overall. Ola was quite impressed and almost buoyantly congratulatory.

"That performance will net both you boys an upside-down peach crumble cake of your own and two days without chores."

Such a prize had greater value for Alex and Tyler than the sixth-place medallions dangling round their necks.

Glory can get on its own roll. Glory sometimes surpasses glory. St. Paul spoke often about how glory does so supremely in and through Jesus Christ. Ola could testify to that from memory and from the convictions of her own soul. But Jesus' glory is more assured by God, than any human glories. Human glories come and go, flare up and just as quickly fade away. Human glory is a flash fire; Jesus' glory, an eternal flame. All the same, go with the glow. On Friday, Tyler sparkled. On Saturday, he would shine.

Saturday evening, before the big country music concert at 9:00 P.M. and a rollicking, kickin' barn dance, the grandstand was crammed with avid spectators fervent in anticipation of the saddle bronc riding competition, pumped with an influx of emotion winding toward release as rushing water feeds the rotors of dynamos spinning in a hydro-electric power plant. Over three thousand citizens from Okotoks had come to cheer on their town's adopted child-of-the-week.

Their boy was engulfed in a smaller, closer-knit hive. Ten riders in the chutes mixed with trainers, coaches, stock suppliers and clowns in a kind of spontaneous fraternal order. Every challenger believed he could win and wanted to. Every challenger encouraged each of the other competitors through every bump, twist and jerk of each ride. A few of them crossed themselves before sitting down on their mounts. Most of them kissed their own regulation saddle before strapping it on. The mounts were the consistently unpredictable factor for each try. Each rider had three shots. Best two combined scores determined the outcome. No one rode the same mount twice. Mounts were randomly assigned. Judges were present in the area but kept aloof from the rest of the gang.

As Tyler Stedman saddled up and settled onto Fishtail, his first mount, the other participants heard a resounding acclamation as to who one of the crowd-favorites was. He did just fine holding on through eight seconds of twelve different equine contortions. A slight slip in spurring in the last second, a bit sloppy in his dismount, but enough to earn him and Fishtail a first round score of 63.5 and a solid footing on fourth place in the standings when the round was done. Several other riders were competing for their first time. Five or six had been at it for almost a year. Two had been on the junior circuit for a little while.

Tyler's second effort aboard Slingshot was less impressive partly because that horse wasn't as feisty during that round as Fishtail had been in round one. He scored 59 but jumped up into second place when two of those who had been leading after round one suffered disqualifications for being bucked off. Bronc riding is often a merciless venture.

There was a huge communal hush when Tyler sat down for his third go astride Hellfire, a four year-old mahogany bay gelding with the worst temperament on display that day. Only one other rider had managed to last out the full eight seconds. Hellfire scored high points, but the rider had not looked all that comfortable or in control. Tyler leaned over the horse's ears and whispered, "I'm all yours and you're all mine." Then he straightened and raised his dull-rowelled spurs high over Hellfire's shoulders, tightened his abdomen into a pelvic tilt as Buck Youngman had suggested, relaxed his jaw and mentally joined in the countdown until the gate sprang open. The ride was on. It began with an immediate rear-high jerk to the left, back towards the chute, often an ominous sign. Hellfire thrust forward head up almost flattening Tyler backwards in the saddle. Tyler kept his body centred, balanced, his free left arm acting as a kind of ballast. He concentrated on rhythmic spurring, down past Hellfire's shoulders, along the flank, and back up again. There was little or no sideways tilt to Tyler's ride until six seconds into it Hellfire lurched into a flying circling manoeuvre, the dreaded sunfish. Tyler felt himself beginning to lean towards the well on the treacherous inside of the horse's twisted body. How he managed to use his left leg and free arm to transfer weight towards the outside, he wasn't just sure, but it was the right move. It was a winning move. One last forward buck almost sent Tyler "through the windshield" and the eight-second buzzer went off. Tyler used the downward incline of Hellfire's neck to sling his left leg over. Extending his right leg into the right stirrup he managed to push off clean and free with only a couple of footfalls on the ground before he was standing upright waving his kerchief at the crowd with a pumped left fist. He even gave Hellfire a grateful slap on the rump as the pick-up men passed by with horse in hand.

There was mass pandemonium before the judges posted the score: 71! This time tears streamed down Tyler's own face as he returned to the chute area. There were still six riders to go, but the final results were already in as far as hands-down champion for the day. The final contestants vied for placements somewhere else in the top five. Nobody caught Tyler's combined best score of 134.5. He was inundated with accolades and congratulations from the other riders and their chute companions. When the event was ended the crowd noise was so loud, it would have shattered all the windows on 17th Avenue SW in Calgary just as they were decimated by public mayhem in May of 1989 when the Calgary Flames won the Stanley Cup in the Saddledome two blocks away. It would have shattered all those windows by volume alone had the event taken place on the Stampede grounds and not some 40 kilometers south at the Okotoks Agricultural Society grounds. The screaming continued until the champion was acknowledged, prized up and given the biggest trophy he had ever seen. In fact, a contingent of overjoyed spectators hoisted Tyler on high and paraded him around the grounds for a full forty-five minutes. Even the spectacle of amazing bull-riding and whirlwind chuck-wagon racing on Sunday couldn't displace the fervour and jubilation surrounding the front-page-local-news-grabbing-tenth-grader from Foothills Composite in Okotoks who had captured the town's heart over Friday and Saturday. Few people fail to embrace a local, regional winner.

The Wojniewski's even phoned their married children with the news, "Dya, ya, dat's right! He ist our neighbour's boy. He vass magnificent, so de paper says. Ve watched some of de clips on TV."

Ola had another circus dream that Saturday night. This one caught her up enthralled at the feats of a daring young man on a flying trapeze playing snatch-and-grab with angels. Four black horses held the corners of the net.

Myra said little, carrying herself around like the one dark grey sock of a cloud in a sky full of fluffy, white cumulus pillows. Stephanie Wells returned home on Monday. Her limp "Good for you, Tyler," muttered to him over the phone hung a second grey sock in that otherwise happy sky.

# Chapter 15:
# Double Dates

Tyler's claim on the heart of Stephanie Wells strengthened nonetheless because she got to hang around in the light of his glory for a while too. Foothills Composite honored him at an in-house assembly on the following Tuesday morning.

"Thank you for your encouragement and admiration," Tyler offered in response. "It's great to be surrounded by good, basically earnest people. I just went after something I've set my heart on for some time now. This time it worked. I hope it works for each of you whenever your turns come. Set your heart where you know it feels fully at home. Go where it leads you."

"Yeah, Stephanie," Enid Evans remarked in a whisper to her friend sitting next to her with a nudge of an elbow into her ribs. "Set your heart. Go where you and I know it's leading you. I bet Tyler's got a very comfortable bed."

"Get out, Enid! That's more in the speed zone of your relationship with Alex."

"No way!"

"Way!"

"Can I walk you two back to class," asked a suddenly-appearing, hope-he-didn't-overhear-us Alex.

"Sure," Stephanie answered.

"Especially if you bring your famous cousin along," Enid added quickly. *Nudge, nudge.*

Tyler appeared almost right on cue for escort duty. And the remainder of the fall, the balance of that whole school year in fact, continued to tumble the four of them together in their budding relationships like two pairs of wool socks held together by static cling in a clothes dryer spinning on medium to high heat, like an irreversible destiny, like Ola's award-winning recipe for peach upside-down crumble cake.

It was Ola who, several weeks later, spent several reassuring minutes on the phone with both Mrs. Wells and Mrs. Evans convincing them it would be perfectly safe and fine for Stephanie and Enid to spend Friday night and a good portion of the next Saturday out at the farm.

"The girls and boys will be well chaperoned and at night the girls will be staying at my place and the boys will be with my father-in-law in his house. And our good neighbour, Mr. Wilton, will be pleased to act as chauffeur as he is going to be coming in and out of town on Friday night and late Saturday afternoon anyway. He usually uses his pick-up truck, but lately he's been driving his recently-acquired late model Jeep Cherokee when he heads into town and back."

"Is he that well-spoken, well-mannered man who's been dating Ms. Morton, the grade nine teacher from Dewdney Junior High?" Doris Wells inquired.

"He sits on the Board of School Trustees with me," Frances Evans added. "He's most reliable and polite."

"Yes," Ola stated, "I believe that would be the same man."

Wilton was dating. Her son was dating. Her nephew was dating. Her sister-in-law seemed happily married to her husband. All around her people she cared about had partners, except for Pops. She had him to care for. That was a different form of love. For a few moments, she remembered her early days of infatuation with Louie, but those days faded fast and that partnership was rightly dissolved. She tried unsuccessfully to hold back tears as she recalled her relationship with Uri: the day he treated her to a carriage-ride on which he proposed marriage, their very sincere Orthodox wedding day, their not-so-orthodox wedding night, the amazing tenderness in his strong hands, the hesitancy in his voice and his touch when they made love, his reassuring presence when Alex was born, one marvellous family holiday to Lake Baikal, the awful ache in her heart when the sad news from Chernobyl reached her. Her heart had known all this terrain as well as a cartographer plotting maps. At age thirty-seven, her emotional journey had been as lengthy and arduous as her move from the Ukraine to Canada. Was she feeling cheated now? Was she sensing loneliness? No. She had another lover. She had known this love since she was a child. It had grown, matured, flourished, established itself as an ongoing experience of her life. Catherine Doherty called it *sobornost*, a Russian word for unity or communion. Communion in the Holy Trinity. For Ola it was decisively Christ-centred. A phrase from Saint Thalassios came to mind with masculine pronouns altered to feminine ones:

> *The person who listens to Christ fills herself with light; and if she imitates Christ, she reclaims herself.* [*The Philokalia*, Vol. 2, page 321].

Ola was not lost, not alienated. She was reclaimed, ablaze with an unquenchable flame.

More common passions smouldered, flared, felt menacing at times within four adolescents venturing for the first time into uncharted territory. The route was littered with warning signs, caution arrows, prohibitions. Those who dared to try offering directions spoke similarly—about detours, amber beacons and stop signs. Scant was the advice about permissible pathways and green lights. Was it all trial and error? Did everyone make it up as they went along? Could you count on your mind to manage your instincts? Could head and heart really handle hormones? Psalm 119:9 set to music asked "By what means shall a young man seek his way to purify?"

Excellent question. Answers to be discovered.

Film at nine, not at eleven. Ola's rule. That was okay for Friday night. Four teens in two pairs squished into a couch shrieked, squealed, and alternately watched and covered their eyes as Jason did his gory, gruesome dirty work in one of the versions of *Friday the Thirteenth*. A lot of popcorn got scrunched, dropped, lost in the cracks, or ground into the carpet instead of being consumed. That was all right, it came with baked in butter not needing freshly melted topping. One ginger ale got spilled. Cuddling was safe. Close cuddling was excitement and stimulation enough. Stolen hugs and kisses in the dark were acceptable, permissible, expected, received with reciprocal acquiescence.

Pizza and pop in the kitchen with lights on after the movie was over gave them settle-down time, time to shift emotional gears from fear and sorrow to silliness and laughter. "No, Alex, put that knife down!" The jury often has mixed feelings on what is funny after watching a horror movie. In this case, the jury was right. When snack was done, so was the evening.

"Good night boys." Two young women at Ola's, two young men at Pops' house went to sleep an hour later after talking each other into pleasant and pleasurable fantasies.

Saturday morning had a late start with breakfast not being served until 10:00 A.M. That left enough time for Alex and Tyler to act as tour guides conducting Enid and Stephanie around some of the barns and grounds. Meet the horses. Visit the granaries. Inspect the garden. View the fields. Take a side-trip through Wilton's chicken coops. Gather some eggs. Hold hands. Wrap arms around one another. Roll down a hill or two. Find out who's ticklish. Kiss good morning. Anticipate the afternoon.

It was late October, but the weekend felt like Spring. In Eastern Canada, they might call it not-so-politically correctly Indian Summer. In Western Canada, people enjoy the phenomenon named Chinook. Warm and breezy air, absolutely azure skies, all nature emitting smells of freshness even though it's dying, sunshine sinking into your shoulders and people as perky as frisky horses. All these make up chinook and cloak the prairie in a spirit of rejoicing.

Horseback riding was the afternoon agenda. Limits of distance and allowable territory had been agreed upon. Pops helped Enid saddle up Charro. Alex would ride Belva. Striker was strong enough to handle two on board, Stephanie hanging on to Tyler from behind. About a half an hour was spent helping the horses and girls become acquainted. Rapport came rather rapidly. The horses were quite willing to treat friends of the family as family. Time check: 1:30 P.M.

"Okay," said Pops, "off you go! Be back by 3:30 so the girls have time to pack up and meet Wilton at four for their trip back to town."

As the quartet of riders left the barn and circled right, Ola waved from her laundry stoop. "Be careful, boys!"

"We will, Ola. We will."

As they rounded the corral, Enid rode up beside Alex and remarked, "Your mother is just so loving and sincere. I don't find her strange at all."

"Strange?" Alex wondered out loud.

"Oh, that's our mothers talking," interjected Stephanie. "Not because your mom is from Russia or wherever, but because she's always so genuine and decent. Our moms can't spot any phoniness in her like they can in their friends."

"Or, in each other," Enid added.

"Oh," said Alex. "Well, she is very religious. I suppose there are a number of folks who might find that strange."

"Well, I don't find it strange," Stephanie commented. "I think it's very… very…admirable. I admire people who can be clear about what they believe in and seek to live it."

"Hookers kind of live what they believe in," Alex jibed.

"Alex!" Enid shot back, "We're not in the boys' locker room, Gutterboy. Stephanie was talking about decent people. If your mother was here, you'd be swallowing soap right now."

Tyler smirked and shook his head. "If his mother was here, he'd be making his own soap for a month and chewing on it daily. In Ola's world, penance accompanies apology."

Alex sought for a slice of decency from within. "You got that right. I'm sorry. Sometimes the quips just pop out before I can catch them."

"Like a hooker's boobs pop out of a bustier?" Enid joked as she slapped Alex on his right shoulder and took off on a gallop crying, "Catch me…if you can."

The chase was on. Three horses, four riders raced down the trail leading to the back woods. Enid was caught before she reached the tree line. Laughter embraced the young lovers like a sun shower. The paths ahead of them would lead them a fair piece further than laughter.

Chinook time, dating time, weekend-away time seemed to four young learners like an appropriate time for embracing. Three hundred yards into the woods the path divided. The way to the left led to small stream-fed pond. The way to the right led to a bush-sheltered view from the top of a foothill, a view of the larger, greener forests to the West and of the mountains rising up behind them, stretching across the horizon like spines on the back of a giant stegosaurus. Time check: 2:00 P.M. Rendez-vous back here at 3:00 P.M. where the way divides. Agreed.

Alex and Enid headed for the hill. Stephanie hugged tight to Tyler as they turned left in search of soothing waters. The smell of fir and pine and tamarack caressed them. The sun sent shafts of brilliant affirmation slicing between trees. Squirrels scampered. A hare looped over the path in front of them then disappeared silently into some secret warren off to the right. Sparrows and finches twittered. A woodpecker hammered at its work. Tyler brought Striker to a halt so they could admire a pair of orioles. Further down the path a lone magpie swooped adventurously overhead. The faint sound of running water entered the range of their hearing.

It took less than ten minutes to reach the pond. It was only four to six feet deep at the most. The stream that fed it ran through the midst of it keeping its surface slightly disturbed. The water glistened cool. "Barstoke's Pond,"

Tyler offered, "named after original settlers around here." It spoke rejuvenation with every ripple, with every vibrant current. A couple of sections of bank were worn smooth from years of human visitation. Tyler and Stephanie dismounted at the second one. Striker leaned over to slurp up some water before Tyler tied him to a nearby tree. Stephanie seated herself on the bank and beckoned Tyler to sit beside her.

"So, how's our latest town hero doing these days?"

"Well, Stephanie, he's still working pretty hard not to let it all go to his head. He's still practicing for the next several rodeos down the road. And these days, he's just feeling very lucky or fortunate or maybe blessed. He's feeling his aunt is probably right in noticing that God is smiling fairly broadly on him right now, and that's a pretty comfortable feeling. At the moment, it's magnified about a hundred times by the fact that he's sitting beside a very beautiful and special young woman from Foothills Composite whom he has the honour of having for a friend, even though she harbours deep dislike for his chosen sport."

"And how is she doing these days?"

"Well, in keeping with the tone you set of being rather formal and polite, she's feeling quite special and blessed herself. She's doing not bad at managing her responsibilities and keeping her activities balanced. But right now, her heart's racing and she's feeling that our relationship could move on to the next level, but she's not just sure what that is."

"Well," Tyler said leaning in closer, "maybe we could start with something like this;" and he proceeded to kiss her gently, fully, lovingly on the lips. It was scintillating. It lasted a long ten minutes.

As they broke apart for a moment, Stephanie asked, "Is this water very cold?"

"Dangle your feet in and see."

"I can do better than that," she said. Stephanie stood up and with a sudden burst of daring stripped down to her undergarments, waded in up to her knees and dove down and resurfaced in the centre of the pond. "The water's fine, but it will be finer when you get out here."

"Ah, I don't know."

"Oh come on, don't be so shy and proper. Besides, the rest of that kiss you started is waiting for you out here."

"Oh, well, since you put it that way...." Tyler removed his boots and socks and was about to wade in.

"No, no, no, lover-boy, lose the shirt and pants too, unless you want to explain wet clothes to Ola."

"Oh yeah, right. Smart thinking." Nervously and hesitantly, Tyler stripped down to his boxers and waded out.

"Whoa, cool boxers, and look at the biceps on you!" Stephanie swam up to embrace him and planted the promised kisses. Restraint drained from her. She pressed her body into his, parted his lips, felt for his tongue with her tongue.

Tyler reciprocated in a more controlled fashion, following her lead, staying tender, venturing some nibbles on her lips, kisses to her cheeks, her chin, the sides of her nose, her ear lobes, her neck, pecking like one of Wilton's hens only more slowly, more softly. Stephanie exchanged the lead with him several times. Blood rushed on both sides of this building equation. Nerves quickened.

In mid-passion Stephanie reached behind her back to unfasten her bra. She slipped it off and looped it over her left wrist. Tyler pulled back just a bit, hesitant, uncertain, not intent on improving his view. He could not help noticing, breasts firm, creamy white with firm crimson nipples in the midst of inch-and-a-quarter wide rose areolae. ("Wow! A pair of orioles and a pair of areolae in one afternoon.... Settle down, Tyler, you're thinking like your cousin." )

Stephanie didn't afford him time to settle down or think. She reached for his right arm with her right hand and brought his hand up to touch her breasts, moving it at her own leisure and pleasure. She grabbed up his left hand and manipulated both his palms in slow, circling motions around each breast and then just around each nipple, tickling, sensitizing, sending rushes of sensual energy into each of their bodies spilling out into the current of the stream as it intersected the pond. Sighs, sounds bordering on shouts came out of her. After several minutes she arched her back, stiffened her torso, abdomen, legs and virtually screamed. Something fluid fled from her. It wasn't blood. It didn't tear anything. It seeped out.

Tyler wasn't resisting, but something within him was fighting, wanting to slow down, wanting to stay in control, something more than mental. The sensual won. He found out what a swollen member really was. He couldn't restrain ejaculatory fluids. Some stuck to his shorts. He watched other small clods of white jizz (he couldn't remember the technical term) bob in the water. Most of them sank. Some of them rose toward the surface first. He hoped Stephanie didn't notice them. She did but wasn't sure what to make of them and resolved not to make mention of them. They had peaked within seconds of each other. As their bodies relaxed, they collapsed into one another, holding on, just holding on.

"Maybe that was a couple of levels further up the scale," said Stephanie, "but I couldn't help myself. It just felt so good, so right...and then so scary, like playing with matches that suddenly catch fire and then you're afraid to drop them. But I don't feel ashamed. I don't regret any of it. But if you want to pull back a bit from here, that would be fine with me."

"Steph, I think that would be smart on both our parts. But like you, I don't regret today. I won't forget it...ever. It was wonderful, scary wonderful as you said, like fire, but like a holy fire. And you truly are beautiful.

"Come on, we'd better find cover where we can wring out our wet skivvies and then get dressed and ride back. It's time."

"There's just one more thing," Stephanie added. Tyler watched her unfasten a hair ribbon. She stretched it out between her hands, lowered it under the water and swiftly brought it up under his crotch looping it tightly around his scrotum. Then she gave it a quick upward yank.

"Yeow!" screamed Tyler, "What's that about?"

"That's just about wanting you to know why I don't like rodeo. That's about helping you feel something of what those bucking horses you ride get to feel. Nonetheless, cowboy, I still find you irresistible." She giggled, kissed him, and said, "Now...let's go get dressed."

They were on time when they got back to the rendezvous point. Alex and Enid had arrived only about three minutes earlier. The conversation was inconsequential. The exchange of glances, smiles, and a couple of almost clandestine winks told them they were four elated teens who had experienced certain degrees of romantic satisfaction.

When they arrived back at the homestead, the girls set to gathering up their suitcases and overnight bags. Wilton was waiting to return them to Okotoks.

"Thank you, Mrs. Davis, and you too, Pops. We had a wonderful time. Your food is delicious and your property is absolutely amazing."

"Thank you, girls," Ola replied. "We thoroughly enjoyed your company. Come again some time. And remember that the town you live in is rather amazing too."

Hugs, good-byes, and kisses followed. Wilton's Cherokee drove out of the laneway. Ola took Pops into her house to help peel potatoes. Alex and Tyler headed to the barns to brush down the horses. As soon as they got into the barn, Alex couldn't contain himself any longer.

"So, how was it, Tyler? Enid told me Stephanie was thinking about moving on to the next level."

"Well, cuz, that's kind of personal and private information, don't you think? Let's just say Stephanie and I agreed we should take it slow and easy and settle for kisses, hugs and cuddles for now. As for what went on at the pond, we didn't really raise our relationship level any higher than we raised the water level. And, there's still a kink or two to work out. And you? Since I know you're dying to tell me."

"Well, cuz, let me just say there's a little grove of bushes on top of that foothill that I will remember as HJ and Stink-finger Hollow"

"Alex! That's not the next level. That only about ten degrees shy of the boiling point. Maybe you and Enid want to think about conserving more of the mercury in the thermometer. Here, hang up these reins in the tack room. Better yet, hang them over your bed at night as a kind of reminder."

"Okay, okay, I hear you, party-pooper. I suspect you're right. It's just that...it's just....it felt so...so...."

"Wonderful."

"Oh yeah, at least wonderful!"

".. and scary."

"Scary? Let me see. Are you talking about Friday night or Saturday afternoon?"

"Both."

"Well, horses, what do you think?"

Charro, Belva, and Striker all nodded agreement. Alex didn't notice Tyler's hand signal. He only knew he had been out-voted and solidly but lovingly chastised. Silence settled in as the boys resumed brushing. As Tyler stroked Striker's hide, he had a feeling he was almost imitating Jesus the day the Son of God drew doodles in the dirt as an adulterous woman avoided stoning.

# Chapter 16:
# Barnstorm

Five days later, the fine weather had evaporated. Fall was fast-forwarding into early winter. Crimson, auburn, purple, golden, orange-green leaves turned quickly brown and brittle. East winds shook them from their limbs, swirling them to the ground, scattering them across lawns and fields and hillsides, swooping them into little heaps in gutters and sewer openings and piles against fence-posts, gates, sides of sheds, and barn walls. Tamarack needles turned brown and dropped to form mats and cushions on the forest floor. Migrating birds were noticed more *en masse*. The gauges on thermometers and barometers plummeted. Chill and frost showed up unannounced etching patterns on morning window panes, forcing drivers to dig out scrapers to clear their windshields. Human breath, cattle breath, horse breath, dogs' breath issued in visible vapor trails. Turtles, newts, frogs and fish fled for deeper water. Overcast skies dominated the weeks. Rain and sleet became frequent features.

Auto garages in Okotoks were filled with vehicles seeking tune-ups, car heater and block heater checks, radiator flushes and anti-freeze top-ups. Some older vehicles awaited a switch to snow tires. St. Paul's United Church Women held their annual Christmas bazaar on the same day as the Okotoks Santa Claus parade and served up a hearty soup and sandwich or chili lunch. Myra and Rebecca Stedman helped prepare and serve. The group netted a profit of $2,500, more than comparable to the special event income of other church women's groups in town and the receipts taken in by the Legion Dinner and Dance on Remembrance Day. Alex straddling Charro accompanied Tyler riding on Striker just ahead of the Santa float. Tyler wore a tawny buckskin fringed jacket, a traditional white Stetson, studded boots and, over his jeans, a pair of dress chaps loaned him by one of his instructors at rodeo school. His two-inch wide brown leather belt was adorned by his prize-winning championship silver buckle. It was difficult to distinguish whether the thunderous applause and uproars of acclamation at the parade's end were generated by Santa's arrival or by the sight of the town's still-venerated local hero ahead of him. Adoration of the Christ-child took a distant third place in the minds of the general public on that occasion.

Pops Davis spent a couple of hours a day in one of his sheds set aside for storing and splitting firewood. He went at it methodically and easy as if he was practicing and enjoying an ancient art. He exhibited a congruence of body, mind and spirit, concentrated and cohesive like a practitioner of Zen meditation. Something satisfying, self-affirming, and transcendental attended his labour. He still had the horses to attend to as well. Seed catalogues got a good thumbing over. Ola was never short on suggesting odd jobs around the houses that he could handle. He would also check on Wilton to see if he needed any help or visit other neighbours up and down the roads offering assistance or just engaging in conversations. "Punky" McAllister had a still going in an old root cellar. A couple of tumblers of his Kickin' Corn Concoction were enough to encourage you to sit down for an hour or so before moving on or getting behind the wheel of your car. Of course Punky was a sympathetic soul who passed around a bowl of breathmints to his guests before they left, making it easier to face whomever was waiting for you at home. Pops figured Punky was one of the most considerate persons he knew, and Punky had a pretty good fix on Ola.

Ola had dug into her stash of worn clothing and scraps of material to begin braiding, piecing and stitching together a 6' x 9' oval rag rug, the first of several at-home projects she had in mind for this coming winter. When Ola was six years old, her mother had started teaching her the craft. Ola could make a rug by rote now in a matter of weeks; wonderful rugs, not haphazard but color-coordinated, symmetric, concentric, artful creations. This one was going feature brown, amber and beige tones and occasional splashes of red, cherry red. It was destined for the floor of the office in her equipment barn, replacing a tatty, worn-out mat that had served its time over the last twelve years. It was being designed to complement its surroundings of varnished knotty pine flooring and wall panels and light oak furnishings.

She would interrupt her project and daily routine for another two-day *poustinia* near the end of the third week of November. She would use a little pup-trailer hauled by a small tractor to carry firewood and extra quilts out to her cabin, just enough to make the chill weather tolerable. Drenching rain the day before had left the ground soft and squishy, another reason for taking the tractor since walking to the cabin on foot would have been exacting and bothersome: slippery trails, wet grasses, soaked footwear, shoes or boots pulled off by sucking mud. Dampness still hung in the air like a weighted net. Wind velocity hovered around forty-five kilometers per hour. For added warmth, Ola took along a red woolen *kutska*, a shawl and headpiece her mother used to wear on their occasional pilgrimages from their farm near Chernivtsi to the monastery of St. Theognostos twenty kilometers southwest into the lower reaches of the Carpathian mountains. The monastery was virtually carved into the hillside and pilgrims got to take shelter in a series of adjacent caves. Simple floor mats were provided, wood and fuel for making your own fire, and a couple of coal oil lamps for light. Meals were taken in the monastery dining hall. The cave became your personal cell for contemplation. The journey was arduous for a small girl and even her mother at times became short of breath and foot-sore. Luggage was simplified: a linen shoulder bag held your blanket, an icon, a Bible, a loaf of black bread and a pinch of salt. Also slung over one shoulder was a wineskin full of water. Stripped down, rudimentary trappings such as these were recommended by St. Theognostos for developing virtue:

> *Regard all you possess as trash in the hope of better things. Shake off even your body when time comes, and follow the angel of God that takes you from it. [The Philokalia, Vol. 2]*

St. Theognostos' ancestors had Spartan blood.

Ola Davis was hardy, disciplined and well acquainted with the ways of pilgrimage. She had the patient endurance of spiritual sojourners branded on her soul. She conversed frequently with several of God's angels. She carried her compassion and concern for others like a tea-cozy around her heart. Among them, she reserved a special place for her step-nephew, Tyler Stedman, whose decency, persistence and no-frills honesty presented her with the image of a potential second St. Theognostos in the making. This was the last of her own thoughts as she dismounted the tractor, carried her meagre provisions into her isolated cabin and began the process of clearing her mind that she might become an open receptacle for light and wisdom from above. *Tikniy [teek-nee]*, that state of blessed and utter quiet made one most receptive to God. She started up a fire in the wood-stove, hung her night-clothes beside the bed then took her icon from her carrying-bag and placed it on the bedside table. It was a picture of Mary in her imagined state of Assumption, a replica of a much revered icon in the Church of Our Lady of Mercy in Dnipropetrovsk, a large town thirty kilometers west of Kiev. "The Red Madonna" was how Pops referred to it. Five cherubs surrounded Mary assisting her ascent. Below her the outstretched arms of farewell from friends and other followers of her son. Only St. John, St. Peter, and St. Mary Magdalene had faces visible in the crowd of onlookers. A classic golden aura encircled Mary's head. A distant white archway perched on clouds in the upper right hand corner. Alex, in one of his unthinking bursts of spontaneity, once commented that it looked like Mary was only heading into St. Louis, Missouri. Fortunately for him, he was only seven years old at the time and thus, forgivable. More readily forgiven by the Virgin Mother than by his own mother no doubt. Forgiveness happens habitually in heaven. On earth it is practiced with hesitancy, and in this instance Ola's heart held back her hand from offering her son an oft-prescribed taste of soap.

Perhaps her unconscious mind recreated a connection between soap and the Red Madonna, for Ola next moved to the wash basin to scrub her hands before seating herself at table with a slice of bread and a glass of water. It was shortly after noon and the ritual meal of poverty, slavery and imprisonment was an appropriate prelude to a pilgrim's silent meditation. Ola was patterning her retreat on the East-West blend of Christian spirituality advocated by Catherine Doherty: a desert experience of *poustinia* in which the goal was to sense *sobornost* or unity with the Holy Trinity. Such was the practice of a *strannik*, a pilgrim—one who wandered into the presence of God in order to emerge as one who embraced others and God's world with love. A passage of Scripture, an icon, a meditation by one of the Church's saints would be the fire-starters for this journey of the soul. Deep, centering breaths followed attentive thought until one blocked out all extraneous noise and sound and sight, unfolded the wings of one's own mind and in a state of blessed emptiness wandered into *molchanie*, the silence of God. In that silence, images and messages and inspirations often came inviting exploration and consideration. Stillness enveloped the cabin for quite some time. Ola's meditation left behind the icon of Our Lady of Mercy as her mind sunk only into the redness of the Virgin

Mother's gown. Redness enfolded her, fiery, fluid, passionate and vibrant. Ola gave herself over to that redness for more than an hour until it picked her up and carried her like a cape on a super-hero. "Come higher. Come further. Come deeper," a voice seemed to call.

She went. She envisioned herself landing on top of Big Rock. The rock levitated and glided into downtown Okotoks. The Sheep River flowed restlessly below her. Riverside Park was sparsely populated by a few seniors out for a stroll and a couple of moms, probably single moms, playing with their toddlers. Ola grew taller. Tall enough that from her vantage point she could overlook the whole town of Okotoks in a glance: commuters travelling off to Calgary, workers and shoppers and students going about their day, stay-at-home spouses doing chores or preparing meals, people with a day off or on night-shift making use of the Recreation Centre or the outdoor skating rink or the cross-country ski trails out at the local golf course, residents in the nursing home being cared for, patients at the hospital being tended to by staff. The old boiler mill was still operative bilging out steam. The Catholic priest was hearing confessions. The Anglican rector was working on his homily. The Baptist and United Church ministers were out making pastoral visits. The Pentecostal pastor was meeting with her associate planning a Youth Rally. And one pair of tourists was engaged in the "Historic Walk." Ola stood there for what seemed like hours just observing, pondering, registering concerns, absorbing the obvious and secret pains of the town; its honesty and its hypocrisy; whatever was disappointing, disheartening, and troublesome; whatever was healthful, hopeful, and amenable to correction. Thoughts and phrases came to consciousness, sentences stretched towards paragraphs, speech was being birthed. "Go ahead," the voice encouraged Ola. "Speak. Speak out whether they hear you or not, whether they listen or not. It is my speech." So she spoke. And no one listened. Some people stared back at her but she was invisible to them, inaudible. They looked through her, past her or around her. The rest just kept moving, sitting, talking, thinking without noticing her at all.

"O blessed, pitiable little city, lukewarm as the church in Laodicea in Revelations chapter 3, listen to me. Your hospitality, comfort, friendliness is one-third genuine and two-thirds show for the sake of reputation. It's a game played to offer you the illusion of living securely and happily. Like the preserved façades of buildings from the old town, you wear them in an ongoing public masquerade. You pin on statistics like ribbons awarded at a country fair: 76 percent of the population under the age of 44 and almost 20 percent ages 45-64, 98% of the employable population engaged in employment, 81 percent church-going or admittedly god-fearing residents, 94 percent actively engaged in sports, arts, charitable organizations. You sit snugly in the shadow of Calgary as an oasis of middle and upper class mindlessness. Forgive me, if I seem to speak to you in clichés, but that is what you persist in presenting to any outside observer—a cliché people living a cliché life in a cliché town.

"Forgive me, I am being too harsh. Beneath the surface of this Teflon town there is much goodness and decency and even a striving after righteousness. But be not too smug, nor blind to the ruder realities also present and fracturing, harmful and ugly: cheating spouses and partners tangled in infidelity, here and there some money-grubbing and embezzling, families infected by abusive behaviours of alcoholism, kids on drugs, neglected and lonely seniors, envy, jealousy, slander, gluttony, people who are over-stressed, people who are depressed, people continually trying to impress, people feeling helpless or hopeless or worthless, and people whose lives are in a mess. How much longer can they bear that freight? How much more is too much weight?

"Listen. My Lord has a message just for you: 'Come to me all you who labour and are heavy-laden, and I will give you rest. Take my yoke upon you and learn from me...for my yoke is easy and my burden is light" [Matthew 11:28-30]. Can you hear him? Can you feel this light as warmth upon your faces? Can you taste this promise a cool, refreshing water running down your skin? Can you take up this invitation to exchange all your striving for holy, peaceful, generous living? I am mindful of a passage from Saint Neilos the Ascetic:

> *Those who travel by sea, when overtaken by a storm, do not worry about their merchandise but throw it into the waters with their own hands, considering their property less important than their life. Why, then, do we not follow their example, and for the sake of the higher life despise whatever drags our soul down to the depths? .... we, who claim to be seeking eternal life, do not look with detachment on even the most insignificant object, but prefer to perish with the cargo rather than be saved without it. [The Philokalia, Vol. 1, pp. 242-243]*

Detach. Detach. That is my prayer and my plea for you, good people of Okotoks. Detach and turn toward the way of Jesus, the way of servanthood and true neighbourhood."

Ola's words now turned to tears, tears of passion and hope, rivulets of tears that spilled down her cheeks and dropped into the water of the Sheep River

160

below her leaving streaks like blood in the passing currents. The currents were picking up pace as the wind gained in velocity. Harder and harder it blew ripping off Ola's headscarf and sending it flying downstream, tugging at her clothes as if trying to defrock her. Rain came, soft-shelled at first, then larger pellets assaulting the body, making Big Rock treacherously slippery. Ola felt her legs give way, felt her butt land hard upon the rock as she began sliding down towards the river. As she slid she heard a creaking, cracking, crashing sound in the distance. She turned to see the old water-tower at the boiler plant teeter on its mooring, tear apart and fall to the ground, as did also happen to a silo in DeWinton for suddenly a wicked storm had come up.

The imagined sight and sound of the tower tumbling, the sensation of sliding jarred Ola out of her visionary state to the seeming security of her cabin. She heard the howling wind, the pelting rain. A hymn came into her head: "Praise to the Lord, who when tempests their warfare are waging, who when the elements madly around thee are raging...." She started to hum it. She knew it continued: "...biddeth them cease, turneth their fury to peace." But that's not what happened next. Instead, a glaring flash of light illumined the window in the west wall and a horrid crack shuddered outside. Instinctively, self-protectively, Ola virtually jerked herself back to the bed by the east wall. Thunder pounded on the roof, only it wasn't thunder, it was the upper limbs and half a trunk of an old oak tree that flanked the cabin eight metres due west. Shingles, struts, planks, crossbeams, and half the west wall crumbled. Sawdust, splinters, branches, dead leaves, and twigs became the cabin's interior decor. One stray branch grazed Ola's right arm, otherwise she was unscathed. Incoming rain provided moisture enough to wash her cut. Quickly she gathered her mother's shawl from the wall hook, flung it around her shoulders, picked up her prayer book, her icon, and her carry-sack, and put on a spare pair of thick rubber boots she kept at the cabin for bad weather occasions. She turned off the oil lamp, doused the fire in the stove and headed to the door. As she made her exit, a section of the back wall fell down. This place for *poustinia* would lie in ruins until it could be rebuilt in Spring.

Ola made several attempts to start up the tractor. It wouldn't fire. The wires and plugs were too wet. There seemed nothing left to do but try to plod heavily back to the farm through muck and sodden fields.

She hadn't gone more than thirty metres when headlights came over a slight rise following the ruts of the tractor trail. Well, sort of, the steering was a little unsteady. It was soon apparent that it was Wilton's Jeep coming to rescue her, but it wasn't Wilton who was driving; it was Alex.

"Mom! Mom! Are you okay?" he shouted out a hastily opened driver's-side window.

"Yes, Alex, I'm fine, but as you can see the cabin isn't. Now, how in heaven's name did you end up trying to drive Wilton's Jeep out to fetch me?'

"Get in. I'll slide over so you can drive back. Quick. I'll tell you on the way back. The storm's a monster, Mom. Lightning struck the barn. Come quick. We've got to get back to help the others."

Lightning had indeed hit the barn. Not far back down the trail, Ola could see smoke and the remains of flames gobbling up air space. Wilton was helping Pops and the local Volunteer Fire Department try to salvage what they could. That's how Alex got sent to retrieve Ola.

"I think the horses got out safely. Pops was leading Tacitus and Charro to safety when I left and Wilton was gathering up the others. The lightning tore a hole right into the roof and the whole rear end collapsed. Good thing the rain is heavy, the fire wasn't spreading too quickly. I think we'll save the tack room and the grooming shed."

Ola was driving faster than Alex was talking which meant she had quite a head of steam going. Mud and grass, gravel and a few small stones flew from the rear of the Jeep like the spray from a power-boat. It wasn't a smooth ride but it was over in half the time it usually took. Ola and Alex sprang from the vehicle and ran to where Pops was trying to keep Tacitus and Charro calm.

"Pops, are you all right?" Ola asked almost breathless.

"Yes, Ola, I'm okay. The barn's busted up pretty bad. Firemen did a good job of keeping the damage contained to the rear end. Tack room, grooming shed, front stalls are still intact, 'cept there's less roof protecting them."

"And the horses? How are the horses?" Alex anxiously inquired.

"Well...Wilton got Belva and Ironstone tethered at the far side of the corral. But Striker...I'm afraid Striker didn't make it. Fire didn't get him though. Smoke might have finished him off. Near as we can figure he burst out of his own stall and smashed down the gate so Belva and Iron-stone could get free. Tacitus and Charro were in the open stalls any way. Before Striker could get away, that back wall came down and one of the cross-beams levelled him. We could see him pinned, heard him neighing, but no one could get to him until we had the flames and smoke more under control. Wilton's in the barn now with a few other men trying to lift away the rubble and drag him out. He died either of a broken back or of smoke inhalation."

Family tears and family silence enfolded them. *And Tyler may nearly die of a broken heart*, thought Alex. Pops and Ola stared back at him entertaining the same thought.

The firemen dispersed when they had done all they could, offering their condolences in passing. Punky McAllister had room for the horses in one of his barns and a ready supply of feed for the next while. Wilton was the last to leave, shaking his head, hugging each of them.

"The special weather report said it was something like a bomb cyclone. There hasn't been one of those out the Pacific Northwest for decades. It's a wild combination of disturbances in the upper atmosphere causing a low pressure system and cold front to swing back into each other creating a negative tilt trough. Wind, water, thunder, lightning, even snow can cut loose. But hell, knowing what happened isn't going to fix anything or restore dead horses to life. If there's anything I can do, don't hesitate to ask. And don't you go messing around in that rubble without me, Pops, okay?"

Agreed.

It was only 9 P.M. and sad news couldn't wait till the next day. Pops, Ola and Alex drove into to Okotoks to tell the Stedmans. More tears. Mutual sympathy. Myra made tea. Tyler couldn't speak for shock.

On Sunday afternoon, a family wake, funeral and interment for one fine young stallion were commemorated. One very good neighbour attended. Just outside the corral underneath a couple of his favorite crab-apple trees, Striker's remains rest in peace.

A couple of weeks later, Tyler could console himself with the realization that Charro was good enough for training in calf-roping, but she didn't have anything near Striker's speed nor instinct for the sport. Bronc riding was always a matter of whatever horses were available for the draw from one event to the next. But a roper and his mount had to have rapport and connection. You could often borrow someone else's mount, but your chances of winning were far better if you rode a trusted and trained companion. Ironstone was too young yet to break into the calf-chasing habit. Rodeo aspirations sometimes wind up relegated to the realm of romance beyond reality's performing ring.

# Chapter 17:
# Mothers at the Mall

Men mourn alone, by and large, often in silence. They also do it mostly while they are moving, and they avoid it by getting busy. Pops and Wilton went on with their days, their chores, with long walks or car rides. Alex buried himself in chores and schoolwork and once in a while went for a ride on Charro when the snow wasn't too deep. Dates with Enid took his mind far away from grieving. Tyler did his homework now at half-speed, spending long hours just sitting, brooding, staring out windows. He started to read Zane Grey and worked his way slowly again through Owen Wister's *The Virginian*. Dates with Stephanie were some relief, but even she noticed that he was uncharacteristically sullen at times.

Women in grief crave company. Ola would have preferred to have Myra come out for tea and maybe Mrs. Berenson who seemed more grounded than many of the other female citizens of Okotoks. What Myra offered instead before the week was out after the storm disaster was shopping. After all, Christmas was coming and several stores at Southgate Mall were already offering attractive bargains. Mrs. Evans and Mrs. Wells would join them. It would be good opportunity for a women's day out.

Ola hardly needed to do any Christmas shopping. Myra would be getting one of the recently- made rag rugs she had admired: "That would look so wonderful in our downstairs recreation room!" Myra had no idea that Ola had already had that in mind. Jules would receive a bulky-knit curling sweater made with Icelandic wool. Rebecca had two splendid new figure-skating costumes and a 10' x 12' quilt for her hope chest lovingly sewn by Aunt Ola already wrapped and in waiting. The families had pooled their resources for Tyler's gift and Ola had put in her share. Wilton would get his usual basket-full of her Christmas baking. He adored her brandied Christmas cake, her Scotch shortbreads, cheese blintzes, and her Ukrainian versions of fried rosettes and bakkelser. Which left Pops. She could shop for him and she knew what for.

His pyjamas and robe had gotten quite tatty of late. New bed-wear and a few baking supplies from the bulk store comprised the short list Ola carried in her head as she met up with Myra for the Saturday spree.

"Would you like a coffee, Ola? We're just waiting for Doris. You remember Frances Evans, don't you?"

"Yes, we have met several times before, and no for now on the coffee, Myra. You are Enid's mother, right?"

"That's right. Your Alex is quite a fine young man, but he sure has energy to burn."

"Yes, he does. I think he gets it from his father. But my mother always felt it was because of his red hair. There certainly is fire in him and clearly he has flames in his heart for your Enid at present. She is a very attractive young woman and impresses me as quite bright too."

"She gets her brains from her father...and her looks from me. Hopefully she won't get the weight too as she gets older."

"Now Frances," Myra interjected, "don't be so hard on yourself. You're not what one would consider fat, just full-bodied and rounded. There are a number of men who like their women that way." (Lie, lie, lie).

"Yeah, Myra, like that painter Rubens and all his cronies and they died four hundred years ago," Frances Evans quipped.

"You'd fit in well in the Ukraine," Ola risked adding.

"There you have it, another country heard from! The jury is in and the verdict is 'Frances Evans, you're not bad for a well-rounded woman. Old World countries would be happy to have you as an immigrant. Just go easy on the chocolate and stay away from Spandex.' I can almost live with that."

"For now, Frances, you may have to. But if you feel moved to sign on with Curves or Jenny Craig, Ola and I would be happy to cheer you on wouldn't we, Ola?" Myra advanced teasingly.

H. Lee Disher

"Oh, yes. I'm sure we would, and besides chocolate you might also want to cut back on potatoes. Oops, there I go thinking Ukrainian again." She was actually feeling relaxed. Maybe Myra's shopping idea wasn't as unlikely a candidate for relief as Ola first thought.

A horn sounded in the Stedman driveway. Doris Wells had arrived with her family's Honda Previa willing to act as chauffeur for this excursion. There was no one to whom to say good-bye. Jules had taken Tyler to High River for rodeo practice. Rebecca was off with the Berensons to her figure-skating lessons and would be spending the day with the neighbour family. The three women got up from the kitchen table, threw on their winter coats and scarves and slipped into their boots. Myra and Frances sported stylish fur-trimmed hats. Ola had a hood she could pull up if a chill wind began blowing. They strutted out the front door in file towards the waiting van as Myra locked the door behind them. They looked like astronauts on a mission. Their pilot was happy to see them and eager to blast off. Doris had the biggest Christmas list of all of them since she hadn't even started gift shopping yet. She tended to live most of her life in a flurry and on the edge of last minutes. For all it was a laid-back place to live, a lot of Okotoks was just like her.

A light snow was falling, not enough to make driving hazardous in any way and just enough to put one in a Christmas seasonal mood. It kept the conversation in the van light and buoyant all the way to Calgary. Conversation of a sort, that is, that drifted through several sprints of topics: who was going to be where for Christmas, other holiday plans such as the Evans family visit to Frances' mother in a nursing home in Red Deer, the upcoming ecumenical Christmas choral concert sponsored by the churches of Okotoks:

"We're even learning a few pieces from Handel's Messiah for this year's offering," (Doris).

"And that's a major stretch for some of our singers and I'm not just talking about the Baptists!" (Myra).

"Singing anything is a stretch for Gerry (Mr. Evans), but you didn't hear it from me and thank your lucky stars you don't have to listen to his daily concerts from the shower," (Frances).

"You believe in lucky stars?" (Ola).

The subject of personal belief systems was quickly side-stepped for the moment. Frances shifted the field to Joyce Parkman's bossy behaviour at the church bazaar. "We have a woman like that at St. Bartholomew's," Ola contributed, still working somewhat at trying to fit in.

The bulk of the remaining conversation was really a monologue as Doris Wells rattled off her entire Christmas list, and God knows what she was going to come up with to give to Richard's maiden aunt in Manitoba this year. The Southgate Mall parking lot was already quite jammed when the women arrived, but they did find a spot to squeeze into not quite on the outer fringes.

"Safe landing, girls," Doris announced turning off the ignition, "I don't know about you, but I'm ready for a coffee before I do anything else." Fair enough.

The quartet made their way to French's Cafés du Monde and commandeered a table where they could enjoy two Colombian decafs and two cups of chai.

"Is this anything like what they make in the Ukraine, Ola?" asked Frances.

"Not exactly. They use a different method of preparation here and the kind of Russian black tea that is grown for export not domestic use. But...it's not bad. It's been nine years since I've been back home. I'm more used to how things taste here and less able to remember there." Three continents were represented at their small table for four, a fact noted by Doris Wells before she suggested they break up to go about their shopping rather than straggling along one after the other which would mean a lot of retracing of steps and periods of tedious waiting and....whatever else she came up with hardly needed to be said. The other three had already reached such foregone conclusions. A rendezvous place was set for lunch hour around 12:30 P.M. and the four women parted company. Doris hustled off to Sears. Frances set out in search of a men's shop. Ola didn't mind tagging along with Myra. As she recalled, the bulk food store was around the corner from The Gap, which was Myra's initial port of call, and Myra would want Ola's help and opinion regarding most of her purchases.

Sure enough, beginning with some new slacks for Rebecca: "What do you think, Ola? Pale blue or pink?"

"Certainly not pink. Do they have navy or forest green? I think Rebecca is starting to favour darker shades. They make her feel more grown up, yes? And they do go quite well with her complexion and hair colour."

"Thank you, Ola, you're so right. Growing up is part and parcel of a child's world, isn't it. I see a ten-year-old girl who was only seven yesterday. You see a ten-year-old itching to be a teenager."

"Without the make-up. At least, not yet."

"For sure, not yet. Only when she and Charlene are playing dress-up. Cindy Berenson and I have let them dabble in blush and lipstick and have kept the cold cream handy. Golly, a couple more years and I'll be bringing Rebecca here to try on training bras."

"*Da, pravda*, as they say in the old country."

Ola popped into the bulk store with Myra in tow to pick up her baking supplies and then they set out in search of the more nebulous gifts for Jules' family. Two brothers had married women from Ontario and moved there in the mid-1980s. Two nieces and three nephews had come on the scene since. Their estrangement wasn't a result of familial dysfunction, just lives taking different paths. Contacts were sporadic and infrequent, but everyone made the effort to be in touch around Christmas. Then there was Jules's sister in Edmonton, the oldest child in the family, the one who volunteered to martyr herself looking after Mom and Dad in addition to looking after (read "controlling") her own "perfect" family consisting of a husband and four kids. Mom died in 1989. Dad was still living, barely. Alzheimer's disease had shown up in earnest in 1994 and was now in its last stages of ravaging old Mr. Stedman's body and mind. Jules visited him once a month in the long-term care facility in which Sis reluctantly and finally permitted him to be placed. But you never visited without her being present, hovering, fussing, patronizing, determining how long the visit would last. Sometimes Jules arranged for Sis's husband to phone during the visit just to get her out of the room long enough so he could have a few words with his father and slip him a couple of contraband chocolates, a piece of Ola's fruit cake, and, on two occasions, a copy of *Penthouse* magazine to stash between the mattress and the box spring. Dad's brain was slowly getting toasted, but there was still some fire elsewhere.

They were about three-quarters through gathering up these obligatory gifts when the rendezvous moment for lunch drew near. Myra had picked out a sweater for Sis, "in colours she will hate and one size too small. But it doesn't matter because she takes back absolutely every gift anyone ever gives her for exchange or refund. One year, I suggested to Jules that we may as well just give her a gift certificate for Sears or The Bay. 'Oh God, no,' he replied, 'that's just gauche, you know. No, it has to be a real gift, or at least an attempt at one.' So, that year I got her a poo-pet, one of those outdoor garden ornaments made from lacquered cow pies."

"Really, people make such things? For a profit?" Ola mulled it over for a half minute or so.

"Myra! You know what that means? It means Wilton has been storing up a goldmine outside his barns and I could figure out how to help him cash in on it."

"You would too, you craft-hungry, natural-ingredient, recycling sorceress."

"Sorcery is for demoniacs. I am just a faithful steward of our Creator's resources."

"Yes, you are. The most diligent I've ever known. I'd love to learn but it would be so hopeless since I'm all thumbs when it comes to handcrafts."

"You do just fine with tending roses and garden flowers, Myra, and you bake a great cake."

"Thanks. I do. Even though I still need someone like you to do the arranging or the icing."

"It's a pact."

"Works for me. Who would have thought Louie could ever find such a treasure? I lose a brother who's hardly good for anything anyway and gain a sister better than I could ever have hoped for."

Ola was deeply touched by this unexpected tenderness in Myra. This longing for sisterhood and female friendship was awakening in her as well. A flash of honesty jostled out of dormancy, a lurking, lingering love that was as needful as it seemed, at this moment, frightful.

When Ola replied, "I'm almost speechless, so let's not go there. Let's go to lunch instead. It's time," she was referring to the mention of Louie not to Myra's disclosure of affection. When Myra and Ola arrived at the Saddle Up Restaurant for lunch, Doris was already there at the entrance covered in parcels.

"Hi!," she yelled unintentionally. "Frances isn't here yet. I've asked for a table for four, non-smoking. If you don't mind waiting for her, I'd like to take most of these parcels out to the van."

"Sure. Let me help you," Ola said not really waiting to be asked and picking up several parcels and bags of various sizes. "Myra will stay here to wait for Frances."

"Why, thank you, Ms. Davis, thank you ever so much. Hang on, Myra, we'll be back in a few minutes."

They were, and by the time they returned, Frances had shown up and was seated at their table with Myra, waiting, menus at the ready. Ola and Doris were barely seated when Frances said, "This place doesn't look like much, but they make a very good Cobb salad and the penne primavera isn't bad either. Of course, if you aren't worried about diet or cholesterol, the best Western sandwich in Alberta is made right here."

This was not new information for them, but Frances went through the rubric ritualistically every time. The waitress brought water for them all and took their orders: Cobb salad for Ola and Frances, Myra settled for the penne this time and Doris chose chicken fingers and fries with honey-mustard sauce and a spinach salad. Three iced teas and a diet cola were their selected beverages *du jour.*

"Well, I managed to get Enid and Eric looked after—one DVD player and a snowboard, both at a discount that made my eyes pop a little. I'm so glad we don't pay provincial sales tax on top of that darn GST like they do in other provinces. Nieces and nephews in our family circle are happy with gift certificates from Future Shop or Sunrise Records. As for my siblings and their spouses and Gerry's sister and her husband, we just put all our names into a hat and draw out one person to whom we aren't married to whom to give one gift. I picked Arnie, my brother, so I'm going to get him one of those George Foreman indoor grills. They're on sale at the Bay today. Which leaves Gerry, who wants a new golf bag and cart but God only knows which kind. What do you think, get something anyway and let him bring it back to exchange if it's not what he had in mind, or just go the Nevada Bob's gift certificate route?"

"You could probably risk picking something out, Frances," Myra submitted, "if you had your own car with you today. Given all the stuff Doris has already loaded into the van, I doubt there would be room for a golf bag and cart."

"Doris, really! You must have done well making a dent in your Christmas list in so short a time," Frances shot out.

"Well…." Doris began, "not exactly. Actually, I only managed to pick up a bottle of Brut cologne for my brother Dietrich in Prince George. His wife would rather he wore Drakkar Noir, or even Jovan Musk, but he likes Brut and I'm not that fond of her, so I aid and abet my brother in this subtle subterfuge. Then I visited that nice jewelry store across from Indigo books and picked up an Omega watch for Richard. Both of those parcels are still right here in my purse."

"So what was all that stuff we took out to the van?" Ola dared to ask.

"Oh well, that was all stuff that was on sale. Sears had percale sheets with a 400-plus thread count at 60 percent off and placemat and napkin sets minus 40 percent. La Senza had the loveliest satin nightgown I've seen in a while for only $89.99. Radio Shack had batteries and blank compact discs on special. Stokes' had dish towels and dish cloths on for half price, and Shoppers' Drug Mart had great bulk prices on Kleenex, paper towels and toilet paper."

Food had arrived a few minutes ago and Doris stopped for a few bites of dipped chicken fingers.

"And, oh yes, Indigo was selling pocket datebooks and magnetic note pads at bargain rates," she continued as she wiped her fingers on her serviette. "They make good stocking-stuffers, you know; so I did manage to get a little more Christmas shopping done. By the way, Ola, that's a beautiful knit sweater you are wearing, I've been admiring it all through lunch hour. No doubt you made it yourself."

"I did actually. Thank you, Doris."

"Did it take very long? Well, what I mean is, you are just about the same size as Richard's maiden aunt, the one in Manitoba I mentioned who lives like a recluse. I don't suppose you could knit one up in time for me to send it to her for Christmas, could you?"

"I think I could manage that. I'd be happy to."

"How much?"

"Oh mercy, Doris, I have no idea. Why don't you just pay me what you feel it's worth."

"It's worth a few hundred just to have the agonizing decision of what to get the old biddy dealt with. How does sixty dollars sound?"

"It sounds like too much, but I can give the extra to our church's refugee relief mission."

Doris nodded agreement with a couple of leaves of spinach flopped over her lower lip.

"You really do take your faith quite seriously, don't you, Ola?" Frances noted. "I mean that in a complimentary way. In fact, it's been quite wonderful to have you join us for our little shopping expedition today. I've so enjoyed getting to know you a little better and I have to confess I don't consider you as strange as I used to."

"Compliment accepted, I think," Ola replied. "I suppose I am strange to people who have never met a Ukrainian up close before...and Eastern Orthodox to boot. Is that how you sometimes say it? And still after thirteen years in this country, going on fourteen, I have to confess I find the pace and style of life here and several Canadian customs rather strange."

"Such as?" Doris asked.

"Such as all kinds of rushing around and noise and not a lot of silence and sabbath time. Such as letting in so much American television, and drinking beer while you're watching hockey or football. Such as not having police on foot or horseback in every neighbourhood or rural district. Such as so much idolizing of Dollar Almighty."

"Touché on all counts and one big bull's-eye," Frances remarked. "I understand you have a place where people can come and spend a day or two in religious retreat. I think that's fascinating. Do you think I could try it some time?"

"I had a place until the storm last month flattened it. But it will be rebuilt in the spring. If you're seriously interested, Frances, I could send you some devotional literature and some sample spiritual exercises you can use anytime right in your own house. Do you have a church to which you are connected?"

"Christ Church Anglican, when I go. Not more than once a month at present I'm a bit ashamed to admit. But I try to do better during Holy Week."

"Well, I won't need to send you very much literature since you already have a very rich resource in your own Book of Common Prayer if you own your own copy."

"I do. I do. I just never thought of using it except when I take it with me to church."

"How sad, and yet how available. All I need to send you to get you started is a few tips on how to develop a personal devotional practice. Would that be okay?"

"That would be wonderful, Ola. I'll look forward to it."

"Yes, well, look forward to an opportunity to make use of my little cabin once it gets rebuilt."

"That sounds even more wonderful. Thank you, Ola."

Myra was keeping an eye on Doris Wells as all this conversation transpired. Doris' eyes seemed unsure about where to focus. Something about what was being shared was making her uneasy, afraid of betraying a similar interest. Not that there was anything particularly wrong with religious people taking their piety in earnest, just that Doris wasn't in that space, at least, not at present. She enjoyed singing in the church choir, the challenge of Handel and Bach and Healey Willan and the joy of less taxing contemporary choral music, but she wasn't all that steady in her own faith or even convinced about the truths alluded to by doctrines such as God's benevolence and Christ's redemptive work, the communion of saints and the possibility of resurrection. The Virgin Birth authored by the same God who cursed Eve and all women with pregnancy and labor pains was just too much of a stretch for the imagination of her heart. The sound of Doris sucking air through a straw in her iced-tea glass brought the church conversation to a halt.

"Oops! Pardon me, ladies. I didn't mean to be rude. Keep talking if you wish. I need to get back on the buying trail if I really am going to make any dent in my Christmas list. What do you say we meet up again at the Deer Valley Trail exit around 3:30?"

Myra glanced at Ola and Frances by way of checking. "That sounds fair," she said. "And don't worry about lunch. It's on me ladies, my treat. Season's Greetings!"

"Thank you, Myra," (Frances).

"That's so kind of you," (Doris).

"My joy," (Myra). "I've been learning some things from my gracious sister-in-law."

Ola blushed a little as Doris trundled away.

"So, I'll see you two again at 3:30 if I don't cross paths with you somewhere else in this concourse during our afternoon rounds," said Frances excusing herself from table.

"Yes. 3:30 or so," Myra agreed. "When you say 'rounds' you make me feel like a nurse in a hospital."

"Force of habit," Frances called back. She was a nurse at a long-term care facility. The kind of nurse who could handle a butt-in, know-it-all, meddlesome family member like Jules' sister so that old Mr. Stedman might enjoy a lot more breathing-room in his final stages of life and the company of at least one son who was not averse to being near to him and saying, "I love you, Dad. I love you."

Such was Myra's tangent of thought as the waitress brought their luncheon bill. She left sufficient to cover the cost plus tip, then she and Ola made their way back out into the mall for their own afternoon foray.

Sarducci's Men's Wear would not have been a shop Ola would have inspected in search of pyjamas and a robe for Pops. It was Myra who had that kind of consumer sense, who knew her father's favorite colours (jade and jet black) and his preferred fabrics (rayon not cotton). It was excellent quality bed-wear for a reasonable price. The robe came with matching black slippers.

"Wow!" Ola exclaimed. "This outfit might make Pops look pretty sexy."

"And why not?" Myra retorted scarcely stifling a giggle at Ola's unusual boldness. "After all he is one grand old Dad to us all, isn't he? Why not give him another shot at being...how would Wilton put it...debonair?"

"Yes, you're right. Debonair it is. This is for you, Pops, oo-la-la!"

"Oh, ho, oh. Ola-la-la!," Myra picked up straining for a pun. "I've never known you to be so amusing. It's delightful. This whole day has been just one splendid blessing after another."

"Yes it has, Myra, indeed. It was a good idea."

The salesclerk gift wrapped Ola's purchases before he rang them in. Ola grabbed Myra's arm as they wandered out into the corridors. They walked together European-style and Myra didn't feel the least bit of embarrassment.

"You know," Ola continued the thread of their conversation, "except for Frances bringing up my cabin during lunch, I haven't thought a bit about anything lost in that storm."

H. Lee Disher

"And there's little need to right now," Myra went on. "Besides, with the insurance and the promises of your neighbours, you know the barn and sheds and cabin are going to be rebuilt. And, once Tyler gets a load of his collective Christmas present from us all, Striker won't be missed half so much."

"I don't know about that, Myra, Striker will always have a special place in Tyler's heart, and yes, in mine too; but God has made our hearts so spacious, there's always room for other loves."

"Speaking of which, and I don't mean to be intrusive, are you any bit envious of Carol Morton getting along so well with Wilton?"

"No, Myra. I don't think so. I'm very happy for her and for him. Wallis is a wonderful neighbour and a good friend. Perhaps several years ago, two years or so after Louie left, I may have entertained the possibility of Wallis being more than a friend, but I've come to realize he's not really my type, as you say. And, at the moment, I'm quite content being single."

Such a splendid day it was. Such a strengthening and deepening of the relationship between these two women could not have been foreseen. Some might say a softening of their protective shields was bound happen someday. Perhaps. But one couldn't force that, nor even predict it given their previous reserved affection one to another. That too had been acceptable and comfortable, and it was still there ready to slip back into should this new honesty suddenly become suspect for no real reason at all. Relationships are seldom progressively incremental, they oscillate. And, sometimes, they shatter awaiting re-assembly, or not.

Suffice it to say that the rest of this day continued along the incremental lines with which it began. The reunion at 3:30 actually took place at 3:25. The trip home to Okotoks featured brief catalogues of the finds of the afternoon and more tales of "some of the funniest or weirdest things that every happened in my family were...." Laughter, a bit of sympathy and intentional listening shared the air space. Four meandering mothers made inroads not only into their Christmas shopping endeavours, but also into those regions of familiarity where acquaintance passes on towards friendship and steps forward towards truer sisterhood.

"Let's do something like this again sometime soon."

"Yes, let's."

Take your pick. Any two of the four could have said such things.

# Chapter 18:
# Uncle Louie

The church calendar is the only reliable, fixed factor about December in Alberta: four Sundays of Advent, Christmas Eve, Christmas Day, St. Andrew's (Boxing) Day and New Year's Eve Vigil at Knox Presbyterian. All else was variable: timetables for hockey teams and figure-skating practices at the Okotoks arena, local school and church concerts, neighbourhood dinner parties, the last day of school before holiday time, garbage pickup, where families would have Christmas dinner, births, deaths, occasional marriages and marital break-ups, crime rates and criminal infractions, Highway Traffic Act tickets and warnings issued, the arrival and departure of illnesses, the price of cheese and produce—all of these differ from one occasion to the next. The weather is likewise highly unpredictable. Sunny and cloudy days intermingle. Maybe rain or sleet or snow or slush and on rare occasions hail will fall. Raw, silent, cold, still days will be followed by frost-bearing winds or chinook-like warmer currents. Some days, one might experience three different changes in weather conditions. Tracking the weather in December in Alberta is like trying to keep up with a chameleon in a square meter of turf containing swamp, savannah, rain forest, Carolingian forest, desert, rocky canyons and tundra. Layers and changes of clothes were regularly thrown on or peeled off as needed and one carried a host of accessories just in case.

For the Stedman and Davis families there was always one other vacillating inconsistency: Uncle Louie. He would show up unannounced, leave almost as abruptly, or hang around for an unspecified length of time, make waves, revisit old wounds or languish in silence emitting only occasional grunts, snorts, one-word responses or non-sequiturs, burps and farts. Somehow or other he commandeered the centre of attention, surprising the children with his generosity and aggravating the adults with his irrepressible, quixotic temperament. He was a burden tolerated rather than borne and seldom, if ever, gladly; a corn awaiting plastering. Plastered was the one thing one could count on either when he arrived or before he left. If you had no liquor to offer or serve him, he packed enough of his own anyway. His one concession to Ola's sense of decency (though Pops, Myra, and Jules held similar standards in the presence of children and young people most of the time as well), was that he relinquished profanity in their presence. Such was not however always the practice of the guests he often brought in tow.

On December 19, 1999, Louie Davis landed at 35 Dewdney Common sober at 8:45 A.M. A small overnight case indicated this would be one of his shorter sojourns. Jules answered the bell. "Well, here you are as irregular as a clock in an Antung prison." (Jules' father had been a Korean War veteran). "Tyler! Rebecca! Uh-hum, Myra!" he called out. "Uncle Louie's here!" Tyler pushed back his chair from the kitchen table and came out to offer greetings. Rebecca, clad in her pale green chenille housecoat, cried down from the top of the stairs, "Hi, Uncle Louie, I'll see you in a few minutes, I'm about to hop into the shower."

Myra made a quick catch of a plate she had just let drop while washing up after breakfast. Her back muscles tightened some as she yelled from the kitchen, "I'm arms deep in dishwater right now, Louis," (she always used his proper name.) "I suppose there's time for a coffee if you'd like one."

"Go ahead," Jules encouraged, "I'll take your bag down the basement guest room." Jules, in fact, had already picked it up and was half way there before he finished that sentence, sighing his own inner sigh of relief. "Good. Myra can manage the first barrage this time," he said to himself, taking his time.

"I have to go upstairs and start getting ready too, Uncle Louie," Tyler offered apologetically. "It is Sunday."

"Yeah, right...Sunday," Louie replied not quite getting it and making his way to the kitchen. "Myra, big sis," he said with some sense of genuine approbation, seeking to cement a modicum of welcome, "there you are, still straight up and gorgeous, apron and dish-soap and all."

Myra wiped her hands on a dish-towel, moved to the coffee-maker and poured a fresh cup for her brother. "Whoops, one slop of milk, right?" she asked turning back to the refrigerator before she handed it to him.

"Bingo! Sis. Great memory."

Her shoulders relaxed slightly in the process of serving her brother reflecting a somewhat- eased atmosphere that had pervaded the house when he stepped through the door. Everyone noticed he was alone this time. No frumpy Klingon floozie in her forties on his arm this time. No blonde bombshell. No red-headed stripper he had befriended in Spokane. No freaky-haired, tattooed, tongue-studded twentysomething still looking like a lost teenager. No native woman he just picked up the day before in a bar in Medicine Hat. Birds of a feather: the washed-out or roughed-up or bedraggled feathers worn by losers. Actually Ms. Twenty-something was the pick of the crop. Unlike the others she was actually working on her master's degree in Anthropology at the University of Alberta in Edmonton. Pressure was on. She had no time or money that year to go back East to visit her folks. Hooking up with a charmer like Louie was simply a means to a Christmas meal ticket. She saw the light before Epiphany and dumped him, heading back to her research and a recently-tenured young professor of chemistry and microbiology she met at the graduate pub on campus on New Years' Eve. Come May the studs were gone and she settled for a more conventional hair style. Losing her didn't bother Louie. So much of his life was characterized by spurts of easy-come, easy-go. Louie is a tiddly-wink.

"Memory might be something you could try to cultivate, Louis," said Myra reprovingly. "It *is* Sunday morning. In forty-five minutes or so, we're all heading out to church. And you know the rule. None of us leaves you alone while we're out. Not since you ripped Ola off for that hundred dollars five years ago."

"Well then, I'll just haul my behind out to the farm and visit good old Dad. Ola will be out too, off to the onion-dome in South Calgary."

"No can do, Lou. Pops is away to a kind of stock auction with Punky McAllister. Shhh! It's a secret we're keeping from one special person in this house."

"Well then, I guess I'll have to go where angels like me fear to tread. Golly, I haven't been to a church service in I don't know how many years. I reckon there's a quiet corner pew near the back where I can hunker down so as not to embarrass you."

"Nonsense. In God's house everyone is welcome. Though, in your case, I wish the Almighty could make an exception."

"Well, ain't that a pretty piece of hypocrisy!"

"Louis! Don't start. We are brother and sister even though I wish it weren't so. Nonetheless, I simply meant that in church we can try to exhibit better, more tolerant behaviour."

"Okay. So do I get a star for good behaviour for going?"

Myra glared like a cobra winding up for a spit.

"All right. I get it! Sorry. I'd better head downstairs to the spare bathroom and see what I can do to freshen up."

"Freshen up!" The phrase shot needles back at him from the mirror. "It'll take more than a shave and a bar of soap to make any real dint in that colossal project."

Going to church was a scary prospect. He knew enough to know that he ought to have knocking knees in the vicinity of an awesome God. He'd been through three or four rehabilitation centres already to get a sense of how huge a lost cause he just might be. Somehow, he never managed to get motivated enough to make any first steps that might matter. Any attempts he had made were comparable to trying to eat an ice cream cone in Ecuador without any dribbles running down your hand. He knew how to survive in the revolving-door world to which he had become accustomed. Bottom-feeders might be able to turn into carp, but not into salmon, that would be a big stretch. And butterfly fish? Never in your wildest dreams. For now he could handle a trip to church like a prisoner's day-out in a botanical garden. Warden Myra would keep her watchful eye on his leg-irons. "Don't even think about secreting a key underneath your tongue." A smile crossed his face. Louie lathered up and stroked his face with care. God knows, he had enough exterior scars and stripes as it was without nicking himself open any more. His interior landscape was too corroded to merit any further thought at this moment in time.

As they were all headed out the door, Louie called Myra aside, "Pssst, sis," he asked as he detained her at the door, "could you spot me some small change or a fiver for the collection? All I have is twenties."

Myra fetched a couple of toonies from her purse and tossed them to him. "God would be quite happy with a twenty. You could see it as, "Here, Lord, have a couple of drinks on me!"

"Now who's hittin' below the belt?" Louie returned verging on a scowl.

"Below the belt is apparently where you think your brains are located."

"Oo! How very Christian of you, sis," Louie responded dropping one of his hands on top of hers. "Let's say we get rollin' and I'll do my best not to contaminate you."

For that he got a smart smack in the rump as he stepped up into the front seat beside Jules and Myra climbed into the back beside Rebecca.

"So, Tyler, what are you packin' these days?" Louie made his inquiry as the van backed out onto the Common and an upper bedroom curtain in the house on the right side fell back into place concealing a snarl and an ethnic "Hrmmph!" "Every year I pop in, you just keep bulkin' up like a prize fighter."

"I'm weighing in around 165 pounds right now, Uncle Louie. I get a little workout in the weight room at school and more at the mini-gym at the training stables."

"Training stables? Oh yeah, that's right, rodeo bound, eh? If you ever change your mind to try driving ponies from a sulky, I could set you up and give you some pointers."

"I doubt it, Uncle Louie. Not my idea of the human-horse connection. And think of the money you'd be betting on me and never being able to collect."

"You're getting to be a bit of a cruise missile like the woman who gave you birth. Point taken. What about Alex? Is he into this rodeo rigmarole too?"

"Not very deeply. He sometimes partners with me in team roping. Pops is all the coach he gets in riding. Once a month he comes with me for roping lessons. Mostly, his heart is set on other interests right now."

"Yeah, I can imagine. Is she cute?"

"She's a knockout for a fourteen-year-old, Uncle Louie," chimed Rebecca.

"Well, there's someone not afraid to give me the straight goods. Could be some stepfather charm rubbed off on him."

"Could be just the usual culprits, Uncle Louie. Raging hormones."

"Tyler!" Myra gasped. "Not in front of Rebecca."

"It's okay, Mom. Mrs. Corsini had a discussion about hormones in our grade six health class about a month ago. She con-fis-cated—is that the right word?—a teen magazine from Vivian Frankenburg wondering what she and a couple of other girls were finding so amusing. When they showed her the article that set them off giggling, Mrs. Corsini read it out to everyone and the lesson was on."

"Opportunity knocks for Louie! Mrs. Corsini sounds like a woman after my own heart."

"Louis," Myra interposed assuming her warden's function, "Mrs. Corsini is, to my knowledge, happily married and, therefore, out of bounds of your heart and any other part of you for that matter."

"Aye, aye, Madame Capitaine. Do you think you could put your sword down?"

Tyler and Rebecca snickered. Jules smirked. The van pulled into an empty space in the parking lot of St. Paul's United. Like all of Louie's surprise visits, this one was shaping up to assume its own inimitable configuration. A lop-sided cubic rhombus comes to mind.

The Stedman contingent made its way into the sanctuary and sat just shy of half-way up the left-hand side. Rebecca was on the aisle so that she could leave for Sunday school part way through the service. Louie sat next to her, then Myra, Tyler and Jules. With five minutes to go before worship began, they watched the rest of the empty spaces in the pews pretty much fill in.

Church-going was regaining ground as a popular practice in Okotoks. St. Paul's United had been experiencing growth over the past six years because they decided to put special emphasis on programming for children and youth; and, because Rev. Fanshawe's leadership had been solid, enthusiastic, caring and generally well-received by the congregation and the surrounding commu-nity. Her ministry among them began six years ago. She was a fairly effective preacher and excelled in people skills and in offering pastoral care support and visitation to her flock.

"Well now, a lady minister!" Louie exclaimed in a whisper as Rev. Fan-shawe appeared at the lectern, "I have been away from church for a while."

"Nora is also married with three grown children and as out-of-bounds for you as Mrs. Corsini," Myra hastened to mutter under her breath.

Smiles and titters spread across their half of the pew. Rev. Fanshawe and some laypeople proceeded to share some announcements and then everyone was asked to greet one another "in the name of Jesus." Louie rather enjoyed that even though it was certainly not his accustomed way of uttering Jesus' name. He allowed Myra to introduce him to the striking, slender woman with silver-blonde hair sitting in front of them. She was quite nicely proportioned in Louie's estimation, almost six feet tall, with a trim, angular nose and pointy chin, wearing a pale blue dress suit of worsted wool and nylon blend with navy accessories.

"Lynda Jenkins (that would be "Lumpy's" mother), this is my brother Louis Davis from...from..." Myra was at a loss, not knowing where Louie was currently hanging his hat.

"Lloydminster, Miss Jenkins, a nice, homey little place," Louie offered.

*Yeah*, *right*, Myra thought to herself, *homey as in it has a race track or an off-track betting parlour there, and a fifteen by twenty room at the Flophouse-and-Floozie Inn.*

"Nice to meet you, Mr. Davis," Lynda Jenkins answered back, "greetings in the name of Jesus, our Lord. Oh, and it's Mrs. Jenkins."

That became obvious as a tall man about six foot five wearing an expensive Armani-type suit and Gucci leather shoes slipped into the pew beside her. Herbert Jenkins had been settling their new-born daughter into the church nursery.

"And this is my husband, Herb. Herb, this is Myra Stedman's brother, Louis Davis. He lives in Lloydminster."

"Good morning. Pleased to meet you. Peace of Christ." Herb Jenkins replied curtly.

Rev. Fanshawe bid the congregation to prepare their hearts to enter into the spirit of worship and the service proceeded. Louie got a few chuckles out of her children's story, as did others in the congregation. Her sermon was informative and interesting as she talked about the difficulties of female peasant life in Palestine being exacerbated (was that the word she used?) for an unmarried, suddenly pregnant teenager like Mary. She shared some stories of some of the peasant women she had met during a recent study tour in Nicaragua in October and connected the feelings of heightened expectations among all such women that someday a Deliverer would come who would topple the mighty and elevate the lowly. Did that mean there might be hope for a low-life like Louie himself, who, unlike those peasant women, had been pretty much the author of his own misfortunes? Was there hope for all kinds of women he knew who found themselves knocked up whether they had been willing participants or not? And for the men who helped them into that predicament, most of whom took off? Was there hope for all his down-on-their-luck drinking buddies back at Ned's Junction in Lloyd? For Slashmouth and Hobnob Hickey and One-eyed Sadie? He had seen them in an exacerbated condition plenty of times and had been a partner in exacerbation just as often. What a word! He liked the "ass" part of it. That sounded bang-on right.

Drifting into this train of thought may have contributed to the trouble into which Louie was about to tumble. Some of it had to do with a build-up of abdominal pressure that began during the receiving of the offerings and which Louie fought to subdue during the pastoral prayers and into the final hymn. It was then that a second major flub irresistibly presented itself.

Years ago, Louie had heard and re-told the joke about the man who got two black eyes at church: one for pulling free a length of skirt and slip stuck in the butt-crack of the lady standing in front of him, and the other for figuring she liked it the way it was *"so he reached out and put it back!"* Well, there was Mrs. Jenkins standing in front of him with a crease in her skirt just like the lady in the joke. Louie couldn't help himself. He reached out and tugged on the stuck skirt until it came free. Lynda Jenkins whipped around and flung her non-verbal shock and reprimand square into his face. He felt like one of those circus performers strapped to a spinning wheel while a blind-folded knife-thrower slings blades targeted to just graze your flesh on all sides. Louie didn't dare move onto part two of the joke. More trouble came anyway. As the congregation launched into the last verse of the closing hymn:

> *Hail, the heaven-born Prince of Peace!*
> *Hail, the Sun of Righteousness!*
> *Light and life to all he brings,*
> *Risen with healing in his wings."*

Louie could no longer restrain the abdominal gases exacerbating his rectal passage. Fortunately the congregation was singing loud enough to muffle the sound of the fart Louie let rip just as they reached the words *"born to raise us...."* But, it spread. It smelled. Louie fled for cover.

Myra was highly embarrassed. Jules and Tyler just barely managed to stifle outbursts of laughter as they accompanied her to the church hall for coffee hour. They avoided contact with Lynda Jenkins and drank up quickly. Louie was nowhere evident in sight around the church, so they headed to their van in the parking lot. There, hunkered down, doubled over between the hedge and the front bumper was Louie. He was wincing from some pain in his stomach. As he stood up, red welts and some swelling was evident on his right cheek and around his left eye.

"Louis! Just get in!" Myra snarled.

"I'm sorry, Sis, Jules, Tyler, Rebecca, I'm truly sorry," he said in earnest contrition as he slunk himself slowly into the front seat, "I just couldn't help it. I...."

"Oohhhhhh!" Myra fluttered in prolonged exasperation.

"I found a men's room and just hid in one of the cubicles feeling awful. I even prayed right there asking God for forgiveness, asking God to make me smarter. I know I'm one of those people whose elevator doesn't hit the top floor, as they say. Heck, in my case, it sometimes doesn't get much past the mezzanine! So, I was cowering there but I guess I forgot to lock the door and the next thing I know, that 250-pound plus Mr. Jenkins bursts in and begins to pound on me. He took all of about thirty seconds to plough me a few times and then he bolts for the door. 'Merry Christmas,' I yelled out at him, 'Jesus loves you too!' I heard him hesitate and just about let the door slam. He stopped it just in time before the noise might have drawn attention to us. 'Shit!'

he muttered softly as he extracted his trapped forearm. 'That goes for you to, Myra Stedman's brother. You just stay right there over that bowl and consider it the home you deserve to dwell in.' He's just about right, you know, I'm not even worthy of a manger."

"Don't be so hard on yourself, Uncle Louie," Tyler risked speaking up. "Everybody makes mistakes. Maybe not quite the doozies you manage to pull off, but mistakes all the same."

"Yeah, and God takes care of them," Rebecca added. "Forgive us our trespasses whether it's kids like me getting into Mom's make-up without permission or guys like you letting go farts in church."

"Rebecca!" Myra screamed.

"Sorry, Mom, my Sunday School class heard of it from Kevin Noseworthy. It sounded really funny at the time, and the thought of a little stench flying up Mrs. Jenkins' snobby nose...."

"I think you've made enough of your point, Rebecca," said Jules admonishingly.

Words ceased. The van headed homeward in silence until after several minutes Myra pursed her lips and let out a mirthful splutter. The tension visible in five sets of shoulders relaxed. Louie was absolved for the moment. Myra had acknowledged agreement with her daughter—a little stink landing on Lynda Jenkins did look good on the woman.

What didn't look good on Lynda were the puffy eyes she sometimes wore to the pharmacy counter, the occasional bruises on her forearms that appeared when her sleeve rode up as she reached for her prescriptions, the frequent presence of muscle-relaxants in her shopping basket, and, once or twice, a bit of a limp in her gait. Was she a more frequent recipient of the outbursts of Herb's temper? Myra considered inviting Lynda for an outing to the local tea-room for serious heart-to-heart. She would pass on the phone number for the community help-line connected to the local Interval House for battered women.

Lunch at 35 Dewdney Common amounted to warmed-up Friday-night-leftover pizza and non-alcoholic beverages of choice. Myra fixed up a couple of ice-packs for her brother and then announced that she and Rebecca still had to go do a little shopping. Tyler was content to curl up in an arm-chair to continue reading *The Virginian*. Jules invited Louie to the rec room for a game of pool. "Not even for a friendly five bucks, though and no double or nothing on anything."

"I can handle that," Louie agreed.

"Oh," Myra said catching herself before heading out the door, "I'd better phone Ola and tell her to set an extra place for dinner. She won't be especially thrilled about it."

"Neither will I," Louie rejoined.

"Well, that's life the way it is for now. So let's see if we can make do with it, shall we?"

After making that phone call, Myra flew away Rebecca in tow. Tyler immersed himself in his novel. Jules and Louie went downstairs and racked 'em up.

• • •

Louie's apprehensions about visiting the farm were genuine. He looked forward to seeing Alex. Pops was always tolerant but difficult to face. Facing Ola was like walking on tundra with only a windbreaker for protection. She wasn't bitter. She was simply like ice in his presence, ice on steel. She still exhibited the patience of Jesus. The compassion of Christ went into hiding when Louie was around. No amount of mental flagellation she exerted on herself for getting herself into such a state could bring about a thaw.

Everyone else got a welcoming hug from Ola as they arrived on the farm later that afternoon.

Louie got a flat "Hello. If you want a beer, you'll have to go get one from your father's frig."

*Fret not yourself because of the wicked, be not envious of wrongdoers! For they will soon fade like the grass and wither like the green herb.* Psalm 37:1-2 came to her mind. Ola was willing to encourage them in achieving their own demise. Louie, in her mind, was already like dried-out, browning summer savory, hanging upside-down by a thread.

"Pops isn't back yet from his excursion with Punky, Louie," Alex chimed in by way of greeting. "Maybe Tyler and Uncle Jules and I can show you the damage the storm did to the barns. If you and Uncle Jules want to grab a beer from Pops' frig on the way by...."

"That's sounds like a plan to me," Louie answered, taking the hint that his stepson was eager to help keep oil and water separated.

They don't mix, and on frozen water oil has nowhere to go but off. He also knew that Tyler and Jules were co-opted as a safety net. Alex was not yet in any space where he was ready for an "I'm sorry I've been so rotten and unsupportive" speech headed for conciliatory dialogue between a step-father and estranged step-son.

They didn't, in fact, stop to grab a beer. They just went and surveyed the ruined barn and talked about what it would take to restore it. They walked on along one of the horse trails, passed over onto Wilton's property and helped Alex gather up eggs in one of the hen houses. Not much talk. Just four guys putting in time.

When they came back to the Davis farm, Pops had returned. He was just coming out of his back porch to meet them when he stopped in his tracks and noticed Louie was among them. Ola and Myra had not seen Pops return in order to give him a heads-up.

"Well, I felt the wind had shifted and started coming from the north-east with a bit of bite in it. Usually an Alberta clipper hits the Dakotas to the south and then turns east, it doesn't often land on us and hover around. Good day, son. I see you're still alive, and I'm thankful for that. It's good you haven't forgotten about us altogether."

"Well, I guess that's right, Dad. If that means you haven't completely given up on me yet, I'll take that as a little incentive. God knows, I've given all of you reason to want to forget about me for good." A generalized confession was the most Louie could venture in Alex's presence with others around.

"Say, speaking of God, Dad, guess what? I was in church today for the first time in I don't know how long. I was just inching closer to believing that there was indeed still hope for me until the service was almost over. Then, I managed, as usual, to make an ass of myself."

Recounting the story, these many hours after the fact, had already taken some of the shame and turpitude out of it. Alex found the whole incident hilarious. Pops considered it highly amusing. Before long, all five of them were engulfed in gales of laughter. Men.

When they entered Ola's house for dinner, it was soon apparent that sound carries.

"What vas so funny?" Ola ventured to ask.

"Oh, Ola," Pops ventured to respond, "just imagine two words and you'll get the idea. 'Louie,' and 'church.'"

Ola glanced at Myra and Rebecca for deciphering.

"I'm not sure you really want to know right now," Myra ventured.

"That's one of the safest bets any of us could ever make," Louie tagged on.

"Some day after Christmas, Ola, you and I will do lunch again," Myra said concluding this segment of repartee.

Tyler and Alex worked at keeping Rebecca from spilling the beans. It was like a short-lived doubles tennis match and the judge had no idea what had just transpired or who had scored what points, if any.

"Vell, okay zen, if you say so. Come to za table. Dinner's ready." Nervousness escalated in Louie's presence. Ola had slipped back into her old country accent.

Dinner was negotiated over guarded conversations. Safe subjects only. The food was, as always, wholesome and delicious. The cherry custard torte Ola served for dessert was almost a propitiatory offering. It had always been one of Louie's favourites. How was she to know that the Sunday she had planned to serve it anyway, would be the day he decided to breeze through their lives again? Or, was this another instance of the Spirit at work in mysterious, fortuitous ways taking her at times into the midst of situations whither she would rather not be placed? Terror lurked in the slightest crack in the ice.

Louie would soon provide her with a means of escaping what she herself was not at all ready to face. After dinner, he went to the van and brought back a small satchel to the parlour where they were all sitting sipping tea, coffee, hot chocolate. "I have gifts this time," he announced.

Ola stiffened as he began to pass out envelopes and a few wrapped thin cartons. There were Christmas cards with crisp fifty-dollar bills in them for Alex, Tyler and Rebecca. Jules and Pops opened rectangular parcels to reveal official Calgary Flames ties, (unbeknownst to Louie, Jules already had one), and gift certificates for the Saddledome Sports Shop. Myra opened a square box to discover a gift certificate for Bijou leather goods and a rather elegant hand-painted scarf.

"The lady at the Bay sales counter helped me pick it out, sis. I hope it's in colours you like." "It is, Louis. It's actually...quite beautiful. I'm...I'm speechless."

Ola knew it was coming her turn. Louie reached into his satchel for one more parcel. She saw the 12" x 12" square box beginning to emerge, she heard it rattle sweet familiarity.

"No!" she shouted. "Please don't, Louie. Take it back. Vatever is in dere uff cash value, redeem it yourself. As for the other, I vouldn't feed dem to Vilton's pigsss! Ze best prezent you could giff to me vould be to get on za next bus back to Lloydminster...and stay dere!"

She dashed out of the room and shut herself up in her bedroom. She would not come out to say good bye. She already had.

Stunned by the awkwardness of the moment, Louie held back for a couple of minutes before breaking the silence. "It's Laura Secord's. She always loved them. Nothing like them was ever available to her back in her part of the Ukraine. The fancy Belgian chocolates that could be found were far too expensive and too rich and sweet to her taste. Uri had once put three such truffles in her Christmas stocking, she told me. They made her sick. Now, it's me that does that. She's right. I'm headed back out on the bus tomorrow. Merry Christmas, folks, anyway."

"Merry Christmas, Uncle Louie," said Rebecca running over to him unable to restrain offering a hug decorated with tears. Pops went to the den to blow his nose. Jules managed to maintain composure. Myra fought to remain unmoved, and won. Tyler gulped, looked at Alex and saw a mirror image of a teenage boy crying unabashed. Not buckets, just several trickling streams accompanied by occasional sniffles.

Pops came back with the Parcheesi board. The table was cleared and three young ones took on Grandpa and an uncle in a couple of rounds as Jules and Myra put leftovers away and did up the dishes. In a couple of hours or a little less, Pops wandered back toward his house and waved "Good-bye" to a van-full of family returning to town. Snow fell lightly. The sky was cloudy and fogged-over. The wind had shifted direction again. The chill in the air had a feel of permanence. Pops's right foot slipped on the snow-covered bottom step of his back entry-way. The rest of his body toppled to the ground.

"Damn!" he muttered. "There's a couple more bruises I'll have to try to hide from Ola."

Feeling foolish and slightly furious he pushed himself upright in a hurry and almost threw himself up through the entry-way into his kitchen. It was all too fast. A twinge of pain shot up Pops' left arm. His left breast tightened. He gasped for breath a couple of times. He grabbed out a chair from the kitchen table and eased himself in to it. Then the pain stopped. Things settled back in order.

*Whew! Just one of them darn spasms*, Pops thought seeking to console himself.

•　　•　　•

Monday morning, the Stedmans bid Uncle Louie farewell. Jules dropped him off at the bus depot in Calgary en route to a half-day of work.

"See you again sometime. Maybe give us a little advance notice next time, eh."

"Yeah, maybe, Jules. Maybe. Maybe sometime."

As Jules drove away he finished his thought, "like when the Flames play the Toronto Maple Leafs for the Stanley Cup." That would be such a longshot, the odds would defy being posted.

# Chapter 19:
# Winter's Challenges

Christmas morning came with its own odd feeling. That's how it struck Tyler as he awakened at 8:00 A.M. to the sound of Rebecca asking her parents "Is it time?" Something else was up. He couldn't get a handle on it. It wasn't related to the absence of Uncle Louie. It wasn't related to the sound of carols coming from the newly-installed carillon at St. James Roman Catholic Church, though he surmised that not everyone in town would be pleasantly stirred by seasonal songs of faith at that time of day on Christmas. There were at least five Jehovah's Witness families that he could think of in town; Herb Jenkins had probably been up late over-celebrating and would be cursing the "crazy dogans" for aggravating his hangover, (Lynda, Lumpy, Monica: beware!); and Old Lady Ellerbeck, who lived in a two-room flat over the bakery downtown, who loved to sleep in, and whom everyone referred to as "Miss Faversham," would rouse up into some spinning state of disorientation and rush to the window to see if angel choirs had actually come for her at last. Nor did the strangeness of this day seem related to Mr. Wojniewski out on his back deck clad in a heavy parka over his nightclothes, bare feet stuck into thermal boots, busy frying fish on his barbecue. For breakfast? Old Polish custom? Or simply another quirk in the idiosyncrasy that defined Wojniewski family patterns? One man's weirdness is another's sanity. Odd was in the air without connection to any of these things that filtered through Tyler's mind.

Pause. Blink. Remove more sleep from eyelid crevices. Stand and file toward the bathroom. A slight sensation strikes him that it may have something to do with Mom, Dad, and Rebecca being a bit more silent this year 'round, with something softer about their Christmas morning tip-toe. Maybe. Proceed. Christmas as usual. Gather around the tree with morning coffee or warm cider and take turns opening gifts. Rejoice with Rebecca as she adores the new skating outfits fashioned by Aunt Ola and dances with delight as she opens her Santa envelope containing a pair of tickets to the Canadian National Figure-Skating Championships in Montreal. Share the joy as Myra opens the pearl necklace Jules picked out for her and Jules comes close to tears over a new full-length leather coat. He had finally parted with his tattered, split-elbowed leather jacket in November. The down parka he had been wearing so far through winter kept him warm, but lacked plenty in the style department. Tyler voiced appreciation for a couple of new sweaters, some compact discs from a couple of his cousins; rolled back his eyes at a rather garish tie from picky Aunt "Sis" and thanked Rebecca for a new set of spurs, silver with imitation ruby insets. Then peculiarity perched square on him. Where was his gift from Santa? From Mom and Dad? From Ola? From Pops?

Jules caught him in mid-wonderment, "It's a wait-and-see Christmas this year, son. That's why we're heading out to Pops's and Ola's as soon as we can tidy up a bit, grab some breakfast, freshen up and switch into whatever we planned to wear for the day."

Rebecca was off to her bedroom and the shower in a shot. Tyler had never seen her so beside herself over someone else's surprise. She had done so exceptionally well under the pressure of keeping a huge secret. She had always caved before. Curiosity seized him like an over-cinched saddle. He helped his mother and father with a little straightening up, wolfed down orange juice, toast, and scrambled eggs and ketchup and then raced into his own personal hygiene and raiment routine noticing in passing that the bathroom mirror was suggesting he might have to learn shaving soon.

Everybody rushed without tripping over anyone else or complaining about being held up. It was like an intuitively-choreographed improvised ballet. Myra packed the angel food cake, the honey-and-nutmeg mini-carrots and broccoli au gratin she had made the day before into a cooler and set it in the back of the van. All hands climbed on deck and the Stedman family sailed off for farm country, smiling and laughing all the way. Had there been sleigh bells, Rebecca would have rung them incessantly.

They pulled into Pops's laneway. Inside Pops's place, Ola, Alex and Pops were waiting with the same intensity of eagerness Tyler had felt at home. There was a decorated tree. There was cider mulling in slow-cooker. There were Ola's Christmas cake, shortbread and Ukrainian pastries on a platter. There were open candy-boxes, thanks to Pops, of ju-jubes and maple buds. But no visible present.

"What is this?" Tyler asked totally perplexed. "Am I not noticing what I'm supposed to see?"

"Nope," Alex answered. "Because it isn't here. It don't fit. An' you still ain't gonna see it right away. Turn around."

Tyler was fully wound now into whatever game was being played. He turned cooperatively while Alex blind-folded him with strip of Pops' handkerchiefs knotted together. "Now, let me help you get your coat and boots back on."

Everybody wrapped up as Alex led Tyler out of the house toward the barns, toward the slightly-more-than-half a barn that was still standing. Tyler's sense of direction and sense of smell told him exactly where he was. Alex removed the blindfold as the family crowded around behind the guest of honor. Tyler opened his eyes and stared at one of Pops's old horse trailers bound up in wide blue ribbon. A large "Merry Christmas, Tyler!" gift tag made from bristol-board and bearing Rebecca's printing hung from the door handle.

"You didn't! You didn't!" Tyler shouted. "Oh my God! You guys. This is too much! Too, too much!"

Pops grabbed up a pair of shears and sliced the ribbon, "Come on now, boy, open it up. We've all been sitting on this secret longer than a vulture waiting for a wounded coyote to die." Tyler shook as he lowered the handle, pulled back the door. There he was: sleek, tan and golden, about thirteen hands high with magnificent withers and sturdy pinions and a head that was already saying, "I'm in love too!"

"Oh my God! Oh my God! Pops, Mom, Dad, Ola, Rebecca, Alex...he's not just a horse, he's a Paso Fino. A Paso Fino crammed with memories of Montana. Oh my God!"

Tyler grabbed up the reins and led the new stallion out into the open for a full inspection. It was magical how this boy and any horse hit it off on contact time after time after time. That just kept the tears of joy flowing around that whole family circle that morning, excepting Myra. Tyler and his new steed fell into instant relationship stroke by stroke, nuzzle for nuzzle, in teardrops and flubber-lips, whinnies, and voiceless exclamations, like watching wax being poured into a mold. He'd never share the thought with her, or anyone else, but, for Tyler, this occasion was more powerful than being naked with Stephanie in Barstoke's pond. The collaborators in this gift subterfuge all concurred though they had no idea about that latter encounter, excepting a somewhat-suspecting Alex. Shared ecstasies are super-savory by virtue of so vast a scarcity.

Yet so short-lived. The satisfactions and delectable gratifications that continued through that Christmas Day reached a rude and abrupt halt on Boxing Day. Winter descended with a whomp and established squatter's rights for the next four months. Most days featured temperatures in the minus 40 range. Far north in Fort McMurray, roads were impassable for three weeks. Those who had ventured out for Christmas couldn't get back home until mid-January. Snows squalls left more than a metre of snow over the southern half of the province. Double that and up once you got past Red Deer and on into Edmonton. Snow so deep you couldn't tell the side of a county road from the beginning of the ditch. Snow so deep some fence-posts disappeared. Snow so deep against some barns you could walk right up to the second-storey hay mow. Snow so deep only the top two feet of goal-post standards were visible on the soccer pitches at the Okotoks Recreation Centre. Snow so deep small children could toboggan, snowboard or learn to ski in their own backyards. And if it melted down some, it was soon replenished. Blizzards recurred weekly. Intermittent sleet added icing to the cold cake piles. Seven skiers, four and then three, died in avalanches in Jasper National Park in February. There had been ten adventurers; rescuers managed to save three. School closures, hydro outages, car accidents in the form of pile-ups, snowmobile deaths by drowning or lost battles with fencing, broken limbs and split trees showed up in random scatterings throughout the season like buckshot. Twenty-two people out of the thirty-six who died of exposure across Canada that winter were in Alberta. "Old Lady" Ellerbeck was one of them. She got lost in a white-out right in the middle of town on March 19. She was found frozen against the wall of the train station at 6:09 A.M. the next morning. Her train came in early. Only two angels on board. That's all the ambulance attendants it took. She was truly light as a feather in her threadbare overcoat and lace-white nightgown and pink fluffy slippers. Wilton lost thirty-two chickens. Other farmers lost cattle, sheep or lambs. Pigs survived. So did seniors who snuck away south from November to May. There's a section of Reno, Nevada called Little Calgary. Stay home and you have to grow hide. Rhinoceros skin is best, especially when covered in grizzly fur. The habits of hardiness form early in the psyche, from toddler stage on. Such is prairie winter, prolonged and unpredictable. Perseverance school. Reality TV devoid of fantasy, as actual experience: "Survivor: Perennial Edition."

Life is lived in the putting on and peeling off of layers. Share-holders in lip balm and skin cream make a fortune. Wine and cider are mulled frequently. Shrubs stay long under wraps. Block heaters are absolutely essential. Plug-ins are provided in parking lots. The soil sleeps but the oil still flows. Jules Stedman continues his weekday commutes to Calgary and back along with sixty per cent of the population of Okotoks. In-town residents who work locally opt for cross-country skis or snowshoes for travelling to and from their places of employment. Or, like Carol Morton and two other staff members at Dewdney Junior High, who reside in the south-west corner of town, they meet up well-insulated, toting backpacks and jog four kilometers across town to school, weather permitting, sidewalks or streets having been ploughed and cleared, cross-trainers waterproofed by mink oil. The rest often just walk or take a cab. Anything but drive. What's the point? Unless you have stuff to transport or an out-of-town appointment to keep.

Myra Stedman doesn't trust herself to any winter sports equipment other than downhill skis. On work days, she walks to and fro. This winter, she slips twice on patches of ice. The first fall leaves her with a bruised hip and slightly swollen shoulder. Left side wipe-out. The second causes a slight crack in her right elbow. Her turn for six weeks in a cast and sling and sympathy for what Tyler went through. Even though she was left-handed, she didn't suffer smoothly.

Rebecca Stedman breezes through winter as if she herself were a snowflake. She cavorts and cajoles with her friends. She delights in schoolwork. She increases her proficiency as a figure-skater. She masters a double loop, a single lutz and a single salchow. Her instructor arranges for her to work with a choreographer. An eleven-year-old prodigy is coming into her own. On Sunday mornings at 6:00 A.M., Rebecca and two other skaters in her club have arena time all to themselves. Myra makes the effort to be primary chauffeur and cheerleader, even when she can barely manage it. Some Saturday nights her Temazepam doesn't quite kick in. Jules only subbed in twice all winter. For three weeks, Rebecca is laid low by a nasty flu virus presumably picked up at school. She practices her leaps around the house anyway (minus the skates). One day she demolishes the lamp on her bedside table. A lutz landed too close to the sideboards.

While others tend to trudge and complain their way through such a winter, Tyler Stedman saunters or struts as seems needful taking every day in stride. He glides through school work, household chores, family contacts, dates with Stephanie, get-togethers with the gang and bi-weekly rodeo training in High River. No traces of anxiety or restlessness appear. No signs of disappointment. Only steadiness. Only effortless measures of appropriate energies, enthusiasm, empathy, attentiveness or deportment as the case may be. Stephanie counts on him and deepens her adoration. Alex depends on him. Rebecca rejoices in having the neatest older brother on the planet. Everybody loves Tyler though it doesn't make for entertaining television viewing. It does settle in the soul like a psalm of confidence. Or rather, he does. Tyler engenders parental pride in the present and youthful hope for the future. He is so close to being the quintessential son, student, friend of anyone's imagination without trying, without in himself recognizing the sheer quality of his own being — not in any way that might sow a seed of conceit or a breath of inflation of ego—that even the mirror-image at which he stares every day would, if it could separate itself off for a moment or two, gaze back completely impressed. Pops often has such a gaze about him when Tyler is in view or in mind. Ola sees an icon of a saint-in-the-making. Each day another fleck of gold mosaic attaches itself to Tyler's aura, another chip of blue-red-violet-green brightness fills in the garments that enfold him, another flake of flesh-tone illumines his facial features, and his eyes follow you and fill you with their kindness, their humility, their assiduity. Something about it won't sit still however. Most saints, as Ola well knows, have been or become subjected to suffering. A fractured patella is inconsequential. An occasional scrape or bruise after falling from a horse matters little. The arena dream repeats itself over this winter season. Where is this circle? What to make of these riders? And a gray horse, a gray horse with eight legs. And where are the clowns?

Ola had no adjustments to make to a prairie winter. In fact, she had known far worse Ukraine winters. She had her full array of indoor-outdoor options and activities with which to fill her time to occupy her mind and to devote the attention of her heart and her spirit. Such a winter as this was a wondrous opportunity for attending to one's spirit. Before the snowfall, Ola had rescued the *prie-dieu*, the red Madonna icon and night-stand, the torch-moon-sun tapestry and her copy of *The Philokalia* from the wreckage of her *poustinia* cabin. She had done some rearranging of the guest room in her home to accommodate these retreat essentials. Pilgrimage for now could happen on site, at home, yet still in some space apart. Ola had set in a store of food for body and soul, for Pops and Alex and self and family and friends. She had a quilt on the go, a knitting basket full of projects, a bake sale to co-ordinate for St. Bartholomew's

H. Lee Disher

at the end of January and for which to prepare her own contributions, farm accounts to review in readiness for income tax time, seeds to select, worker interviews scheduled for late March, a copy each of *Anna Karenina* and of *The Brothers Karamazov* which she promised herself she would re-read for the fourth time this winter, and her spiritual ghetto temporarily re-located to her spare bedroom.

The bake sale, the quilt, the first half of *The Brothers Karamazov* (how comparable were Alyosha and her nephew?) and looking after Pops and Alex filled up January. For the first two weeks of February, she had the added pleasure of Tyler and Rebecca's company. Tranogco's head office in Houston had selected Jules and another senior vice-president in the Calgary office, Roger O'Connor, to participate in an oil industry convention in Maui during that time. Spouses were welcome to come along—all expenses: flight, accommodation, meals paid; three days of green fees also, but alcohol, other tourist adventures and pleasures not covered. So Jules and Myra got to enjoy two weeks of total respite from winter weather. Fortunately for Myra this happened before fall number two, bruised hip almost healed, shoulder still somewhat tender, nothing to hamper her enjoyment of sun and surf as an arm in a sling would have. During that time, Tyler and Rebecca had two weeks of wintering at the farm. How wonderful! Pops' tender wisdom and tours of the Parcheesi board, and Aunt Ola's cooking, and Alex' hijinks and good humour were all as reliably present as soap operas on afternoon television; and, yes, Charlene Berenson could come for a visit one weekend; and also for Tyler, access to the horses, to his newly beloved Paso Fino as yet unnamed. "Blizzard" came to mind but that didn't seem quite right for a tawny-coloured horse. "Lazy J" would capture a fond memory, but that adjective hardly applied to such a spirited steed. Nope, nothing came in early February that would settle the question. But time on the farm came, time neither Tyler nor Rebecca would trade for a trip anywhere else in the world. Time they relished more than a month of luaus in mid-winter.

Time for a man and his no-name horse to get better acquainted. By February, Tyler's new Paso Fino was accustomed to being saddled, sat upon, led around and paced around Punky McAllister's indoor corral of sorts, well more like an empty barn. There wasn't much room for getting up any head of steam, but space permitted practicing a few "giddy-ups" and numerous "whoas." What the horse valued more was being unconditionally loved. Spring, though it would be much later coming this year, dangled before them both like the proverbial carrot-on-a-stick, a pregnancy of anticipation, each one eager and waiting to show the other just what he could do. Engagement intent on marriage.

When the sojourn of her niece and nephew were ended, Ola had a week back at the routines she had inaugurated for the season until Frances Evans was due to arrive for her guided retreat.

Ola was apprehensive about being a kind of spiritual mentor. Others who had visited her farm for retreat purposes previously were already part of network of persons familiar with the practice of *poustinia*. All Ola had to do for them was act as a Bed and Breakfast provider and then leave them to their own devices and desires. Frances was a first time pilgrim. She agreed to bring along her own copy of *The Book of Common Prayer*. Ola would recommend that Frances set aside morning, afternoon, evening and compline prayer times each day using that resource with which she already had some familiarity. Knowing Frances's love of food, Ola reckoned rightly that offering an option of only one day of bread-and-water fasting during the week-long ordeal would be plenty for a novice retreatant to handle. For the rest Ola figured having a one-hour morning consultation during which she hoped the Spirit would guide her in selecting Scripture passages, sections of *The Philokalia*, and such that would be appropriate springboards for Frances's daily meditations. As for offering guidelines for the practice of meditation such as deep breathing, mind-clearing exercises and jottings and journaling, Ola was quite comfortable giving help in that regard.

The last week of February, a car bearing Frances Evans to her destination with solitude and quietude crept up Ola's laneway, not out of fear of the unknown, but because freezing rain overnight had made traction slippery and slick. County road crews had salted the roads early in the morning, but neither Ola nor Pops had had a chance to spread cinders and salt on the lane yet. Besides, Frances had shown up three hours earlier than she had indicated.

"My P.T.A. consultation with the principal and guidance staff at the high school was cancelled because of the weather, so I figured I just might as well boogie on out here. O God, Ola, if you only knew how much I really need this time out! I'm just so raring to get at it even though I've never done anything like it before. I just know it's going to be rich!"

All these mouthfuls tumbled from her profusely as she bustled up to the porch bearing a suitcase, an overnight bag, a well-stuffed shoulder bag and a large teddy-bear tucked under her left arm. "Can't go anywhere without Micki to sleep with. Guess I'm just still a big kid at heart." Somehow the notions of simplicity, self-denial and detachment hadn't quite registered with Frances as aids to a spirit of *poustinia*.

"Welcome, Frances," Ola offered charitably. "I'm glad you came. I truly hope this time will be helpful for you. Come, give me a couple of your cases and we'll set them down in your guest room. I expect you won't need even half of what you've brought."

"Oh, I know that too, but that's me. Gerry says I'm a super-graduate of the Girl Guides with the biggest brain tattoo of 'Be Prepared' he's ever witnessed. Then I remind him that 'Be Prepared' is a Boy Scout motto. And he says, 'You'd have made a marvelous Boy Scout too. Now sign me up for two cases of your cookies.' And I say, 'So where did you learn to excel at taking it easy?' And he says, 'I'll show you.' And then we usually get all snuggly, and one thing starts leading to another and then to...you know...THE other! and, Whew! I'm sorry, Ola, that's probably heading into the realm of too much information. See, that's me. I pack too much, I talk too much, I cook too much, I eat too much, I commit to too much, I spend too much while Gerry tries to save too much, I fuss too much, worry too much, spoil my kids too much, maybe even believe too much. If someone started up a chapter of Over-doers Anonymous, I'd be the first one to sign and wind up volunteering to be President within half an hour."

All of this issued voluminously forth as Frances slipped out of her fur-lined boots at the door and followed Ola through the house to the guest bedroom, placed Micki on the pillow shams, set her cases and bags down, removed her scarf, gloves, and goose-down-filled three-quarter length winter coat, and hung it on a hook behind the bedroom door.

"Well then, whew, as you say Frances," Ola replied, almost butting in, "we could be in for an amazing week since my role is going to be to try to help you to do as little as possible and to get by on as little as possible. So to begin with, why not take off that heavy sweater, slip into those comfy woolen slippers poking out of your shoulder bag, and come to the kitchen and sit with me over a hot cup of tea. Okay!"

Ola had been in Canada long enough to mimic some of the more frenzied speech patterns of natives like Frances Evans, and she let all of this fly with joyful mock gusto hoping that it would build rapport and not cause offense. It was a safe risk to take.

Tea time afforded Ola opportunity for taking Frances' personal and spiritual temperature. Talk turned to sharing stories from each of their childhoods as well as present family matters. Frances was fascinated how Ola's tales from Chernivtsi bore similarities to her own formative years growing up in a sizable family on a hand-to-mouth farm near Boisevain, Manitoba: everybody pitching in as soon as they were able, having one's existence determined by the wiles of nature, wearing home-made clothing, pretending poverty was other people's problem or accepting it as a soul-and-character-building discipline.

"If it hadn't been for the generosity and familial love of my mother's mother who with my grandfather had operated a successful small real estate office in Winnipeg, I'd have never been able to go through nursing school. Gramma paid my whole way. Helped put my two brothers through agricultural college and my sister, Kate, through a law degree too. There was always some uneasy tension about it though, like she was making up for the mistake she thought my mother made in marrying a farmer. It was no mistake, my father was a hard-working, gentle, caring man. My mother adored him, relished the simple life, fitted herself into home-making like a debutante's hand slipping into a satin glove. They gave us kids a home, a no-frills happiness, a wholesome existence and their hearts. Dad died in 1992. Mom came to live with Gerry and I two years later. Within seven months she started slipping downhill, getting repetitive and more forgetful, wearing different-coloured socks and her blouse buttoned wrongly. When she got snarly and apt to wander off, it was time to place her in Cedarview Home. I see her every day at work now and she doesn't have a clue as to who I really am. I'm just that nice lady who comes to clip her toe nails, check her blood pressure, and wheel her to the tub room for a bath. It's my turn to give back love, just plain and basic love."

Tissues attended to two sets of temporary tears.

"I think you will slip into *poustinia* time the way your mother nestled into homemaking," Ola interjected. "It will re-cloak you in the spirit of those earlier years. Solace may settle around you silencing some of the frenzy, fretfulness and fearsomeness that presently enfolds your life."

It did. Frances followed instructions and suggestions faithfully embracing the process. Day by day she poured herself into the rhythms and routines: waking to proper prefaces, meditating on the psalm of the day, consuming simple meals, taking fresh air breaks, contemplating Scripture and Ola's selections from *The Philokalia*, keeping a journal, passing through Nones and Treces, Evensong and Compline, concluding each night with "*Lighten our darkness, we beseech Thee, O Lord, and let Thy mercy defend us....*" She underwent the bread-and-water fast on the Thursday. She blanketed herself in a week's worth of blessed benevolence, centering herself and her soul in God as snow continued to augment the pile of white carpeting covering the prairies.

Frances' farewell steeped in gratitude seemed a fitting finale to February.

Ola moved onto the more mundane matters of March: seed selections, worker interviews, preparations for tax time. She worked in some rug-hooking, a stretch of needle-work, the end of *The Brothers Karamazov*, and the opening

H. Lee Disher

two sections of *Anna Karenina*. Was Canada compared to Chernobyl and the Ukraine for her something like Kitty returning to Moscow less confused, less weighed down by the sorrow and dreariness of others having completed her convalescence in Germany? Was Varenka taking shape for her in the form of Frances Evans? Comparisons ceased there. No prince, no Mihail Alexeyevich took tea with her luring her into temptation. The Alex in Ola's life was a completely different ball of wax, or - what was that children's play material? Silly Putty? Kitty's illusory icon of Madame Stahl came softly unveiled. Ola's once-idolized second husband had plummeted ingloriously into disgrace.

Such rueful ruminations were displaced for Ola near the end of March by her annual ritual of fashioning decorative Ukrainian Easter eggs. They are called *pysanky* and Ola painted up a dozen of them every year. Alex, Tyler and Rebecca had a collection of them, one for every year Ola had known them. Ola had a collection of several dozen, some she had made herself but many had been made for her by her mother or passed down from her maternal grandmother. The tradition is that the woman of the house stays up on Easter Eve to make them. Ola liked to work on them even further ahead. No design is ever repeated. Red is the most favoured base colour.

Eggs have long been a resurrection symbol in Christianity, signs of hope, rebirth, new life and recreation. The yellow yolk represents the sun; the egg-white represents the moon. Fresh, fertile eggs are used and each one is individually blessed. Each design is outlined by melted beeswax applied with a special stylus or *kistka*. Waxed eggs are dipped in dyes in clay pots and then set in a bowl in a warm oven. When baked and dry, the eggs are removed, the melted wax is wiped off and fresh wax is reapplied elsewhere around the next section to be colour-dyed. The process is repeated until all chosen colours have been applied and set. It truly is at least an all-night project. The most prevalent designs include stars, birds, sheaves of wheat, flowers, suns, moons, ladders and even spiders. Each egg has its own particular story.

The legend behind *pysanky* tells of a young village girl who ventured out into a deep snowfall to gather wood with her grandfather. She began to find numbers of frozen golden birds buried in the snow. She and her grandfather scooped up as many as they could and brought them home.

They co-opted their whole family in the rescue mission that soon embraced the whole village. When people ran out of shelter room in the rafters of their homes, the village priest opened the church as a place of avian hospice. The birds recovered and sang thanksgiving. Their chirping in the church was regarded as praise for God. When the snow melted in Spring and mud reappeared the captive birds flew against windows begging for release. "Let them go," counselled the priest. "Let them all go." The villagers knew it was the right thing to do though it saddened their hearts.

On Easter morning, the little girl ventured outside to fetch wood for the stove once more. On the lawn she found one brightly decorated egg after another. All the villagers discovered the same blessings, gifts of thanks, gifts of new hope, gifts of new life, each one unique like every creature God has ever made.

Helping God plant seeds of resurrection hope, Ola put in time preparing *pysanky*.

Prairie winters protract themselves over hours as long novels extend over paragraphs. Prairie people make do.

H. Lee Disher

# Chapter 20:
# Rodeo Readiness

Usually by the end of February or early March, the sap in maple trees in Eastern Canada flows free and ample following tapped lines in its transformation into maple syrup and maple sugar. As winter wound out its calendar days in Alberta in 2000, Tyler Stedman's systems ran with copious amounts of adrenalin. He would turn sixteen before the end of June. Having spent several years in apprenticeship in junior ranks at rodeo trials and events, this would be his entry year into the novice division. Entry fees increased as did possible prize money. The circuit to travel would widen. The competition would be tougher and more intense. The rush engulfed him.

The need for new and extra equipment took a dinosaur-like bite out of Tyler's bank account. Fortunately, his saddle did not need replacing. He did however purchase saddle pads, a fly mask, three pairs of medium-soft 3/8" roping gloves (used by headers), a supply of hand powder, a 28' heading rope nicknamed The Striker (a memorial to his previous mount), a new cinch, and a large tote that including a rope bag insert. The most important piece of equipment was a protective nylon shell vest with shock-absorbing foam and puncture-resistant armour. Being unceremoniously thrown to the ground from a bucking horse can hurt plenty. Being kicked by flying hooves can make even the toughest cowboy cry; can wound, maim and damn near kill you. In fact, that too, has been known to happen.

Now Tyler travelled twice a week to the High River training centre. Roping practice took place on Wednesday evenings with his own new mount now trial-ready beneath him. More of the same occupied an hour on Saturday mornings followed by group bronco lessons and an additional hour of private session for which Jules was fully prepared to pay. Rodeo readiness was the all-consuming focus.

From both standing and riding positions, Tyler spent hours and hours seeking to perfect his side-arm lariat toss. He was amazed at how many precious seconds could be saved by not raising one's arm overhead and still having enough slack and fly to catch that runaway calf. His new Paso Fino caught onto Tyler's signals and roping routine as if it was already in its blood: making swift and effective starts while seldom breaking the barrier, zeroing in on the quarry they were chasing, knowing instinctively when to come to a halt and help pull the lasso taut.

"Whew!" exclaimed Pat Chalmers, Tyler's instructor after observing the first few runs, "that's one bright and speedy horse you got yourself there. And you still haven't named him?"

"No, Pat, I haven't. I just can't seem to come up with a name that really suits."

"Well, maybe you might try giving up on English. His origins are Latin American you know. Maybe something Hispanic might fit the bill better."

"Si, si, señor, I theenk ju may be right," Tyler shot back suddenly enthused. "I'll dive into a Spanish dictionary in our school library during my spare period tomorrow morning."

Which he did. His first few forays seemed feeble translations out of English: *"El Rapido"* (Swift One), *"El Viento de Oro"* (Golden Wind), *"El Fino Argentino"* (Silvery Splendour in rhyme, except there was no silver colouring anywhere on Tyler's horse). Exasperated, Tyler let loose a heavy sigh thinking to himself, "Golly, I'm not very good at this."

"Something I can help you with, Tyler?" asked Ms. Donaldson the head librarian who had observed and overheard him.

"Well, uh, it's not really school work Ms. Donaldson. You see, I own this wonderful new horse, a Paso Fino—a special Latin American breed, smaller than most but very smart and especially fleet of foot. He almost floats across the ground."

"Raising little dust? Silent, subtle then suddenly overwhelming? Somewhat hypnotic?"

"Yes, yes! That's exactly how he acts."

"*Sirocco.*" She bent down to spell it on a page of notepaper as she spoke.

"What's that mean, Ms. Donaldson?"

"It's an Italian word really. In Spanish it's spelled with only one "c." It's origins are Arabic for that smooth and sly east wind that creeps over the desert and takes you prisoner."

"*Sirocco. Siroco.* That's perfect! I kind of like it with two "c"s instead of one. Thank you, Ms. Donaldson, you're a genius."

"Well, let's just say I know a few things about a lot of things. That's kind of how librarians are. By the way, you're no shabby young scholar yourself, Tyler Stedman."

"Thank you, Ms. Donaldson. And now that you've saved me a pile of time and effort I can use the rest of this spare period to apply myself to some of the work assigned to me that belongs in this environment."

"Life is more than school, Tyler. It's the biggest classroom of all. All pieces of our lives offer us opportunities to learn. Common sense and horse sense are just as important as any knowledge we find in textbooks or school-rooms. So far you seem to excel in all of these."

"I think I'm starting to blush, Ms. Donaldson. Thanks for your encouragement. I feel like I should neigh in agreement or something, but that might look silly, so I'll just nod and shake my mane a little bit and then we can both get back to our work."

Another student at the main desk was beckoning her attention anyway as she smiled and turned from the affable prodigy who was giving his head a little shake.

Tyler would report his decision at the Stedman family dinner table that night, but before that, as soon as he arrived home from school, he telephoned his grandfather. "Pops, I did it! I found a name for my horse thanks to our school librarian. *Sirocco.* I'm going to call him *Sirocco.*"

"*Sirocco,* eh. That's sounds pretty nifty."

"It's perfect, Pops. It's what the Arabs call a wind in the desert, but we spell it the way the Italians do in their language only with two "c's" instead of one as the Spanish do."

"A desert wind. Hmmm. By golly, Tyler, that is perfect. *Sirocco,* the paso fino who came straight out of the pampas of Argentina, smooth and swift and breezy."

"And captivating too, Pops, don't leave out the captivating part."

"Right...and captivating like the belly dancer the management brought into the Spur and Saddle over in Black Diamond a couple of weeks ago. Ol'

"Punky" McAllister was just glued to his chair for an hour and a half."

"I can just imagine. And where were you, Pops, roped onto "Punky's" back?"

"I reckon we'd better just put your imagination to rest in the first instance. There's only so much of that kind of stimulation to which a young lad like you should be exposed sight unseen and I probably overdid it already."

"Pops, it's me you're talking to not Alex. It's a good enough comparison as it stands, I won't get carried away with it. At any rate, I'm quite content with the name *Sirocco*."

"It's a truly great name, boy. I'll see you Saturday when you come to load him up."

"You bet, Pops. Whoops, I didn't mean to conjure up the image of Uncle Louie."

"It's okay, Tyler. It's only an expression. Seems like both of us kind of managed to ride up to a barrier and pulled back on the reins before we jumped over."

"Right. See you Saturday, Pops. Good-bye. I love you."

"I love you too, Tyler, and I can't think of anyone who doesn't."

When Tyler hung up the phone he went and gathered up the daily mail that had been shoved through the brass slot in the front door. Among the bills, the flyers and a late birthday card for his father from one of his aunts in Ontario was a letter in an envelope addressed to him.

*Silver Crown Ranch, RR 2,*
*St. Albert, AB, T4A 3B5.*
*February 23, 2000.*

*Dear Tyler:*

*I'm a bit slow in following up on our conversation during the Stampede, and I apologize if this is too short notice but I'm wondering if your parents would permit you to spend the March school break period this year at my ranch here near St. Albert just outside Edmonton. There will be several of us gathering including a couple of other novice rodeo riders. We'll be working at getting ourselves in shape for the Royal Rodeo in Calgary the weekend following the break. I know you're not entered there, but you are planning to compete on the novice circuit come April, and I thought you might welcome an opportunity to sport around with some of us pros who are already deep into it. Word's already out that you're one of the up and coming riders of promise, and a major part of rodeo is about cowboys helping other cowboys. A couple of hundred dollars will cover your room and board and mount expenses for the week. Let me know if you're able to join us or not as soon as you can.*

*Sincerely,*
 *Randall Lecroix*
*Phone: (805) 442-6767, Fax: (805) 442-2909,*
*e-mail:* broncorbust@westlink.com

Rebecca came in from school in the midst of one of the loudest outbursts of "Oh, my God! Oh, my…I can't believe it. Oh, yes! Yes! Yes! Yippie-ay-yo-ky-yay!" she had ever heard from her brother's mouth.

"Becca! Becca, guess what?" he asked her as soon as he noticed her.

Of course, she couldn't guess…didn't get time to before he blurted out the whole exciting prospect.

"Holy moley, Tyler, that sounds awesome! In fact, it sounds like another of Aunt Ola's showings taking real shape."

"What? Aunt Ola had a showing I didn't hear about."

"There hasn't been a chance to tell you I guess, but, yes, last weekend she shared one with us while you were off practicing rodeo in High River. It was about this huge red-tailed hawk that seemed to keep circling and circling the farm until it swooped down and carried something or someone away, not in its claws because it wasn't hungry, but on its back. The more Ola stayed with the vision, the clearer it became that it was a person, but she couldn't tell if it was male or female. It was a person riding a hawk like an angel straddling a cloud and heading northeast away from its home territory among the foothills and mountains which seemed strange because hawks are particularly territorial she pointed out. The rider did not seem frightened or endangered but expectant and yet fully at ease. The hawk seemed to be like a messenger, a sign of some form of divine protection and companionship. Wherever they were headed was destined to be all right. That's about all she could say about it. So, you see, Tyler. It was about you—about you being invited away to the ranch near Edmonton. If it's an okay event, if it's like something that's meant to be, according to Ola, it's a sure thing Mom and Dad will let you go."

Tyler reached out and hugged his sister as tears began to roll.

"Okay, brother dear. I'm happy for you, but let's not get over-emotional here. Save the goopy stuff for Stephanie 'cause this also means I'll be going off with Mom and Dad by myself during March break."

"Right," responded Tyler releasing her, "but we'll see about that."

So, as newsworthy as coming up with *Sirocco* as a name was, there was this larger stop-the-presses announcement corralling centre stage over dinner that night.

Myra looked across at Jules and then said, "Well, even though I'm out-numbered here, especially since this venture appears to have the blessing of my almost-goddess of a sister-in-law, I voice my objection and invite you to remember what we had being planning to do."

"Yes, Mom, and I was truly looking forward to spending the break with all of you in Banff. We've had wonderful times whenever we've done that be-fore. But a week with Randall Lecroix and other rodeo pros...that's a dream realization for which I will be forever grateful to you both for letting me grasp onto. And maybe, maybe if Rebecca asks her soon, maybe Charlene can join you all in Banff. She'd be super company for Rebecca and she's a better skier than I am so the two of them would be safe and quite happy off on their own as much as when you could all be skiing together."

Rebecca's eyes widened to the size of old 45 rpm records. "Oh, Mom, Dad, could I? Could I ask Charlene to come along? Would that be all right?"

Before they could fully say "yes," Rebecca had planted a big sloppy kiss on her brother's right cheek saying, "Tyler, you are the best! Here's some of that goop back at ya!" and dashed off into the kitchen to dial up her friend on the phone. She talked so loud, she might just as well have opened the back door and hollered over the fence.

An affirmative response from next door came within a half hour. Joy spread itself on at least two homes on Dewdney Common with every flake of accumulating snow that dropped on Okotoks that night. An e-mail sailed to Silver Crown ranch near St. Albert as if on hawk's wings. Hope hummed with a quiet kind of restlessness. The night had positive ions in its neurons, except between the synapses of Myra's mind.

# Chapter 21:
# Banff Breakaway

T he first Friday night and Saturday morning of the March school break were
  spent getting laundry done, clothes pressed, suitcases packed in the Stedman
household. Jules tidied up some paperwork. There was always paperwork needing tidying. By 11 A.M. on Saturday, the family was in their van heading to the
Brian Orser Arena in Northeast Calgary. Rebecca was competing in junior
ranks figure skating. Later that afternoon a bus would arrive at Massingale Mall
in the same quarter of that widespread city ready to load up Tyler Stedman and
other hopeful young bucks who were St. Albert-bound for rodeo training week.
The rest of the Stedman family, with Miss Charlene Berenson as guest, were
trip-ready to turn around after the competition, find the Trans-Canada and
make a beeline for Banff. Everybody was as happy as they were excited.

It was Rebecca's turn to shine. She aced her compulsories. She floated almost flawlessly through her free-style routine performing the required elements with technical precision, landing her first single-salchow, double-loop
combination in competition and almost nailing a difficult single axal except
for touching a hand down and landing with a wobble. Her choreography was
fluid and graceful as she toured the ice surface to the tune of "Circle of Life"
from *The Lion King*. Her costume was yellow and beige with gold epaulets and

a cincture of gold phalanges resembling a gladiator's over-skirt. She was lioness guaranteed to bring heart-throbs to any young Cimba within sight. She won bronze. The gold and silver medalists were a couple of years older than her. Did promise pass on from brother to sister in a manner similar to osmosis?

After a late-lunch/early-dinner celebration at East Side Mario's, Tyler was escorted to his destined pick-up location, hugged farewell and witnessed boarded and departed. The Stedman van ran on towards the mountains. In less than an hour, it pulled into the parking lot of the Timberlodge resort just off the Trans-Canada and east of the renowned year-round tourist mecca town. The Stedman group checked into their two pre-booked, sumptuous-enough rooms in a tastefully-decorated, all-amenities-included facility that would set them back about half the cost of staying anywhere within the town limits and one-third of the cost of the Banff Springs Hotel. Jules and Myra had been there, done that on a couple of anniversary weekend occasions. Mount Norquay was overtly in their face whenever they peered out the front window of their suites. On clear days, the Three Sisters were visible staring southwest-ward down the highway, wearing their snow-caps like proud Mother Superiors sporting starched wimples. Space, place, atmosphere, crisp, healthful mountain air enshrouded and exhilarated four temporary refugees from Okotoks for seven nights and six rapturous days except for Tuesday when it poured freezing rain, made the slopes precarious and impassable and forced all vacationers in-doors or to the hot-springs and a bout of boutique-hopping.

Sunday was a tolerable, minus 4 degrees Celsius, virtually windless, blaring sunshine day. One could get by without thermal under-garments beneath one's ski-wear. Shaded goggles were a must to counteract snow blindness. Charlene and Rebecca had a whale of a time on the beginner, intermediate trails and the junior moguls section. Tyler was right. Charlene kept watch, took good care of his sister and taught her how to tighten and smooth out her parallel turns. They only fell twice, just for the fun of bumping into each other at the bottom of a couple of runs. One time Rebecca took a little tumble when she caught a tip getting off of the chair-lift.

Jules and Myra tackled longer and more expert slopes. Jules enjoyed skiing and had enough proficiency to manage most of the challenges before him. Ski-ing was Myra's great release. What presents itself to many others as intimidat-ing and anxiety-escalating was a cakewalk for her. She had been skiing since she was four years old. She handled any slope with the expertise, calm, balance and control comparable to a professional surfer's wave management in Cali-fornia or Hawaii. She could turn on a tack, stop on a hairpin, use sharp, clean, unwavering edges and control her speed as if she had a gearshift in her knee joints. She was a liberated woman without worry, without fear, without doubt weighing her down, visiting her spirit as they did in her day-to-day life. She had qualified for ski patrol during high school and made decent money in the Crowsnest Pass resort areas. She headed her high-school ski team and, during her university days as she studied pharmacology, she won numerous medals and trophies skiing for her alma mater, and financed a good chunk of her own education with patrol duty in Banff and Canmore. She knew the Banff runs like Ola knew pie recipes. Snow was her element. She looked like a duck in a down jacket swimming in it. She wore an elbow brace as a precaution. Her gimpy leg had healed.

Later that evening, back at the lodge, the phone in Jules and Myra's suite rang.

"Dad? Is that you? It's Tyler. Silver Crown ranch is amazing! Randall's got all the practice equipment you could imagine and a mock arena to die for. We all got settled into our places in the bunkhouse and then met at the main indoor corral to get acquainted with our horses for the week as well as with each other! I can't thank you enough for allowing me to have this opportunity. Do what you can to stop Mom from worrying. A lot of the cream of the amateur and professional crop on the Canadian circuit has gathered here. After dinner, we went to this large instruction hall in one of the barns to learn about all the safety equipment we have to wear on the mechanical bucking broncs. Randall has four of them! And they're all surrounded by four-foot-thick foam crash pads covered in dirt just to simulate something like the real thing. Tomorrow's going to be so awesome when we get to have our first goes at it. After safety lessons, we watched a couple of videos of winning performances on the Canada circuit in 1997 and 1998. There will be lots of in-class video lessons every afternoon including rides that failed as well as ones that succeeded, and later in the week, Randall and some of his buddies are going to risk live demonstrations and invite us to critique them. Greg Dugan is a second-year novice rider out of Red Deer. He's my bunk mate on the top bunk. We've already hit it off very well. He's quite funny and he makes up his own running commentary on the videos. If he ever falls out of the competitive ranks, he's already grooming himself to become a rodeo announcer. God, I must be excited to go rambling on like this. How's skiing?"

"It's wonderful, Tyler, just wonderful. Well, in your mother's case, you know, even better than that."

"Right. In her case, it's like having a chance to go dancing on clouds."

"How true that is, son, and tomorrow maybe I'll try to carve your initials right in the middle of a couple of slopes, wishing you were here. I'm so glad you've had an exciting introductory weekend. Sounds like you're in for a *majorly* stimulating ride of your own as Alex might enthuse about it."

"I expect I am, Dad, and you can use your usual adult language to imagine it instead of aerated adolescent talk. I am getting as giddy as Alex though as I anticipate the rest of this week. I'll call again in a couple of days. Good night, Dad, I love you."

"I love you, Tyler, and so does your mother, despite her reservations. She'd be here to talk with you now if Rebecca and Charlene hadn't talked her into a few two-on-one matches of ping-pong. Good night."

Monday was colder, minus 12 degrees, cloudier, and therefore not as bright. The ski slopes were still blessed by a foot-and-a-half of natural powder on top of a couple of feet of artificial base. Jules, Myra, Rebecca, and Charlene didn't go back for evening runs after reveling on slats all morning and afternoon. They went to the movie theatre in Banff to see the first installment of *Lord of the Rings: The Fellowship of the Ring*. Charlene developed a crush on Frodo. Rebecca got the hots for Sam. Gandalf was, like, superbly cool.

"Why don't you use your left ski pole as if it was a magic sceptre tomorrow, Dad? Think about how you could clear yourself a nice safe path unobstructed by other skiers!"

"Your father does just fine using his ski pole as a subtle ("What-was - that?") bum prod on any number of unsuspecting other skiers as it is, Rebecca. Don't encourage him to increase his powers for self-serving route-making. He's the same on the slopes as he is driving on the expressways."

"I am not!" retorted Jules leading into a lingering lull. "Well…not always."

"Yes, dear. Not always. Only about 90 percent of the time."

Jules lifted an imaginary ski pole to his chest as they made their way to the van in the theatre parking lot. "*Touché.*"

Tuesday, however, was that sleet and ice and wipe-out-outdoor-recreation day. Tyler phoned again at night.

"Hi, Dad."

"Hello, son."

"Dad! It's absolutely excellent here! I came second in the friendly competition roping trials today. Mind you, it only involved lassoing calves from a standing position twenty feet away from the chute once they were released. And yesterday, I held on to the bronc machine twice for the full eight seconds; once with a saddle, and once without. Six other times I got bucked off. Once

I went through the windshield. Man, that's the scariest throw of all being launched head first over the horse's own neck and head. Greg, my bunk-mate, he got thrown twice the same way and tried to turn his misfortune into a front flip. He landed smack on his back the first time and square on his arse the next. "Tailbones and lower spines can take a long time to heal, son," Randall had told him. "Better to settle for trying to get your arms out front and your hands down first and turn it into a front roll if you can, or a belly flop if you can't." Thank God for all the padded safety gear we get to wear here. Still the impact after buck-off is harsh enough."

"I'm glad you're safe and uninjured, son. That's what they promised at Silver Crown: maximum safety, even though all parents or participants had to sign an insurance claim waiver. Sounds like they're true to their word."

"They are, Dad, and tremendously helpful and encouraging. These cowboys not only cheer each other on, they really care too. Well, not in any forthright way that most of them would admit. But it shows anyway in what they don't say, in how they look, in how they act."

"Yes, that's the often secret lining under the saddle of rodeo, the saving grace of a sport that like any sport has its share of fierce competitors, bitter rivals, occasional cheaters on steroids or clusters that put in a fix from one corral to the next, taking turns so each one gets enough points and prize money to qualify for semi-finals and larger events. Any cowboys that get caught in some kind of fraud or swindle get sternly admonished in the first couple of instances. After that, they're rousted out and blacklisted pretty quickly. It's a long time before they ever compete again, if ever, and some can't even make a comeback as a clown."

"Well, as far as I can tell, there's nobody like that on this ranch right now. There's a few that will compete fiercely, but that's about pushing yourself to excel more than it's about having to beat the other guy."

"Including you?"

"Yes, Dad, including me. And whom do you think I got that from?"

"Oh my, *touché!* Twice in twenty-four hours! Good night, son. We love you."

"Ditto, Dad. My heart's like ever-rising shares of Tranogco stock. My family is my company, we invest so much in each other. Good night. I'll check in again on Thursday."

"His family is his company." Jules pondered the image. "I can't quite make the same equation. My company makes demands that tear me away from family. My family pulls me to counteract the expectations of my company. That's business, but I don't know that it's what life's intended to be. I'm too much of a juggler not an artful acrobat."

He poured himself a night-cap, double single-malt Scotch on the rocks, and moved across the room to sit in the armchair next to Myra to catch her up on Tyler's news. They watched the nightly television news report before tucking into bed, before meaningful and heart-felt love-making that had not been so frequent in their relationship of late.

Wednesday offered limited but enjoyable skiing while crews worked at re-grooming and restoring all the trails after Tuesday's storms. Some of the more expert runs were closed until Thursday. Jules slipped out on one of them on Thursday in the middle of the afternoon. His right leg went underneath an artificial snow pipeline bruising his shin and wrenching his ankle just severely enough to incapacitate him for the remainder of the week. The first-aid applied by the Banff ski patrol sufficed to contain his sprain. He rented crutches from the local medical centre, sat around the lodge reading a couple of novels he had brought along, watched Myra, Rebecca and Charlene continue to delight in their closing days of sporting fun, and kept a recurring cycle of ice-packs resting on his injury.

By Saturday morning, the swelling and discomfort had disappeared, he could put weight on his right foot again and walk without limping. He returned the crutches but didn't buckle up his boots again and step into the harnesses for a last few downhill runs. Instead, he rented a pair of cross-country skis, shoes, and poles and did some solitary, soul-searching trail-walking. The family-company conundrum needled him. Hazy outlines of bigger pictures inserted themselves into his thought-frames like slides in a Microsoft PowerPoint presentation. Life, however, could not be organized by PowerPoint. Maybe he'd have a chat with Rev. Fanshawe at St. Paul's, or a heart-to-heart consultation with his sister-in-law. Questions scrounged around for more clarity.

During Tyler's Thursday evening check-in Jules heard about the live demonstration rides put on by Randall Lecroix and his rodeo running mates at the Silver Crown corral, about how Tyler and his bunkmate Greg won the friendly team roping competition, about how sleek and fast the riding horses on the ranch were, about too many beans being served for dinner and too much farting in the bunkhouse at night and about a tentative circuit schedule Tyler had already sketched out for his first year as a novice competitor. That too was organization that would likely have to be altered which would be okay with Tyler who well knew that life did not revolve around his needs and expectations and who more than anyone was willing to compromise and accommodate and forego his plans if someone else in the family had a more pressing agenda or need or even a sudden inspiration. Jules thought he had been like that in his earlier years, but couldn't quite convince himself that that was true. It seemed he had always overloaded his boat, had trouble saying no. That's what had gotten him transferred a year ago from sales and marketing to the explorations and research division of Tranogco. So often, Jules had sacrificed a good-sized chunk of himself trying to satisfy others' needs and expectations at the expense of his own aspirations (whatever those really were). Frequent flashes of irritability accompanied by short-lived heavy sighs or muttered exasperations dogged his life like mosquitos you can hear but not see in the dark. Pleasantness was his game face. Going with the flow, taking things in stride, rolling with the punches was what he appeared to be. He didn't always manage that with the grace of Rebecca on ice nor the effortless synthesis of Tyler on horseback. He imagined himself a contestant on that old television show *To Tell the Truth* that his grandparents used to watch. *"Will the real Jules Stedman please...stand up."* He could visualize himself standing amidst two impostors, yet he was all three. All this recurred to him, made race-car figure eights in the circuits of his mind during his Saturday cross-country ski trail ruminations and caused him to pause several times for a nip of Scotch from a portable hip-flask.

They had all packed their bags and locked them in the van that morning as part of checking out of the lodge before noon. Jules finished his stroll, returned his rented equipment and found Myra, Rebecca and Charlene drinking hot chocolate in the main chalet at the rendezvous time of four o'clock. Each one had something significant to share about their last day of downhill runs. They had already stashed skis, poles and boots in the overhead carriers so by 4:30, three Stedmans and a Berenson were homeward bound with a stopover in Canmore for dinner at a fish and seafood restaurant recommended as "Where to Eat in Canada" for seven years running. Tyler would be returning to Massingale Mall for pickup on Sunday afternoon kitbag, riding gear and saddle in hand.

His family met him with Stephanie Wells also in tow. He was still overwound, uninjured and glad to be reunited with them. He hugged them in the here and now. By a parallel process of mental mapping, he was writing the screenplay of his dream for the coming months. A cloudless sky hung its indifference in the air.

# Chapter 22:
## Following the Circuit

T yler had envisioned competing somewhere twice in April and three or four times a month from May through September. In his zealousness, he had overlooked the fact that he was still in high school and that being a student had its own set of demands and responsibilities. He had neglected to consider that his family might have some vacation plans during the summer that could include him. He had forgotten that Rebecca's primary figure-skating competition was scheduled for the same weekend he had set his sights on his first competition in Coleman 160 km south and a bit west through the mountains in the midst of the Crowsnest Pass. Rebecca's venue was taking place in Red Deer which was pretty much the same distance in the opposite direction north. So Coleman got deleted from his inaugural year on the novice circuit. A trip to Red Deer would afford him a chance to hook up with Greg again.

That actually happened sooner. A novice bronc rider from British Columbia was a late scratch for the Royal Rodeo in Calgary the very first weekend after Tyler returned from his sojourn at Silver Crown ranch. Greg phoned that Thursday night to inform his new friend that he had been invited to be a last-minute entry to complete the novice roster.

"So, do you think you'd be able to come watch and cheer me on? I mean, I could get you a ring-side view right from the starting-pen area."

"Just try to stop me. And say, if you haven't arranged accommodations just yet, how about staying here with us in Okotoks. I'm sure that Mom, Dad, my grandpa, my aunt, or my aunt's neighbour will take turns taxiing you back and forth."

"We'll what?" Myra interjected by way of interruption.

Tyler's recitation of the arrangements was so excited and rapid, she had to ask him to slow down and repeat himself.

"And you think this will work? Don't forget, you've promised to work with Stephanie, Alex, and Enid on that group science project this weekend."

"Don't worry, Mom, I've already figured out how to make it all fit."

"I'm sure you have. I just hope it's a better plan than the scheme you thought you had worked out for your own competitions this year."

"It is. Trust me, Mom."

"As usual, I don't think you've given me many other options." Worry remained intact.

"Thanks, Mom, you're the greatest. Greg? Greg? Are you still there? It's all set, you can stay here. I'll come watch whenever I can. It'll be like our St. Albert days hardly ended, only better because this time you'll be riding in earnest not just for fun."

"You got that right, pardner. I can hardly wait to see you again."

"Nor I you. See you tomorrow night even, spurs, spunk and saddle and all."

"I already feel like I'm half-way there. See you tomorrow, Tyler. Bye now."

"Bye, Greg."

It was a hectic weekend but Tyler did manage to make it all fit. Greg arrived on Friday night in the midst of the first group session having a go at their science project—making a cardboard boat that would float and hold at least two people. It was a grand opportunity for Tyler to introduce his new, older friend to some of his own gang. He thought he detected a more-than-passing interest of exchanged glances between Greg and Enid. Alex didn't miss it either and made sure to position himself always between them and to insert himself in the middle of any of their getting-acquainted conversations.

"So," he risked commenting, "I hear there's a lot of rednecks in Red Deer."

"Really," Greg offered by way of rejoinder. "Well, I figure there aren't no more rednecks there per capita than anywhere else in Alberta. This is cowboy country to a large extent. Cowboys can tend to be tough, rough around the edges, opinionated, not fussy about others who seem to shy away from hard labour. Most of the population of this province seems to have conservatism in their bloodstream, the hardnosed kind. Heck, we've not only had a few Conservative governments, we've had long, long runs of Social Credit parties running the show. Ralph Klein and company are only bobcats compared to some of the cougars in office before them. So yeah, we got rednecks in Red Deer, and just plain conservative folks and some Liberals, and, guess what, I even know a few cowboys and citizens who support the NDP! You know, wanting to be seen to be sticking up for the little guy, the blue-collars, the down-and-outs."

"My grandpa's friend, Punky McAllister, he makes no bones about supporting the NDP. He's come home from a few taverns with broken bones to show for it. When he heard that Kelly Sutherland, the chuck-wagon driving king had named one of his lead horses Prairie Premier and nicknamed it Ralph, Punky said that at least Sutherland's eyes in the wagon seat were staring at the right end."

"Um, hello!" Stephanie inserted, "Do you think we could get back to our project here, I have to be home in half an hour."

"Sure, right," Alex agreed re-orienting himself. "Hey, how about duct tape? It sticks to anything."

"Actually, if I can offer a suggestion," Greg ventured, "there's a special adhesive tape used by auto body repair guys that's stronger, moisture-resistant and virtually waterproof. It tends to come in fluorescent colors though, so it would sure make the seams of your boat stand out."

"Or..." Alex re-implanted himself, "we could paint over them."

"Yes, we could," Enid added, "and then we'd need to coat the whole boat in some kind of glossy, waterproof sealant, the kind of stuff my father just applied to our renovated recreation room floor using those snap-in Pergo blocks and strips."

"Snap-on flooring, eh? My, my what will they think of next? Snap-on drapery? Snap-on bedding?" Alex commented by way of grabbing the floor again. "Oh! Oh! I got it! Snap-on, snap-off clothing! Wouldn't that be great when you're in a hurry to get to school, or out of the locker room after a soccer game, or out on a date!"

"They already have it, Alex," Greg dared mentioning. "For babies."

"Uh, Steph, why don't you go get Cokes for everyone while I show Greg to his room," Tyler chimed in rescuing a situation of mounting tension.

"Actually, Greg, Alex, they have tear away clothing for adults too. Stage actors use it all the time for quick costume changes. Perhaps there would be a wider market for the general public if someone wanted to take a chance on it."

"That's my cousin who said that, heart set on being a rodeo hero, smoother of ruffled feathers and ever a businessman's son."

"I'd say you've got one very impressive cousin there Alex," Greg noted.

"I'd say we've just found something we absolutely agree on," echoed Alex extending his right hand. "Nice to meet you, Greg."

"Ditto, dude."

"Oh, he's not much of a dude," Enid blurted out half-snickering. "Cowboys intrigue me, but I'm more at ease around clowns like my lovely carrot-topped tabby kitten here."

"Enid!" Alex shot back somewhat embarrassed. "You promised you wouldn't talk like that in front of our friends."

"Oh yeah, right. And you promised to take me glow-bowling tomorrow night, so we won't be able to come and watch you do your thing in the ring, Greg."

"That's okay, I don't like having too many familiar faces in the audience, even recently familiar ones."

The study party broke up shortly after that. After a good night's rest, it was Jules who volunteered to drop Greg off at the arena in the morning. Office work beckoned him to the city anyway. Tyler and his classmates would be going at their project again Saturday morning. After lunch, Myra would take Tyler to the Royal Rodeo for the afternoon trials while she and Rebecca went off shopping. Wallis Wilton had agreed to bring both boys home to Okotoks after the evening rounds of competition. Carol Morton had given him tickets for the event for his birthday and was more than happy to accompany him there for a different-than-usual Saturday night date. All these fortuitous pieces fell in place, making Tyler's weekend plan almost a no-brainer.

Sunday was a bit trickier beginning with convincing two out of three sets of parents and Aunt Ola that completing the science project was more important than attending church. Sunday morning was the only time all four of the students had free simultaneously. Actually, they could have gone at it Sunday afternoon except that Tyler was determined to observe the final rounds of the Royal hoping Greg would qualify to participate in them. It was Pops' turn to play taxi driver and they took Jules along for a well-needed respite from figures and paperwork. Greg had, in fact, qualified and wound up fourth in saddle bronc and fifth in bareback out of eight final competitors in each event. An admirable start to his year on the Canadian circuit and already a few points and prize money accumulated towards his final ranking.

Tyler's itinerary didn't get started until the end of April with a three-day event in Stavely. It gave him almost a month-and-a-half of preparation time, which proved to be a blessing. Aunt Ola could hardly have prayed it into existence any better. Perhaps it was more adrenalin boost on top of natural and acquired skill, but Tyler Stedman scored very well in his first outing on the novice circuit. He netted a sixth place finish in bareback bronc mostly because his mount wasn't as difficult a challenge as those of the riders who placed ahead of him. He wound up third in saddle bronc after an impressive pair of scores in the two opening rounds and a dazzling display of dexterity and balance atop a torturous black Arabian dubbed Killer Instinct. He and *Sirocco* were a surge of synchronicity in the calf-roping finals netting a fault-free time of 34.5 seconds, the second fastest initial time for a rookie on the novice circuit ever and good for second place honors. Tyler came home beaming, points racked up, money in his pocket, medals in hand, and a new, bright silver buckle on his Wranglers.

His May and June outings had to be tapered down from three to two. Victoria Day weekend was spent at the family's rented cottage on Lake Kananaskis even though it was still chilly. June exams took precedence over rodeo ventures, though his test schedule made his appearance at the Brooks rodeo on the second weekend of that month feasible. May appearances took him through the Crowsnest Pass to the competition in Falkland, B.C., on the weekend after Victoria Day weekend and eastward to Taber, Alberta at the end of the month. He didn't fare nearly as well in May as he had for openers. In fact, he suffered buck-offs in Falkland, and a missed rope toss in one round of calf-chasing. He managed however to snag seventh place in the final day of calf-roping. At Taber, he took fifth place in all three events entered: calf-roping, saddle bronc and bareback bronc. A rough landing in the final bareback event aggravated his old right-knee injury. Dr. Krupka arranged for intensive physiotherapy for the subsequent several weeks. Myra reiterated her fears and protests.

His bouts at Brooks bode better: third in saddle bronc, fourth in bareback, and his first ever victory in calf-roping as a novice! Two hundred dollars to his credit and newspaper feature in the Calgary Herald sports pages. Tyler was being touted as a real up-and-comer. The article showed up on notice boards all over Okotoks. The month-end event in High River was a total wipe-out which was very disappointing because it was so close to home, where he had had success before. That too is rodeo. Some days are diamonds. Some days are simply dust. Rave revues and wild Yahoos switch to simple but courteous applause. Myra's lack of support and Stephanie's dislike for his chosen sport stung worse.

There was scarcely much time after the High River rodeo for the Stedman family to head home, pack up again and head off horse-trailer in tow for a week of R & R in the Cypress Hills of Saskatchewan and an opportunity for Tyler to strut his stuff again at a more major venue in Swift Current. Greg Dugan was there as a friend and as a fellow competitor. Randall Lecroix was there to mount his own charges and to cheer on a couple of his protégés. Uncle Louie and his drinking buddies from Lloydminster were in Swift that weekend on a bender. Hearing of the Rodeo, Louie hustled them over to the corrals where they huddled surreptitiously at the back of the viewing stands without making contact with his sister's family.

It went very well. In the end, Greg and Tyler placed second and third respectively in their division. More points, more medals, advances in the cumulative standings and more attention. The sports news notices on Okotoks bulletin boards were overlaid with Tyler Stedman updates.

Greg was off to the Stampede the following week. Tyler wasn't sure he was Stampede-ready yet, and hadn't acquired enough qualifying points to get an automatic invite. He settled for an event in Benalto that took him and his family back across Alberta, but north of home and west of Red Deer. His final standings there weren't his best, but added into the mix served to inch his cumulative point totals up a few notches. He placed eighth in saddle bronc and sixth in roping.

In his original plan, Tyler had set his sights on returning to Saskatchewan later in July for the round-up in Estevan. But it wasn't in the cards for anyone else in his family circle to be there with him. Besides, Ola needed his help around the farm again and his body had been bruised and beaten enough by then to deserve a stretch of time for healing and re-strengthening. What he also needed and had been neglecting was some spiritual mentoring from his God-connected aunt.

One day after supper, she said, "Tyler, why don't you let Pops and Alex look after the horses tonight. Stay here at the table with me and have a little chat." Even a little chat with aunt Ola was as personal and profound as a reflective walk through a labyrinth. Tyler was not averse to her suggestion. He welcomed it like an invitation to Silver Crown ranch.

"How is your body, Tyler — somewhat bruised, slightly battered, but basically still intact?"

"Yes, Aunt Ola. I've done all I can to keep in shape and it appears to be paying off."

"Yes, and even your rodeo debut is paying off too. You must be quite happy."

"I am very happy and, if it's not particularly sinful, proud of myself."

"A healthy respect and love for oneself, tempered by humility is never sinful, Tyler. Without a measure of self-love we are unable to truly love God and others. That is different from the kind of pride that entangles us in sin. Let me see," she continued as she reached for a volume of *The Philokalia* from the bookshelves. "Yes, here it is in the teachings of St. Thalassios:

> *Pride deprives us of God's help, making us over-reliant on ourselves and arrogant towards other people. There are two remedies against pride .... prayer with tears, and having no scorn for anyone. (Vol. 2, page 327)*

You seem to manage both of those rather well, Tyler, which frees you from having to bear with the third remedy for pride of which St. Thalassios speaks, chastisement. In heart and mind, you seldom if ever sink into haughtiness. You have a good heart and a keen mind. Speaking of which, I also understand you're keeping up your grades in school which is also testimony to balance in attitudes and concentration."

"Yes, I am, Aunt Ola, thank you."

"And what about your spiritual life?"

"Oh, that's where I may have gotten a little shaky. I say prayers almost every day. I read that devotional literature you gave me for Christmas on occasion. I get to church with mom and dad and Rebecca when I'm not tied up in a rodeo event on the weekend. But I'm not as consistent as I might be. What can I say, I'm a teenager. This isn't stuff I share with my friends."

"Consistency is often a casualty in one's spiritual life. So many other demands, pressures and responsibilities crowd our days. With practice it comes. What matters most is focus, frequent focus. Here, Tyler, I have something else for you. I've been saving it for just such a time as this. It is an icon, one that is quite special in Orthodox faith. It is small enough to carry with you, to lean up against an alarm clock so that you notice it first thing every morning, or to place on a dresser when you bed down for the night."

"It's a picture of Jesus isn't it? It looks like it's copied from something rather old, it has several cracks in it and there's a chunk of paint missing from Jesus' hairline and forehead."

"Yes, Tyler, it is old. The original was painted in the fifteenth century by Andrew Rublev who has gifted his people with countless precious icons. This one was part of a whole tier of images of which only three have survived: a portrait of St. Paul, a conception of the Archangel Michael and this picture of Jesus that used to be flanked by images of the Virgin Mary and of John the Baptist. The tier had its home in a Russian church in Zvenigorod. The iconoclasts during the Russian Revolution ripped it down and flung its remains into a barn near the Cathedral of the Assumption. An art restorer found it quite by accident in 1918. He decided to preserve it but not to restore it. Replicas such as this one you now hold duplicate the image as the restorer found it."

"It's quite marvelous, Aunt Ola. Jesus' face is flat and sad and still beautiful. Despite the damage to his head and chin those eyes stare out with great love and a deep desire for peace."

"You are already quite perceptive even at first glance, Tyler. Many look at this picture of our Savior and fail to see such things for quite some time. It is known officially as "The Savior of Zvenigorod" yet through Russia, the Ukraine, and other former Soviet republics, it is more beloved as "The Peacemaker." So simple with its varying shades of brown and chipped blue tunic. So profound, as you have already noticed, despite is damages and discolorations."

"I will treasure him and carry him with me always, Aunt Ola. I remember once in Sunday School our teacher gave us small wooden discs with crosses on them called "The Cross in My Pocket" to remind us how much God loved us, but this, this is a more precious, more intriguing image to have on hand. It will remind me daily that Jesus is close to my heart, wants to be at the centre of my life."

"Yes. And if you continue to spend time with it, this icon has much more to teach you. Now, would it be all right if you and I shared a little prayer right now.

"Certainly."

Ola's hands enfolded Tyler's on the table top. With bowed heads she invited God in Christ to indeed stay close to her nephew, to protect him in the rodeo ring, to keep him humble and healthy and vibrant in body, mind and spirit, to unfold more of the treasures of divine wisdom that would steady him and steer him and enable him to continue to be such a blessing to others. Tyler took a moment to bless and thank God for the love and counsel of Aunt Ola, for the simplicity and sincerity of her faith that embraced everyone she met and everything she did. They thanked God for the gift of Jesus Christ to the world and repeated the Lord's Prayer together. Amen.

The right balance of rest, manual labour, and rejuvenated prayer life helped Tyler mend well enough to compete in the calf-roping go-rounds in

Strathmore on the end-of-July first-of-August long weekend. The purse was not as rich as the one in Medicine Hat around the same time and the points up for grabs in the overall standings not as many, but Tyler managed a third-place buckle and a prize of one hundred and fifty dollars, more than enough to cover his entry fees for the August outings in Olds (August 11-13) and at the more major marbles Lethbridge rodeo (August 25-27). He fared quite well in Olds with a fourth overall rating for his efforts in saddle bronc, bareback bronc, and calf-roping. In Lethbridge, he upset several of the favorites placing second in saddle bronc, suffered two buck-offs in bareback and took sixth in roping. Prizes and points totals mounted in his favor. And an unanticipated surprise.

"Well, hello there, Hero!"

Tyler, leading Sirocco into the paddock behind the main ring after picking up his calf-roping ribbon, did a double-take. There was no mistake. There, before him, was Allison Kershaw, to whom he returned a cordial greeting.

"So, got any plans for tonight?" she asked.

"Well, actually, Allison, I believe that after dinner with my family, I'm heading home."

"Oh, that's too bad! I was hoping we might have a chance to become re-acquainted."

Hopes don't always materialize according to human designs. However, that brief encounter sufficed to send Tyler back to Okotoks fighting no un-certain amount of sexual stimulation he was powerless to subdue. Allison held hers in abeyance like a deferred parliamentary motion.

Labour Day weekend, September 2-4, set all Okotoks ablaze with excitement. It was time for their annual rodeo, and this year their golden-haired boy had been distinguishing himself as a rookie on the novice circuit attracting more local media attention than the pros coming to town.

True, some of the tougher competitors were off riding for notoriety in Armstrong and Merritt, B.C. that same weekend and again the purses there were more lucrative, but Okotoks was not to be outdone in hype when it came to putting on the town's best face and hospitality aprons for the show of shows it was hosting. Eager advance planning had procured performances by Prairie Oyster and k. d. Lang for the evening grandstand shows. Center stage for three days would be in the riding and roping corral surrounded by a sea of "We love you, Tyler!" and "Stedman reigns" placards and such the like. Tyler himself was buoyed up by Greg Dugan's decision to switch venues from Merritt to Okotoks to spend some quality time with his new-found rodeo buddy and knowing that the two of them would provoke each other to putting out their best effort

It worked. Sometimes there's nothing like a hometown crowd and a bonafide cheerleading friend to spur one onto unexpected success. Tyler and Greg between them virtually blew the competition away. Tyler snagged his first ever victory in saddle bronc, another first in calf-roping and second in bareback, though he almost got shoved out the back door at the end of his final mount. Greg snapped up first in bareback and second in the other two shared events. Novices were all the news out of Okotoks on rodeo weekend. The pros that won did well, but not one of them dominated the ring the way Greg and Tyler did.

This time, Myra had not been able to steel herself and refuse to watch her son compete. It was happening in her hometown too. She agreed to appear supportive. Her son's victories began to crack the granite she had grown around her heart. Her hugs, her congratulations were to him a greater triumph that any of his trophies and prizes.

The stage was set for the last series of go-rounds at the Hanna rodeo near month's end. All Tyler had to do was manage any kind of placement in calf-roping and a sixth or seventh place finish in bareback and saddle bronc and he would be a shoo-in for the novice events at the Canadian finals in Edmonton in November. He qualified for the final rounds in all three events and did what he needed to do with a little insurance. It was like watching a musician write a new song in her sleep. The inner satisfaction of accomplishing what one set out to do was as much reward as all the gathered points and prizes and purse monies. *Sirocco* got treated to six fresh bales of quality hay for being such a reliable co-pilot all season long. The Savior of Zvenigorod was thanked with a few private kisses. Tyler was swamped with hugs from his family (though his mother's felt forced), and a couple of clownish smacks from Alex.

"You're the greatest, Cuz!"

"If you say so, Alex, but in future say it with handshakes or a few thumps on the back, okay? Pops, could I borrow your hankie?"

H. Lee Disher

# Chapter 23:
# The Frontiers of Love

Kissing, hugging, cuddling, holding hands, conversation—that's what Tyler and Stephanie's relationship came to comprise after that one bolder foray into intimacy. When rodeo events began to consume more and more of Tyler's weekend time, it cooled into good friendship. For a few months it unofficially broke off and Stephanie went out with Kevin Noseworthy a few times. Once, she went farther with him than she and Tyler had ever gone, though it wasn't very exciting for her. Love resembled a single-lever twisting faucet water tap. For Stephanie it seemed to swing widely back and forth from hot to cold. For Tyler, it had a demeanor that seemed to be stuck somewhere around lukewarm. The tap stayed on, the threads held, but the washer was thinning. The whole romantic apparatus could someday easily spring a leak.

Alex and Enid became more deeply attached and settled into the teasing and playful mode that was part and parcel of their nature. They never went all the way but experimented and indulged in just about everything else but. It was sometimes like kittens at play and sometimes like cat and mouse and sometimes like a couple of alley cats on the prowl but not wanting to get caught or bit or trapped. *"Catch us the little foxes"* as it is written in the Song of Solomon, except, for these two foxes, the vineyard remained unspoiled throughout their high school years.

The school trustee and the junior high teacher surrendered themselves into a relationship resembling a wilderness canoe trip. They kept things simple, let them unfold naturally, unrushed. They came to value one another's resources and innate wisdom. They figured out how to paddle in synchronized fashion regardless of who seemed to be in the lead or who was managing the rudder. They spent increasing amounts of time in the comfort of one another's company, building trust, sharing dreams and disappointments, letting go of the past, embracing the present, trembling less about the future confident they could steer around the next bend or through any sudden change in current. If they hit rapids, they headed for shore and portaged around them.

They sensed early on this could be a fit. Every passing week corroborated their hunches. It was a journey of mutual self-offering and they wanted it to last. Christmas 2000, Wallis Wilton was ready to relinquish widowhood if Ms. Morton was willing to abandon singleness. A proffered proleptic diamond was joyfully accepted.

Within two years of Louie having abandoned her, Ola gradually suppressed and finally forsook all romantic interest in men. Simultaneously, she embraced and augmented her higher love for her Lord, Jesus. Daily devotions at morning, noon and night were established. Half- to full-day *poustinia* experiences were implemented weekly along with a weekly day of fasting. She adopted her own adaptation of Catherine de Hueck Doherty's "Little Mandate." Instead of selling all she had and identifying with the poor, Ola lived simply and gave generously. She sought fervently to turn her life into a living gospel and an attentiveness to God's Spirit. She prayed plenty and approached life with a childlike simplicity. "Little—be always little!" were the words that had come to Catherine over time as she fleshed out her discipleship. "Do little things exceedingly well for love of me. Love...love never counting the cost," Jesus had instructed her. Words that likewise chimed sense in Ola's ears were: "Be hidden. Be a light to your neighbour's feet. Go without fears into the depths of people's hearts. I shall be with you." Ola became caught up in agape. She could not count the times she was absolutely certain she never walked, spoke, moved, or even breathed without sensing a close companionship with Jesus.

H. Lee Disher

# Chapter 24:
# Routines, Rituals, Reveries

Life anywhere is more than wedding rings, friendship rings, and rodeo circuits, but it does travel as much in circles as it does along various lines. Routines and rituals demarcate the repetitions. Goal-setting, personal objectives, spontaneous surprises and unanticipated detours define the straighter geometries by which people live and move and have their being. Some will argue that sometimes the unexpected and the sudden send us in curves and loops rather than on zig-zag courses The populace of Okotoks pursues the planes and patterns particular and, at times, peculiar to its citizenry.

Business people attend to business. Teachers teach. Students learn. Athletes exercise and play. Ministers minister. Priests do priestly things. Doctors doctor. Nurses nurse. Pharmacists dispense. Politicians politic, shake a lot of hands and say what's safe and helpful towards getting re-elected. Functionaries attend to their respective functions. Managers manage. Workers work. Farmers farm. Craftspeople tend to their craft. Salespeople sell. Consumers consume. Media people report. Police, firefighters, ambulance attendants are either on duty or on call. Childcare workers care for small children. Social workers meet with clients and uphold qualifying criteria. Researchers research. Programmers program. Cooks cook. Waiters wait on tables. Bartenders tend bar. Technicians and tradespeople fix things or build things. Engineers inspect, study, plan, engineer and troubleshoot. Consultants consult. Transport industry workers perform what they variously do. Hoteliers operate hotels and motels. Funeral directors arrange funerals and seek to offer immediate comfort to the grieving. Retirees do as they please (usually). The sick receive care. The poor are always with us. The down-and-outs run in their own ruts. Okotoks has all of these and more though the latter two are few and somewhat obscured. Commuters abound.

Week after week, month by month, Jules Stedman travels to and fro between Okotoks and Calgary and wherever else Tranogco sends him. The transition to supply and exploration from sales and marketing is not beyond his expertise or capabilities. He simply doesn't find it as stimulating. It also requires travelling farther afield. Monthly jaunts to the main mines and processing plants in Fort McMurray and near Peace River are necessary. Meetings with managers and supervisors to discuss targets and quotas, to review production procedures and to gather estimates on reserves determine Jules' agenda. He has a working knowledge of the steam-assisted gravity drainage system Tranogco uses in most of its sites to extract and separate bitumen from the clay, mineral matter and traces of water that enclose it. He knows that in two of their Peace River plants, Tranogco is experimenting with thermal injection methods through vertical wells as a means of extraction. Bitumen is a viscous, liquid hydrocarbon that requires further processing to convert it to upgraded crude oil. Jules is aware of the likely inefficiencies: that only about ten to twelve per cent of what is mined is convertible; that approximately two tonnes of soil are mined for every barrel of oil. Much of the rest is stored until it can be returned to the environment when the site is returned to its natural state. Jules is pleased that Tranogco has been an industry leader in reducing carbon dioxide emissions, one of the environmental hazards of recovering oil from tar sand. An ethical environmental consciousness is the one part of this job that Jules seriously embraces. He is resolute and thorough when it comes to site restoration projects. He values the north Alberta landscape as much for its wilderness ethos as for its mineral potential. He knows he could not live there now as he did during his first two years with the company. He expects to get stranded during some of his winter visits. Jules marvels at the hardiness and endurance of the managers and workers who have settled into this isolated northern outpost for the long haul. After around thirty-six hours there, he gets itchy to get home again.

The discovery of rich bitumen deposits in age-old tar sands in late 1960s jolted the Alberta economy into international corporate competition almost overnight. The reserves are among the richest in the world estimated at 1,700-2,500 billion barrels but not all of them are recoverable by means of current technology. They are more commonly referred to as oil sands now. It created a whole strata of *nouveau riche* and completed the quiet coup by which agriculture was overtaken by business, banking, and industry as the primary source of fiscal provincial health. A steady rush of out-of-province job-seekers and fortune-hunters flocked in. Parochial powers still held control of the reins and reaped the bulk of the new benefits. Nonetheless something akin to a cultural revolution seeped into the fabric of prairie life in wild rose country.

The gaseous decomposition of deceased dinosaurs even in as rich a bed as the Alberta oil sands is not alone enough to ensure adequate supplies and reserves to compete in the commercial arenas of international oil and gas corporations. Like its competitors, Tranogco has contracts and agreements with other nations. Saudi Arabia is not one of them. Only a select few American firms have access to that multi-million dollar mecca. Tranogco's connections with Qatar and Kuwait have been re-established after the temporary disruption caused by the Irani-American war of 1991. The conflict that would be inflicted upon Iraq by the United States subsequent to the disaster of September 11, 2001, would serve to close up international access to any oil and gas reserves in that Mid-Eastern nation. More recently, the quest for other fields has begun to shift to Africa. In 2000, Jules is sent to establish contracts with infant refineries in Liberia and Djibouti, so he misses Tyler's engagement in Stavely and his convincing triumph in June in Brooks. An investigative trip to Mali is planned for late January 2001. More certain finds have been opening up in the former Soviet republics, notably Russia and the Ukraine. Jules arranges for Wallis Wilton and Carol Morton to look after Tyler, Rebecca and Alex for week in October 2000 while Myra and Pops and Ola join him for a week-long junket to Ola's homeland.

Ola finds it nostalgic but not very rejuvenating. She is convinced emigrating to Canada was a healthful, ameliorative move. Four million citizens of the Ukraine still live in dangerously radioactive areas. Twelve percent of once arable land remains contaminated. Poultry and fowl farming predominate all ventures in agriculture with chicken operations in the millions. There are more ducks being bred and raised in the Ukraine than cattle or sheep; more turkeys than there are pigs or goats. Independence was regained in 1991 after the break-up of the Communist-dominated Soviet Union. Democracy is having a steep learning curve and uphill struggle.

Oil is the new mineral darling in which the nation is hoping for golden goose prospects. Coal, manganese, lignite, mercury and peat while still important, have been displaced. Jules participates in the opening of a new refinery in Luhansk in the former coal-rich Donetsk basin on the eastern border and re-negotiates three five-year contracts with firms in Odessa and Mariupol, a port on the Sea of Azov. He continues to long to leave wells and drills, pipelines, hard-hats, $CO_2$ emissions, blueprints, and speculations behind so he can return to balance sheets, market analyses and stock market trades, and transportation and delivery services; to the more antiseptic corridors of gas companies and plastics manufacturers who use petroleum derivatives, to the mercantile yards and warehouses of those who sell bulk oil in drums.

Wallis Wilton is totally immersed in the former Alberta. His poultry and egg venture is just large enough to pay most of his regular bills. His bread and butter and gravy comes from cash crops and Simmental beef. His returns are sufficient to keep ahead of the large loan repayments required by the Royal Bank. His profits bolster his RRSP and investment portfolio, enable him to buy his new Jeep Cherokee outright and treat Carol Morton more than decently. She doesn't need his money and that isn't what keeps her attracted to him and in love with him. It's his manners, his intellect, his genuineness and fairness, his tenderness in intimacy. She is responsible for drawing him out of his routines by addition not by substitution. He attends plays and operas instead of merely watching them on television or listening to them. He finds a niche for his leadership and supervisory skills on the council of school trustees. His literary bent is whetted. Romance evokes a writing spirit within him. Once a month throughout their courtship, Wallis pours himself into the production of a sonnet.

Witness these lines which Carol receives in August 2002:

> Your slender form slides by as lithe as larkspurs
> as you pass by my window to my door.
> My heart is power-surged with curious wonders.
> Your love unlike that which I knew before
> enkindles something different in my soul
> without diminishing the former flame.
> To have two partners helping make me whole,
> each one unique, neither quite the same,
> is blessing, grace and fortune without measure.
> I cannot but rejoice and soak in solace
> awash in peace, security and pleasure.
> Amazed, affirmed where loneliness can't menace,

my life feels like a garden condominium
where daffodil's succeeded by delphinium.

Myra never received a poem from Jules, but she knew she had his undying affection and love. The flowers and gifts that came by surprise, the pecks on the cheek "Good Morning," the hugs and kisses when he came home at night, the continued times of earnest love-making and simpler intimacies—all these sought to ground her, to affirm her importance and specialness. She sought to reciprocate, but was never quite sure that she wasn't always holding some of herself in reserve. For whom? For what? Where did that originate? She couldn't say or ascertain any satisfactory answer. She was a part-time wife and mother, community volunteer, and part-time pharmaceutical assistant.

Tuesdays, Thursdays, Fridays from 9 A.M. to 1 P.M. and through some Saturday shifts, she left behind the laundry that needed washing or ironing and folding, the mending, the cooking of meals, the housecleaning, the taxiing of her children to their extra-curricular activities, the lawncare and gardening that she agreed to undertake, and whatever else she did to attend to her family and share their love, their laughter, their trials and disappointments. She left all that and stood at the back counter of Kingman's Pharmacy dispensing prescriptions, consulting with doctors and customers over the phone, offering advice and drawing attention to warnings and special concerns connected with the drugs being issued, stocking shelves and ordering supplies. Her boss, Irving Kingman, one of three Jews in all of Okotoks, was a fair, honest employer, affable, and knowledgeable enough yet definitely businesslike. Still working at seventy-one, he wasn't as keen to keep up with the ever-advancing, changing realm of pharmaceuticals. He depended on support staff to keep him informed. Myra was happy to oblige. She knew there was precious little room for error and found the whole field of pharmacology fascinating. Her mind was like a constantly churning stomach Irving told her: consume, indulge, then spew or excrete at will. She would have preferred a less graphic, more pleasing image but she knew what he was getting at. She relished being up-to-date, took time to scan the frequent newsletters of Canadian and American Pharmaceutical Associations and reacquainted herself with the contents of the two drug encyclopedias the pharmacy kept on hand (on computer disc since 1995). She also knew Kingman's customers and what ailed them, and took her oath of confidentiality with utter seriousness. One of Irving's other workers waffled about that, tried to draw her co-workers into discussions of various clients and what probably contributed to causing them pain or discomfort and, at times, was highly suspected of spilling the beans in public. Proving it was always just out of reach. News reporters aren't the only ones who diligently protect their sources.

Myra might only go so far as sharing what anyone might reasonably conjecture, that heart and cancer medications, water pills, and anti-depressants were the most common drugs dispensed. Shift by shift, she faithfully counted ninety patches of Nitroderm four for customers with weak hearts; ninety 20 mg tablets of Tamoxifen for cancer control; ninety 20 mg hits of Furosemide (Lasix) to prevent fluid build-up and ninety 20 mg doses of Ludiomil (Prozac) to keep the depressed and over-anxious calm and mellow. Each prescription represented a three-months' supply. Some notices from pharmacology publications to which she gave attention during 2000-2001 included new approved drugs such as Fenofibrate (Tricor) to help reduce cholesterol; Orlistat (Xenical), another diet pill designed to help reduce hydrolized fats and increase the absorption of fatty acids; Sirolimus (Rapamune) an immunosuppressant, to be taken in conjunction with Cyclosporine, that had proved helpful to recipients of organ transplants; Clopidogrel (Plavix), a platelet function inhibitor administered to stroke recovery patients and persons with peripheral artery disease, and Omeprazole (shelf-name Prilosec) for episodic heartburn. There was a study that indicated estrogen therapy could be helpful to postmenopausal women suffering osteoporosis; warnings about AIDS-sufferers who combined medical treatment with alternative therapies and herbal remedies; hopeful research into medications that would target dopamine receptors and certain amino acid transfers in the brain to improve memory-enhancing agents during the early onset of Alzheimer's disease; and a heads-up regarding the addictive properties of certain psychotropic drugs that promised stress reduction. In this last instance, Myra immediately prepared a staff memo. Having had her own bouts of high anxiety on occasion, the whole realm of treatment for mental disorders fascinated Myra. Bulletins for 2001 included the approval of Pramipexole (Mirapex), a dopamine receptor agonist for use by sufferers of Parkinson s disease; Mirtazapine (Remeron), an anti-depressant dissolving on the tongue when ingested; and, a study of the neurological and biochemical basis for the success of Sildenafil (Viagra), Tadalafil (Cialis) and such in treating male erectile dysfunction. Almost all of this got filed in Myra's cognitive compartment labelled "Important." She took special interest in research and treatments for novel outbreaks of disease such as the search for an effective anti-biotic against West Nile virus, for instance. SARS would be the surprise and riddle around the corner in 2003. The greater riddle for Myra was, "Who am I, really?"

Whereas Myra seemed dedicated to active engagement in keeping herself and others healthy, her brother immersed himself in just about every possible bodily-abusive and addictive behaviour one could other than drug addiction. True enough, nicotine, caffeine, and alcohol are habit-forming drugs in their own right, but Louie never got hooked on anything else as some of his friends and acquaintances did, diminishing their neural capacities with marijuana, speed, cocaine, or heroin for instance. Tack on the exterior addiction to gambling and the risks he ran sleeping around the way he did, and you would have to consider that Louie Davis was a walking recipe for disaster. Maybe so, but it seemed he was also wired for high tolerance and survival. Was it simply his other daily fix of beef jerky, pepperoni sticks, and pickled eggs that gave him metabolic balance? Or was he being guided and protected by some invisible hand for some undeserved purpose? Neither. Louie just lived on luck.

Finding reasonable lodgings, a small circle of free spirits with whom to chum day after day, and a bartender that would run you a tab for a month was the kind of luck that kept Louie in Lloydminster longer than he had stayed anywhere since he left Okotoks and Ola behind. Over a year he had settled in now (frightening thought that—settling in), landing in the soup and pickled egg barrel so to speak at Ned's Junction, a ramshackle tavern and cheap hotel operation two blocks south of the main intersection downtown. His room-mates, dining and drinking buddies, were free-range rovers like himself cut loose or ostracized from family connections, worlds unto themselves with atmospheric pressure so thin it held them hardly accountable to anyone or anything. Screwy Louie they dubbed him, a form of knighting that took him into their circle.

They all had nicknames used so frequently, Louie could scarcely remember their real names. Slashmouth (Conrad Hilton von Helmond), son of German immigrants who fell far short of his father's high entrepreneurial expectations, bore a jagged scar that ran up the left side of his cheek from the corner of his mouth, remnants of a broken beer bottle polka that he won when he was nineteen. The scar was like a medal to him. Hob-knob Hickey (Albert Ransom) walked bow-legged with his knees protruding and took a red-neck approach to life just for the fun of stirring the pot. "Hickey" was a tag end he added on himself knowing that his red-neck attitude was one that came and went like an evening shower. Hob-knob, orphaned at birth, was graduate of twenty-six foster homes by the age of seventeen, never really fitting in anywhere until he landed in the cozy circle of companions lodged at Ned's Junction. One-blue-eyed Sadie (Sandra Cooper) was a boarding school drop-out and run-away from somewhere in Yorkshire, England. She had a droopy lid on her right side through which one sometimes caught a glimpse of an iris that seemed to be different in colour from her left eye. She wound up in Lloydminster two years ago jumping ship from a transport driver that offered to take her to Edmonton from Saskatoon and who got far too frisky after dinner on the way. Having sex was always her call. She shielded herself by taking charge of situations and was savvy enough and tough enough to do it. When she walked into Ned's, she negotiated a part-time barmaid and waitress position in exchange for room and board. She had several other sources of income: as a free-lance dresser of store windows, a tombstone engraver, a police informant and as the organizer of random games of poker in a back room off of Ned's kitchen where she wheedled the wallets out of numerous unsuspecting customers. For protection, she carried a battery-operated engraving drill in her hand-bag, (that transport driver was left steering with a bleeding hole in his left wrist). Sadie was the one who pulled the little support group together one by one as they came to stay at Ned's. Albert, Conrad, and, lastly, Louie became her mini-harem to which she played beneficent sultan, randy dominatrix and mother hen. No one dare accuse her of the latter to her face.

Louie was as content to snuggle under her wing as any of the others and to nest at Ned's as long as his luck allowed. Ned's was a nexus for all sorts of clientele likewise bitten by the betting bug and, since his arrival, Louie had been riding a string of luck unparalleled in his life thus far. He cleaned up in the hockey pool, the football pool, had several ponies come in and nailed several exactors. A number of times he drew a $50 Nevada ticket from the plastic-box fund-raiser that sat beside the till and in March 2000 (the best win of all) Louie bought a winning federal lottery ticket that paid out $20,000. Ola nearly fell off her kitchen chair when a cheque arrived in the mail enclosing $2,000 towards Alex' savings for college. Louie had enough sense to bank $15,000 of the remainder and only keep $3,000 of liquid assets as his floating fund. He had been around long enough to know about a gambler's rainy day itches and dry seasons. Lady Luck had washed over him at Ned's in Lloyd and he was prepared to ride every blessed wave.

Ned's was so situated in that border town that shared the same name with a Saskatchewan city that the owner-operator, Neville Edward Hammersmith, claimed the provincial boundary ran straight through the middle of his establishment. That led to all manner of trite jocularity along the lines of: "So did you fall out of bed and land in Saskatchewan this morning?"; "Got a tough day ahead. Might have to go over to Alberta for the afternoon and a late dinner" or, "Ned, this has got to be the only place where the Tory supporters sit on the left and the NDP Socialist adherents gather on the right." Once or twice a month, Ned got in on the act, threatening to move his cash register to the other side of the bar: "You guys better just keep counting your blessings that I keep my till, buy my business licence, and pay my property taxes over here in Alberta, otherwise you'd be getting dinged for provincial sales tax on all your grub and grog."

One cold night in April, 2000, Louie did fall out of bed in a drunken stupor. He didn't realize he hit his head on the window ledge en route to the floor. The force of the extra smack was severe enough to knock him right out. He had no idea where he was, let alone what province he was in. He came to in mid-hallucination. He saw himself walking knee deep in snow in some foreign country. Behind him was a forest trail he had recently exited; before him, the slope of a mountain. He mounted a jagged ledge of rock and turned to review his steps. In the distance, beyond the forest was a small village. The sunlit landscape stretching beyond that led his eyes to the profiles of a larger city on the far horizon. It bore some of the features he recalled from his visit to Kiev years ago when he first travelled to meet Ola. He clambered off the ledge and headed back to the forest on a different trail about fifty metres to the left of the one he had taken previously. Footing became easier when he found the woods as the snow-cover thinned. He wound his way along until the path came to a rather steep decline. He made two or three tentative steps and then slipped and began to slide. Sliding turned into tumbling and he was bumped and jostled further downwards by occasional roots and trunks of saplings bordering the trail. It seemed to take some time to hit bottom. When he did, he heard the sound of rushing water. He had landed beside a partially frozen stream and the ice closer to shore felt solid and thick enough to walk on. Flatter ground came as welcome relief at this juncture of his vision. Up ahead the stream made a sharp right turn between two small tree-topped promontories—a gateway of sorts. Louie made his way gingerly to the gap not particularly certain of the thickness of the ice beneath him.

As he rounded the corner he bumped into something long, solid and leathery that could not be an overhanging root. He stepped backwards about ten or fifteen paces to get a clearer glimpse of the obstruction. What he saw left him breathless and agape. Protruding on slanted, anchored poles were the eyeless heads, forelegs, and hollowed-out body cavities of two horses. The hind legs were missing, but calcified testicles testified that these were the shells of a stallion and a male colt. Skin hardened into leather still covered most of the skeletons though in some spots it had rotted away and in other places it flapped loosely. As Louie's eyes glanced across to the other side of the gap, he noticed a similar pairing of hollowed horses suspended from the promontory on that side of the stream. Horrific as the sight was, more frightening still in Louie's imagination were the four separate ossified hearts that hung on tethers between each set of forelegs. Louie reeled, felt sick and sensed the ice beneath him giving way. Balance deserted him. He was falling backwards into the rushing, frigid water. At which point, he woke up.

"Holy Ghost on a month of Sundays!" he muttered as he shook himself and scrambled to stand erect. Already wearing a T-shirt, boxers, and a pair of woolen socks, he stuffed himself into his jeans, slipped on a pair of old brown loafers with splits in the outer seams, headed to the sink in the corner of his room where he splashed cold water on his face and proceeded downstairs for the blackest cup of coffee Ned could brew and whatever bite of breakfast was destined to be the special of the morning.

After placing his order, he sat down at his customary table where he was soon joined by Hob-knob Hickey. Dressed rather nattily in a light brown suit and yellow dress shirt, Louie's comrade in survival leaned forward wide-eyed in his chair and asked, "What's up with you making all that commotion? Sounded like someone who suddenly got religion or somethin'."

"I didn't get no religion, Hickey, but I might just have to go find me some real quick."

"How so?"

"Must of fallen out of bed and into some kind of hallucination."

"You must have fallen all right judging by that red goose-egg on your forehead. What do you mean, hallucination?"

"Well, it was in between a dream and a nightmare since I was half-conscious at the time. I can remember it clear as the mirror behind Ned's bar."

"Scary?"

"More like weird, but, yeah, kind of scary too. You see I was wandering these wooded trails in the Ukraine I think. Only it seemed longer ago, long before I went there to fetch my Chernobyl bride. It was winter and I slid down this snow-lined path to the edge of a stream. I followed along on the ice near shore to a gap up ahead of me framed by two juttings of tree-covered rock. When I passed through the gap, I bumped into something and had to move back to figure out what it was. My God! Hickey, it was a pair of hollowed out horse carcasses hanging on poles with their fossilized great big balls still attached and hanging between their forelegs on tethers were their hearts turned hard as stone. And there was a similar pair suspended over the other side of the gap. I gasped, started falling backwards ... and woke up."

"Sredni Stog."

"Huh?"

"Sredni Stog. They were tribal peoples in the Ukraine during the Copper Age. Bred horses the way we raise some cattle—for the meat. Revered them so much they'd stick up gutted horse carcasses on poles as guardians and purveyors of the dead to sacred burial grounds. Your guess is as good as mine or any anthropologist's as to whether they tended the gates of heaven or Hades."

"Srednecks pog? Or what did you call them? No matter. I told you it was weird. But what's more weird, Hickey, is how come you know anything about them."

"Bummin' around you get to spend a lot of time in libraries and Christian Science Reading rooms. I like reading *National Geographic* and *Scientific American* magazines. Two weeks ago I told you about an article on those horses you saw. It was in a 1991 *Scientific American* I believe. Fascinating stuff. I read it several times till it kind of stuck in my memory. Remember I almost graduated university till I flunked out in my third year as an anthropology major. I always loved reading and participating in seminars, just hated the essay work and the exams."

"Fascinating for you. But, tell me, O wise one, how come I got so lucky as to have such a lurid vision, even if I was recalling something you told me while I was in a drunken stupor?"

"Beats me, Louie. It was stallions and male colts you saw, right?"

"Yeah, why?"

"I don't know. When's the last time you had a heart-to-heart with your old man?"

In April, 2000, Pops Davis read through Ola's copy of Constance Garnett's English translation of Ivan Turgenev's *Fathers and Sons*. He wept at the end. Should his rebellious son wind up buried in some untouched tomb, Pops might not know where to find it. No trees, no flowers would bend in the wind whispering prayers of reconciliation.

In the usual daily patterns he traced out, Pops was not the kind of working man who took time out to sit around reading. There were always the horses to feed, groom and bathe and stalls to keep clean, though sometimes Alex helped with those chores and Tyler always did when he was around. There were several visits every week shared among Pops, Punky McAllister and the gang of three others who had all been farming on that same rural concession for decades, who always had a cooperative approach helping one another out with projects: seedings, harvests, barn-raisings, stock auctions, trips to the local abattoir, whatever. From late May till the end of September, Pops had his vegetable and flower gardens in which to putter around and some patches of grass to keep trimmed with his riding mower. In late October and through the winter when the snow wasn't too deep nor the weather too raw, he could hitch Tacitus up to a sleigh, head into the wood-lot to fell and chop firewood with a chain saw. This activity caused Myra no little worry. Ola harbored similar concerns when she first came to live on the farm, but by now she had seen Pops go into and out of the woods without incident and with several fresh cut cords in tow, that her anxieties scarcely surfaced.

What she had witnessed closer at hand was Pops' chain saw skill and safety measures when it came time to cut Christmas trees for shipping. That project always consumed almost all of November and the early weeks of December. The trees grew on her property but it was by and large Pops' enterprise and hobby. She helped drag some of the cut trees to the baler and load them on a wagon or sleigh so they could be dragged to waiting refrigerated tractor trailer trucks parked on a gravel lane that led to the Christmas tree plots. She arranged the transportation contracts and bills of lading, set up foreign markets in Mexico and America and domestic markets in Alberta, Saskatchewan and Manitoba. On weekends in December, the plots were open to the locals to cut their own tree, which often meant having Pops saw one down for them.

One might think that Christmas tree farming is rather low-risk, low maintenance compared to other agricultural and horticultural endeavours, and it likely is. But it still takes vigilance and a good deal of work. As one of about 15,000 growers in North America, Pops and Ola had a hundred acres worth of evergreen produce on the go. Approximately 2,000 trees are planted per acre of which as many as 1,500 and as few as 750 can be expected to survive. Seedlings and saplings are planted five to six feet apart and take six to seven years to mature to Christmas tree stature. As with market gardening or grain-growing, crop variety and rotation are important to faithful stewardship of the soil as well as consumer demand. Ten of their hundred acres were left fallow for a year. The other ninety were planted in successive stages over a six- to seven-year stretch and comprised four varieties: firs, balsams, Scotch pines, and Colorado blue spruce.

Do the math and that means that out of 180,000 trees on site, somewhere between 70,000 to 112,000 are going to survive. If it takes seven years to maturity, then in any one year only 10,000 to 16,000 trees will be harvested; 1,250 to 2,000 of each variety on average. Wholesale price: $8-$10 per tree. Some of your profits get eaten up in buying seedlings for the subsequent year's planting, sprays to protect against diseases, fertilizers, gasoline, equipment maintenance, baling twine and plastic wrapping and, in Canada, the ubiquitous federal goods and services tax. Costs of shipping are recovered from the vendors. During the year there are particular times for shearing the tips of trees to control height and width. There's also trimming the ends of branches to induce the conical shape buyers prefer. Imperfect trees are weeded out, fed through a chipper and sold for mulch. Diseased ones are removed away from the growing site and burned. Fallow fields are burned before planting to encourage new growth. It's no hobby for slackers, yet comfortable and busy enough to keep Pops occupied and feeling useful within his capacities.

Cash-cropping is agriculture in a much higher key. Eighteen hundred acres is below average for those who indulge such a venture, but it was plenty for Ola to manage and the returns on her efforts were more than sufficient to sustain her simple life-style. Some of what she knew from growing up on a farm and attending business school in the Ukraine was transferrable to her new life situation in Canada. The land now under her care lay at different latitude with somewhat different climatic conditions and required adjustments on her part plus the acquisition of new knowledge. Pops' accumulated agricultural wisdom was invaluable to her during the process of transferring the operation into her hands. She was also wise enough early to consult with a local provincial agricultural representative and have an aerial photograph taken of Pops' acreage.

She knew that crop rotation was key and worked out a circulation that maximized the conversion of former horse pastures into fields so that virtually all 1,800 acres went through alternating rounds of oats, feed barley, canola and hay. Grain fields continually resown in grain rather quickly give diminished returns. Putting oilseeds and forage crops in the mix serves to enhance soil nutrient and moisture retention, guards against erosion and, because different herbicides are required, deters the spread of resistant weeds.

Ola was in charge of the enterprise but it was not a one-woman show. She had three hired hands for about nine months of the year, three young, married men she met in the congregation at St. Bartholomew's. From November through February, they supplemented their income with part-time employment like delivering fried chicken and doing odd household repair jobs for other members of the parish. Two of their wives had year-round employment. Two of them had grown up on farms outside of Melfort, Saskatchewan but marriage and their wives' careers brought them to Calgary.

The third young man immigrated with his family from the Ukraine in 1991 and married a Canadian girl he met in high school who was willing to embrace Eastern Orthodox faith.

Anton, Andrey, and Vladimir were a blessing to Ola as she was salvation to them. She kidded them about being three characters that had just stepped out of a story by Dostoyevsky called *The Double* and welcomed them like younger surrogate cousins from the old country. In fact, Andrey and Anton looked enough alike that people often mistook them for brothers. They were familiar with the circuits of ploughing, seeding, fertilizing, spraying, cutting, and harvesting. They brought the requisite array of mechanical skills to operate and maintain farm machinery. They welcomed her shared bits of spirituality. She treated them well and paid them very fairly, taught them all she knew about cash-cropping and enjoyed the conversations they sometimes had about faith and life.

Andrey was the worker who kept those copies of magazines featuring naked men and teenage boys in his bedroom in the Bunkie. That part of his life never came up in conversations with Ola. Vladimir and Anton sometimes teased him about it, made it clear their orientation was other-wise and generally preferred to "let sleeping gay dogs lie" as Anton had once remarked.

"This farm is blessed with a fairly decent mix of black soil near the waterways and dark brown soil elsewhere. There is sufficient irrigation available except in one large section in parcel three to which we pump water from Barstoke's Pond that you will find within our woodlot and which is fed by an underground spring. The soil on average has a pH level of 6 which is excellent for growing oats. In about three hundred acres, we add chemical supplements to make sure a pH level of about 6 is sustained. Copper content is generally favorable for growing barley and it helps guard against ergot. The canola fields receive an supplementary application of sulphur. We do deep tilling here by and large and take time to cut grasses around pathways, stream beds and the roadside, all of which also helps control the spread of ergot. There are some crop diseases that scarcely, if ever, affect us in Alberta such as Anthracnose, Aster yellows, and stem and crown rusts *(puccinias)*. Rusts require an alternate host in order to reproduce and germinate. It's called buckthorn and unless someone is stupid enough to bring it into this province from Ontario, Manitoba, eastern Saskatchewan, or parts of the United States, we will stay clear of them. Fusarium head blight is uncommon but just to be sure, I use treated seed. As for Barley, Yellow Dwarf virus which is also known as Red Leaf on oats, we use seeds from resistant cultivars here and rarely have a problem with that infection. The same practice of using treated and resistant seeds is used to guard against smut. As for problems that can arise from root rot or that bacterial blight that sometimes shows up on barley crops in late July especially around the edges of fields in shaded areas, crop rotation is our best defence. To protect our crops against damage from other potential predators, I devise an annual schedule of fungicide and herbicide applications indicating times, locations and amounts. It needs to be adhered to strictly. We focus our attention mainly on the *septoria* complex of fungi that make barley and oats susceptible to leaf and glume blotch, on preventing barley stripe mosaic and brome mosaic on oats, against scald and powdery mildew on barley and blast and leaf spot on oats. As for disease-control in canola, it's pretty much the same process. We have found that Argentine canola fares better on our land than Polish varieties which have a shorter growing season. We use treated resistant seed to stave off blackleg and red canola blight. We apply foliar sprays when flowering plants are between 30 to 60 percent in full bloom. These applications help cut down damage from *sclerotinia* stem rot and *alternaria* black spot. To date we've had very good success in the disease-control department. If we've had years of lower yields, they have been far more attributable to unfavourable weather conditions than any other factor. Too dry, too wet, too bad." [Notes from Ola's lectures].

Vladimir and Anton took charge of disease control, knowing that some of their work also contributed to pest control. The matter of pest, insect and weed control was taken up by Andrey who had gathered particular knowledge and aptitude in those departments. He knew, for instance, that even treated canola seed could use a foliar spray like Ripcord during early growth stages to mitigate damage attributable to flea beetles. He had combat strategies for other canola-favouring pests like diamondback moths and cabbage seed pod weevils. He was prepared to do battle with grasshoppers, green-bug aphids and redbacked cutworms if needed. He rejoiced when he saw natural predators in the fields: ladybug beetles, green lacewings and ichneumon wasps, for example. He was ever out in the fields scouting for insects and keeping an eye on weeds.

Weeds are an ever-present farming hassle. So many of them are highly ubiquitous: Canada thistle, wild mustard, dandelion, quackgrass. Scentless chamomile can be a terrible nuisance if it shows up in quantity. Andrey scoured roadsides and ditches and the perimeters of fields, cutting, mowing, handpulling as much as possible seeking to minimize weed intrusions into the midst of Ola's crops. Threatening populations were given the appropriate herbicidal treatments of 2-4-D, or glyphosate or Curtail M and such. In 1999, he took on an infestation of yellow toad-flax that showed up and won.

His deepest sense of satisfaction, however, was derived from controlling larger pests: mice, moles, voles, and Richardson's ground squirrels; i.e., gophers. He was very adept at constructing and setting traps near the entry-ways of burrows and around the edges of storage facilities and under raised buildings. Moles in particular had to be trapped. He built wooden nests to place on fenceposts for natural predators like hawks and owls. Ola was not in favour of using poisons, but she did permit fumigation of burrows with carbon monoxide which was best done at the time of emergence from hibernation. Then, in the process of spring plowing, many a gopher burrow was deep-tilled into non-existence their inhabitants having already succumbed to noxious gas. Andrey so enjoyed this challenge he used his calendar as a place on which to keep score. For April 23, 2000, for instance, he wrote: 20 gophers, 10 voles, two moles and about 55 mice. Some of them he had killed with the grass-mower.

Keeping the farm machinery clean and in top working order was Vladimir's department, though Anton was more skilled in tending to hydraulic mechanisms. Ola had no small inventory of equipment on hand more than adequate for the size of her cropping operation: three large tractors, three smaller ones, two balers, two windrowers, two tillers, two seed-planters, one giant sprayer, a couple of harrows, two manure spreaders, hay-wagons, grain hoppers, and a state-of-the-art combine. It was her good fortune that the inheritance she received from the sale of her parents' estate in the Ukraine enabled her to purchase outright what Pops didn't already have on hand as she gradually overtook management of the farm. Profits from her operation had been sufficient to purchase replacement or up-graded equipment, repair or improve her sheds and storage facilities and two tall silos. She owed no bank anything except seasonal start-up loans for seed, fertilizers, herbicides, insecticides, fungicides and such. These she promptly paid off when the returns from a growing season came through, which sometimes meant mid-August of a subsequent year. Yields from her acreage were consistently higher than provincial averages.

She exercised maximum thrift wherever she could: recycling seeds; converting the former stables into a sanitized storage facility for canola, the horse stalls becoming aerated but well-sealed bins; and using manure for a natural fertilizer base. She had worked out a contract with some horse stables in Spruce Meadows that she supplied with hay. So many bales were bartered in exchange for so many tons of piled horse droppings. She always sent the manure to a lab for testing to gauge its nitrogen, phosphate, potassium content and then calculated how much extra chemical fertilizer she would have to purchase each year for each of her various crops. She abided by provincial government guidelines not spreading manure too close to any watershed, digging it in within four or five days, or spreading it in winter on light snow cover.

Cash-cropping is a gargantuan kind of juggling act, but Ola had the wisdom and the tenacity to keep it all straight. She consulted agricultural representatives and had tracking programs installed on a forty-gig computer and read government and other agricultural publications voraciously. She found the Ag-dex blue and green books invaluable guides to crop rotation. In 1998, she risked seeding her canola fields in the fall instead of early spring. It worked for her, freeing precious spring time for seeding barley and oats. She read almanacs and crop-year predictions and only took out insurance if it seemed prudent and did not tie her into any kind of contract with certain suppliers. When the provincial department of agriculture developed its crop-cost calculator and other helpful tables, hints, and information sheets as an on-line web-site, she mentally devoured it, consulted it frequently and praised God for its creation. She was even better at following the grain price index based in Chicago where selling and buying prices for all North American grains are controlled. She had a knack for marketing her crop at near optimum return moments.

By the year 2000, Ola was well on her way to practising precision farming. Upgraded or new equipment was outfitted with global-positioning system and geographic information systems technology. Sensors, monitors and such all linked into her main database enabled her to monitor and map yields, track weeds and vary sprays accordingly, control variations in fertilizer applications for particular segments of her fields through an on-board computer outfitted with a topographical map of her acreage and to keep tabs on borders, ditches, access lanes and possible alterations she might consider. Cumulative records from one year to the next enabled Ola to analyze successes and failures, compute trends and make cash-cropping economics a fingertip ready enterprise. In her hands, the farm flourished.

In late September 2000, Ola's post-harvest respite was interrupted one Wednesday morning by the sudden arrival of Frances Evans. Ola was quick to recognize the signs of spiritual malaise in her student of meditation: whitened cheeks, tension across the eyebrows, twitching hands and some shortness of breath which could have been occasioned by Frances' dashing from her car into Ola's kitchen except that it persisted for a while as the reason for the visit unfolded. Ola poured out two cups of hot tea from a just-made fresh pot and bid Frances sit down.

"Oh mercy, Ola, I'm so glad you're home. I just took a chance, but I knew I had to come to see you. I had the strangest vision last night. I think it was like one of your showings. In the middle of the night, I dreamed a strong wind stole into my bedroom, crept up my nightgown and turned me into a human parachute as it carried me out the window and up, up, up high above Okotoks. It was a friendly wind more than a frightening one and I knew I could trust it wasn't going to suddenly withdraw and send me headlong to the ground. It was like it just wanted to show me something.

"As it held me hovering over mid-town, I was tilted at about a 35-degree angle to improve my vision. Slowly, something dark like oil slipped in over the whole town from the outer edges to the centre. It lingered there wavering, wobbling like fresh black pizza dough. It was semi-transparent, not opaque, like film. Then from the north, then south, then from the east and west a cry sounded, cries joining onto other cries that also made their way steadily toward the centre.

The dough by now was floating on an underlay of salt water. The wind seemed to reach out a hand and scoop some of that water up to my lips. And everything below me began to sway.

"Then the wind gave me a gentle half twist and I could see what I had not noticed before because it was hidden by the billows of my nightgown. There was a new clock tower that had been constructed above the face of our town hall. It had a carillon in it that was playing some lazy classical tune like Pachelbel's Canon in D, but slower and less melodic. And then it began to thunder, not in the sky but beneath the streets. The cries turned into wails and the carillon music crescendoed. And white light flashed across the salt water under the film of black dough. Then suddenly the clock tower began to split, from the bottom up, brick by brick, row by row until after, I don't know, perhaps an hour it seemed or two, the clock-face itself cracked and the steepled roof-cover was rent apart. But, instead of crashing to the ground in pieces, each half of the tower just bent over backwards till it touched Elizabeth Street in front of town hall. It looked like two symmetrical green halves of a fresh-split tree limb curved and taut like twin mechanisms on a pair of catapults. They didn't spring forward. They just lay there as if they were super-glued to the pavement.

"That was all. The wind took me back home and set me down in bed. That's when I began to shiver and woke myself up. Gerry was out of town on business. Besides, he's not given to being an audience to my dreams, not a very attentive or sympathetic one at least. He kind of just grunts and nods and gives me the impression that he's really disinterested and would rather I just get on with making breakfast.

"So I thought of you, Ola. Ola Davis, I said to myself. Ola Davis! Now there's a woman who will listen to the likes of this and maybe even help me unpack it. It was a weird one, wasn't it? I told you. Really weird, eh?"

"Yes, Frances, it is quite strange. I doubt that it is a vision from God, but we never know for sure. There is a little petition one can offer for assistance. It goes, 'Holy God, grant me Your Spirit of discernment, that I may know if this vision is from you. If so, help me to understand it. If not, help to dispel it.' Other than that, I'm afraid I can't help you much. I've had a weird, recurring vision of my own that continues to bewilder me."

"Really? Care to share it. I'm not bad at listening either."

"Why not? I keep seeing this kind of arena. There are rows of polka dots in two or three colours that seem to be a kind of impressionist idea of faces in a crowd. In the centre there are three horses with riders on them. They are engaged in a circular chase raising all kinds of dust that sometimes obscures the crowd's view. The lead horse is so pale it is virtually transparent as if made of rubberized plastic. You can see its interior muscles, its bones and some of its internal organs as it moves. It's quite, how do young people say it? Gross. The rider is thin and gaunt with his head facing backwards and a rather bizarre smile pasted across his face. He has long, blond flowing hair that imitates the long, white hairs on his horse's mane. Behind him, the rider on the second horse is hazy, rather indistinct, but the horse is strong, gray and, strangest of all, it has eight legs. The trailing horse is blazing white, the kind of blinding whiteness you get when the sun hits fresh snowfall so that, at times, it seems to be a four-legged flash of light. Its rider, who seems to be female, is on fire with flames dripping from all four limbs, from her mouth, from the tips of her hair and pouring out of her breasts. She is also carrying a lariat which is also ablaze. The fire does not harm the horse she is riding, instead it seems to energize the two of them. Hot pursuit, if ever there was an image of such. I have asked God repeatedly to help me comprehend this nightmare of mine, but so far, I have received little clarity."

"Well, isn't this an amazing coincidence! I come to you with my vision and it opens a door for you to share yours with me. I can't pretend to understand it all, but I'm pretty confident that horse with eight legs in the middle of your arena is Sleipnir."

"Sleipnir?"

"Sleipnir, the legendary mount of Odin, king of all gods in Norse myth. You see, before I I married Gerry I was Frances Sigurdsson. I was raised on Scandinavian myths by my grandfather who shared them with me as bedtime stories. Sleipnir is the gray, eight-legged super-horse that Odin is reputed to ride: exceedingly swift so that when all eight legs go full out, the horse soars; exceedingly strong, strong enough to surmount high walls, trees, and even to trot on clouds; a race horse, a work horse, a bucking horse and, when necessary, a fighting horse. As for that pale horse in the lead and her grinning seducer in the saddle, my guess would be that that is Loki, the trickster god in Norse legend. There is a legend that once the gods of Valhalla engaged in a wagering contest over a mortal who owned Sleipnir and who had a dream of building a large, fortified farm. He was given three weeks to complete the project. The gods who were not on his side were at a loss as to how to thwart the dream until Loki offered them his services. With just a day to go to complete the project, Loki turned himself into a mare. He sprinted up to the outer walls where Sleipnir could fetch a good look. Then, Loki the mare tore off into the forest and seduced Sleipnir into a chase. Loki led Sleipnir so far away from the farmer that even with his great speed, Sleipnir was not able to return in time to complete the work."

"Yes, a trickster grinning on the lead horse in my disturbing vision," Ola remarked. "That could make some sense. Why is it tricksters are so popular? Native people in this country have legends like Napi and Big Rock. Your ancestors have this Loki character. I even read somewhere that Jesus could be regarded as a kind of trickster figure: teasing his disciples and listeners with his intriguing parables and shorter, earth-bound aphorisms; turning the tables on his opponents among the scribes and Pharisees by answering their questions with questions as if to fling their baited hooks straight back into their own ears; and, near the end of his earthly days, engaging Pontius Pilate in some serious mental fencing."

"Well, if it's true that it takes one to know one," Frances submitted, "then keep on praying, Ola, because Jesus just might be able to help you figure out what Loki and Sleipnir are up to and about in your strange vision. But what's with that third, flaming female rider?"

"I'm not sure, Frances. She is the most mysterious figure of all. I suspect I will need a very precise discernment of spirits to determine whether she is a positive or a negative character. More tea?"

Real horses need a great deal of direct attention on a regular basis, far more so than their mythical counterparts. These responsibilities were picked up primarily by Pops, Alex, and Tyler. Occasionally, Rebecca and Myra helped out. At least four times a week, and always before and after a ride, Tacitus, Charro, Belva, Ironstone, Striker (as long as he lived), and Sirocco received a careful grooming. At least once every two weeks, they were bathed.

H. Lee Disher

Grooming has several purposes. It removes debris and loose hair, it enhances the animal's blood circulation and it brings up natural coat oils to produce body sheen. From the horse's perspective, it also feels wonderful. For owners and riders, grooming engenders bonding. They also become familiar with a horse's conformation so that cuts, blemishes, contusions, cracked or split hooves, injuries and such become readily apparent. An average grooming session lasts about forty minutes. Tyler could often extend that to almost an hour just by brushing and rubbing down more slowly and interjecting several minutes of encouraging and affectionate chatter while he worked. This was particularly so when he groomed Striker and Sirocco.

In the Davis horse barns, horses being groomed are secured with cross-ties with quick-release snaps. The general practice is to begin with a rubber curry at the top of the neck on the right side and work back towards the rear of the body. Tacitus, however, always preferred to be groomed on the left flank first. Using a slow circular motion, dirt beneath the animal's hair is gently loosened. Even gentler strokes are used on the shoulder and backbone areas. In the Spring, Pops works carefully with a shedding blade to loosen and remove excess hair from the horses' bodies built up over the winter months. To remove the dirt from the coat, the second step is to use a dandy brush in a flicking, sweeping motion in an up and away fashion. Small dust clouds should appear with each flick. The dandy brush is also applied to the horses' tails. Only a soft-bristled body brush is applied to face and leg areas. Then manes are gently disentangled and teased out with a mane comb. Should one of the horses decide to roll around too much in mud, there were mud brushes for removing caked-on dirt, but only after it had dried. Alex once got too anxious to clean up Charro after the mare had indulged in puddle play. He only succeeded in smearing her black coat an ugly, dingy brown. "Now that really is a horse of a different colour!" Pops remarked.

When the whole body is groomed, it's foot care time. Hoof care is a daily duty since long-term exposure to dirt and debris in that anatomical area makes a horse susceptible to the kinds of bacteria that can cause infection and rotting. "Caress one leg at a time by running your hand down to the fetlock." That's how Pops instructed Tyler, Alex and the others. "Give a gentle squeeze and lift the foot just about this high so the horse doesn't lose balance. The hoof pick includes a brush, so after you have loosened grime and dirt from the hollows on both sides of the frog and around the sole, flick it away." End of lesson, except, of course, to check each hoof for cracks or other signs of damage and go for the glue bottle to protect the affected areas. Watch for loose shoe nails and tap them back in place. "If the nails are badly worn or missing, get me to replace them."

Pops never let anyone else affix horseshoes, he had seen too many injuries to human limbs and faces received by well-meaning amateurs. The touch of arthritis in his right calf was attributable to a swift kick he received when he was learning how to shoe that cracked his tibia and put him in a cast for eight weeks when he was fourteen. "Armie" Allbright in Pops' neighbourhood farmers' circle was so nicknamed not because he had served in World War II (which he had), but because it was short for Armadillo. "Armie" was the only man in the vicinity tough enough to take on the shoeing of all the skittish horses. Parts of his arms and legs resembled a toad's back and his nose bore the signs of being broken in three places. Yet he withstood all manner of abuse and never backed down from a challenge. "Hell, basic training and those Gerries never roughed me up half so bad as some of those damn stallions and mares around home," he would boast. His lumps were more precious to him than the string of medals with which he became decorated for distinguished service overseas.

The last act of grooming is a final toweling of the whole body. Pops Davis believed in the restorative properties of nylon-cotton blends. "A subsequent application of coat polish serves to repel dust and stains, reduce static and speeds up grooming procedures thereafter."

Bathing was another regular horse-care ritual. Pops had had a special 20' x 20' cement pad poured half inside the barn and half out with a connecting door in the west wall. There were run-off gutters and an inside and outside hitch for tying horses up during bath time. One might think that warm water would be best, but actually lukewarm is preferable. On sunny days, outdoors, cold water works well. The Davis barns have a combination sprayer and scraper brush so that excess water can be removed as bathing proceeds. The first wash includes a mild shampoo and is sprayed slowly and steadily out of a nozzle working from the legs of the horse up. The sprayer is then flushed to remove shampoo residue and reapplied in the same fashion as a rinse. Once a month, each horse receives a sponged-on application of skin conditioner that is let stand before a second rinse. Horses are given a snack as they are lightly toweled and then wrapped in an anti-sweat sheet. Weather permitting, an outdoor, hand-led walking or some grazing time speeds drying. Wet and wintry days mean extra toweling and lateral pacings along the barn floor until the coats are dry. There are three no-nos. Don't expose a wet horse to drafts. Don't transport a wet horse in a trailer. And, never, *never*, let a damp horse into a stall for a roll in the hay, or you will have to repeat the whole process again. Alex made that mistake a couple of times as well over the years of his horse-care learning curve. Rebecca also once put Belva back into her stall in a damp condition. During the second bath, the back-spray that had left her own clothing moderately moist the first time managed to soak her right through. When she came into her aunt's kitchen looking drenched, Ola and Myra were perplexed.

"Did we miss something?," Myra asked her sister-in-law. "It's a bright, summery day. Was there a sudden sun-shower while we were so caught up in talking?"

"No, Mom, I had to wash Belva twice so I kind of got a bath of my own as well. Do you think I could get a couple of towels designed for humans? Please. Or should I just walk around smelling like a wet horse for a while?"

Rebecca wasn't really cut out for rural life. She liked visiting the farm, but much preferred staying and playing around home in Okotoks, or, even better, trips to Calgary or anything the size of a city. Skating rinks, time with Charlene, school and shopping excursions, such were the excitements, concerns and preoccupations that routinely defined her weekly schedules. At times, she acted older than her age; seldom younger. Mostly, she was in body, mind, behavior, and spirit pretty much as old as she actually was. In November, 2000, she had just turned eleven the previous month, she was in grade six and she still slept at nights with a stuffed toy dog, with one black eye and curly, tawny terry-towel fur, named Cuddles.

One rather chilly, windy November night that year, she too was visited by a bizarre, somewhat unsettling dream. It wasn't especially terrifying—not as bad as *Arachnaphobia* which she had watched at a friend's birthday party when she was nine; nor as hair-raising as parts of the *Alien* series of movies which she had also seen. Truth to tell, she didn't lose too many winks of sleep in the aftermath of any of those films. Her eerie dream didn't seem to be the kind of experience a young girl would share with her mother; but, she did tell Charlene.

"Honest to God, it was totally weird! It was like a twisted version of *Toy Story* in which all the toys go bad. They were all residents of this blue-gray city with tall buildings and narrow streets and smelly sewers. There were Muppets who were all mean to one another and who formed a street gang. Mr. Potato-head just went around farting on everyone with noxious gas. Teddy Ruxpin was like a mad scientist. And G.I. Joe wore a dress behind his grenade belt. Buzz Lightyear and a whole army of other robots were in charge. They could just zap any other toy with their ray guns and turn them into slaves or killers or whatever. Their wish was their command. Precious Pony spit fire like a dragon and the Groovy Girls all dressed and acted like hookers. They were chasing Barbie all over town. She had cried out for help on her cell phone to Woody, the cowboy, who was meeting on the far side of town with the Muppets and Teddy Ruxpin to plan a rebellion against the robots. Oh, still such a cowboy hero thing to do! Woody set off to the rescue, commandeering a remote-control car. He sped through streets and back alleys and tore up parkland. He rounded a corner on the other side of town just in time to see Barbie ducking down into a tunnel at the far end of the street. But as he turned the corner, Mr. Potato-head rear-ended him with a blast of knock-out gas. When he came to, he straggled down the street to the entrance of the tunnel. He descended a set of steps and there on a kind of landing in front of him was Barbie, all melted with her hair singed off and blood, real blood, pouring out of her neck and abdomen.

"G. I. Joe came out from behind a pillar and sympathized, 'You're too late, Woody. So was I. She got caught in a cross-fire. Strawberry Shortcake was in the middle of a big row with Buzz Lightyear. She came from that end up there riding Precious Pony and he flew in from this end over here. She pulled back on the reins and brought Pony to a halt. He landed and spread his legs like he was preparing for a showdown. They start cursing and swearing at each other when all of a sudden Barbie rushes down and runs right into the middle of it. Buzz whipped out his ray-gun just as Shortcake pressed a button on Pony's neck to set the flames free from his mouth. Between the blasts of a laser and the burst of blaze that both hit her square on, this is all that's left of your girlfriend and the woman I could only ever dream of. As she went down, them other two rascals beat it the heck out o' here.'

"Woody bent over Barbie's seared body and cried."

The front door-bell rang at the Berenson house. Myra had come to fetch Rebecca. The Stedmans were off to Edmonton to watch Tyler in his first National Rodeo Championship.

# Chapter 25:
# Heigh-ho, Edmonton!

Edmonton has its own rarefied air. It is not quite the geographic centre of the province, but it is the political centre. Conservatism colours most of the rest of the province and often comes with a capital "C." In some instances, there is a definite tilting as far right as one might go before crossing the line into Fascism. Here is the seed-bed out of which curious Canadian partisan out-croppings have sprung: Social Credit and, in more recent years, the Reform Party. It can be like right-wing Republicanism gone rabid. Jacobites, Jebusites, and Up-tights welcome. Red-necks may also nestle in nicely, particularly around Red Deer apparently. Some say it has something to do with drinking water. More likely it's about latitude—sitting far enough north to convey an image of being the True North. The True North strong and regulated. Top-dog types can flourish here. Lovers of having influence, "right"-thinking, tight-fisted solutions, and calibrated attitudes grow up here or gravitate in. Birds of a feather do flock together.

In Edmonton, the rare birds who vote Liberal and those who promote political positions of a socialist nature congregate, cogitate, and sometimes agitate. It's a bit like streaking through the middle of a fundamentalist prayer meeting, but these intrepid Edmontonians persist in flying against the Tory blue atmosphere that predominates and rules from halls of government on the edge of the North Saskatchewan River. In "Punky" McAllister's pub circle in Turner Valley, they often raise a glass to those citizens of Edmonton who are so "un-Ralph in-Kleined as we are; and if taking the name of a provincial premier in vain is a sin, the Devil can have us."

This may be overstating the case. What is truer is simply that while Calgary is a bustling rather homogenous place Edmonton is a more eclectic community. Where in other pockets in the south of Alberta liberals have a niche or two, once you hit Edmonton liberals have a home. Wild-eyed, broad-minded or radical-thinking professors are more likely to get tenure at the University of Alberta than at campuses in Calgary or Lethbridge. Unfortunately, Klondike Days, Edmonton's version of annual hoopla, is to the Calgary Stampede as oatmeal is to blueberry cheesecake.

Nonetheless, Edmonton is a city worth visiting. The legislative buildings are magnificent, almost uncharacteristically rococo. The arts have several admirable homes and exhibition venues. Sports franchises in this provincial capital do have a history of winning ways and showpiece stadia in which to perform. When the Eskimos win the Grey Cup, or the Oilers win the Stanley Cup, ecstasy erupts. Gardens abound in this city. Parks are plentiful. The West Edmonton Mall is rightfully world-renowned, a shopping and tourist mecca second-to-none. Fort Edmonton offers the almost obligatory tourist trap dedicated to pioneer days and the old West. Local residents are friendly, high-spirited and helpful to visitors.

Near the end of November the Canadian Rodeo Finals always come to town. The temporary migration of national title hopefuls and their coteries of horses, stock suppliers, judges, reporters, trainers, coaches, tack-and-gear-schleppers, medics, clowns, roustabouts, wives, children, family members, mistresses and lovers does wonders to take the chill off the early onset of winter and to elicit genuine Edmonton hospitality. The spirit of celebration is more apropos in this venue.

Klondike Days tends to make a mountain out of a molehill event in terms of national and provincial history. Yes, Edmonton came into its own as a significant terminus and trading post on the Macleod Trail during the Gold Rush Era at the end of the nineteenth century. But cowboys and cattle drives had far more to do with shaping the history and cultural ethos of Alberta than did that four-year explosion of economic wanderlust. The Gold Rush in the history of Alberta resembled what in reality it turned out to be for many of its actual participants, a flash in the pan.

H. Lee Disher

A national rodeo finals event is much closer in character to a provincial religious experience. It is about heritage and pride, hopefulness and mystique. It is the Stampede at its highest level transposed into this capital locale. It is to the winding down of fall in Edmonton what the Stampede is to the onset of summer in Calgary. Of course, coloured leaves have long since disappeared from the landscape. Barren branches and a few dead, brown-leaf stragglers are all you see on deciduous trees. The conifers are covered in cotton swabs. Snow banks on the roadside may already be well over ten feet. Slush, salt, sand and cinders make traction on wheel or on foot a soggy, slippery, adventurous experience. The undampened, undaunted adventure takes place in the Agriplex, which until 1998 was the Northlands Coliseum and home ice for the Oilers' hockey team. Line-ups at ticket windows are twelve deep or more. Scalpers are already at it twenty metres from the vending booths. Hotels, motels, bed and breakfast operations are all fully booked. Traffic is heavy. Parking lots are packed. The local economy laps up every tourist-and-local-populace extra dollar like an alley cat finding a pail of milk. Ka-ching! Jackpot! The national rodeo finals are a gold rush bonanza for many.

The competitors come likewise starry-eyed envisioning significant purses and silver buckles and trophies. It's the recognition that matters most, the acknowledgment that you're the one who is at the top of his or her game. King of the ring. Queen of the corral. Title is what titillates them most. Even a top-three placing also gives one an invitation to the biggest rodeo circus of all: the World Finals in Oklahoma City in December. The Canadian Nationals are comparable to an Olympic Games trial. Bucking horses and bulls are every bit as keen to garner premier honors, to have their shot at appearing in other really big shows. Stock suppliers have almost as much at stake as riders and ropers who have qualified. Coliseum is a great name for this stage, for this North-American contemporary version of gladiators, chariot races, Christians verses lions. The ancients seldom got applause however just for trying. The risk factors in Rome in antiquity were higher by multiples than those at play a couple of millenniums later in Edmonton. *Sic est historia timoris.*

There are no qualifying rounds, just the best two out of three aggregate scores, winner take all. It's a kind of sudden death playoff. A grand parade and demonstration events occupy the Friday evening. Initial rounds for novices, women's barrel racing and team roping are held on Saturday morning. All other pro events are run on Saturday afternoon. The novice finals take place Saturday evening; pro finals are Sunday morning and afternoon. Judges come from across the nation. Even clowns have a kind of honorary rotation so that every four or five years, the best in the business each have a chance to appear at the Nationals. Mike "Micky" Leeder has been the national announcer for twenty-five years already. National television, radio and newspaper crews jam the press boxes. Cameras occupy strategic places throughout the arena.

The Stedmans, Pops, Ola and Alex Davis, and Wallis Wilton and Carol Morton checked into their pre-booked rooms at the Jasper Arms after dropping Sirocco and trailer off at the stables adjacent to the Agriplex. Tyler stayed at the arena with his horse and met up with Greg Dugan and other competitors for pre-rodeo check-ups scanning riders, mounts and tack. The scan included a mandatory urinalysis and blood work. The judges held a rules seminar and noted special regulations specific to that particular indoor arena. Before the grand parade at 8:00 P.M. there was a government-sponsored banquet for competitors, stock providers, officials, and other rodeo assistants and their families and guests. The Federal Minister of Culture, the provincial Premier (or his representative), the mayor of Edmonton, the CPRA President sat at the head table and made welcoming and encouraging remarks.

It was the mayor who broke predictable words and formalities adding a bit of comic relief to the festivities by saying, "I'm sure looking forward to the weekend's competitions. They're bound to be far more exciting than sitting through a municipal council meeting; though, if you've been reading the news recently, you cowboys and cowgirls know you've got to raise some dust as well as a stadium full of eyebrows."

Two weeks previously, the lead story in *The Edmonton Journal* was about three city councilors who just about came to blows during a pre-budget debate session. After the meeting, one councilor did rough it up with another behind a snowbank bordering the city hall parking lot. A female councilor broke up the row by bashing both of the combatants with her purse. "Budget this you idiots!" she reportedly screamed in the process.

"Certainly," added the mayor, "you'll all be wrangling with more prestigious purses in view."

Tyler was rather full after dinner and already on the edge of yawning. He excused himself from his personal supporters to go to suit up for the evening's serpentine introductory procession. Immediately thereafter, he was off to the stables to spend some time in the stables grooming *Sirocco* before heading to the hotel to retire early. He checked *Sirocco's* shoes and hoofs. Still polished. No cracks. No loose nails. After combing out the mane and brushing the tail, Tyler made smooth even strokes with the body brush. "That's it, boy. Look at the shine coming into your hair just like you're going to shine in that arena tomorrow getting me out of the gate and up close and personal on that running calf in record time. You're the best, *Sirocco*, a born champion." Nuzzle, whinny, front right stamp—the equine body language of agreement. And a kiss good-night.

The stables the next morning were like rush-hour traffic—grooming sessions, baths being administered, roadies fetching tack and other gear, spurs spinning and jangling, boots being polished, hats being punched and folded into shape, stalls being cleaned, feed-bags tied on and removed later, chaps getting a last-minute shine-up, all mingled in with cowboy banter, chatter and occasional whoops and yee-haws. Stable hands were kept busy spreading non-toxic, environmentally-friendly dust-bane up and down the aisles. Through the open doors of the next barn, one of the clowns emerged from putting on his make-up and yelled, "Golly, pardners, that's one hell of a pile of bullshit!" He was referring to the real thing from the oversized bovine tenants harbored there as it was being gathered and hauled away in front-end loaders to waiting dump-trucks from the municipal works department. The dung was headed to city greenhouses for fertilizer stockpiles.

"I reckon what grows out of it will wind up smelling a whole lot better," Greg commented to Tyler in passing.

"No doubt, buddy, no doubt," Tyler replied. "My aunt's been turning similar stuff into garden and patio ornaments."

"No kiddin'?"

"No kiddin'. She gets fifteen to thirty-five dollars apiece for them."

"So she's into cash-crappin' as well as cash croppin', eh."

"Yes, you could say that but your pun smells as bad as that load that just left."

"Agreed. Come on, Ty, let's get our horses over to the corral and get ready to ride and roll."

The smell of the Agriplex was different from the usual outdoor rodeo venues. Lots of leather, horse hide, calf and bull flesh, and fresh-raked turf and the random clods of animal dung had an odor akin to ozone after a summer rain with a slight tinge of sulphur. Contained by four walls, a vaulted steel-strut ceiling and continually circulated by air-conditioning the aroma would only become more intense as the day progressed mingled with the sweat and excitement of human spectators, participants and officiants. The additional oddities were the scents of perked coffee, hot chocolate, baked donuts, bagels and pretzels from the outer corridors where concessionaires operated their stands. Even at 9:00 A.M. the smell and crackle of buttered popcorn was evident, if rather incongruous, for that time of day.

By then, the first assortment of witnesses and cheering sections had taken their places in the arena seats clutching and scanning their daily programs. Ten novice competitors were pacing behind the stalls holding the selected mounts for the saddle bronc trials. Media crew, judges, and corral crew were in their places. Micky Leeder was launching into words of welcome and introduction. A rodeo clown came to the centre of the arena, interrupted Micky, and set off a few forays of early-morning humour intended to put the crowd at ease. In fact, he served to heighten the anticipatory intensity of the pre-event by carrying on for fifteen minutes. Before he got on into his fifth joke, two other clowns raced to centre, slapped a strip of duct tape over his mouth, picked him up and stuffed him in a plastic oil drum and rolled him out the south end of the arena. "Phew! Thanks fellas," Micky exclaimed. "I was beginning to think that joker had *me* over a barrel... Okay, folks, the riders are ready, the stallions are eager," his voice boomed over the public address system, "Let's rodeo!"

Of the ten novice riders entered in the saddle bronc finals, two Americans and one Canadian had secured their spots by travelling the Canadian circuit on the thirds. That meant they shared expenses, entered all the same events and shared prize winnings among them regardless of who wound up in the money. There were similar all-Canadian trios competing in the pro bareback bronc and bull riding events at this year's nationals. Two other novice riders were protégés of Canadian pros who sponsored them for a percentage of whatever they might win. Randall Lecroix had offered to sponsor Greg Dugan, but Greg had turned him down for this season. Only half of the novices were there completely on their own behalf, but that didn't necessarily mitigate the amount of pressure they felt.

There was only one chance to score in the morning rounds. Tyler and Greg scored admirably well placing sixth and fourth respectively. Two of the riders suffered buck-offs, one of them being ripped out the back door from a wild steed named Blitzkreig. The rider who placed second was one of the Americans who was awarded a re-ride on account of a skittish horse who reared up and misbehaved in the pens before the gate was opened. His reassigned venture netted a score of 78.5 and signalled he was the one to beat given that his balance, spurring and grit seemed superb.

The women's barrel-racing event gave them a breather before the calf-roping round. Greg and Tyler and another young rider from Stavely, the one who suffered the simpler buck-off, conferred with each other on their way around to the portion of the arena where their roping horses awaited them. Consensus: "that cocky little American from Idaho is going to be tough to overcome."

"Right," Tyler added, "and he's got two other competitors not just rooting for him but keen on helping him secure the victory."

They did use their breathing time to put saddle-bronc thoughts behind them and find their focus for the next event. This time Tyler and Greg traded places. The lad from Okotoks placed fourth. The young luminary from Red Deer came sixth. There were no competitors working in tandem in calf-roping, but there were four sponsored participants, two of whom placed 1st and second. Third place went to one of the ever-regenerating Butterfields. While he was tying off, Tyler thought he saw a familiar face in the crowd a few rows up from where his family were seated.

With two out of three events behind them, Greg and Tyler took consolation that they were still very much in the running. The first round of bareback riding would wind out the morning competitions when the pro team roping initial runs were completed. Both of them had drawn temperamental mounts. Tyler also had the number one position. He made a valiant effort aboard Black Sabbath hanging on for six-and-a-half seconds before being dumped into the well in the middle of a fish-tail move. One of the clowns yanked Tyler clear while two arena hands rushed at the horse to commandeer it out of harm's way. In the stands, Myra closed her eyes and held her breath, Ola and Rebecca covered their faces until the voice of Micky Leeder yelled, "What a gutsy try, Mr. Stedman! You're safe! Let's give this lad a whole mess of applause folks and wish him better luck in the next two rounds."

Greg managed to outlast his bucking fiend but only scored enough for fifth place when his spurring became ragged part way through the ride. His dismount was more like a catapult from an ejection seat and he seemed to land hard and display a slight limp in his right leg as he walked out of the arena back to the pen area.

"Are you all right, Greg?" Tyler asked.

"I think so, pal, just a little strain I expect. Good thing we have the afternoon to rest up."

They went to the stables to groom down their calf-roping confederates. Greg watched Tyler and Sirocco with great admiration. He thought he saw something like flashes of light in the exchange of their eyes.

"I'm heading to the showers," Tyler informed Greg.

"You go, pardner. I'm headin' for lunch. I'm famished. See you in the stands this afternoon."

The locker room for competitors was at the east end of the stables. Tyler took his time lathering up, massaging his body, rinsing off, and running shampoo through his hair. His mind alternated between images of himself competing and that face he thought he saw in the crowd —a young, very familiar face from home.

He had just gotten back to his locker wrapped in a towel when he was startled by a pair of hands gripping his shoulders from behind, and surprised by the sound of a female voice saying,

"Well now, handsome, you did just fine out there in that ring this morning."

As his heart began to settle, he turned and met another familiar face. "Allison! I am surprised to see you here. Uh, especially here right in the locker room. Would it be all right if I just…."

"Shhh! Just relax, Tyler," Allison was quick to interrupt as the fingers of her left hand travelled up and down Tyler's chest. "I do follow some of the rodeo circuit, you know. A good friend of mine is entered in the barrel-racing finals." Then she cupped her hands around his face and said, "I don't believe I thanked you properly for rescuing me."

Initially, he sought to resist, his legs went rigid, his hands moved into position to push her away. But when she planted her kiss on him and began running her hands up and down his spine, he began to melt. He shuddered some, fought for control he sensed he was going to lose, felt helpless and then captivated as Allison stripped off one article of clothing after another. Those fabulous breasts did him in. He had to hold them, fondle them, taste them. As he did that, Allison removed the towel from his waist.

"Oh my! Surely a cowboy like you should know that a horse like that needs some good exercise once in a while."

Tyler was fully, almost achingly erect. Next thing he knew, he was lying backwards along the dressing-room bench, engulfed by Allison. She was shimmying, gyrating, riding him as if he were a bronc. Yee-haw. Yowee!

"No! Allison, please…this isn't right! I don't want…."

They didn't hear her footsteps, probably because she was almost tip-toeing since she wasn't sure she was allowed to visit the competitors' locker-room. But she too wanted to see the young man who was kind of hero-like to her. And she heard the noise. She heard the sounds of moaning and oohing and aahing, and then, something like screaming began. She hastened her step towards the shrieks. She thought someone might be in trouble or pain. But what she saw… what she saw as she rounded a bank of lockers…shot pain through her heart like a gunshot.

Tyler lifted his head and took her in in mid-shout. "Tyler! Tyler Stedman! How could you? How could you?" And his helpless agony was counterbalanced by the agony of seeing that face in the crowd, of watching the back of Stephanie Wells disappear in high-tailed flight.

Back at the hotel Tyler was sullen and rather uncommunicative during lunch. There was still time for a bit of rest and relaxation in the room he and Alex were sharing. They changed into swimming trunks and climbed into a Jacuzzi shared with Tyler's parents' room next door.

"What's up, cuz? You did well this morning, but I've never seen you so glum."

"I screwed up, Alex, figuratively and literally."

Tyler wanted to just leave it at that, wanted more time to process the circumstances. But he knew Alex wouldn't give up needling the story out of him.

"Whoa! That's bad, cuz. That's really bad. But right now, there ain't a darn thing you can do about it until you get back to Okotoks. And tonight, you've got a competition to complete." It was difficult for Alex to hold himself to offering such immediate sympathy and encouragement. What he also wanted were the details about the "ride" Allison had taken Tyler on. But this was not the time and place for that. He could, however, sort of imagine how amazing it must have been.

That was part of Tyler's problem. Despite his resistance, his intimate encounter with Allison had been amazing. He had travelled to far-flung galaxies and back and seen vistas of territory previously unexplored. She wasn't unattractive. Their relationship possessed many of the ingredients of a recipe for friendship...but lovers? He wasn't at all sure. Stephanie...Stephanie had held his heart in thrall for several years now. They knew the positive pieces of each other's personality and the quirks. How could he? How could he have extricated himself when Allison was so overwhelming? Maybe it was time to let Stephanie go, to think about moving on, to head off into a different yonder than the one he had been contemplating. Riddling questions. Dizzying thoughts.

"Yeah, you're right, Alex. Thanks for understanding, I think. I know where else your mind is wandering, but I'm not going take you there. Actually, I'm just tired now. Would you mind going off to the mini-arcade in the hotel lobby while I have a nap?"

"Gotcha, cuz. I'm on my way."

By 2:00 P.M. Tyler and Alex were back at the arena with Jules, Pops, and Wallis Wilton to take in the afternoon pro rivalries. Greg met them in the stands. The women from Okotoks had begged off for the afternoon. The whole crew would be together for the pro final rounds on Sunday. But this was the provincial capital, home of the world-famous West Edmonton Mall. For shoppers and consumers around the globe that meant Mecca. Buying and browsing pilgrimages were mandatory whenever one was in the vicinity. So for that Saturday afternoon, Myra, Ola, Rebecca and Ms. Carol Morton —

soon to be Mrs. Wallis Wilton—joined the ranks of hundreds of gawkers and devotees making rings around the indoor roller-coaster, water park and skating rink. In fact, Rebecca had brought her skates along and managed to dazzle a number of onlookers and passers-by for her hour on the ice, treating them to several displays of fancy footwork, double loops, occasional single axals and salchows. Credit cards secured several purchases made by the adult females in the group. Ola was virtually overwhelmed by such a plethora of stores. There was nothing like it in the old country except the crowds, the lines. But when you reached the front of the line back home it was usually only for bread or meat or milk.

The women rejoined the men for dinner back at the arena around 5:00 P.M. They ate at a restaurant just down the street. Tyler and Greg had a light dinner of Chicken Caesar salad before heading back to the Agriplex for the evening showdowns. The order was somewhat altered: calf-roping, bareback and then saddle bronc. It was all novice riding all evening. All eyes were on them. All the pressure was present as well.

Greg improved his placement in calf-roping with two quicker times than his morning outing. As he hit the turf for his second tie-down he winced and seemed to stagger favouring that right leg again. Tyler's first evening run was three seconds longer than his morning time. During his second attempt, some kid out in the concession corridors stomped on an empty milk carton just at the moment *Sirocco* dug in to pull the noose around the calf's neck taut. The popping sound of the burst carton was enough to cause *Sirocco* to lunge backwards a bit toppling the calf on its side. Tyler lost precious seconds waiting for the calf to stand up again before he could throw it down and tie off. When all was said and done for the national calf-roping novice finals this time around, Greg Dugan had finished in third place, displacing another budding Butterfield, and Tyler Stedman had slipped to sixth.

En route to the bareback pits, Tyler convinced Greg to consult the on-site medic and head to the first-aid room to have his right foot taped up. Their assigned horses for the evening rides were less testy than their morning mounts, so style points would matter a lot. Greg's first outing was rather uneventful as he slid easily off a low-spirited horse at the end of the requisite eight seconds. His second ride netted him a score of 74.5, enough to secure fourth overall. Tyler managed to stay aloft on both his bucking opponents but didn't score highly in the judges' estimation. Ninth place was where he wound up. "Well, it's only my first time at the nationals," he consoled himself in private, "and I wasn't last." Other preoccupations had also interfered with his focus: Allison's bold advance, Stephanie's shock, and his mother's continued reserve.

Nonetheless, Tyler knew he had served notice that he was indeed a rider to watch in the future regardless of how the outcome in the saddle bronc final might go . He also knew that Greg had a shot at the all-around title. Cheering on his friend claimed a larger priority that night.

As it turned out, Tyler had two exceptionally laudable rides which the judges rewarded placing him fourth overall. Greg's performance was likewise commendable and his aggregate scores gave him another third place finish. After being thrown from his second evening mount however, he landed hard and awkwardly again on his right foot. His leg buckled beneath him and when he got up and tried to walk, he fell down again. Arena assistants came to his side to help him hop off the turf straight to the infirmary. The doctor on call removed Greg's footwear and examined the injured extremity.

"I can't say for sure," he assessed, "but I suspect you cracked the metatarsal bone earlier in the day, and by hanging on and competing and continuing to land on it, you've succeeded in fracturing it. I'll wrap it as tight as I can and ship you off to Edmonton General for x-rays and, probably, a cast."

That was exactly what had happened. Pops and Jules took Tyler to visit Greg in the emergency room while plaster was being applied.

"Hey, buddy, you missed the presentation ceremonies. Here's your trophy and prize buckle; you placed second overall. Unfortunately that cocky little American grabbed top honours and our national trophy will have a resting place over the border and out of the country for a year."

"Hey pardner, that's okay. Next year, you and I will run the rest of the competition right out of the ring."

There was one other visit for the Stedman family to make after enjoying the pro finals on Sunday. Pops, Ola, Alex, Wallis Wilton and Carol Morton, who had travelled together, bid farewell in the Agriplex parking lot and headed home. Jules, Myra, Tyler and Rebecca took a side trip to visit old Mr. Stedman in the nursing home. He didn't recognize them at first. Something about Rebecca's voice clued him in for a few moments.

"Oh, oh my, that sounds like my lovely grand-daughter, Rebecca. Jules, is that you? I'm sorry. I get so golldang forgetful. Oh, and Myra's with you today and, and your boy .... uh ..."

"Tyler, Grandpa."

"Right! Tyler, the young buckaroo who loves ridin' horses."

"Yes, Dad," Jules cut in, "he sure does. He's been competing in the national novice rodeo finals this weekend. He wound up eighth overall, but he made a bigger impression than that on the crowd and the sports reporters."

"Sounds like he keeps impressing you too, son. Good stuff. Keep telling him when you're proud of him. Sons often don't get enough of that. I'm still awful proud of you, Jules, yessir, awful proud."

Jules broke into an accepting smile and almost let a tear drop when his father's face went suddenly quizzical. Turning to Myra, the old man shouted, "Nurse! Nurse! Can you get me out of this damn bed. I gotta use the commode. Now!"

Myra quickly pressed the call button as the family stepped out of the room. A nurse came by soon enough to deal with the old man's emergency.

When the Stedmans re-entered, the old man, lying back in his bed, stared up at them. "Do I know you? Are you that singing group from the Salvation Army? I'm too tired today, and I don't want any more of your *Watchtower* magazines."

"Dad, we're your family, Jules and Myra and ...."

"Family! I don't have no family. The Nazis blew my family all to bits in the war. You must be Ollenbach's family. Ollenbach's in that other bed over there across the way. He was a Nazi you know. Maybe his family blew up my family, heh? Rotten kraut!"

"Yes, Dad, we've been through that story before...many times. Myra, Rebecca, Tyler, come on, he's gone from us now."

Jules nudged them out of the room. At the doorway he called back, "Bye, Dad. I'll see you again in a couple of weeks."

"That's the longest I've seen him lucid in the past couple of years," Myra remarked.

"You're right, dear, and we should likely treasure it for it's the best he'll probably ever get from now until..." Jules couldn't hold the tears back any longer.

Tyler took pride in his father for that. Pride sat on top of his heart and shame at the bottom like a burgeoning storm cloud, white above, grey underneath—the foam of betrayal.

# Chapter 26:
# Heart-Stopper

February 2001 surrounded Okotoks in a blanket of its own indifference. A cold snap came early and lingered hardening in thicker and thicker layers of ice on top of January's mounds of snow. Studded ruts of gravel, mud and ice formed grooved incisions in the laneways on the Davis and Wilton farms. The horses had to be bathed on the indoor pad in warm water run through hoses connected to the laundry taps in Pops' place. The oil tanks for the furnaces emptied almost weekly and fuel bills were the highest they had ever been. Twice Ola took laundry into Jules' and Myra's house because her pipes had frozen. She marveled at and ached for the young women at St. Agatha's Catholic High School as she passed them waiting for buses or standing around the school-yard with bare legs and knees between the ankle socks and plaid short skirts of their uniforms. They reminded her of Russian peasants lining up for staple foods in Moscow in winter. Her mother had taken her there a couple of times when she was an adolescent to see the Bolshoi ballet. It cost a small Ukrainian fortune but then, Ola's mother never intended to send Ola to university. Her grandfather managed to scrape enough together to enable her to spend two years at an agricultural and business institute in Kiev. If there had been any uniform for Ola to wear to school, it would have been head-to-toe wool and flannel in winter. Most of the rest of the residents of Okotoks bundled up appropriately against the cold, the dry subtle chilling cold that leaves any exposed skin frost-bitten within a half hour or less. Those Catholic girls hopefully kept their exposure time to less than fifteen minutes per outdoor stint. It was grin and bear it weather, not skin and bare it weather.

Twice a week Ola and Pops donned insulated coveralls, heavy work gloves, and fleece-lined boots, strapped on metal snowshoes and trudged out to the Christmas tree plots. Accumulations of snow on the branches were getting too heavy. Firs, spruces, and balsams especially had to be shaken and brushed to remove most of the excess. Scotch pines were hardier and their more upward-curving branches were more resistant to collecting snow. But this winter, they too had to be relieved of their uncustomary burden. Pops carried along a hack saw for removing the odd dead limb. Your feet, your legs, your back, your arms get to know how large a hundred acres really is when you have to tend to each individual tree planted thereon. Pops still believed in mustard plasters which Ola got the knack of preparing. She herself preferred Epsom salts and bathing in lavender oil.

Wilton collected eggs daily, cleaned out cattle stalls and kept a watchful eye on the pregnant cows in his herd. Calving usually didn't start until March, but there were always two or three mothers-in-waiting who freshened early, almost always at some ungodly early morning hour. Even so, Wilton still had plenty of time to go around ploughing lanes for others, removing snow from roofs, tending to equipment repairs and barnyard maintenance. Then he still had time to confer frequently with Carol over wedding plans, sending out invitations; visiting the tuxedo rental shop with his best man, Norbert Pedersen, who operated a large ranch next to Punky McAllister's spread; choosing a wedding cake design (Ola had offered to make it); attending a couple of pre-marriage seminars sponsored by a group of churches in Calgary. This latter was interesting to Wilton, who had been married before. He and Carol were also the oldest couple in the seminar group and the most financially sound couple, and probably in many ways the wisest couple. They admired the enthusiasm and vigor of the younger adults preparing for marriage and fretted and prayed about their naiveté. Discussion during the segment on sex and intimacy varied: cautious and reserved, fearful and laughable, embarrassingly frank, hopeful and earnest, something like a national assembly of a Canadian religious denomination. Communication—the main emphasis over and over again was on communication. Wilton surmised that most of the young men in the seminar felt that certain forms of non-verbal communication resolved anything. "They'll probably find out the hard way," he thought to himself, "just as roosters discover most hens have minds of their own. And beaks."

Alex and Enid still dated, but less frequently. Tyler and Stephanie had put their romance in the cooler and their friendship on hold. The chill of the season was a contributing factor. Another raw truth was that Biology, Math, World History, and Family Studies as a second semester course load in grade ten was exceedingly demanding homework- and project-wise. Stephanie had developed an interest in hip-hop dance lessons. Tyler persisted in bi-weekly rodeo training: Wednesday evenings and Saturday mornings in High River. The winter was not past, and the sound of the turtledove was still murmuring for one pair and virtually mute for another.

*Friday, February 8th*

*Dear Diary:*

*I talked Alex into going to see* Legally Blonde 2. *It was pretty dumb, but he says he still likes Reese Witherspoon. "So, should I dye my hair blonde? I asked him. "No way. I like Reese as an actress. I like you as my girlfriend. And I like you brunette and smart just the   way you are." "I'm not that smart," I said. "You get better marks than I do," he replied. "And your body's better than Reese's." "Careful, smarty-pants," I said to him, "you're thinking with your other brain." "Huh?" he went acting all innocent. "The one beneath your belt," I said. "Oh, right. Sorry. Or would you like to see it?" "ALEX!" I screamed, "We're sitting in Flear's Restaurant having cherry Cokes and fries with gravy. This is hardly the time and the place even if I were interested." "So you are interested?" he says. And I said, "Alex! Shh! Keep it down. Your voice and your ...other thing as well for that matter. I have seen it," I whispered. "Several times, if you recall. And we've done more than that." "So we can still do more some time?" "Maybe. I don't know, it is kind of like playing with fire." "Yeah, and if I'm hot and you're hot, what else are we  supposed to do?" "Hope to God one of us is handy to a water bucket. Don't pressure me, Alex. Are you pressuring me?" "Uh, no, Enid, I'm just kinda wondering when or if ever...." "Maybe someday. I don't know when. It has to feel right. It has to feel special I guess. I don't know. Say," I said, "would it be all right if we changed the subject." "Sure. I guess. What's the subject? Not math I hope." "No, not math. Good God, Alex, it's only Friday. Homework can wait. What about dreams, Alex? Not the weird or fantasy kind when you're sleeping, but like plans for the future. What would you like to do with your life, or be?" "The publisher of* Rolling Stone *or a reporter for* Sports Illustrated *perhaps." "I don't know." he says, "I can't say I've given it a lot of thought. Heck, I'm only sixteen. It's going to be a job just to graduate senior high." "Well, I kind of like working with numbers. I think I might like to become a chartered accountant or an investment counselor like my Uncle Earl." "Oh, well," he goes on, "if it's about doing what you like...don't buzz this around any of the guys, but I like cooking. My mom's been teaching me some. Pops doesn't know it, but some of the soups and casseroles he's been eating this winter are my creations with Mom's help." "I think that is so cool, Alex. So, are you going to bake me a cake for Valentine's Day." "Right, and roll it and pat it and mark it with me....I don't think so. That would let my secret out. I'm happy as a closet chef for now."*

*I hope that's all he's keeping in the closet. Oh, there I go, diary, thinking with my second set of brains. Hmmm. Just between you and me, Diary, I don't see the harm in it once in a while. If Alex is doing anything sexual in the closet I hope it's me he's thinking of. Me and him. Him and me. Oh yes, some day. Some day when it feels right and special and oh, oh, oh, oh Alex, yes, yes, yes, don't stop, don't stop, don't ....*

*Stop. I'm getting a bit silly, Diary. And sweaty. Stop. Stopping is good. For now. There's the near future that might involve...uh, yes.. what I was just fantasizing about. But there's also the more distant future. Will Alex still be in it? I hope so, Diary. I hope so. I really do feel I love him for all his quirks and idiosyncrasies [is that the big word we just learned in English last term? I hope I spelled it right]. He makes me laugh. He puts me at ease. I'm always comfortable around him. And happy, so happy, deep, deep down inside, right to the bottom of my soul. If that's what makes love real, then I really am in love, Diary, and it's wonderful, ab-*

H. Lee Disher

*solutely wonderful. And I don't have to dye my hair. He likes me just the way I am. Reese, eat your heart out, I've got a Ryan Philippe of my own, a red head who really loves me. Nobody around here is acting."*

There were other pages prior to that one analyzing Stephanie and Tyler's breakdown. Maybe he couldn't help himself. Maybe Steph should forgive him. Maybe not.

Ever since his reflective experience in Banff, Jules was unsure about his commitment to his work. He seemed less enthralled by it than he was when he was rising rapidly through the ranks and more like he was going through the motions, like an actor performing to the same script in a long-running production. He hoped he was good enough at masking his latent ennui convincing his superiors, co-workers, customers, contacts he was still one of Tranogco's primary cheer-leaders. "Go team, go." "Go, company, go." "On we go with Tranogco. Go. Go. Go." His enthusiasm had cooled long before the deep freeze of February, 2001. February was always the month to begin gathering cold, hard data for year-end audits and financial reports. Statistics stiff as steel were summoned to speak. Graphs and pie-charts were called upon to put order into chaos. Let there be profits. If not, let there be a positive future prospectus. Speculations had to be teased into trends. It struck Jules that his recent transfer (promotion?) to the exploration division could be the cause of his dis-ease. Explorations were highly tentative and not always cost-effective. Seven fruitless searches may often be undertaken before an eighth one hit pay-dirt or, in this business, pay-spurt. Ministry of Environment officials were always watching over your back and confounding the discovery process with new pieces of legislation. Estimating the longevity of current sources and reserves was an economic crap shoot. America meddling in the Middle East wasn't helping oil prices. The race was on among oil industry competitors to find alternate sources and supplies, especially outside the Middle East. Russia, and other former Soviet republics were certainly being courted. Fresh fields of endeavour were being opened in parts of Africa. Tranogco was just one dog among many chasing after the same foxes. Jules had secured that one healthy contract with a supplier in the Ukraine. Actually, Ola had provided Jules with the lead connection he needed. She had a cousin who had married into a Ukrainian oil exploration firm. Putting all the facts and figures for exploration futures on paper was nowhere as neat, crisp and tidy as it was in the sales and marketing division Jules had left behind. It was always easier for an oil firm to know where its products were sold and sent than to know where their raw material was going to come from for ever and ever. Presenting and promoting best guesses to upper management, shareholders and the Board of Directors was like trying to sell water as an aphrodisiac. Jules worked robotically. His heart just wasn't where his head was. The cold front that swept over most of Alberta that month affected his moods and mannerisms. He talked less, used one-word responses and sighed or grunted before replying to questions. He seldom hummed along to songs on the radio, or made rustling noises as he read the newspaper. He got a prescription for barbiturates from his family physician. He scarcely got to the gym for a work-out. At work, he succeeded at charades. At home, his altered state was less disguised.

"What's the matter with Daddy?" Rebecca would occasionally ask.

"February," Myra would answer. Her perception of the truth was limited to that. Her systems were somewhat off that month as well. She never considered engaging Jules in conversation over the possibility of more bothersome concerns.

He likely would not have confided in her if she had tried. He feared that his discontent would disturb her, strike murmurs to the heart of her bourgeois security. She was troubled enough with the rumours that some national drug store chain was considering buying out Kingman Pharmacy. There was no one left in the Kingman family wanting to continue in the business and Mr. Irving Kingman was becoming increasingly crippled up with arthritis. He could barely sign cheques any more. If the takeover happened, the floor personnel jobs would likely be kept, but the pharmacy staff themselves would probably be replaced by the company's own imports. Myra had visited the family physician too to negotiate an increase in the dosage of her tranquilizers. Jules was reluctant to dump his own load of manure onto the full hod Myra was already shouldering. Ola, on the other hand, might be someone who could hear him, might even have some way of helping him. Or, maybe he was just suffering some passing dissatisfaction.

Rebecca was only fleetingly affected by her father's underlying malaise, if at all. February was recital and competition month for her figure-skating club. She had continued to gain in grace and proficiency. She was one of the star attractions. Heads up! Another Elizabeth Manley in the making? Tyler readily yielded the spotlight to his younger sister for the time being. She deserved it. She too had worked hard and learned well. Her performances burned some puddles of joy into her mother and father's otherwise congealed spirits in that bleak mid-winter.

H. Lee Disher

Tyler plugged away at honing his rodeo skills, applied himself to school-work with his usual diligence and helped out around the house often without being asked. He made a couple of stabs at mending fences with Stephanie. By mid-February at small crack appeared in the ice.

On Friday, February 21, 2001, the clouds over southern Alberta let loose. Gallons of snow fell all day, halting or impeding highway travel, making town streets impassable, and closing schools and a number of businesses. Almost forty centimetres of snow piled up on level and scraped ground. Drifting complicated matters. People like Ola and Alex and Pops simply hunkered down indoors and let it all fall down.

Saturday morning, February 22, the three of them suited up after breakfast and headed out to clear the laneways. Ola and Alex used shovels to clear the walkways to the back porches. Pops plodded to the equipment shed to start up the small tractor with a snow-plough attachment. He had to shovel the doors clear in order to open them. The tractor was an older Allis-Chalmers model before electric-start engines became a regular feature. This old gas-fired unit called for letting out the choke and then yanking several times on a pull-cord to get the engine to turn over. Once it was running you applied the clutch, threw it into gear, and pulled on the throttle to regulate your rpms and your speed. The knobbed levers representing the throttle and the gear-shift came up beneath the steering-wheel right between your legs. A cup-holder anywhere near the driver would have been pointless.

Pops set the choke and gripped the handle of the pull-cord. One yank. Two. Three. A faint whirr. Rest. Another yank. Five. Six. Seven. Lucky number seven. The engine churned. Ah. "Aaaah!" Pops sensed strain in his left arm, made a gasp or two for air. "Damn rheumatism!" he muttered. He climbed into the seat, slid through first gear into second and accelerated forward. The new snow was deep yet light and fluffy, easily pushed aside. The depth of fresh accumulation was sufficient to begin to melt the frozen, rutted remains of January's precipitation turning it mostly to wet slush. Occasionally, the plough would strike a hardened knob or chunk of ice temporarily jarring tractor and driver. Persistence won out. With Alex and Ola clearing walk-ways and doorways and Pops making pathways in the lanes, they had clear access to the two houses, garages, sheds and barns within a couple of hours.

"How about a warm cup of cider?" Ola asked as they surveyed their excavations. "I'll go in and warm some up while you two put equipment away."

"Sounds good to me," said Pops. "Here, Alex, you run this old tractor back to the shed. I'll just go widen the entry way at the end of the lane and make sure there's access to the mail box."

"Aye, aye, sir," said Alex with a respectful salute hopping onto the tractor seat.

Ola went inside. Alex drove off toward the shed. Pops walked down the lane shovel in hand. There wasn't much widening to do. It was the mail-box that was of more concern to Pops. That old-age pension cheque was due to arrive on Monday. He had not opted for direct deposits—didn't trust computers all that much. Little did he know how banking had been functioning for the past couple of decades. He fussed around the mail-box giving it more than ample visibility.

He had built it and painted it up himself twenty-five years ago, a scale replica of his own horse barn complete with cupola and miniature weather-vane. Over the years, he kept the paint-job freshened and touched up. Visitors on the back roads of Okotoks sometimes stopped to take photos of his mail-box. That pleased him, made the effort worth it. If you positioned yourself at the right angle, you could get a picture of the mail-box in the foreground and the full-sized barn in the background. In 1997, a picture just like that appeared in the June edition of *MacLean's* in a feature story titled *Rural Route Whimsies.* Fading copies of that picture were tacked to the wall of the tack room and to the bulletin board at Rompin' Roger's Roost in Turner Valley. Hal Miller, part of Punky and the gang, had stuck a caption beneath it: "Davis' Zippety Doo-Dads!"

"Pops," the drinking buddies sometimes teased him, "you could make more money banging fancy mail-boxes together for folks than you do pandering those scraggly excuses you got for Christmas trees." Pops doubted that. Every time he went to the bank with revenue from tree sales, he shook his head and chuckled. "Scraggly excuses, eh? How come they've put more money in the pork barrel than I ever made from breeding horses?"

Just as Pops turned up the driveway to head in for cider, the inevitable appearance of a county snowplow rumbled by filling in the end of the lane. It was Hal Miller giving a smilingly ironic "Hello and sorry about that" toot on the horn as he passed in the course of his part-time winter job. "And may the bird of happiness poop on your hat too, Hal," Pops cussed and set himself to clearing away the newly-made pile of debris.

When he was about half done, that shooting pain visited his left arm again briefly and went to his jaw like a bad toothache. Dizziness, shortness of breath followed, then the feeling of weight against his rib-cage, like the plough on the little tractor was pressing him back towards the snow banks. He stumbled back until he was propped up against the west bank, dropped the shovel and stood there sort of half-sitting. Alex came running down the lane to fetch him for cider, wondering what had held Pops up. He saw the part pile of new-ploughed snow, the fallen shovel and then his grandfather stock still against the snowbank, pale-faced and staring into space.

"Pops! Pops! Are you okay?"

Just then Wallis Wilton was driving by heading to Okotoks for groceries. He braked, got out, sized up the situation and pulled out his cell phone. "Alex, you go get Ola and get your coats and boots on. I'll stay here. I'm dialing 911. Pops is heading to the emergency ward at Foothills General. You two can follow the ambulance."

"What? What's going on?" asked Pops, coming to. "Alex, tell Ola I'll be right in. I thought you might wait and walk back with me. Oh, hello, Wilton. Nice day, eh? Hell of a pile of snow though. Why are you looking worried? Why do you have your phone out? Heck, I'm okay. Just that damn rheumatism acting up again."

"Maybe so, Mr. Davis. But perhaps we'd better just be sure. I stay right here with you until the ambulance arrives."

The ambulance and paramedics were there within fifteen minutes. Ola and Alex had managed to get Pops to sit in the warm car at the end of the lane until help arrived. Wilton had said he would hold the fort for them till they got back. He'd put the winter blankets on the horses and let them out for a stroll in the yard. He'd keep an eye on the place and a log or two in the stove. In fact, one of the first things he did was to pour himself a cup of cider and remove the pot from the burner where Ola had left it simmering in her haste.

The trip to Foothills General seemed to take two minutes instead of twenty. Emergency staff rushed to take over the gurney from the ambulance attendants and whisked Pops into a vacant cubicle where a cardiograph operator was already standing by. A nurse removed Pops' coat, unbuttoned his shirt and began to apply goop and electrodes to his chest. The attending physician kept her eye on vital signs.

"What's all this fuss about?" Pops complained. "I feel fine, just a bit light-headed."

"We're just taking precautions, Mr. Davis. Nothing's going to hurt," the doctor remarked. "Try to relax. These are your Medicare dollars at work." It had become part of that physician's usual patter. Older patients often seemed to become less tense at the mention of bang-for-your-buck taxation.

Ola met with the receptionist who did the hospital intake on Pops: name, address, social security number, hospital card, blood type, et cetera. Alex sat in the emergency waiting-room swinging his legs nervously beneath his chair. It was larger than the last similar setting he had been in a couple of years back in Brooks. Two mothers with colicky crying babies sought to hush the disturbing sounds. A whole family of Greeks or Italians were jabbering on, some of them pacing, cracking knuckles, tapping toes, wringing hands, working themselves into a sweat. An older woman among them was muttering away pushing a bunch of beads around. A couple of Saturday morning hockey players were there nursing fractured arms or bruised hips attended by mom or dad or an assistant coach. A young woman was sitting there with her boyfriend who looked exceedingly pale and nauseous. She kept checking with the receptionist as to where her man was in the triage order. A forty-something man wearing a slightly soiled and bloodied apron sat opposite Alex applying pressure to a hastily bandaged sliced finger. A couple of drops of blood leaked from that finger onto the floor between his knees. A friend waiting with the man went in search of more gauze. Several other people were there appearing anxious about someone already being tended to. A couple of them heaved heavy sighs, bothered more by the fact that, whatever the incident, it had interrupted the flow of their day and altered their plans. "Hmmph!" Alex found that rather amusing. Ola joined him within fifteen minutes after phoning Myra at work and telling her not to panic. That's like telling a coyote not to howl at the moon. But Myra was at the pharmacy counter alone that day and couldn't spring free.

"We will call you later when we've heard from the doctor who is examining him. I have a very strong feeling your father's not in any great danger. He's a good man, a strong man. He's in the palm of God's hand."

A little over an hour later, after a rather poor excuse for tea from a vending machine, one very sugary cola, a couple of Krispy Krunch candy bars, and a small bag of ketchup potato chips, a nurse summoned Ola and Alex back into a cubicle for a consultation. Pops was there sitting up on a gurney with more colour back in his face.

"I told you I was okay," he said with a wink. They hugged him.

The attending physician came in. "Hello, I'm Dr. Lawrence, and you are?"

"Ola Davis, Pops' daughter-in-law, and this is his grandson, Alex. Oh, sorry, I mean Zac's daughter-in-law. Family and friends call him Pops. Zac is short for Zachariah. His parents were Baptists."

"And the Mr. Davis whom I presume would be your husband?"

"Last we knew he was in, how do you say it, some flophouse in Lloydminster. Zac also has a sister here in town but she's tied up at work right now."

"Oh. I see. Well, Zac here, or Pops as you say, has had a mild heart attack. I use mild advisedly because we don't have all the evidence we need to make that a firm diagnosis. Pops, we need to keep an eye on you for a few days so we are going to give you a bed in our Intensive Care Unit where we can do blood work every three hours or so and continue to monitor your breathing, your heart rate and your blood pressure. The cardiogram we took today says there's been some damage to your heart but we need to run other tests to determine how much. Then we can prescribe a course of action and whatever medications might be required. Any questions?"

"Yeah. Can I eat? How's the food? And are the nurses as pretty as you are?"

"Small amounts with no salt. I understand the food is tolerable. I let you make your own judgements about our nursing staff, Mr. Davis, and thank you for the personal compliment."

"How long do you expect he'll be here?" Ola asked.

"Three to five days is the usual stint. Someone will need to bring him sleepwear, shaving kit, changes of underwear and whatever else might be useful."

"I will put that together and see that Pops gets it all somehow."

"You aren't going to strap him down are you? Pops will hate that. He's got to be able to move about some," Alex commented looking worried.

"No, he won't be strapped down, or totally confined to his bed, but his movement will be limited. Short walks, little trips to the bathroom, that's about it. Where he goes, the monitors usually need to go."

"Can we see?"

"Sure, if you wish. Someone will be along soon to wheel him to the unit. You can stay until he's settled in but visits are limited to five or ten minutes."

It wasn't just movement limitations that caused Pops some anxiety; it was more about not having control of your day-to-day life. For a short spell he guessed he could put up with it. As he was being settled into the unit he turned to Ola and said, "Make sure you pack that novel I've been trying to read for three months, some crossword puzzles and *The Farmer's Almanac*." Then whispering he said, "perhaps you could sneak a flask of whiskey into my shaving kit."

"I'll see that you get the books, Pops." She knew that he knew that the alcohol would interfere with any medications being administered.

After hugs and kisses farewell, Ola and Alex left Pops in the keeping of the Intensive Care Unit. From the lobby of Foothills General, Ola phoned

Myra to fill her in. Myra insisted that she would meet them when they got back to the farm and look after delivering Pops his hospital-stay suitcase. "Jules, Tyler, Rebecca, and I were heading into Calgary tonight for a movie anyway. We'll stop and check in on Pops along the way." She was doing her best to keep her panic in check, but she did have to see her father and his current condition for herself.

February 1984, Sarah Davis, Myra's mother, Pops' wife, suffered cardiac arrest after clearing out a couple of closets. She sat down for a cup of tea at the kitchen table and died in her chair. February 1991, Gertrude Stedman, Jules' mother, died of an aneurism in her aorta on a bus trip through the Jasper ice-fields. February 1994, Ralph Stedman, Jules' oldest brother in Edmonton suffered congestive heart failure and died after three days of hospitalization. February 1997, Shaggy, beloved Cocker spaniel of the Stedman household developed coronary thrombosis in her ventricles. She keeled over dead on the family room floor. February 2000, baby Nancy Jacobsen, six-month old daughter of Myra's niece Tammy and her husband Barrett in Ontario did not survive an operation seeking to correct a heart defect with which she was born. "Don't panic, Myra." Really? In the Stedman family, February was heart month. Brutally so.

# Chapter 27:
# Wilton's Wedding

"**M**ake us glad as many days as Thou hast afflicted us, and as many years as we have seen evil." Psalm 90, verse 15. These were the words that caught Ola's attention as she closed her Bible after bedtime devotions that night. For all that life is raw and rude and rabid at times, there are on balance numerous days of delight, dazzle and depth. The Eastern Orthodox saints were keenly sensitive to this. Jesus told that story about the gardener who pleaded on behalf of the fruitless fig tree: "*Let it be just one more year till I dig about it and put on manure, and if it bears fruit next year, well and good....*" Into every life a load of crap must fall. Ola could barely believe she entertained such a thought on those terms. But it is the manure: the pain, the sorrow, the sin and suffering and such, that fertilizes the soul, that fosters maturity. It is the sunlight and oxygenated air: the joys, the flights of the human spirit, the ecstasies internal and external that water and feed the heart. Her own son's heart continued to swell.

The chemistry between Alex and Enid was as simple as sodium chloride (Na + Cl): one body-soul full of sauciness, impishness, humour, and restless energy combined with one body-soul full of assertion, a bit of brassiness, self-confidence, and liquid kinesthesia created a relationship fated to fusion. Theirs was a protracted and incremental process, nothing like smelted metals or nuclear amalgamations. It grew like the boreal forests nearby despite an obvious impetuosity resident in them both. There was scarcely any material for a mother's dreams there. Ola simply knew that someday.....

As for the man next door, for whom for a few fleeting months her own heart felt flutters some years back, Ola was fascinated by a more complex chemistry between a wholly ruralized man and a thoroughly urbanized woman. She knew as much as anyone else how Wallis Wilton and Carol Morton met. She witnessed the silent transformations each one wrought in the other, how he adapted to dressing up, going to the theatre, fine dining, night-clubs and such; how she adjusted to dressing down, leisurely woodland strolls, the excitement and smells of a cattle auction and chomping on a slice of raw turnip with a sprinkle of salt on it. Though there was nothing caustic nor acerbic in either of their characters, their relationship entailed a melding of backgrounds and upbringings in the way an alkali can neutralize an acid. She remembered one time when, in the midst of cleaning her kitchen counter, she reacted to the compound in use: "Whew that smells like the inside of a stove-pipe on a damp day with a bit of sting to the eyes stronger than onion juice!"

"Show me the label," Jules had asked her since it was a time when the Stedman family had been around for dinner. He had come into the kitchen to fetch a couple of cans of beer for Pops and himself while Ola was cleaning up. So she handed him the bottle and listened as having perused the ingredients he said, "Ten percent ammonia. That accounts for the stinging sensation. 60 percent carbolic acid or phenol we sometimes call it. That's the coated chimney scent for you. It's one of the derivatives from coal tar, one of the by-products Tranogco extracts and markets to chemical companies." ($Na_6H_5OH$ was the formula he rattled off which Ola couldn't remember). "Quite often it gets used in any number of disinfectants."

It was the disinfecting image that came to mind as Ola reflected on how Wallis and Carol's relationship had transpired to the point of engagement. Already relatively pure as far as her observations had concluded, now the two of them were becoming something holy, something fragrant in God's nostrils, something supremely satisfying. If Ola had hit upon or witnessed the experiment of mixing a clear solution of vinegar, starch and a bit of iodine with a likewise clear solution of half as much sodium hydroxide punctuated with a few drops of sodium thiosulfate and phenolphthalein and watched the liquid turn burgundy, she may have nailed down the chemistry exactly. Carol and Wallis had merged in such a way over the past few years that it resembled water becoming wine.

H. Lee Disher

Their wedding would not take place at Cana but under a canopy in the yard of the Wilton homestead on what used to be Macmillan Line until 911 regulations called for all roads to be renamed. Thus the location was currently a rather boring numeric: 434 Avenue West. And the date was set for June 30 when the school term was over, report cards completed, and final marks and recommendations for each of Carol's students submitted and filed. In the coming September, Rebecca Stedman was slated to attend Dewdney Junior High and inherit Ms. Morton as a teacher.

Ola finished up a wedding-band quilt for the soon-to-be-married couple as winter 2001 truly melted away and conifers and grain fields would consume the bulk of her springtime attention. Post-Easter she had committed to loaning out her restored cabin to a couple from Salmon Arm, B.C., for a week-long *poustinia* of their own design and to overseeing another personal retreat weekend in early May for Frances Evans. Sleipnir, that's what Frances had told her was the name of that eight-legged gray horse that kept recurring in Ola's visions. Icelandic mythology she had said. "Yes, yes," Ola promised herself several times already this year, "I must take some time out to do some research." But that spring flew by faster than Elijah's heaven-bound chariot, and the next thing Ola found herself setting out to do was to go to the beautician's shop on Palmer Street in Okotoks with Myra. They were getting ready for Wallis Wilton's wedding.

The weather was as tailor-made as Wilton's new suit. Cars bearing the sixty-two guests, including the Stedman family, parked in neat rows on a patch of flattened hay field just north of Wilton's laneway. Carol's brother Dan had flown in from Chicago and booked a room for the weekend at the Okotoks Best Western. He was going to give the bride away in lieu of her deceased father. Her mother came in a wheelchair accompanied by and attended to by Carol's sister Alice, who lived in Medicine Hat. Cardboard cut-outs of Greek gods (Zeus, Juno, Aphrodite, Apollo) on wooden stakes directed the guests past the main house and the chicken coop to the lawn and garden area out back where the ceremony would take place. Hint. Hint. The newlyweds were headed to Greece and the Aegean islands for their honeymoon. The cattle barn was a hundred yards away and the wind that day was blowing from the southwest minimizing a certain set of country odours under the rented canopy. The canopy was a large, white, peaked canvas stretched over twenty-four aluminum poles anchored to the ground by guy-wires. It measured 40' x 30' and provided covering for the ten round dinner tables for six, the head table, sixty-four chairs, a rectangular table for gifts, another rectangular table in a corner where the DJ would set up shop and a sturdy card table in one corner on which was placed a three-tier wedding cake made and decorated by Ola Davis. All the tables were covered in white linen as were the chairs with large roseate bows tying the cloth around the backs. Strings of white mini-lights entwined with garlands of ivy covered in white tulle were draped liberally around the top inside edge of the canvas and along the length of the head table. Two large standing-basket bouquets flanked the head table and separate vases graced each round table and the cake table. Two arrangements in baskets sat on the head table. The flower arrangements were comprised of $500-worth of purchased gardenias and background emery leaves interspersed with cuttings of pink sweet-pea which grew on the fence-lines of Wilton's property and slips of wild rose of which there were several bushes around his house and out-buildings. All arrangements were lovingly prepared and gifted by Myra Stedman. The senior art class at Dewdney Junior High had painted 140 feet of faux fresco that was fixed around the outer edges of the canopy and twenty-four mock Ionic columns fashioned from carpet rolls and painted papier maché back-slit to wrap around the aluminum poles which gave the reception area an Acropolis look. Tyler and Alex had helped Wilton during the late winter and early spring to fashion a separate open-roofed replica of the Temple of Diana out of plywood and balsa and plaster of Paris. They made and assembled it in Ola's implement barn keeping it a secret from Carol until that day when, in the morning, they loaded it on a trailer and transported it to Wilton's backyard to be the actual locale for the ceremony itself.

Carol had thought she and Wallis were going to be married beneath a rose arbor that adorned one of his gardens. She was utterly astounded when she caught sight of the little temple, choking back some tears and having her sister apply tissue to some mascara that had run in the process. That's part of what matrons of honour are for. What amazed her and her sister even more was that Wilton had designed the floor so that an inner circle was fixed to a slow-rotating axle driven by a three horse-power belt motor. It meant that while their guests enclosed the outside of the temple on an imaginary circumference, the whole wedding party of four plus the officiating minister spun in a protracted manner as the service proceeded affording everyone present equitable video and audio opportunities from all angles. There was a section of floor space off the inner circle of the temple where Soft Echo, a cellist and flutist duet from the Calgary Symphony, provided a mix of classical and popular music suited to the occasion.

Reverend Fanshawe from St. Paul's United in Okotoks had been contracted to conduct the ceremony. She met and shook hands with Wallis and his best man, Norbert Pedersen, and led them up the temple steps to await the bridal procession.

She couldn't help smiling as she remarked on the surroundings, "This is absolutely lovely, Mr. Wilton. Rather pagan mind you, but lovely. Then again pagan in its Latin root is associated with country-sides and rural living, like the French *pays* and *paysan*."

"Yes, I believe that's right, Reverend," Wilton replied. "We weren't really thinking of that when we planned the ceremony. It had more to do with Carol's bachelor's degree in Classics and with our honeymoon plans."

Just then the processional music, the ever-popular "Water Music" by Handel, began. The trio and duet in the little temple and the assembled guests turned and moved to watch Alice stroll across the yard from the back porch to take her place on the dais. Then Carol entered escorted by Dan, grinning broadly, nerves of Jell-O.

(For those who are curious about such things, the Okotoks Herald would record in its weekly edition in the local pages:

> The men were dressed in tuxedos, the groom in white, and the best man and bride's brother in black. They sported white fluted shirts with onyx cuff-links, teal bow ties and cummerbunds. White gardenia boutonnieres were pinned to their lapels. The best woman, the bride's sister, wore a full-length, low back satin teal bridesmaid's gown set off by a black sash belt and black gloves. Her bouquet featured gardenias, sweet-peas and Alberta wild roses. The bride carried a similar but larger bouquet. Her wedding-gown, from Loreen's Bridal Salon in Calgary, had a strapless cinched bodice of white sateen decorated with thirty sewn-on pearls over a full-length tapered white skirt of damask silk dotted with tiny pink roses. A seven-foot veil fell from a silk-wrapped headband studded with pearls. An elegant emerald pendant on a silver chain gave the bride's neck a regal demeanour.

> Soft Echo, a flute and cello duet from Calgary offered splendid ethereal music for the occasion. Guests at the wedding included family, neighbours, friends, numerous teaching staff from Dewdney Junior High and several local School Board

trustees. A sit-down dinner of....served by Germaine's Cater-ing of Okotoks....[There followed a detailed description of the "Acropolis" and the "Temple of Diana," with which the social reporter was especially fascinated].)

"Welcome one and all to this celebration of marriage this day for Carol Morton and Wallis Wilton," Reverend Fanshawe began. "I must say before we go on that I'm not quite sure I'm in the right place. Or perhaps, I feel like I should be reading that bit of the Bible where Paul preaches to the Athenians from the Areopagus part way up the Acropolis hill." A few snickers passed through the crowd among those who knew that biblical reference. "Uh hum, well, yes, be that as it may, in the name of the one true God who made the world and everything in it, being Lord of heaven and earth, yet who does not live in shrines made by humankind, let us gather together to celebrate this covenant marriage between Carol Morton and Wallis Wilton this day."

The ceremony proceeded with dignity and decorum. Wallis managed a nervous Freudian slip in the opening phrases of his vows: "I, Wallis, take you, Carol, to be my life." Truer, perhaps, and deeper than "wife," or in this instance, certainly synonymous terms. The rooster, for some unknown reason, let out a loud cock-a-doodle doo at the very moment when the groom kissed the bride. Laughter erupted all around. "Hey," Reverend Fanshawe commented, "at pagan weddings all nature participates!" More smiles and chuckles.

Dinner was delicious. The dancing was diverse given the range of ages present. No one recalled ever seeing Wallis Wilton blush so much. There was no one present to welcome Carol into Wallis' family, but Pops Davis offered a toast and a speech *in loco parentis*.

"I've known Wallis since he was about four years old when he and his folks came to settle in here next door. Even then he was smart, eager to learn, ready to pitch in to help with chores, housework, barn work, whatever, from sweeping floors to cleaning stalls to setting up fences. Once when he was about five, he turned to watch a couple of gophers playing tag across the field while he was holding up a fence post and slipped right into the hole. Well, I reckon today he's gone and slipped in the biggest hole he'll ever fall into, but I got no intention of yanking him out this time. He don't want out. In fact, I reckon he wants you right there in it with him Ms. Morton. So, if you don't mind being adored and pampered and respected and loved by one of the most decent men on God's good earth, by one of the most earnest, hard-working farmers I've ever known and about the best neighbour anyone could ever have, well you

H. Lee Disher

just jump right in there beside him and enjoy this marriage for all it's worth. Hell, if he weren't so darned humble and unassuming, he'd be an agricultural legend from Cardston to Camrose. As it is there ain't anyone in farmin' for at least a hundred mile or more around here who doesn't hold Wallis Wilton in the highest regard. He tells you straight. He'll come runnin' to help in a flash. He's wise.

"His mother didn't really take to country life. Within three years of comin' here, she kinda broke down and took off. Died about a year later. His father did everything he could to raise Wallis right. Taught him all he knew about farming, scraped pennies and nickels together to send him off to Agricultural College when he was seventeen. Imported Grandma Wilton to teach Wallis how to make a bed, a stew, a neat pile of washin' and ironin' and how to sew on buttons and such. Darned if he didn't turn out to be as good at that domestic stuff as he did in the sheds and fields and chicken coop. A year and a half into Ag College and his father died all of sudden of pancreatic cancer. So at nineteen going on twenty, Wallis was left with a farm to operate on his own. So he put mind, muscle, shoulder and soul into that like he does just about everything. He's pretty much the best I know at getting' bulls to breed when it's time. You might wanna watch out for that, Carol, when he gets a little frisky hisself. He'll take a sick calf into the house to heal rather than leave it out in a cold barn. He raises quality beef, quality grain and quality eggs and has been through several randy old roosters. He's a one-man band when it comes to fixing machinery or repairing homes and barns or putting in weeping tile. Now he's got you to share it with Ms. Morton and someone else who enjoys going to the opera to boot. I can't say I abide his taste in music, or rather, he's not so fussy about mine. Country and western music we agree on—that's indigenous to your bloodstream in this part of the world. But I also kinda like jazz and blues, but Wilton don't have much truck with that. Funny, he's about the only man I know for miles around who likes drinkin' that rot-gut bourbon that's part of jazz culture. Which just goes to prove he ain't perfect. He's just awful damn close.

"This here ain't no bourbon, it's just dinner wine, but I'm raisin' my glass to one world-class neighbour, friend and human being. Ms. Morton you've made a spectacular catch. Folks, here's to the groom, the brilliant, the smashing, the debonnaire, the one and only...Wallis Wilton!"

Cheers. Applause. Tinkle and tipple. And *tink, tink, tink* went forks on glassware.

Those who had been Ms. Morton's students enjoyed seeing her at ease, kissing her groom in public, letting her hair down. She even hiccoughed dur-

ing her thank you speech. "That darned red wine. I should know better. Bu..
(hic!)...ut, darn it it's my wedding day. Let's party!"

Tyler, Alex, Stephanie, and Enid just about fell off their chairs at that
point, a moment when they were all completely relaxed. The whole affair was
fabulous. The ceremony was wonderful. Yet there was something about the
whole event that visited each of them with a smidgeon of proleptic fear. Not
that it intruded on their enjoyment, just that it was subliminally present. Yes,
Tyler and Stephanie had become an item again during the Spring. Enid had
reminded her several times about her little fling with Kevin Noseworthy and
how far it went, and about the fact that it wasn't like there was a ring on her
finger or anything, so what if Tyler had a temporary cheating moment. He
had apologized as best he could — "Somehow, at the time, Allison was just
too overpowering, I told her to stop but couldn't manage to break free."
Though Stephanie felt reassured, she wasn't one hundred per cent convinced.
Neither was Tyler. Perhaps, he did have affection for both young women in
different ways. He had known Stephanie forever it seemed; yet Allison was
more mature and certainly shared his passion for horses and rodeo and…. It
was too difficult to make up his mind and his heart completely. Maybe a young
man his age should keep his options open.

Myra and Ola's worst fear failed to materialize. Louie didn't show up. It
was a glad day undisturbed by any affliction. Praise the Lord!

H. Lee Disher

# Chapter 28:
# Blaze of Glory

During the winter and spring of 2001 Tyler Stedman had bulked up by 35 kilograms. Seventy percent of it was added to his upper body (chest, shoulders and arms) by working out. The other 30 percent was distributed on his thigh and calf muscles, around his lower back and through three inches of a growth spurt that took him from 5'10" to 6'1". He was truly a strapping and handsome young man. All that added muscle translated into greater fitness for the rodeo challenges awaiting him on that year's circuit. Calves would be thrown down precious seconds faster. A tougher and more flexible body meant greater endurance and shock absorption on the back of bucking horses.

His coach began fine-tuning Tyler's technique: a slight adjustment in his grip, paying attention to his centre of gravity during bucking events; keeping a 45-degree angle in the saddle while chasing down a calf rather than positioning himself almost parallel to Sirocco's neck and perfecting an over-the-neck frontal pass with his outside leg before dismounting rather than kicking over the horse's back. This latter move enabled Tyler to slide rather than virtually jump off Sirocco *en route* to grabbing a roped calf and saved more precious time. The practice corral in High River added a mechanical roping calf to its training equipment. It was placed about 25 metres out from the chute and offered ropers opportunities to rope a dummy with a head that sometimes bobbed down, sometimes twisted to one side or the other, and sometimes took the rest of the calf's body sideways with it. Computer programming enabled practicing ropers to have repeated tries at any of these real-life simulations and trained them to watch a running calf's head while preparing to throw their lassos. Given all that, Tyler Stedman was a profoundly improved novice rider heading into the 2001 circuit.

His first few forays served notice that he was a novice on a mission. He wound up second overall in the kick-off rodeo in Red Deer. His pal Greg still nicked him by a few seconds here and there to capture first. During the March school break, he took on the rodeo in Camrose and took top honours in calf-roping; a third in saddle-bronc, and a fourth in bareback. April saw him score well again at Coleman and, instead of Stavely, he took on tougher competition in Leduc just south of Edmonton where he pulled off his first overall title with firsts in saddle-bronc and calf-roping and a second in bareback. He was stronger. He was more savvy. He was the toast of the novice circuit and tagged as a rising star in every Canadian rodeo magazine and every newspaper sports report that bothered to include rodeo events in its coverage.

He suffered let-downs in May. To compete in a Kelowna, B.C. event over the long weekend Tyler and his father flew out while Pops and Chuck Leverton, Tyler's coach, drove Sirocco over the Rockies and back. Maybe the travel upset his equilibrium, maybe the more arid semi-desert air and higher elevation factored in. He wound up in seventh place overall. He returned to the corrals of Taber, Alberta at the end of the month but didn't fare much better placing fifth, sixth in calf-roping and saddle-bronc respectively. In bareback, he wound up disqualified through buck-offs. The second one, a nasty surprise flight out the back door over the rump and haunches of a chestnut Canadian bred stallion named Danger Zone, wrenched his lower back and re-aggravated his right kneecap again. Taber was shaping up to be a venue that took its toll on him and perhaps a place to be avoided in the future. This time, it served to rekindle Myra's resistance.

Thus, the month of June was primarily spent focusing on his grade eleven exams and visits to the physiotherapist and the chiropractor. He had to scratch himself from returning to the ring at Brooks where he had captured his first silver buckle in calf-roping a year ago. That's rodeo!

By month end, Brad the therapist declared him fit enough for the go-rounds in High River or Wainwright except that that was the weekend of the Wilton-Morton wedding.

Doctor Punkara was not so sure. Raja's father had brought his family to Okotoks in 1996 and set up his chiropractic practice in one of the units of a small strip mall on Riverside Drive. Dr. Krupka had referred Tyler to him for x-rays and treatments following the mishap in Taber. Describing his backwards flight off of Danger Zone to Raja's father, Tyler remembered hitting the ground hard with his heels. The toes of his boots pointed upwards as his legs straightened, pain jarred his lower back before his bum landed in the dirt smack on the tail bone. He laid down supine for a few seconds before propping himself up on his elbows and shaking his head. Rags the clown had come over to check on him and help him to his feet. He was a bit winded and sore, but not limping. He expected he was badly bruised.

"Yes, young man, there is a large bruise on the skin and muscle tissue around your coccyx, but here, look at this x-ray showing your lower back. See here where your sacrum joins your last two independent vertebrae," Dr. Punkara indicated the location with his right index finger, "there's a lot of in-flammation, there's compression and subluxation as we call it which means a degree of misalignment between those last two vertebrae, and your sacrum is sitting further forward than normal, a condition of dislocation we call sacrum-anterior. You'll need to take muscle relaxants for several weeks and I will need to see you for treatment every day for the first week, then every second day, then every three or four days towards the end of the month. You'll have more flexibility, less pain, but it may take most of the summer to fully heal. If you plan on riding again you'll need to wear a brace. Your knee, by the way, is only somewhat inflamed. Physiotherapy should fix that. If you like, I can give it a couple of ultrasound treatments."

"That would be great, Dr. Punkara. Whatever you have to do, do. I want to get back in the rodeo ring as soon as possible."

"I suppose you do, but I have to say it all surprises me very much. Accord-ing to Raja and from what I've noticed in more detached manner over the past several years, you're a sensible young man. You've got manners, friendliness, intelligence, and the admiration of your peers who trust you completely. So why rodeo? Why this reckless abandon that seems out of character?"

"I don't know for sure, Dr. Punkara, but keeping up my grades, being friendly and polite and trustworthy, well that just seems to me like normal, or-dinary living. I suppose it's influenced a bit by faith, you know, being caring and as righteous as possible as God wants us to be. But beyond all that there's a fire, a passion within that completes you, that draws your soul to over-reach itself. You can suppress it, I suppose, but by denying it you cheat yourself. Rodeo is my fire, it crackles in my root-fibres. There's a part of me that's as wild and intrepid as the broncs I ride. That's where I truly come alive—in the challenges, in the clash of wills and wits between undaunted humanity and animal abandon. How about you, Doctor? In your case perhaps there's a tiger inside?"

"There could be. Back in India I was a fierce player of cricket, which may seem like a very boring and listless game to you. Let me assure you, it is very intense and requires all manner of strategy and concentration. Here, cricket opportunities are few and far between, so I've taken up Tae Kwan Do in the last four years. The difference may be that my tiger is still very much like a circus performer over which I can still exercise a measure of control. Yours however is very much at large in the jungle and a highly endangered species. It's so marvelous that you can be so philosophical about it, which proves that you are a sensible, thinking person. Rodeo, however, doesn't fit for me in the categories of logic and good sense. Perhaps, I'm reflecting my age. I forget being young. I forget my crazier days of heading out hunting on the back of an elephant. That too, Tyler, is a very wild ride. Tell you what, do you have video recording of your performances?"

"Yes. My coach and my dad often film the events in which I'm entered."

"Good. Bring me the one from Taber. I'd like to have a look at it, to see what happened, in case I've missed something."

"Can do, Dr. Punkara. So should I go get ready for my first treatment?"

"That would be a most excellent thing to do. You can use room number two. I'll see you in about ten minutes."

Tyler brought Dr. Punkara a copy of the Taber event video the next day. When he came in for his fifth treatment three days later, Dr. Punkara asked him if he had a few extra minutes.

"Sure, it's Friday."

"Good. Come with me into this office over here."

Two chairs against the wall inside the office door faced a television monitor and video-cassette recorder across the room next to a computer screen on an adjacent stand. Dr. Punkara turned on the television and set the video player to play.

"That's you at the Taber rodeo, yes?"

"Yes, sir, that's me. That's the calf-roping event. Black calf means it's my second go."

"Okay," said Dr. Punkara pushing the pause button on the video machine. He moved to the computer monitor and switch it on. What showed up on the screen was a replica of Tyler chasing down that calf only he and Sirocco, the calf, other people around were all in skeletal form. It all looked rather ghoulish. "I sent your video up to the lab at the chiropractic training school in Edmonton. There's a program there connected to the sports medicine department that can translate video tape into these skeletal images so we can observe what's going on inside an athlete's body. Very useful when injuries happen."

He let the computerized replay catch up to the point at which he had put the video on pause. Then he let both machines run simultaneously. "Watch...[a lull of five seconds during which Tyler had roped the calf, slid from his horse, and was in the process of throwing the calf down and tying off.] There!" Dr. Punkara hit pause on both remote controls just as Tyler stood up from tying off. Then he rewound both tapes back a few frames. "Watch the computer while you stand up after making your knot. Look! See how you arch your lower spine inward by getting up so fast! You pushed yourself backwards instead up shoving straight up through your bent knees. Very hard on backs that."

Then Dr. Punkara took Tyler in slow motion through the sequences of his saddle bronc mounts. "Eight seconds is a very short space of time. I suppose it feels like a small eternity of minutes up there in the saddle. But notice how your arms get twisted with every gyration of that horse, how your neck can suddenly flop sideways, forwards or backwards with every pounding hoof-beat, and how your spine takes a thrashing with every lurch, spin, toss off the saddle, and heavy landings back on again."

Tyler was mesmerized.

"Eight seconds, or less if you get bucked off. Not long. But it's the equivalent of being jerked and jostled around on an old roller-coaster for ten straight two-minute runs. It's like trying to steer a careening car with a stuck accelerator and no brakes fighting for control as you glance off hydro poles and parked cars, jump curbs and take out fire hydrants, fruit carts and newspaper stands, negotiate tight turns and crash through road work barriers until you run into a mound of earth or heaved up broken pavements. Before you even got on that bronc that bucked you off, you were an accident ready to happen, some of the damage had already been done. You sure you want to keep doing this?"

Tyler remained speechless.

Dr. Punkara proceeded to show him the computerized skeletal version of his bareback riding fiasco. "There. You were right, the main compression happened when you landed thump on your heels. Probably a good thing your legs got in the way of landing square on your tail bone."

"Rodeo is high-risk adventure, Dr. Punkara. No one who goes into it is unaware of that. Week after week, we see companions and fellow competitors suffer fractures, injuries, bruises, body bashings, the lot. We all take our share of lumps and liabilities. I'm sure we give our families no end of worry and drive insurance companies berserk. But, like I said, it's a fire inside and I can't put it out. I can only do my level best to stay in tip-top shape, use my wits as well as my muscle, maintain an ongoing conditioning program and learn from my mistakes and miscues. Actually, my coach would welcome a copy of that computer visualization. It will help focus my conditioning and training exercises when I return to the circuit."

"He's welcome to have it. But all the conditioning in the world can't prevent the inevitable. However, I expect a strong, determined young man like you would be caught up in ice hockey or rugby or some other punishing sport if he wasn't immersed in rodeo. I treat those casualties all the time too."

"I expect you're right, Dr. Punkara, and I appreciate your concern. All I can promise is I'll do my best to be careful and to protect myself. And, if it's any consolation, I don't foresee doing this past the age of twenty-five. I'm riding pretty high in the novice standings this year. That might be my ticket to turning pro in one or two more years and then I'll take on more events in America as well as Canada, perhaps Australia and Germany where rodeo has also been catching on. Several years of that and I call it quits to pro riding; maybe turn to coaching or clowning, or God knows, maybe by then I'll just be married with children with a university degree and a job and a more regular, less hazardous kind of life."

"Well, in that case, you untamed Humpty Dumpty, I'll likely be here to keep putting you back together again until your sensible side finally wins out."

"Deal, Dr. Punkara. I'll count on it. You're a pretty decent egg yourself."

They shook hands, holding each other in high regard as well as sincere concern. Treatments continued. Tyler's joints healed faster than expected. Physiotherapy added its blessing. An extra week away from the circuit because of Wilton's wedding was as helpful and welcome as an additional hot stone massage.

Swift Current, Saskatchewan, was slotted as the circuit stop again on the weekend following Canada Day. This time out, Tyler and Greg impressed the crowd again with an outing improved from the previous year placing second and first overall again, just as they had in Red Deer in March. What was also clear was that Tyler truly seemed fit and ready again, fierce as a wolverine on the prowl.

The highlight of July was the invitation to contend at the Calgary Stampede based on his previous year's showing and his standings in 2001 to date. For Tyler this dream-come-true had all the impact of an athlete making one of Canada's Olympic teams. He set his face to head to the Greatest Rodeo Show on Earth (well, in Canada at least). Fully three-quarters of the population of Okotoks assembled themselves throughout the grandstands for the novice go-rounds on Tuesday and Wednesday. They were rewarded when their hometown hero squeaked into the finals in the tenth and last position.

High hopes splinter on the rocks of high pressure. During the Saturday finals, Tyler got bucked off in both saddle-bronc attempts and wound up last in bareback bronc. He did however manage to pull off a bronze medal and trophy in calf-roping, triumph enough, victory worthy of hometown celebrations for at least a couple more weeks. Tyler accepted all adulation with his characteristic humility knowing in his heart he could have, should have, would love to have done better. He and his coach decided to take the rest of July off from the circuit and concentrate again on training, conditioning and weight-lifting. Readiness is a mercurial condition.

It was a plan similar to the previous year and it paid off when Tyler re-entered the ring in Medicine Hat and came away with a third overall trophy and buckle to add to his growing shelf of honours in the family room at 35 Dewdney Common. The lower back brace proved helpful though Dr. Punkara detected some re-aggravation and fresh stretching in the lower spine area when Tyler stopped in for a check-up on the Monday following the event. Caution was advised.

Tyler's coach concurred. Guided exercise and conditioning continued alongside a scaled-down schedule. Jules took a week off work while he and Pops accompanied Tyler up the spine and down the sternum of the province so to speak. The first leg of a restful three-day journey took them from Banff to Jasper on the spectacular Jasper Highway, "perhaps the most magnificent stretch of road in the whole country" according to Pops. The next day they travelled from Jasper on over to Highway 40 up to Grande Prairie which got them into Peace River country. Poplars, lodge-pole pines and birches standing as perpendicular as comb's teeth. Cows in pastures, clear waters and fresh air in a somewhat freakish climate that far north thanks in part to South Pacific trade winds searching for a resting place. A day pass at a local health club got Tyler some hot-tub and gym time. A short jog on day three got them over to Grimshaw where Tyler entered the calf-roping event in a two-day affair. He won hands down. The locals truly appreciated someone that talented travelling that far to grace their event. The return trip towards home ran from Peace River down over to Edmonton then straight south for a repeat appearance at the Olds rodeo. Again, Tyler only entered the calf-roping contest. Came in second. Racked up more points to maintain his number one novice standing in that category. There were still two weeks for more practice and conditioning, a few sessions of physiotherapy and several check-ins with Dr. Punkara before the more significant telltale outing in Lethbridge.

He fared much better in his second appearance at Lethbridge holding onto his second-place standing in saddle bronc and winning the calf-roping event like it was getting to be a foregone conclusion. When his number came up in the more treacherous bareback event, he was not feeling any pain and had his mind cemented on not getting bucked off again. Try, technique and sheer determination kept him aloft for the full eight seconds on both challenging mounts: a gray, spotted Appaloosa with a temper named Dust 'n Ashes and a brazen brown Standardbred called Trainwreck. His net aggregate score of 80.4 netted Tyler the third-place bronze medallion and combined with his other two victories to place him second overall, once again behind his friend and toughest rival, Greg Dugan. This time they were only fractions of points and seconds apart destined for a significant showdown in Tyler's own backyard on Labour Day weekend.

Success in other forms had visited others in Okotoks that summer. Stephanie, Enid, and Alex all got their driver's licences. Myra was promoted to chief assistant pharmacist. Jules was transferred out of explorations back to the Tranogco marketing department with advancement and an increase in pay. Frances Evans was made director of nursing for the Cedarview long-term care facility. Wallis Wilton was elected incoming chair of the school board trustees. Rebecca grew ten centimetres taller, burst out of her training bra into a "B" cup and finished off her Red Cross swimming training by garnering a Bronze Medallion. Pops took Ironstone to a horse show in Cochrane where the healthy two-year-old took second prize. The soggy part of August came after Ola's barley had all been harvested and marketed and in time to give a good soaking to the root systems of the Christmas trees optimizing their growth prospects for the coming fall. As August wound down in that burgeoning retirement and dormitory town, the vast majority of its citizenry were caught up in contemplations and preparations for their own rodeo.

More top-name pros had entered the 2001 Okotoks rodeo than ever before, Blue Rodeo had contracted to play the Saturday evening dance at the curling rink, but the bulk of local attention was focussed on the novice competitions. Home-boy Tyler was shining up his saddle and chaps and set on whoopin' his buddy Greg Dugan's ass. Those weren't Tyler's words, but they were the scuttlebutt in the local billiard hall, bowling alley, taverns, seniors' home and camp grounds. Bets to that effect were put down at the RCMP detachment office, the Chamber of Commerce and the Hillsdale Golf Course. Tyler spent the Wednesday previous in silent retreat and prayer with Aunt Ola. Thursday was spent with a session of physiotherapy, some practice roping, video reviews and two-hours of conditioning. Friday morning, he visited Dr. Punkara for chiropractic treatment and a G-5 relaxation massage while Polk Rodeo Stock unloaded trucks and trailers full of competition animals into pens and makeshift barns around the Recreation Centre and area hotels, motels, guest homes and bed and breakfast operations filled up with other competitors, their entourages and fans, press representatives, sponsors, and a wad of interested tourists. Cash-flow eddied all around town because of the hype. High spirits gushed from one corner to the next because of the hope. The Sheep River ran languidly with low water and utter obliviousness. Frances Evans, home in bed after working a night shift for a nurse on vacation, dreamed she saw the ghost of Napi sticking his tongue out at Big Rock.

At 5:00 P.M. Central Time, at Ned's Junction in Lloydminster, Alberta, Uncle Louie, Hob-knob Hickey, Slashmouth, and One-blue-eyed Sadie raised and drank their sixth half-pint of Grasshopper Wheat on tap from the past hour. "Here'sh to Tyler St-st-st-ste-edman, my broncccco-busshtin' nephph-phphew who-wis shabout to blow the fffrickin' comp-pet-t-tition away at the ol' Okotoks-shhh rodeo! (Hic!)" After they downed their glasses, Hob-knob Hickey's head fell smack down the table. The other three bodies toppled onto the floor. Slashmouth fell against the outside wall hard enough to dislodge a small television from its shelf. The resultant crash startled a passing waitress who dropped a whole pitcher of beer. One-blue-eyed Sadie's left arm had landed near to where the smashed television fell. When the beer met up with broken but still connected television, the resultant electric shock travelled up her arm, singed her red bra strap, sent sparks flying from her dangling silver-plated ear-ring and shot the hair on the left side of her head straight up. Louie managed enough consciousness to roll her out of the puddle in time to minimize the damage to a temporary paralysis of the left side of her face.

"Next round's on me, boys," she yelled as she hauled herself up, tugged at her blouse and lumbered to the women's room to straighten herself barking to the bartender, "Set 'em up! Ned, ain't no minor buck-off's gonna keep this ol' broad from climbin' right back onto the saddle."

Buck-offs did dishearten the first three novice competitors in saddle bronc in Okotoks that night. The crowd still applauded then broke into a deafening roar. Tyler Stedman was fourth up.

"Here he comes," declared the announcer, "your hometown hero. He'll be sitting on top of a nasty beige nag named Sacrilege. Hold your breath. Hold onto your seats until chute number three where you see the Coors Light sign springs open."

Ten seconds later it did. The eight-second clock kicked in. Sacrilege kicked out and up, then right, then left. Tyler held fast with his right arm and worked his spurring legs up and down the mare's neck and flanks. His upper body was yanked every which way in the opposite motion or direction from those in which that horse bucked and jerked itself. He was flung smartly forward just as the eight-second horn sounded. He flung his right leg up and over the golden mane of Sacrilege and vaulted to the turf clear and free. Grubby the clown and two ring workers shooed the still-spirited horse into the exit lane. It was a likewise spirited ride which sent the crowd into jubilant cheering. The judges recognized quality and awarded an 82.5, a mark that would not be eclipsed by any other novice competitor that night. In fact the contestant closest to Tyler only scored 80. And it wasn't Greg Dugan, who wound up fourth with a 78.

In calf-roping that night Greg and Tyler pulled off the two top times with Tyler only a three-tenths of a second ahead. In bareback bronc rounds, Greg edged out Tyler for top spot with a score of 79.5 to 78.5. The crowd was euphoric. If Tyler could pull off similar performances tomorrow afternoon, the hometown hero's triumph was in the bag. When Tyler rode around the recreation centre in his two victory laps, his face emanated not only appreciation but positive assurance that their hopes as well as his own were destined to be met.

There were some exceptional performances in the pro events that night, and one record-setting team roping victory. A hushed and worried moment followed one of the bull rider's taking a horn in the left thigh. He emerged with only a long surface scratch and a two-day limp. From hotel room to tavern stool to restaurant booth to bedside prayers the whole town remained awash in Tyler-mania. Tyler and Ola said their prayers that night and slept soundly, undisturbed by visions, nightmares, random thoughts or even the need to go to the bathroom.

Mania verged on hysteria as the throngs assembled the following night churning over the second and championship novice rounds. Raja Punkara sat with her father in the second row near the centre on the north side. In her blue jeans, Western shirt and brown stetson she might have passed for a native Canadian, but her father, while sporting a tan cowboy hat and lariat tie over a pale yellow shirt, chose to wear a cream-coloured Nehru jacket and suit pants making their ethnicity obvious. It was his first time viewing live rodeo.

H. Lee Disher

He winced several times and occasionally closed his eyes as the saddle bronc rounds proceeded. He was as impressed with Tyler's championship-winning outing as was the rest of the delirious crowd. He made a note-to-self to offer Tyler a special, private Sunday afternoon session of treatment the following day. Or morning even, if Tyler wanted to watch the pro finals during the afternoon. When Tyler's calf-roping time squeezed out Greg Dugan again by tenths of seconds to capture that title, Dr. Punkara tossed his hat in the air in the midst of grandstand-wide ecstasy. He tossed it safely enough to catch it again, turn to his daughter and wrap her in a huge hug. "He's rather amazing for a daring young man, isn't he!"

"Yes, Father, he's all that."

A clown routine, a trick riding demonstration and the pro women's barrel racing finals preceded the novice bareback event. Even a fourth-place finish would probably garner the all-around title for Tyler. And he had drawn the last ride this time. He knew what was needed.

Two of the first six competitors were bucked off and one of them fell hard to the ground with his left arm bent beneath him. Dr. Punkara turned his head and grimaced visualizing the damage. Greg Dugan was sitting in second place after his turn in this round. If Tyler hung on and pulled off a fourth-place standing the all-around prize was guaranteed. The seventh competitor out of the chutes hung on for a ride of mediocre excitement and only scored enough points to stand fourth at that moment.

"Here we go again, folks," the voice of the announcer rang out. "It's the last ride of the night and you know who right now is setting himself down astride Recharge. It's your boy, and you can be sure he knows as well as you do what's at stake here. It's for all the marbles, folks. I'm not trying to add to the pressure. I'm just acknowledging the pressure. This kid has a habit of excelling under pressure. So set your gaze on gate number five and listen for the horn."

As Tyler set himself onto the back of Recharge, Greg Dugan was hanging over the fence extending his right hand. "It's your night, pal. Go grab the glory."

While they clasped hands Tyler replied, "Damn straight, buddy. Thanks."

"Ther-ere's the horn! There goes the gate. And look at Recharge wriggle! Man, it's like watching a fifteen-pound pike caught on a Sassafras spinner and Tyler Stedman looks like a hapless leech stuck on the pike's back. Yeow! Look at that wild lurch to the left. Hold tight boy. Mark that horse out!. Heads up! Recharge is curving into a well-hole...."

Dr. Punkara formulated a different commentary: "Oh my God! Crunch to the sacrum. Wrench right upper thoracic. Strain right triceps and deltoids.

Wrench left upper thoracic. Compression between third and fourth lumbar vertebrae. Aaah! Collapse forwards over your abdominals then get flung straight back, that's almost enough to cause an abdominal tear, not to mention slipped discs in the lower back! Oh Raja, Raja, I can hardly bear to watch!"

"Hang on, Tyler, only two seconds left. Careful, careful, don't slide too far sideways. Whoa, what a torpid frontal rear-up by Recharge! But it helped him regain his balance folks. Five, four, three, two, one. There's the buzzer! There's the leap of a tough, young cowboy. There's a victory dance already happening folks. The judges can't let that ride go without a great score!"

"Oh, oh, pulled rib muscles on the left side, more cranking of the upper thoracic adding stress to the latissimus dorsi. Careful, careful how you land again after that horse rears up, Tyler. Ouch! Right on the coccyx! What punishment to your right forearm. Let's hope your lower back holds up, son. Let's hope...Was that the buzzer? Yes! Yes! Oooh! Don't land so hard on your heels. Even with bent knees that impact's going to turn your whole spine into a closed Slinky toy. And the ligaments in your knees will...."

"There it is, folks ... a score of 84. It's a new novice record! It's a clean sweep. First in saddle bronc, first in calf-roping, first in bareback, and *first all-around!* Ladies and gentleman, salute your absolutely A-one homegrown cowboy, Tyler Stedman. And look out Edmonton come November, there's a new king in the novice ring and he's the pride and joy of Okotoks, Alberta."

Pride exploded into pandemonium, a jamboree of jubilee.

Hugged tightly by Pops, Wallis Wilton, his father, and his coach, embraced by his aunt, tackled by Alex, and then hoisted aloft by Alex and Greg and marched right out of the arena into a waiting convertible provided by one of the local car dealers and on through a spontaneous street parade that rode ceremoniously down Mulligan Drive out to Highway 2A, up to the parking lot in the new mall at Highway 7, back around to the centre of town where several tours of Elizabeth St. and Riverside Drive were completed, Tyler received the hand-slaps and other adulations of hundreds of adoring fans amid thousands of whoops and hollers and honking horns. But the best praises of all were the kisses he received from Stephanie, who couldn't watch but listened to it all at home on the radio, and the tears of relief and joy he saw in his mother's eyes.

The aftermath may have been as rough on his body as the competition had been. Tyler was glad to accept Dr. Punkara's offer of a Sunday morning treatment. He had a big silver buckle and wad of prize money and a gleaming all-around trophy to soothe his soul.

All of Okotoks held Tyler in awe for the rest of the month as he set his sights on the round-up in Lacombe. He and Greg would do battle one more time that season for the number one novice title in Canada before the national finals. At the moment, Tyler was ahead.

He was given permission to miss school the week ahead of the Lacombe event so he could travel to Red Deer to stay, work out, and train with Greg. Why not feed a friendship that fed their competitive juices and their mutual respect? They both knew that finishing in any of the events in Lacombe would secure a top spot in that event in the nationals. Finish well in any two or all three, and they would definitely wind up seeded number one and number two. Finishing anywhere in the top three in the nationals would get them to the grand National Finals Rodeo in Las Vegas in December. Neither of them seldom got thinking that far ahead. The focus was always on the event in the immediate future. While Tyler was off in Red Deer that week, eight-footed Sleipnir revisited Ola's nightly dreams attended by those other strange charioteers.

When the Friday night rounds were completed at Lacombe, Greg and Tyler stood in first and second position in their three usual events, calf-roping being the one in which Tyler superseded his friend. Saturday shaped up to be another foregone conclusion on the novice circuit. It didn't fail to draw out large audiences alongside tag-along fans.

"Second up in the saddle bronc rounds tonight, behind gate number one," the announcer bellowed, "is the wunderkind of Okotoks, Alberta ....TY-LER STED-MAN! He'll be in for a tough test on top of Bresnall Stockyard's dun gray stallion, Loki's Revenge; a rising star in the stock stables and a real fuzztail."

Ola twitched without knowing why.

"All eyes are funneling in on gate one now. The rider is set. The horse's nostrils have begun to flare. And there's the buzzer...."

Just before the gate flew open, Tyler glanced to his left a saw Allison Kershaw in the middle of a hot embrace with an American competitor who was slated to ride two mounts later. His head had not yet come back fully forward when Loki's Revenge seemed to leap straight up and out from the chute for a good twelve feet landing on his forelegs and flicking his rear end almost ninety degrees in the air. Tyler leaned flat back, marked out rhythmically, and praised God this was saddle bronc as the horn that pressed hard into his crotch kept him from sliding straight over the stallion's ears. As Loki's Revenge brought his hind end down he gave it a strong half twist left that bolted Tyler up off the saddle and tipped him twenty-five degrees to the right. Tyler's sacrum felt severely scrunched as he landed in the saddle again. The bronc was working up into a furious frenzy unlike any ride Tyler had experienced to date. Every buck and twist was torturous. Tyler was concentrating so hard on holding on he only saw the horse's neck. He didn't realize his mount was getting closer and closer to the side wall just past the chute area. Six seconds into the ride, Loki's Revenge threw himself high and forward once again. Tyler felt his right hand let go, felt his body leave the saddle, saw his legs disappear beneath him as his head and shoulders passed over the stallion's mane, felt the ego-puncturing disappointment of being thrown, then saw the dirt no less than a foot from his face, and then...felt his hatless head crack up against the wall and felt something else crack. Then he saw no more.

"Oh no!" the announcer screamed. "Look out, Tyler, you're goin' straight through the windshield! Watch out for that wall!" Screams permeated the audience. Shrieks came from one particular row, none louder than Myra's. Then, a moment of stunned silence. "Just stay steady, folks. These boys are in tip-top shape. Let the attendants do their work. What an amazing exhibition of try, folks. Give Tyler Stedman a huge round of encouragement with your applause."

The crowd clapped less than enthusiastically, not able to shake off worry. The announcer noticed that the doctor-on-site had been summoned, saw the St. John's Ambulance personnel fetch and carry in a stretcher.

"Okay, folks, sit tight. I know this doesn't look good. Perhaps, if you feel so moved you might offer up a little prayer or two right now. Young Mr. Stedman will get optimum attention from our medical personnel. Let's send out another round of support and encouragement as they set Tyler in that stretcher and carry him off to the infirmary. And, yes, we'll keep you posted."

Jules, Greg, and Tyler's coach were already in the chute area and following fast behind the stretcher-bearers. Mr. and Mrs. Wallis Wilton helped escort a frantic Myra, Rebecca, and Ola through the crowds and around the inside of the arena to where the infirmary room was. Myra was screaming and shaking all the way. Rebecca was crying out loud, shouting "Tyler! No! Tyler! No!" Ola shuddered from head to foot. The rest of the saddle bronc competitors agreed to hold off continuing, as anxiety spread itself over the whole arena as an incoming tide overtakes a shoreline foot by foot, rock by rock. No one left their seat. The announcer had a booth technician play soft country music over the public address system.

The cluster of concerned onlookers huddled in the infirmary didn't have a long wait before their worst fears materialized. The doctor's examination was brief. Grief gripped the whole room. "I'm afraid he's dead." Within a minute, when the doctor's pronouncement became public announcement, that incoming tide turned an arena into a trapped pool of tears.

The agony of family and close friends was prolonged and augmented as an ambulance came and bore Tyler's body to the emergency department at Red Deer General Hospital. The coroner had been called in. An autopsy was required: Canadian Professional Rodeo Association protocol. The contingent of those most concerned followed the ambulance, wept, paced, raged, and emoted variously for over two hours in "the family room." A hospital chaplain attended them mainly in presence only. Words truly failed.

The coroner came in. "Mr. Stedman, Mrs. Stedman, I'm Philip Verbeek from the coroner's office. I'm very, very sorry for your loss. I can't imagine how upsetting and sad it is. If it's any consolation at all, I can tell you that he died instantly, felt nothing, didn't suffer. The impact of striking the wall fractured this neck bone right back here. (The doctor turned around, pulled back his shirt collar with his left hand and pointed with his bent-over right hand). This is the C3 vertebra in the neck or cervix, small but very vital. When it shatters or fractures it virtually always severs the spinal cord. Death is instantaneous."

It was very small consolation.

The Dugans and their neighbours housed three Stedmans, two Davises, and a pair of newlywed Wiltons overnight. Communication was minimal: brief stuttered words, tears, hugs, arms on shoulders, the exchange of sympathetic glances and guttural expressions of sorrow and disbelief.

Ola was utterly silent, lost in inward contemplation. "Loki's revenge. I should have realized. I should have begged Jules to stop the ride. Oh, Loki, your seductive prank has now become transparent. You have suckered Sleipnir and our own precious Odin. You are truly a cruel and heartless trickster. God, if only You had revealed the meaning of this showing, I would have known what to do with my restless fire. God, if only You could have.... God, it's only You we do have in such a time. God, have compassion on us all and grant us strength. God, receive Your servant Tyler with rejoicing."

Myra Stedman was totally numb, like a cloud hitting the Arctic sea and becoming iceberg.

# Chapter 29:
# Down Town

By the time Tyler's death became headline breaking news on the 11:00 P.M. television and radio broadcasts, a good portion of Okotoks already knew. Alex had phoned Enid Evans at home and managed to spit out the sad story in spurts. Enid dialed immediately after that call ended. The hot potato of grief was passed on quickly from the house of Evans to Wells to Jenkins like a triple-play in baseball. From there it ricocheted throughout the whole Parent- Teacher Association network, church women's groups, the local figure-skating club membership, and the men's section of the golf and country club. Magda and Yannis Wojniewski may have been the last citizens in town to hear. As soon as the news clip was finished, Yannis pressed the power button on the remote off. The two of them lay transfixed in bed, silent, staring blankly.

A major thunderstorm broke loose over southwestern Alberta that night. The whole town of Okotoks could have changed its name to Ice-burg, a population was fast frozen in shock, the epicentre of a stunned province.

When the Stedman contingent arrived home around 9:00 A.M. Sunday morning, there were bouquets, homemade wreaths, ribbons on every house and storefront, and candles detectable in virtually every window. Flags at half-mast flapped limply in low-gusting wind of eight kilometres per hour. The message mail-box on the answering machine at 35 Dewdney Common was full. In the midst of many "if there's anything I can do…" recordings was the voice of Rev. Fanshawe saying she'd be over right after worship was concluded or at whatever time in the afternoon might suit them if they'd like to let her know.

"Right," Jules muttered, "I suppose we'll need to start making arrangements."

The only arrangement made thus far was to have Tyler's body transferred from the morgue at Red Deer General to the R.T.P. Governor Funeral Home on Northridge Drive. Pranksters on the night before Hallowe'en and other sporadic occasions often painted out the top bar on the letter "T" on the illuminated front lawn sign. In 2001, they removed that line with rocks. Rick Governor was a fourth generation funeral director for this local family business that had helped carry the community's grief for almost a century. This one would be the heaviest to bear in all his memory.

At 11:30 A.M., he picked up the funeral home phone to receive a call from Jules Stedman. He offered his condolences and suggested a meeting with the family at 2:00 P.M. The local paper was extending its usual deadline for notices till 4:00 P.M. that day in case there were details available for publication by then. Rick Governor didn't share that information with Jules just then. Other concerns were of greater importance to the bereaved family.

When he had finished that call, Jules dialed up the office of St. Paul's United Church, leaving a message for Rev. Fanshawe appreciating the minister's regard and asking her to meet them at Governor's at 2:30 P.M. instead of dropping around to the house right after worship. For the moment, the resources of faith seemed more like social window-dressing, a bit of detail not that different from deciding whether to have Tyler dressed in a suit or in rodeo garb.

The family settled on a suit, a lariat string tie with a pewter clasp featuring a bucking horse, and a silver buckle won during his first appearance in the Lethbridge corral. Pops wondered about placing a pair of chaps and Tyler's first saddle in the coffin. Neither happened for, in truth, there wasn't exactly room. One of Tyler's high school rodeo trophies was nestled into his left arm. His hands folded across his abdomen held his cowboy hat. All of this was only seen during a private family viewing on Tuesday evening that included a select few close friends. There was no public visitation. When Alex approached the coffin to pay his respects, he slipped in one more object—an ammonite fossil in a piece of ironstone.

The funeral service was set for Wednesday morning. After several rounds of discussion, St. Paul's United Church and the Foothills Composite Gymnatorium were passed over as venues too small in favour of the Community Recreation Centre. Classes at Foothills Composite were cancelled for that morning so that students and staff could attend. In fact, except for a couple of service stations and a donut shop, all the businesses and offices in Okotoks were closed until noon or 1:00 P.M. A closed-circuit broadcast of the service would be fed to an overflow crowd seated in the gymnasium at Dewdney Junior High. The front lobby of the recreation centre featured six easels full of photo montages honouring Tyler. Alex and Enid and Stephanie with ample help from Ola had spent a number of mixed emotional hours assembling them. Hundreds of flower arrangements and wreaths surrounded the coffin set on a low raised stage formed from a dozen wooden risers at the east end of the arena. The Stedmans and Davises felt tremendous support from the thousands of mourners who showed up but were thankful there had been no visitation. They could never have stood that much grieving traffic. They were sorry they had to restrict the numbers of people invited back to 35 Dewdney Common for a post-funeral reception. There was comfort in knowing that a number of other forms of celebration and gathering had been arranged. The mourners began arriving at the recreation centre a full three hours ahead of time just to pass by Tyler's coffin before finding themselves a seat.

Ten minutes before the start of the ceremony, Louie and a brace of companions breezed in from Lloydminster. There had been no known way of contacting him and the family wondered whether or not he would catch the news any way, and worried that, if he did, he would show up.

Looking as spiffy as one might imagine for a down-and-outer, Louie approached the front row of family and introduced Hobknob Hickey, Slashmouth, and One-blue-eyed Sadie by their proper names and by their nicknames and then sent his three companions off to find seating somewhere in the stands. "If there's room for me near here, I'd like to stay, if that's all right."

Pops shrugged in ambivalence and turned away. Myra twinged and glanced at Ola, who returned a quiet nod. "I suppose we can find you a seat somewhere handy," Jules offered.

"I was kinda wonderin' if it would be all right if I could be a pallbearer."

Myra and Ola's eyes widened with numbed incredulity. "He is still family," Jules whispered. Sister and ex-wife commiserated as if by default. If Jules could arrange something, they could tolerate it. Jules walked over to where the pallbearers were seated and held a brief conference. Gerry Evans graciously offered to back out and allow Louie to take his spot.

"Thank you, Jules," said Louie, bowing slightly as if he was a diplomatic attaché who had negotiated a pact. "Myra, Ola...Pops...I truly appreciate this. Tyler was one heck of a good nephew and an extremely talented rider. Oh, and, don't fret, after the ceremony, me and my buddies gotta head back to Lloyd. We'll not be staying for any reception."

"Some things never change," Jules muttered to Ola as Louie strode off to take his seat among the pallbearers.

"Sometimes that can be a good thing," Ola replied.

"Amen to that!" grumbled Pops. "Praise the Lord."

Organ music from the loft indicated that it was close to time to do just that. Soon Reverend Fanshawe would open the service with words of welcome, an expression of shared community sympathy, an invitation to join in worship with openness to the promises of God in times like these, an acknowledgement of gathering to honour Tyler Stedman, and the words of John 11:25-26. Then, after an opening prayer, Reverend Fanshawe stepped aside as Wallis Wilton came to the podium to offer the eulogy.

"A few months ago, my good neighbour, Pops Davis, got up at my wedding reception and gave a speech and a toast in my honour that was truly humbling. I thought to myself, some day, before too long perhaps, I might have the privilege of paying tribute to him in return when death finally got its hooks into him. I never dreamed, nor I'm sure did anyone else here, that today we'd be here in deep and earnest grief, in shock and disbelief, in full-blown sadness and sorrow to pay tribute to his grandson. I never dreamed that death would just get greedy and brutish and stretch out his great big gnarly fingers to rob us of Tyler Stedman. But...here we are.

"Jules, Myra, Rebecca; Pops, Ola, Alex, if nothing else let me reassure you today that no one of you nor even all six of you together have to travel on from here alone. There are neighbours, friends, a whole town, and God only knows a whole county, three-quarters of a province and an international network of rodeo participants and afficionados to help bear your grief and share in carrying your sorrow. Lean on us, please. Twist two weak strings together and you get the start of some mighty strong rope.

"Perhaps I don't need to say much. Perhaps I'm not going to say anything that anybody here doesn't know already. If a roper sitting on top of his trusted steed gets wound up with the kind of intensity I'm feeling inside right now waiting for that barrier to snap as the calf he's about to chase down bursts out of its gate, then I have some degree of appreciation for the deep, obvious ardour for Western life and all things rodeo that churned inside Tyler Stedman twenty-four seven. That's a good part of the truth about his utterly impressive life that I'm about to let loose, but not all of the truth.

"The truth about Tyler Stedman might best begin by admitting that he was not the kind of person who ran away from you trying to elude you, he ran toward you seeking to enfold you. He met you with a sincere interest in who you were, what you were up to, what you dreamed of, what energized you, where your life was headed. He met you with his winning smile, his decency, his honesty, his trustworthiness, his own enthusiasms, his keenness to learn and drew you straight into his heart. The closer your relationship with him became the more he took you in. The subsequent truth is that whatever he filed there he used to build you up, encourage you, egg you on to be your better self: a better parent or close relation, a better friend, a better teacher, a better neighbour, a better fellow competitor, a better human being, a better horse. He had instinctual ways of relating to horses that are inbred, that can't be taught. He had more faith in humankind and in God in his little finger than I sometimes have in my whole body. He had faith in himself that was confident but never cocky, stalwart but never boastful. Faith and instinct are a third truth about him that formed the foundation beneath his ability to relate companionably and equitably with everyone he ever met. And with every horse. Yes, out at Pops' farm there are five others who are going to have just as difficult a time handling Tyler's death as we are. Their names are Tacitus, Charro, Belva, Ironstone, and especially a dearly loved Paso Fino called Sirocco.

"Like a totally non-subtle breeze, like a fast forked-tongued tornado, Death has lapped up Tyler Stedman and spirited him away from us. So Death thinks. But Death is wrong. Tyler's spirit, his infectious (in the best possible understanding of that word), passionate spirit has lodged itself within us as an abiding influence and presence. He left a large chunk of his heart inside all our hearts. It's uncanny that one who only graced this earth for seventeen years could have done so, but he did. And he did it indelibly and forever.

"If we embrace the consuming passion that resides within us only twenty-five per cent as much as he embraced his fire for rodeo, we will do him great honour and do ourselves immeasurable good. If we love others even half as well as he loved others, we will do him great honour and do the world immeasurable good. If we have even ten per cent of the faith that he exhibited, it will honour Tyler immensely and be enough to move all manner of mountains and put a permanent smile on the lips of God Almighty. I am here fumbling around trying to pay him tribute. We all have the rest of our lives to do him honour. God help us."

There were moments during the eulogy where Wilton paused in mid-sentence with a glottal click as emotion caused the words to stick in his throat. There were more moments during his tribute when outbursts of crying came from the assembled crowd. Several came from Stephanie Wells. Myra gripped Jules' right arm tightly and sobbed into his shoulder once or twice. For the most part, she remained as mute and dazed throughout the ceremonies as she had become when the coroner in Red Deer delivered his verdict. Jules held a stolid appearance but the traceries where tears had dribbled down his cheeks were visible on his face. Rebecca at times buried her sobbing face in Aunt Ola's lap. Once or twice Pops reached for his handkerchief to dab his eyes. When Wilton finished, he approached the family who stood to thank him, Jules and Myra with sincere handshakes, Rebecca by hugging his left leg, Pops with an arm to Wilton's shoulder, Ola with two small pecks to each of Wilton's cheeks.

Reverend Fanshawe went on with readings from Scripture, a meditation on Christian hope and the strength faith affords us, prayers and a benediction. The mood in the arena remained hushed, attentive, and emotionally charged throughout.

"If we could turn back our clocks to last Saturday morning and start over, we would," Re verend Fanshawe's meditation began. "If we could wish we did not have to be here in mourning today and have that wish come true, we would will it into existence. But we can't. God knows. God would wish it could be otherwise for us. But it can't. Accident happens. Tragedy strikes. A much loved son, brother, cousin, nephew, companion, classmate, neighbour, community sports hero, Tyler Stedman died tragically, and far too young, in the midst of doing what he loved to do. We are saddened, numbed, stunned, caught in a whorl of emotional and spiritual upheaval.

"God knows. God's heart has cracked again just as our hearts have. God's heart cracks whenever parents lose a child, whenever someone dies too young. God also lost his child, his Son, at an age older than Tyler Stedman, but still quite young. And God said, 'That will never do. Death can never be allowed to have the last word. Life must be the last word.' And so, out of death, God raised God's own Son. And so, out of death, God is intent on raising all who die. This belief, this hope is part of the very core of faith we call Christianity. Some of us here truly believe it. Some us would like to believe it. Some of us likely harbour doubt or simply aren't sure. To believe means to trust that, indeed, what God did for God's own Son, will happen for any of us and any of our loved ones when death strikes them down. Death will not be the last word. The last word and the final outcome will be life—ongoing, everlasting, perfected, eternal life. Go ahead. I urge you to believe it. It may defy logic, but it makes its own enormously powerful sense. It turns life as we know it into an experience filled with meaning and value and purpose no matter what happens. It is God's way of gifting us with the ability to handle all the messy, sad, painful or tragic, unfair, and evil events that disrupt our lives. It is about living more from the heart than from the head.

"Wallis Wilton has spoken not so fumblingly but rather eloquently recalling to our minds how Tyler Stedman lived from his heart. Tyler got up every day and got at it prepared to roll with whatever came, wearing his heart out on his sleeve. Remember this wonderful human being with whom you shared life in so many forms: eating, learning, playing, laughing, riding, travelling, making choices, sharing sorrows, loving, striving and all other ways that come to mind. Remember how he supported you and had faith in you. He counted on you. He counted on himself. He counted on God. Remember that once embraced by a heart like his, you remain forever embraced. Remember that once someone like Tyler Stedman has taken you into his presence like an angel enfolding you in his wings, you remain forever enfolded.

"Yes, we can feel the pain we share here today. But let us also feel the love that permeates this place: not only our love for Tyler, but the love were are called to share with one another and God's love beating in and through our own hearts. It is the beating of God's own broken yet hopeful and steadfast heart. Can you also feel the hope here today? And the faith that floods this arena? Faith in each other. Faith in ourselves. Faith seeking God and faith that has already found God. Believe it. It is here. It is for real. It works.

"Let faith, hope, and love propel and drive our own lives. They will not let us down. They will get us through this day, this time and on with the rest of our lives. They will keep us connected with the God who truly cares, who blesses, who forgives, who reassures, who comforts, carries and strengthens us. They will keep us connected with the love and the life we knew as Tyler Stedman. They will give us confidence that life is indeed the last word. Thanks be to God."

Ola pondered the pastor's words, broke into a small warm smile and stared at Tyler's coffin. A word formed in her mind describing that Life [she visualized the capital "L"] he would now enjoy: *sobornost*, (union). She sank into her seat at ease.

When the Stedman family and a few close friends gathered back at 35 Dewdney Common for food and continued community support, the door-bell rang. Jules answered. There were Yannis and Magda Wojniewski. She held a platter on which was poised a marvellous five layer torte.

"Ve are very sorry for your loss, Meester Stedman," she spoke up. "I know ve have been somevat difficult at times as neighbours, but your son vas always polite to us and often shovelled snow off our walk bevore Yannis got out to get at it. Please accept zis cake and perhaps ve can try to get to know each ozzer better in ze future."

"How very kind of you, Mrs. Wojniewski, Mr. Wojniewski. Perhaps you'd like to come in."

On the long journey north to Grimshaw earlier that summer, Tyler, Jules, and Pops had held a very serious conversation about the risks of rodeo, Pops' heart attack experience and those uncertain, unsettling periods of life such as Jules had been passing through of late. The day they headed out from Peace River for the Olds rodeo, Tyler had handed his father an envelope that morning for safe keeping, the kind only to be opened just in case.... It was an incredibly mature act for one so young and Jules hoped it was exceedingly premature. When that hope was crushed, Jules took the letter out of the locked stationery box in his office at home where he had stored it and opened it. There were words of deep gratitude and love for his ever supportive family and a few requests for the distribution of Tyler's worldly goods: his country music and CDs to Rebecca, his Western literature collection to Wallis Wilton, a prize buckle or garnered trophy to any member of the family who wanted one for a keepsake, his educational savings bonds and GICs were to be split between Rebecca and Alex, and Alex was to have Sirocco, if he chose. If not, would he please give that wise and winning Paso Fino to Greg Dugan.

As for funeral and burial arrangements, Tyler was rather open-minded other than that he asked that his remains be cremated at some point with half the ashes to be spread out at Big Rock and the other half to be scattered over the corral at Pops' farm. On the Saturday following the funeral service, that is precisely what happened.

The Western World was still reeling in shock from the events of September 11 in New York City. The good folks of Okotoks now had the death of one their own heroes to mourn. They were suspended in time for a while as if working by a cracked clock. They were swimming in a sea of salt-water tears beneath a sullen atmosphere that was somewhat supple like black pizza dough. Frances Evans, on the evening of the funeral, was leafing through a volume of *The Philokalia* Ola had loaned her. She was reading by candlelight in a chair beside her bedroom window. She was caught by the words of St. Diadochos of Photiki *On Spiritual Knowledge:*

*"For glory befits God because of God's majesty, while lowliness befits humankind because it unites us with God." (Volume 1, page 256)*

"Be that as it may," she said to herself, "there is another form of lowliness, this present emptiness and sadness. God, draw near and hold us all and raise us up from this despondency."

She clutched the *pysanka* Ola had given her that year at Easter.

# Epilogue

At the town council meeting the following week, it was moved, seconded and carried to name the paddock and practice ring area at the Agricultural Society property on the outskirts the Tyler Stedman Corral. Area high school rodeo athletes would train there. The annual Labour Day weekend rodeo competitions would sometimes be held there. Once designated, the fences were lined with memorial wreaths and crosses.

In 2003, Wallis and Carol Wilton adopted two mentally challenged native children who learned as much in the informal classrooms at home as they did in the Alberta educational system. They caught on quickly to feeding cattle, gathering eggs and country music. They sang, or rather bellowed, mock opera in the shower.

That same year, Pops suffered a stroke which left him physically incapacitated. His mind and his speech were unimpaired. He became a resident of Cedarview Nursing Home, delighting staff and other residents with jocular repartee and his acumen as a raconteur. No one has beaten him yet in a game of Parcheesi. He was visited regularly by Myra, Jules, Rebecca, Ola, and a small circle of farming friends who are still kicking as he is. When Punky and the gang show up, it's always Happy Hour. Punky became the proud, new conscientious owner of Tacitus.

When Myra and Ola had decided what to keep out of Pops' house there was a country auction. Ola then moved from her place into Pops' smaller house clearing out some of her accumulated goods through a church yard sale at St. Bartholomew's. She keeps up a brisk business in Christmas trees and lives with the vagaries of owning and operating a cash crop operation, including the province-wide desolation of 2002 when yields were less than half usual amounts. Wallis Wilton still leases parcels of her land for his crops. A few months after Pops' stroke, Ola and Alex decided to let the horses go. *Sirocco* was handed over to Greg Dugan. As a horse and rider team they continue to blow the competition away in calf-roping. Belva and Charro found a new home at some stables in Claresholm. Ironstone became a resident at a horse farm in Spruce Meadows. He is being groomed to become a championship show-jumper.

The bigger transition for Ola was to renovate her former residence into a spiritual retreat and counselling centre. She herself is making annual trips to a seminary in British Columbia to become a licensed spiritual director. Already her *poustinia* enterprise has been of great benefit to a number of couples from the prairies who have lost children.

Louie Davis collected handsomely on a exactor in the Fall of 2002. He and Hob-knob Hickey caught a train out of Lloydminster and headed out to Vancouver. They fell in with another Skid Row kind of crowd lodged in a men's mission just beyond Gastown. In the Spring of 2004, Louie would be one of two local indigents named to the mayor's task force on homelessness.

Alex Davis and Enid Evans continued serious dating for the rest of high school. She went on to receive a Master of Business Administration from the University of Calgary. He got a diploma in restaurant service and hotel management from Athabasca College. They would buy out the roadhouse-style saloon on Riverside Drive in Okotoks and turn it into a profitable fine-dining and bed and breakfast operation. The menu features Ukrainian and Russian specialties alongside Western Canadian food. In 2007, their first child, a son, was born. They named him Zachariah Tyler Davis. Francis and Gerry Evans would make fantastic grandparents.

In January 2004, Jules Stedman was offered a transfer to Tranogco's Houston office. After a few days deliberation and consultation with his family he accepted. The citizens of Okotoks had been sincerely sympathetic and supportive, but they felt they needed to move on, move away from daily reminders and remembrances of the life and family they once were. Myra would continue with intensive personal therapy after the move. Within six months, marital therapy would be added into the mix. Houston and America don't seem to sit well with her. She is headed for a serious mental breakdown and a divorce.

Jules settled well into his lateral move. He always enjoyed marketing and sales. Marital tension with Myra caught him off guard. He would be generous and accommodating in the divorce settlement.

Rebecca remained tough. She would weather the family storm; never date a cowboy; embrace alternative music, Lee-Ann Rhymes, Randy Travis, and Vince Gill thanks to the CD collection she inherited from her brother; and turn her figure skating skill into an assistant coaching position. She would study library science in a community college. She would sleep with a silver buckle under her pillow.

Raja Punkara entered medical school. Martha Yellan followed a path leading to outstanding women's fashion design. Lumpy Jenkins and Kevin Noseworthy would wind up as actors on the British Columbia theatre circuit. They would pass Louie Davis sometimes in the downtown core of Vancouver without any kind of mutual recognition. They would room together. They fell in love and accepted their gayness.

Herb Jenkins was found dead in his car in an abandoned garage in North Calgary on a cold winter morning in March 2004. The coroner's report will read: suicide by means of carbon monoxide asphyxiation. Lynda Jenkins was free.

In the Spring of 2003, Stephanie Wells had a major falling out with her mother. She quit school, packed her bags, and left home. She would phone her father from time to time to say she was all right but would not disclose her whereabouts. By pressing the redial button, Mr. Wells knew she was calling from Toronto. Without Tyler, her world collapsed. She would fall into all the potholes a young woman on her own in an unfamiliar big city could find: drugs, prostitution, pornographic videos and films. In November 2003, her body was found raped, beaten, and dead on an East End Toronto subway platform. Barbie's meltdown. It took two weeks of police investigation to hunt up Richard and Doris Wells to come to identify her.

Richard and Doris were among the early beneficiaries of Ola's retreat centre. They would also conclude, after Stephanie's death, that staying in Okotoks would not work well for them. They sold everything, relocated to the hot-spot community at the southern base of British Columbia's Okanagan Valley, the one that has a similarly strange name where "o" is the only vowel: Osoyoos. They had considered Orono, Ontario, and Oromocto, New Brunswick, but opted for remaining in Western Canada. They hoped healing might come in the semi-desert. They planted a vineyard.

Okotoks reached its optimum growth target within eight years. Cloud patterns overhead continued to vary. Like the Sheep River in its midst, the town flows on through joy and sorrow, economic shifts, changing demographics, fluctuating fashions and trends, worry or confidence—whatever comes; acknowledging and celebrating the old West, welcoming and encouraging the new; engulfed by that greater wave that carries humankind towards occupying three seconds to midnight on the clock-face of geological time.